THE SHORES OF PARADISE

SHIRLEY STRESHINSKY

BERKLEY BOOKS, NEW YORK

Grateful acknowledgment is made for permission to reprint an
excerpt from the following copyrighted material: *The Polynesian
Family System in Ka-u, Hawaii,* by E. S. Craighill Handy and Mary
Kawena Pukui, © 1958 Charles E. Tuttle, Inc. All rights reserved.
Used by permission.

This Berkley book contains the complete
text of the original hardcover edition. It
has been completely reset in a typeface
designed for easy reading, and was printed from
new film.

THE SHORES OF PARADISE

A Berkley Book/published by arrangement with the author

PRINTING HISTORY
G. P. Putnam's Sons edition/July 1991
Published simultaneously in Canada
Berkley edition/July 1992

ISBN: 0-425-13331-1

A BERKLEY BOOK® TM 757,375
Berkley Books are published by The Berkley Publishing Group,
200 Madison Avenue, New York, New York 10016.
The name "BERKLEY" and the "B" logo
are trademarks belonging to Berkley Publishing Corporation.

PRINTED IN THE UNITED STATES OF AMERICA

10 9 8 7 6 5 4 3 2 1

" From the prenatal period, throughout life and beyond
death the individual is regarded as a free, whole, independent entity. . . . Everything relating to this individual
is within the matrix of 'ohana: an individual alone is
unthinkable, in the context of Hawaiian relationship."

—*The Polynesian Family System in Ka-u, Hawaii*
E. S. Craighill Handy and
Mary Kawena Pukui, 1958

" Butterflies are found everywhere that plants suited to
the nourishment of the caterpillars are found. There
are some species which are arctic and found in the
brief summer of the cold North. . . . Most of them are,
however, children of the sun, and chiefly abound in
the temperate and tropical regions of the earth."

—*The Butterfly Book*
W. J. Holland, 1898
Revised edition, 1931

FOR MY 'OHANA
*on the Mainland
and in the Islands*

THE
SHORES OF
PARADISE

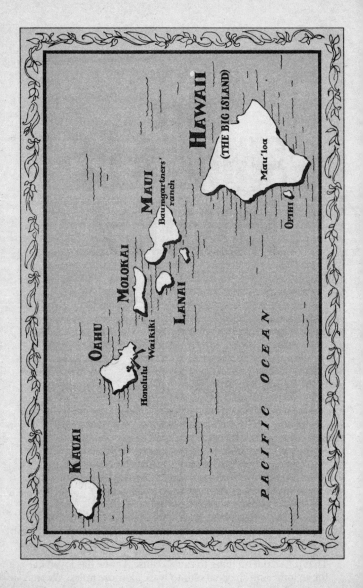

Prologue

Sunday, August 7, 1898

True was married yesterday, in a bower by the beach at Ainahau. She said her vows in a strong, clear voice, never once hesitating or faltering; her face glowed with purpose. The trade winds stirred the warm air. Chinese jasmine and tuberoses and plumeria—all the thick, sweet, sad scents of the Islands—filled the big house and the gardens. The ceremony was at sunset, when the breakers were tinged with pink as the waves washed ashore; at dusk, lanterns were lit all about the grassy lawns and the peacocks shrieked and the Royal Hawaiian Band played and there was much singing and celebrating. I went through the motions, as I had promised I would. When the newlyweds left, the Queen sang "Aloha Oe." That was when I lost my courage and began to weep. Tears come easily to the Hawaiians, so I hid in their midst and hoped that True wouldn't notice.

This room which True and I shared for many years, which has always seemed small, now seems big and empty and still in the afternoon heat. Even with the shutters open to catch the sea breeze, the air is heavy with the perfume of my fading ginger lei and her absence. A frayed green ribbon lies, dusty and discarded, on her writing table. The quilt is gone from her bed, and the mosquito netting lies folded on the mattress, along with the box this journal came in. I don't know why these leftover bits should make me feel so forlorn, but at this moment I doubt I'll ever be able to take a full, deep breath again.

I wish old Auntie Momi hadn't come to see True married. That is a shameful thing to say, because Auntie has loved me for so long, and she is so old, to walk all those miles. We sat together, looking out to the ocean, and when she started talking her voice was so thin and cracked that it sounded like the whisper of the palm fronds brushing against each other. Then I heard her say what I had been afraid to tell myself: The path True has chosen to take up the mountain is a hard path, filled with brambles, not well trod and with no clear view of the top.

True made me promise not to fret. She said if I was to start feeling seedy, I should ride the grey pony down the road to Ainahau and coax Vicky into going sea bathing with me. And she left me this journal, with a smooth cover of koa wood and Florentine marbled endpapers and thick cream pages, things she knows I set store by. Her note said, "It is time to put Auntie Momi's talk stories on paper, as you always said you would. And while you're about it, story-teller, talk our story. Write it all down, from that first day—do you remember? You stared at me so, I thought you were the most curious, big-eyed little thing I'd ever seen! Tell it outright and honest. I'll expect to read some in the spring, when we come back. *Aloha nui loa.*"

This is just True's way of keeping me busy. Aloha nui loa. *I love you very much.* True does everything *nui loa*. I never knew anyone like her, for saying what she means or for plunging headlong into things. When I said that to Vicky, she only laughed and in that proper English accent she's acquired said she'd never known anyone the slightest bit like True, either, and wasn't that a joy?

Old Auntie's talk stories I will write, for they are Hawaii's and deserve to be remembered. That I should talk True's story, our story—well, that will require a certain considera-tion, especially if it is to be "outright and honest." Some-times I think True should learn to hold back, but that's like telling the waves not to wash in or the sun not to shine. I swear she only knows how to walk into the wind, that fine white hair of hers flying. My legs are shorter, I can never keep up, and she never waits so I have had to learn to run fast.

Our story. How shall I begin?

Martha Moon is what I am called, but it is not my name. Only Sister Catherine Joseph knows what that is and she won't tell. This much I know: When I was too small to remember, a woman brought me to the Convent of the Holy

Names in Honolulu and gave me to Sister Catherine Joseph. Auntie Momi, who was old even then and had raised many children, cared for me. The sisters called me Martha; Auntie added "Moon" because she said the night I was given to her care had been bright with moonlight.

Auntie and I shared the room behind the kitchen, which was set apart from the convent. When I grew old enough, I began to ask Sister Catherine Joseph to tell me the name of the woman who had brought me. She would not; she said she could not.

I spent long hours studying my face: coarse dark hair, black eyes, full lips, a nose that is small and straight. Little Sister Maria Therese liked to say that I had an aristocratic nose and elegant wrists, but even then I knew she meant only to comfort me for my plainness. My body was small and my skin dark, but not so dark as Auntie's or any of the native girls. I was *hapa* Hawaiian, certainly, and *hapa haole,* half white, and you would think that two halves would make a whole, but I didn't feel whole because I knew nothing of either half.

I'm certain I have a mother somewhere, I would say to Sister. I must have a father. Perhaps I have sisters, brothers, an *ohana*—a family. "Say if they exist, only tell me that much," I would plead.

Sister grew ever more silent, until she would scarcely speak to me at all. When I was not receiving instruction in the school or in church, I was left to the keeping of Auntie Momi. She cleaned and swept and cared for me and comforted me and told me the old stories, in a voice so lulling and low that for a time I could escape the fears that came of not knowing where I had come from or who on this green earth belonged to me.

In the end, it was one of Auntie's stories, shamefully embellished for my own purposes, that caused me to be sent away. On the thirteenth anniversary of the day I had arrived at the mission, I arose at five, pulled on my dress and ran across the courtyard, so full of excitement that I did not feel the sharp rocks that cut into my feet. I knew Sister would be at matins; I slipped quietly into the church as she made the sign of the cross and rose, her lips moving silently. I was at the door when she stepped out.

"I have prayed to our Sweet Savior that you will speak to me," I said, piously, as I had practised.

"Martha . . ." she began, wary.

"I cannot go on without some notion of who I am," I said, too loud.

Her face closed, her eyes blinked slowly, like an old sea turtle's, and when she looked at me again it was with reptilian indifference.

"Then you must pray to Almighty God to sustain you," she finished coldly. I suppose that was what set me off.

"I have prayed to God," I answered, the words spitting out of me, aimed straight for the cold heart buried in the black habit, "and He has answered me in my dreams. An angel hovered over my bed last night, an angel with a dog's face, and it told me I am an abomination, an evil thing that was never meant to see the light and that you took me into the convent against the will of God."

The muscles around her mouth began to twitch; I saw but I could not stop myself. My voice began to rise and tremble:

"The angel said I was the child of King Kamehameha the third and his sister, Nahienaena, a Christian. The missionaries taught her that her soul would burn in hell for her sin. The angel said that I died at birth but that my spirit has lived on, wandering in the Pali, and that you sent someone to find me and bring me to you, so that you could punish me for my mother's terrible sin."

Sister's face grew red and her hands began to shake. Holding to the wall, she staggered away, letting out short whoofing sounds, like a cat trying to clear its throat of a hairball. I remember standing there, wondering what awful thing I had done, and how I should be punished.

I had not long to wait.

That same morning one of the young sisters came to my room with a basket and a new missal with a sealed envelope tucked into it, addressed to "Mr. and Miss Wright." I was told to pack my Sunday dress and my shoes in the basket and wait in front of the church. Within the hour the old Chinese who made deliveries for the church arrived with his mule and cart. Sister Maria Therese came running out as if to say something to me, but then she pulled back into the shadows and only lifted her hand, in some lost motion of remembrance. Auntie was away visiting one of her daughters; I didn't know how she would ever find me.

The old wagon creaked and rumbled through the streets

of the city, down Beretania and onto the District Road, on and on into the country, past duck ponds and banana groves and taro patches, always within sound of the sea. Great palm trees lined the dusty road; still we drove on, into the afternoon. I felt neither hunger nor thirst. The sun was full up and I had no hat, but I scarcely noticed. We passed small farms and houses and, now and then, a farmer or a fisherman. Finally, when we had gone so far down the beach road that the thick green leaves of tropical plants were brushing against us on either side, the old Chinese signaled his mule to stop and, turning to me, pointed toward the sea. I sat, stunned. He made a sharp, angry sound then and took my basket and threw it by the side of the road. I climbed out and watched as he turned the old wagon in the narrow roadway and drove off. Then I sat down next to my basket to wait.

After a time I moved into the deep shade of a hau tree. I think perhaps I drifted into sleep, because when I opened my eyes I found myself looking up into the branches and saw, perched high in the tree, a small person with a large head and very short legs staring down at me.

"Aloha," he said and dropped to the ground in front of me. Had he not been so small and had he not been wearing such a goosey smile, I might have been afraid. "Have you come to stay?" he asked.

I could not find words, but he seemed not to notice. "My name is Liko. Come," he directed, swinging my basket over his shoulder and starting off down a path, his stout little legs churning in the sand.

Soon we stepped into a wide clearing marked by tall coconut palms, a profusion of flowers and, scattered about, several small cottages in the plantation style, with thatched roofs and wide verandahs. Three children ran up to us, but Liko waved them away importantly.

"Uncle," he called as we approached the bungalow nearest the beach. A tall, big-nosed white woman came out, flapping her apron in annoyance. "Shush, child," she said in a loud whisper. "Uncle is working . . ." Then she saw me and said, "Oh my," and shouted out "Brother!" as she might have called "Fire!"

A small man, slight and balding, emerged. I stood, face burning, as the two haoles asked me questions I could not seem to answer.

I had clutched the missal so tightly that my fingers left wet marks on the black cover. I looked at it and handed it to the man Liko called "Uncle." He found the envelope.

"This is addressed to my sister and myself," he told me courteously, peering over his spectacles, his bushy eyebrows raised in question. He read the letter and handed it over to his sister.

"Oh my," she said as she read, her eyes fluttering wildly.

"Do you know where you are, child?" the man asked, and the kindness in his voice made me suddenly thirsty and hungry and aching with woe. Tears flooded my eyes and slipped down my face. I shook my head furiously and began to hiccough.

"You are at Hale Mana'olana—it means House of Hope," he said. "It is a home and a school for any child who needs them. I am Jameson Wright and my sister is Miss Winona Wright. The children call us Aunt and Uncle. We hope you will want to stay here and be part of our family."

I closed my eyes and bit my lip. Hale Mana'olana—at the convent they called it "House of No Hope." The children no one else wanted came here—the cripples and the outcasts, the unwanted and unloved. Misery washed over me.

"Would you say that Sister Catherine Joseph is well versed on the subject of blasphemy?" he asked me.

I looked at my feet.

"Well, I'd have to say I agree with you," he went on, his voice coaxing me to look at him. When I did I was confused to see that he was smiling. He went on: "I for one am most happy to be getting a student with such an advanced imagination. I can see that our writing classes are going to be much livelier, don't you agree, Winona?"

His sister gave me a cup of water and steadied my hand when I couldn't hold it. She said she had to admit that she couldn't see the humor in my getting myself banished from the Catholic Mission and the sight of Sister Catherine Joseph.

In a weary voice, drained of the laughter that had been there a few moments before, he told her he felt it was kinder to look for humor in another's righteous indignation than to admit to the cruelty that was at the heart of it, and that in his view it should not be a sin to want to know who your people are.

Winona Wright's face filled with contrition. I thought then, and I think now, that I've never known a person more intent on pleasing another as Winona Wright is in pleasing her brother. She touched me kindly on the shoulder, murmuring all the while that of course he was right, when you look at it that way, but it certainly was a wild story, that was all. She began to talk as if she had been wound up and had to wear down, about how not everybody in the world understood children the way he did, and I believe she would have gone on all afternoon if he hadn't held up his hand, palm out, a signal that cut her off mid-sentence.

It took Auntie Momi four days to find me. Jameson Wright brought her to the bungalow in which I had been assigned a room. After that she stayed nearby, doing small jobs, cleaning the school rooms. In the afternoons she would sit with Uncle Jameson on the lanai looking out to the ocean, and I could hear her familiar voice—flat and even, talking, talking. Her presence steadied me.

The Wrights were as peculiar as people said they were. Uncle Jameson didn't hold with organized religion or with what he called "Protestant progress." He favored the Hawaiians over the haoles, and made it plain that he did not approve of the Hawaiian Islands being annexed by anybody, not even his own countrymen. It was not the first time he had taken such an unpopular stand—the brother and sister had come out from Georgia after the war. It was said they opposed slavery, which made them misfits in their home state.

When I came to Hale Mana'olana, there were only four girls and six boys, none save Liko more than ten years of age. All had some mark—a small boy with tiny stick legs, a girl of ten with a face so pocked she tried to hide it with her hair. Liko, who is near to my own age, is a dwarf with the constitution of a small bull. The one tall, muscled Hawaiian boy who looked to be perfect could neither hear nor speak.

We were, all of us, in some way damaged. That was how we happened to find ourselves on this wide stretch of Waikiki far out from the city, past the taro patches and fish ponds and all the summer places of the Hawaiian royalty. Separated and protected from the world on this island within an island, we were young outcasts governed by old ones.

We children were expected to spend our mornings in the

schoolroom, our middays splashing in the ocean or playing, and late afternoons doing our chores. Liko, more fish than boy, coaxed me into the sea and showed me how to float, then how to turn my head this way and that to catch little breaths, and finally how to swim far out and let the waves lift and carry me back to the beach. Aunt and Uncle remained on the periphery of our existence. Their rules were few, but, we soon enough discovered, inviolate. We were never to do anything that would endanger ourselves or others, or do damage to the school. When the boy named Moku, who could not speak or hear, set fire to Uncle's cabin, we all worked furiously to save as many of the precious books as we could. Moku ran away, but came back the next morning, his sooty face streaked with tears, his eyes filled with remorse and misery. The Wrights sent him to the boys' reformatory.

I was able to help in the classroom by teaching the younger children their letters. Uncle began to select books for me to read. The days were never long enough; there was so much to do.

After a time I began to forget what the pattern of my days at the convent had been. No longer did I wake so often in the night with the questions sending sharp pains through my head. One afternoon I came out of the ocean to find Old Auntie waiting.

"I go now," she told me, touching her wrinkled old face to mine. I traced the tears that flooded her cheeks and kissed her good-bye; when she left, I found I felt sad but not afraid.

Write it all down, from that first day—do you remember?

I remember.

I thought you were the most curious, big-eyed little thing I'd ever seen . . .

And I thought she was from another world, with skin so pale and luminous you could see into it, a faint sprinkling of freckles scattered just beneath the surface, and eyes of such a strange, warm green that once you had looked into them, it was hard to look away. And the hair, the spun-white hair hanging long down her back so that she looked like the princess in Uncle's book of fairy tales, the one kept locked away in the tower.

The day Uncle came riding in with True, Aunt Winona came out to meet them, slowly and without saying a word. I remember thinking it strange that she should be speechless.

The little children gathered around staring, then Liko charged in, hands on his squat hips, challenging the strange girl to say who she was and if she planned to stay. True stared back, and ignoring Auntie's outstretched hands, jumped off by herself, tumbling and falling at my feet.

She looked up at me with a terrible wild anger in her eyes. I wanted to look away, to run away, but I could not. "If you come with me," I said so softly I could scarcely hear myself, being careful not to touch her, "I will show you where you will sleep."

She was to share my room, but for three days and three nights she did not stay there, nor did she speak to any of us. Early on the morning of the fourth day, I opened my eyes to find her sitting on her bed, watching me.

"This is where we are to live," she said. I couldn't be sure if it was a question.

"Yes," I answered, carefully.

She looked around the room, scanned the rafters lined in tapa, and the shutters that opened out to catch the sea breeze, and studied the titles of the books on my writing table. Her eyes returned to mine. "I do not believe in God," she told me.

I blinked and, not knowing what to say, said nothing. "I thought you should know that, if we are to share a room."

"I blasphemed," I croaked, the words crumpling as they came out of me.

She stared at me with her steady green eyes, and then she said, "Perhaps we could collect some seashells." Seeing my confusion, she explained, "To hang on the walls for decoration."

Six months later our walls were covered with seashells, each carefully named and labeled, and I had found—in this girl who was unlike me in every way—my much-needed friend.

BOOK I

Waikiki

1887–1899

1

June 1887

Lord, listen to me, True began her first prayer in four years, clamping her toes tightly around the edge of the rock, bracing against the sudden hard crack of a wave as it hit and surged and sent a fine spray into her face. *Please, Lord . . .* she started over, *help me to believe.* She could hear her mother's soft laughter, "He is listening, sweet child, no need to shout. He will hear" . . . *let me do this thing I must do. Keep me safe.*

She cupped her hand around her father's pocket watch and counted as the next wave surged in, pushing through the narrow channel with such force that it exploded on the rocks below, filling the small cove with a boiling and churning flood of seawater which rose and lifted for a long moment before pouring out again in preparation for the next rush. If she had calculated correctly, after a count of seven the fury of the wave should subside enough for her to swim out to the rock, where she would wait for the second wave to come back. If luck . . . *and God,* she added quickly under her breath . . . were with her, she would not be swept into the maelstrom and crushed against the rocks.

For six days she had sat on this ledge at the edge of the sea, the pocket watch that had been her father's wrapped in a handkerchief to shield it from the salt spray, timing the interludes between waves, thinking hard to decipher some pattern, some clear sign. Today was the seventh day, the Sabbath. She would pray to her mother's God to help her do this; she hoped He would understand her need.

The skies behind Diamond Head were massed with grey clouds and heat lightning pulsated through them. Out to sea, great cumulus giants piled high in the sky, dazzling white against the hard blue. She stood, squinting to the west, and the trade winds riffled her hair, lifting it in fine white strands. Behind her, the fronds of the coconut palms clacked as if restless in the breeze. It was time. She pulled her dress over her head, wrapped the watch carefully in it, raised her face to the sea and felt a sure, sweet surge of excitement.

He arrived at the moment when her body lifted high over the rocks, the flash of her skin reflecting the light like cool, smooth marble; he saw the first sweet swelling of breasts, her hair a spray of white, caught by the sun. For an instant (he was a practical man, not given to flights of fancy) he thought he might be seeing a mermaid. *Holy Christ,* he swore as soon as he realized it was a child, a girl, and that she would be crushed against the rocks. Fear sent the blood surging into his head. He broke into a run, cursing the deep sand for slowing him, but he pulled up short when he saw she had climbed onto a rock and was standing, perfectly still and naked, her sleek body glowing against the dark stone, watching the water and waiting.

He stepped into the shadow of a palm so she would not see him; his breath was coming hard. He wanted to call out, to tell her to stop, to wait. Then she was airborne again, defying all the laws he knew anything about: the law of gravity, the law of the sea, the law of logic and survival. He was not a man for memories, but that memory would remain: the luminous young body in flight over a rushing sea.

He waited, and watched as she pulled herself up and dropped her head on her arms, exhausted; after a few moments she looked up and he saw a face shining with such triumph that he looked away, embarrassed. When he turned back, she had slipped on her dress and was transformed into a girl of a dozen or so years, different from other girls of her age in these Pacific Islands only by her fair coloring.

"I think you must be True Lindstrom," he called out to her. "Miss Winona sent me to find you." She stared at him, her eyes warm and alive in her cool face, her steady glare challenging him to tell her how much he had seen.

But he was collected now, and he was not going to let this girl—this wild, pale child—know what fear she had struck in him. "My name is Evan Coulter," he said. "I have a message from your father."

He waited for her to speak, and when she did not he went

on, "I met him in Port Townsend, on the Washington coast. He was on a lumber schooner, and when he heard that my ship was sailing for Hawaii, he came aboard and asked for someone to carry a letter to his daughter on Maui." He smiled, but she did not respond, so he continued. "When I got to Maui, they told me you were here, on Oahu, which was just as well, since I had planned to come here to see my friends the Cleghorns, just down the beach at Ainahau."

She looked away, pretended to concentrate on a brig working its way down the coast. She had to breathe carefully to keep her body quiet after the struggle with the sea. Now, with the news brought by this man, she could feel her victory ebbing.

Her father had sent a message. Her father was alive. Her head dropped, her eyes closed, her legs grew weak. "Sit down," he told her, in charge now, and when she obeyed he blurted, "Why would you take such a monstrous risk?"

Her head snapped up, the eyes flecked with anger. "Don't tell," she commanded and saw the disapproval register in his eyes. Then she repeated, struggling to swallow a rising panic, measuring out the words in that peculiar child's voice with its echoes of silence: "Please do not tell."

"I don't know how you did it," he said, grudgingly, "or why you did it . . ."

She allowed the silence to hang in the air until finally he exhaled, took an envelope from his coat pocket, handed it to her and finished tersely, "Miss Winona said to tell you to come for tea. There is someone she would like for you to meet."

True took the envelope and vanished into the foliage like some wind wraith, and the air she stirred scattered the scent of jasmine, sweet and wistful. Evan Coulter couldn't say why, but the girl had unnerved him, and he felt uneasy and annoyed with himself.

Words issued from Winona Wright like water over a fall: in a rush, splashing and spraying, freefalling and, finally, running off into assorted babbling byways before finding its way into the mainstream.

"Did you find her, yes, Mr. Coulter?" she asked and then answered for him: "Yes, of course, or you wouldn't be back so soon, our True can be seen from a distance with that remarkable hair—Scandinavian, you know, Swedish in True's case. Her mother had those same fine, white tresses. A beautiful woman, True's mother. Did you know her? I suppose not, they were so isolated out on the farm. Amazing, that the father turns up now . . . No one seemed to know what happened to him . . ."

She paused long enough for her brother, Jameson, who had learned over the years how to gauge his sister's monologues, to break in: "Perhaps we should have tea now, Winona. Miss Barrows and the Princess must be thirsty. I suggest we move to the lanai, where it will be cooler."

"That would be lovely, wouldn't it, Kaiulani dear?" Jenny Barrows said, in a voice meant to ingratiate herself with the beautiful child who one day would be Queen of the Hawaiian Islands.

Jenny was small, with large eyes set in a heart-shaped face and a small, pursed mouth, soft pink and pliable. She was pretty in the way women with sharp features can be: a China doll prettiness, attractive in her middle twenties.

"Where are the girls who are my age?" Kaiulani asked, a tremble of petulance in her voice.

"True was sea bathing," Evan Coulter said, and Aunt Winona put in, "Wherever you find True, you can be sure Martha Moon will be close by. We don't always know where they are, but we know they will be together. I'll send one of the children to find them."

The young Princess Victoria Kaiulani, oblivious of her white dress with the insets of lace, sat down impatiently on one of the dusty porch steps. Except for Evan, who had lived with the Cleghorns for two years while he finished school at Punahou and treated Kaiulani as if she were his little sister, the adults were deferential to the princess.

"I've asked the older children to join us for tea," Aunt Winona answered, then laughed. "Perhaps they will come, and then again, perhaps they won't. We try not to make rules that aren't terribly necessary, and afternoon tea doesn't seem to either of us—" she nodded at her brother to show their solidarity—"to be necessary. Did True say she would come?" she asked Evan. "Did you happen to see Liko and Martha Moon? Such a strange little trio, as different as night and day, yet like three cherries on a stem . . . Oh, they'll be ever so pleased to make your acquaintance, Princess Kaiulani. They know you are our neighbor—though it is a good ride down the road to your place. True is the leader, no doubt about that at all, and you would be surprised where she leads sometimes . . . they get into a certain amount of mischief. Lately she's spending a good bit of time out at the cove and it makes me think . . . what was True doing when you came upon her?" she asked Evan and, to everyone's surprise, waited for an answer.

Burrowed in the warm sand in the crawl space beneath the lanai, taking shallow breaths so we would not be heard, True and Liko and I waited to hear what Evan Coulter would say.

"She *was* at the cove," he began, a trace of discomfort in his voice, "but the others, I don't know . . . I didn't see them—who are they?" he asked, rather obviously trying to coax Aunt into one of her monologues.

"Tell us first about the girl True," Jenny broke in. "I remember when it happened—everyone was talking about it in such a hush . . ."

"Why was that?" the Princess Kaiulani, who had not seemed to be listening, asked, suddenly interested. "What are you talking about?"

"Nothing you need to know about, Big Ears," Evan Coulter said, grinning.

With an exaggerated sigh, she answered, "Oh, Evan. Can't you do something? You always used to play with me. Now I have no one to play with and no one to talk to."

"Poor little princess," he mocked, teasing a smile out of her. "Maybe you could go down to the pond and catch yourself a frog. I've heard that a real princess could turn one of those into a prince."

"I am a real princess," she said sharply. "You know that very well, Evan. I am third in line to the throne of Hawaii . . . after Uncle David and Auntie Liliuokalani . . . then me." Evan pulled one of her dark curls and chucked her under the chin until she had to laugh. She tried to be angry with him, but couldn't. "I am never going to say anything nice about you, not ever again," she said, trying hard to be serious. "Miss Jenny, if I were you I wouldn't spend another minute with this not-nice person."

"I have a new game," Jameson broke in. "Actually it is an old game called Chinese checkers. True and Martha are quite the game players, but they haven't had a chance to learn this one yet. I wonder if perhaps you would like me to teach you, so when those two show up you will already know how to play?"

Uncle had figured Kaiulani perfectly; she settled down at the table across from him, and they were quickly absorbed in sorting out the marbles and setting up the board. Jenny Barrows rose and moved close to Evan, whispering, "I didn't mean to . . ."

Evan silenced her by saying, "We'll talk later."

Rebuffed, Jenny turned to ask Aunt, "How many bungalows do you have in your . . ." she hesitated for a moment, not quite knowing what to call it, and settled finally for "school?"

"Three, four counting this one," Winona began. "It was such good fortune, finding this place with its wooden structures, close enough to Honolulu to attend church and get medical help when we need it—far enough away so the children can roam free. Jameson teaches the natural sciences and mathematics. I teach grammar and reading and writing. We brought our father's library out from Savannah— though we lost part of it in a fire some months back, we can scarcely bear to think of it—but we feel we can give our children the rudiments of an education. Martha Moon is a great help with the little children. True would much rather be outside all day. She has taken charge of our menagerie— Jameson says he's never seen a child with such an understanding of animals. And of course we keep a garden, and each child has a plot to care for, so we have a busy little enterprise, as you can see."

Jennie smiled; it was pleasant enough, she supposed, nicer than what she had expected from all the talk about the Wrights. Feeling expansive, she lifted her arm and pointed, "What a lovely flowering bush—such beautiful big blossoms."

Jameson chimed in from across the lanai. "Belladonna," he drawled. "Quite poisonous, you know. Said to induce strange waking dreams. The old Hawaiians would heat the blooms and breath in the vapor. They believed it could cure all manner of lung ailments."

Kaiulani skipped a marble two, three jumps, looked at him triumphantly and said, "You must pay better attention, Uncle."

"Indeed I must," he answered, in the tone he always uses when he lets you win.

"You said you had recently been to the Big Island, Evan," Aunt Winona said and changed the subject. "I've always been curious about that great, empty island—we should love to be able to see an actual volcanic eruption."

Evan Coulter's voice betrayed his fascination. "I'd done some business with Colonel Wakefield so when he invited me to Mau'loa—the Wakefield ranch—I took him up on it. I hadn't planned to stay quite so long, but . . . it was hard to leave, I admit."

Jenny laughed and added, significantly, "We were all beginning to worry."

Evan Coulter, at twenty-four, was still boy enough to blush. "I admit it surprised me, the Big Island and Mau'loa ranch," he began, "I'm not sure just what I expected. The wildness, yes. But not . . ." He paused, and then, as if he had just figured it out, "not the grand sweep of the land, the mountains rising up in the distance, into the clouds—all snowcapped. We rode out on the high plateau, the grass was belly-high on the horses and it was so clear you could see Maui in the distance. It was like . . ." he was struggling for words to describe what he felt but when they didn't come he settled for ". . . nothing you'd ever imagine."

Jenny, eager to take part, put in, "Maudie Ingram went over on one of Colonel Toby's riding parties—she's a friend of his niece Malama. Maudie said the horses were half wild, and the trails went through such tangled brush that she got all scratched up, and it rained something terrible too."

In our nest, Liko rolled his eyes and made a face and True glared at him fiercely to keep him quiet. Liko had taken exception to the tone of Miss Jenny Barrows' voice. So had True, and so had I.

"But you never did answer Miss Winona's question, Evan," Jenny suddenly put in, "about what our strange little Miss True was doing when you came upon her."

True wrapped her arms tightly around her chest, to still the beating of her heart. I slipped my hand into hers and held on tight. We did not know what would happen if Evan told; Auntie Winona had warned her once, and Uncle had been stern about True's wildness.

"I didn't find her strange at all," Evan began in a voice he managed to keep free of reproach. "And to answer Miss Winona's question—she was standing on a rock, looking at the ocean. I'm afraid I startled her, coming up with a message from her father so abruptly. I thought about making up a story—telling her that her father said he missed her, something like that. But the fact is, Miss True Lindstrom was well named; it isn't easy to lie to her."

"Seems to me our True has caught your fancy, Mr. Coulter," Aunt Winona said and laughed. "I'd watch out, Miss Barrows."

Under the floorboards, the three of us rocked back and forth to keep from crying out with relief. That night, True got down on her knees by her bed and thanked God for sending her Evan Coulter.

2

On the following Tuesday, without announcement, Kaiulani rode in on the pony she called Fairy, followed by one of the retainers who went with her everywhere. Her long slim legs were brown against the pony's white flanks, and there were beads of perspiration at her hairline, causing her face to be ringed by small, damp curls. She was hot and, though she would not admit it, tired. Liko saw her first and stood staring, his mouth dropped open.

"It is not polite to stare," she chided him. Liko, struck dumb, began swinging his big head this way and that, rolling his eyes to keep her in view. She looked away, as if he were too silly to be bothered with, and craned her neck to scan the yard, wishing someone would come soon so she could ask for a drink.

"Princess Kaiulani!" Uncle called as he came out of the schoolroom. "What a nice surprise."

"I've come to play with the girls," she told him. "Checkers. I should like to play Chinese checkers."

Uncle smiled, settled her on the lanai, told Liko to get her a lemonade and came to fetch us.

"I am going sea bathing with Liko," True told him flatly. "She can come along if she likes."

Uncle frowned. "She seemed a bit tired, I think. It's quite a long ride she made, just to see you girls. And Liko is with her—you remember how he stared at you when you first came? Well, the Princess is getting Liko's full attention right now. We'll have to see if he wins her over as well." Thinking about it, he chuckled. Then, more seriously, "I believe she is looking forward to playing a quiet game, True. She is not as robust as you are. It would be nice if you and Martha would change your plans for the afternoon." He paused for a moment, then added, "She is the

21

Princess Royal, you know. One day she will be Queen of these islands."

True lifted her chin. "Are you saying we should play with her, because she is important?"

Uncle did not answer. Instead, he looked at me and shook his head slightly; I knew what it meant. It meant he was counting on me to win True over. I sighed; it would not be easy. She had set herself another challenge, this time riding the waves on a long, smooth surf board that Liko had managed to acquire, and very little could deter True once she had set herself a goal.

"I choose blue," Kaiulani said.

True looked at her with unconcealed annoyance. "This is how we choose," she explained as if there were no other choice. "Each of us picks a card. The highest number chooses first, the next highest second and the lowest, last."

Kaiulani collapsed into her chair, glowering, but when Liko fanned the cards out in front of her she pulled one out.

It was a six. I drew a ten and True, a jack.

"I choose first," True said, ignoring the frown on Kaiulani's face, "and I choose red."

"Green," I put in quickly. "My choice is green."

Kaiulani sat up very straight, her face radiant, and said, "Blue is my favorite color. I choose blue." And then she added, regally, "I really am a Princess, you know. My name is Victoria Kaiulani—Pa calls me Vicky. You may call me Vicky too."

At that moment, I knew I had never seen anyone more exquisitely beautiful than this girl—this *hapa haole* like me—who was, as we were becoming increasingly aware, the last hope of the Hawaiian crown. There are pictures of her which give a small measure of her beauty—the great eyes, which seem even larger because she is so near-sighted and has, most of the time, to wear specs; the long, graceful neck; the delicate mouth. But none of the photographs convey the lights that play in her eyes when she is happy, or the excitement that wells up when she has mastered a challenge, or the sweet sadness that sometimes overtakes her.

Vicky became our friend and playmate that summer. Whenever she came, Uncle allowed us to do much as we wished, although we were often cautioned to take care not to tire her. The three of us, sometimes with Liko and always with Vicky's retainer trailing after to keep her safe, explored the far reaches of the beachlands. Sometimes we would take along a lunch and spend the whole day out, swimming and fishing and exploring and talking.

We quickly learned that Vicky was not strong. True seemed to take that as a challenge and became determined to prove that Vicky was stronger than she imagined herself to be. In the ocean, where Liko reigned supreme no matter how hard True pushed to equal him, he was never far from Vicky, in case she needed help.

After sea bathing, we took turns brushing each other's hair with an ornate, silver brush that glittered in the sun. It was a gift to Vicky from her uncle, King David Kalakaua. She smuggled it out of her house each day, she explained, "Because Mama has such a temper, and if she knew I was taking it to play, she would be angry and make us all unhappy."

One day as she was brushing True's hair, Vicky said, "If this were the old days, I would be a chiefess and wear a shark's tooth on a braided strand of this beautiful white gold hair of yours."

True laughed and said, "You've pulled out enough of my hair to make six necklaces. Besides, I'm sorry to have to tell you this, Vicky, but you're not fierce enough to wear a shark's tooth, so maybe you'll never be a real chiefess."

A sudden summer squall moved across Vicky's beautiful face. "I *am* a chiefess—you know that," she insisted angrily, her dark eyes flashing with fury. "I really am, and you must understand. I am not like you at all. Not at all. One day I will be Queen. I will be!"

"We know that," I interjected quickly. "True didn't mean . . ."

"You don't have to explain what I meant," True said. She was hurt by Vicky's angry words, and I could tell by the square thrust of her chin that this storm would not be allowed to blow over quickly.

The two of them sat on the sand at water's edge, their backs rigidly straight, looking away from each other. Miserable, I searched for some words that might clear the anger, blow it away over the ocean. "We still have the whole of the afternoon," I fumbled. "Let's not ruin . . ."

As if mobilized by my words, True stood up and began gathering her things. Vicky watched, waiting for some conciliatory gesture, some small move that would make it easy for her to dismiss her tantrum without accepting blame. When True began walking away, Vicky knew she had lost. "Go, then!" she lashed out, "but I know about your mother, about what happened to her. I know!"

True stopped, her head fell forward for an instant, but she lifted it almost at once and, without turning around, walked on, her feet digging deep and hard into the sand.

I wanted to run after her, but Vicky's eyes had filled with tears and she begged, "Don't leave me," in such a small, sad voice that I stayed. True would want to be alone—I had learned that in those early weeks with her. Patience was the key with True; she could not be rushed. I had known from the beginning that something terrible had happened to True, and I had known from the beginning that I could not ask. She would tell me when she was ready, and I would wait.

That night True did not come to the cottage until she thought I was sleeping. She climbed into bed and turned two or three times before she settled down.

I said, "I'm sorry."

She let the silence grow. My eyes were growing heavy when she said, "Why?"

It was my turn to ponder the question. "Because," I finally said, "Vicky was trying to hurt you with something that I think must hurt you too much already. So I am sorry for your pain and sorry for Vicky that she couldn't help but do something so mean."

"Didn't she tell you?" she asked, and I knew from her tone that she was frowning.

"No," I answered.

"My mother was killed."

A little gasp escaped me.

"My mother was murdered by the *luna* on our farm. When it happened, my father was on the Mainland. He never came back for me." Her voice was flat and hard.

After a while I ventured, "The letter that Evan brought?"

"There was no letter," she said, a tightness in her throat. "There was a bank draft for fifty dollars—that's all."

I slipped out of my bed and into hers, and held her close when she started shivering and crying. Her pillow grew wet with our tears; I wrapped my arms around her and waited; sometime in the early morning hours her body seemed to sigh, and soon I could hear the soft sounds of sleep breathing. When it happened I cannot say, but sometime during that long night a loneliness that had been lodged inside of me left. When I woke the next morning I felt bone tired and free.

The next day Vicky's pa, Archibald Cleghorn, came. He was tall and craggy in a formal longcoat, his beard and gentle smile giving him the appearance of a wise and kindly judge. He talked with Uncle for a time, and then he asked to speak to True.

In his soft Scots accent he said, "Ah, lass, my girl Kaiulani is fair ashamed of what she did to hurt you. She has a quick temper, that one, but she is a bonny girl, you know. And she values her friendships here, with you and Miss Martha. I've never seen my Vicky so strong and lively. I know we have you to thank for that, lass. So as a selfish old man, I've come to ask your forgiveness for the hurt my daughter did you. She is more sorry than you can know, and she will tell you herself if you'll come to visit us—you and Miss Martha and the boy, if he wants to come along. Mr. Jameson and Miss Winona have given their permission. Vicky is sitting home now, waiting for me to come back, praying you'll say yes."

Vicky and Evan were waiting at the gate at Ainahau. Evan stood back, his long frame leaning against the stone gate, and I could tell from his smile that he knew all that had happened. "We've been waiting all morning long," Vicky called out even before we got there, "but where is Liko?"

"He wanted awfully to come," I told her, "but at the last minute he was too shy. He says you are to come visit us soon."

"We're just on time," True added uncertainly. She hadn't expected Evan. I suspected that Vicky had brought him along because she knew, from all the questions True asked, that she was partial to him.

We rode through the gardens of Ainahau, which Vicky's pa had planted with a profusion of flowers and trees and shrubs from all the far corners of the world. Evan told us some of the names; I looked up at him, and saw what True would see: smooth skin stretched taut over a strong jaw, light brown hair that was thick and unruly, and brown eyes filled with fun. He spoke to us as if we were grown-ups, except for Vicky, whom he treated as a pesky little sister.

Now and then I noticed him glancing at True, as if he found her curious. She was just beginning to relax and talk back a little when we got to the house, and Jenny Barrows came running out to claim Evan.

Vicky's pa welcomed us as if we were ladies, making certain we met Vicky's half-sisters (his daughters by a Hawaiian lady named Elizabeth, Vicky would tell us later), and her mother, the Princess Miriam Likelike, who was small and dark and would have been pretty, had she not scowled and fretted so.

"Have we done something to make your mother angry?" I asked Vicky.

"No, no," she answered, sighing. "Mama's like that; even when she isn't angry she seems so."

You could tell that Vicky wanted nothing so much as to be off with us; she could scarcely contain her impatience. Her mother did not seem to notice, for she kept asking Vicky questions about how she was feeling and telling her what she should or should not do to conserve her energy, and then she told us that she expected us to be especially careful when we played with her little princess. At that, Archie Cleghorn winked at us and said very tenderly, "My dear, I think the girls would like to be off to have a look at the gardens."

True scarcely heard; her eyes were following Jenny Barrows and Evan Coulter, who were walking arm-in-arm down a path that led to the beach, Jenny's small, neat little head bent possessively against his shoulder.

Released, we raced across the wide lawn, True in the lead, me holding back so that Vicky could be second. "No, no," we heard her mother call from the lanai, but it was too late—we were free of them.

Vicky did not apologize. I think she was too afraid, for fear True would bolt. Vicky had not yet learned what I already knew: that it was over, that True did not harbor resentments. Vicky took True's hand in hers, comparing the dark to the light as she liked to do, and True said, "I would like to be in your skin for a time. Shall we trade?"

"I would like that," Vicky told her.

"No," True answered. "You wouldn't. It would be too lonely for your pa and your mother." Near the end of the afternoon we broke off some branches of a tamarind tree and were fencing with them, lunging and poking each other, laughing when the leaves tickled our faces. Vicky jumped from a low wall and attacked me from behind; yowling, I turned and thrust my leafy branch, and she yelped in pain.

Blood gushed from a small gouge just above her eye and ran down the side of her nose. My heart started beating wildly. "It's all right, it's all right," Vicky kept saying. True pressed the cut with leaves dipped in seawater, and we walked as fast as we could back to the house, me saying how sorry I was and Vicky saying it was all right, that it was just a little cut. But before those sitting on the verandah could see us, Vicky made me promise to be silent, to let her do the explaining.

"Please," she pleaded, "I know exactly what to say, not to get Mama riled, and you must not contradict me." She smiled then, a whimsical smile dissected by a rivulet of blood. "Remember, I am a princess. You must obey."

"Who did this?" Vicky's mother demanded. She was looking at True.

"No one did it, Mama," Vicky said. She was taller than her mother and slipped her arm easily around her waist. "I was silly enough to run into a low branch, that's all. It's just a scratch."

"Archie, come," the Princess Likelike called, her voice edging to hysteria. "Kaiulani is bleeding!"

Although she had wanted to play, Vicky allowed herself to be bandaged and propped on a chaise to watch the croquet match; I sat on the ground next to her, feeling abashed, but mostly glad because Vicky was basking in the glow of True's pride. ("You *are* a real Princess," True had whispered to her when she protected me.)

While Jenny did some practice shots, Evan was instructing True on how to play the game. She listened intently; games were serious to True, and even her fascination for Evan Coulter did not break her concentration.

From the first stroke, it was obvious that Jenny Barrows was a very good player, and True was not, and I knew that meant trouble.

True's first strokes were wild and strong. "You're trying too hard," Evan told her once, and again, when she missed, "Don't be discouraged, you're doing well for your first game."

Jenny was not so agreeable a competitor. She had a habit of pressing her hands together and emitting a small, ecstatic "Oh!" when others did poorly. On True's next shot, she stood very straight, took aim and slammed the croquet ball hard. We all heard it crack into Jenny Barrows' ankle bone.

Jenny limped off the court, biting her lip with pain. Evan helped her to a chair.

"She did it on purpose," Jenny told him.

"What?" he said, as if he couldn't have heard right.

"I said she meant to hit me," Jenny repeated calmly.

"You also said she couldn't hit the wide side of a barn, remember?"

"She did it on purpose," Jenny insisted.

"Did you mean to hit Jenny?" Evan asked.

"What?"

"Hit Jenny with the croquet ball?"

"Why would I?" True said.

"I don't know. Maybe you don't like her."

"Maybe I don't," she agreed. "I did not mean to hit her. I'm not good enough to aim that well. But I think she deserved it."

Evan looked at her and frowned. Once again, he was awkward in the presence of this girl and it unnerved him. "That's not a nice thing to say," he finally told her.

"She is not a nice player," True came back. "She expects the advantage from those who play better than she does, but she won't give it to those who aren't as good."

Evan looked at her. She could see the questions flickering across his eyes, like the shadows of clouds on the ocean. Then he turned and walked back to Jenny.

Vicky had to think hard to answer True's questions. "Pa says Evan is smart and levelheaded, and I know he trusts him," she said. "I think his father had a small business, or maybe it was his uncle, I'm not sure. Evan lived with us for two years—that was the best time! He would play with me, and when Mama would get really angry with Papa, he would take me out of the way. He left our house to go to see the world—on lumber ships, I think. Since he's been back he's been asked to serve on some committees—Pa says he's not political, but that he is quick and fair, so he is in favor in both camps—the Reformers and those who support the Monarchy."

"Is he white?" I asked.

"Yes, but Pa says he has a sympathy for the Hawaiians. I always tease him about being Hawaiian, and he always says he wishes he was."

True sat with her chin in her hand, thinking. Finally she asked, "Is he going to marry Jenny Barrows?"

Vicky looked at her curiously, hesitating before she said, "Well, I suppose so. I know Mama thinks so. The Barrows are strong Monarchists. If you met Jenny's father, you'd be surprised . . . he's a giant man, big and red and fat, and he hasn't a spit of manners. He just ups and speaks his mind, and it doesn't matter a bit what you think. But he's free with his money—he owns the big slaughterhouse, and the butcher shop . . . We need all the good people we can get, you know." Vicky's tone took on an edge of self-importance, "You can't always choose your future. Mine is all planned out for me, I haven't much to say about it and I suppose when it's time, I'll be told whom to marry. I do hope I love him, of course . . . but that's a long way away."

True would not let Vicky distract her. "What about Evan, does he care about her?"

"Why are you asking so many questions about them?" Vicky came back, tired of the subject.

"Does he want to marry her?" True repeated.

Vicky sighed and answered, "When I asked him, he said he couldn't think of marrying anybody until he gets back from Yale. He's decided to go to law school—he'll be leaving in a few weeks. Pa thinks it a good thing."

True sat up straight, fighting a small, satisfied smile which struggled to escape. Evan Coulter would be away four years. When he returned she would be eighteen. There was still time.

3

As I think of it now, that summer was the last of our childhood, days and weeks of sunlight and laughter bubbling up out of us for the sweet joy of being together, the warm air and soft rhythms of living. We would run barefoot through the hot sand to fling ourselves into the surf, or gallop the ponies full-out along the edge of the water or run until our sides ached and we could run no more, so we would drop in the shade of a coconut grove, sprawled out, and when we had caught our breath either Vicky or True or Liko would ask me to talk one of Auntie's old stories.

Without her specs, Vicky could not see well at all. Sometimes we managed to outrun the retainer that followed Kaiulani, but we always watched over her, so she was safe. Sometimes when I was telling a story the heavy lids of her eyes would half close, and I would wonder how much she heard. When the time came that I had talked all the stories and had to start over again, I would discover that she remembered well enough to correct me.

True says I have a talent for mimicry; I know that when I talk Auntie's stories I take on her tone—low but not melodic, rather the opposite. If I close my eyes even now, I can hear Auntie's voice—steady and droning and as inexorable as the wind blowing down from the Pali.

Vicky's favorites were the stories about Kaahumanu, the queen who had most influenced her own fate. Though Kaahumanu is dead now these fifty-five years, there are those still living who knew her, whose old eyes glow bright when they speak of her, as if they cannot believe it still, all that she was, all that she meant to the people of Hawaii. Old Auntie Momi is one such; Auntie's mother was a member of Kaahumanu's court, a favored friend, a keeper of her secrets in the fearful days at the end of the Great King's life and the months following, when life in these islands was changed forever because of the strong heart, the courage and the ambition, of this one great woman.

She lay on her stomach in the warm sand, the first of the Kaahumanu stories begins, *wishing the slow ache at the pit of her belly would go away, wanting the time of the blood weeping to end so that she could return to her father's house.* She was lonely for her cousin, who had been confined at the same time for all these months past. Now this cousin was with child, and it would be long months before she would be *kapu* again and would be required to remove herself to this place—the *hale pe'a*—away from the life of the village.

Kaahumanu touched the place between her legs and felt it wet and thick. She frowned. It had been four days, the bleeding should be finished, she felt angry that it was not. She dipped her fingers in water to rinse the blood from them, and began a rough kneading of her stomach as if to punish it for keeping her imprisoned.

She stood, stretched, reached high to the branches of a kou tree, grabbing it with her hands and lifting herself until her large breasts were swinging free. The weight of their movement made her look down at them, two large full globes with great nipples at the end. She smiled to herself, knowing that the size of a girl's breast told how many boys she lay with. She blew on her nipples and watched as they grew hard and erect, then she laughed, remembering how it was with Kaiana. His tall, hard body; her legs wrapped around him. She had a fine, big body, she knew that. Men could not keep themselves from looking at her; it had been this way, even before the time of the bleeding. She caressed her long arms, her long legs, her stomach of rippling muscles. Even the King was looking at her, and she knew the look. He wanted her, and he would have her. She was sorry he was such an old man, in his thirty-fourth year. His body was not a boy's and his face not so fierce as it had once been; but he had not reached the fullness of his power, nor had he reached the fullness of his desire. She knew that, more than he. She would be his next Queen, and she would be the last; she would make certain of that.

Kamehameha the Great, the most powerful king the islands had ever known, wanted her. He would get her, but she would say when, and how. She felt another surge of blood pushing out of her and let out a small cry of anger. *She had not thought to stay kapu this long. She was to have been out of here, and away, by the time of sunset this day and already, the sun was casting long shadows on the sand.*

"Kaahumanu," a woman's voice sounded soft and tinged with fear. "I am sent to bring you to the King. Come quickly, now."

As the messenger bent to come into the hut from the sunlight, Kaahumanu did not know who it was that spoke in such troubled tones. Then, slowly, the woman's face came into view. She saw that it was the mother of the young chief Kaiana, and she knew what the King was threatening.

She looked at the woman for a long time. Seeing the sweet likeness of the son in the face of the mother made her speak more gently. "Tell the King that I cannot come, that I am kapu, and unclean."

The woman's voice tightened. "It has been four days. The King says it is long enough. You are to bathe and appear before him. You cannot disobey."

Kaahumanu spoke with a small edge of anger: "Say that I am unclean still, that I will present myself when I am not kapu."

The woman's eyes were large with fear, and Kaahumanu knew it was for her son. She made her voice warm and sure when she said, "Go, tell him. You can say I wished to come, but I was afraid of what the gods might do, if I should break the King's own law. Tell him I wailed with sorrow, not to come when my King sent for me." The woman stood, uncertain of herself. "Go!" Kaahumanu urged.

She watched the sun move closer to the sea; a crease appeared in her broad, smooth forehead. She touched herself again, and again pulled away fingers marked by dark blood. She went to the pool of brackish water, removed the tapa cloth from her waist and, naked, lowered herself into the spring water. The coldness caught her in the throat and she had to stifle a cry. With her hand she rinsed the hair that was stiff with dried blood. She stood then, walked across the grounds to the sandy beach, walked very slowly into the water, felt the salt froth of the waves lap at her mouth, felt the water lift her. She swam with strokes that were strong and sure, moving until the palm grove she had left behind was like a small twig; she swam along the coast until she saw the white rock in the shape of a turtle, caught between two trees.

She pushed herself up, both arms lifted in greeting, and sent a strong, piercing, joyful wail out and over the water to where he waited. As she rode the long wave in, she saw him remove his malo; as she stood he ran to meet her, and she could see that his want for her was great.

That night she did not tell him that his mother had been sent to her as a messenger, did not tell him that the King wanted her, or that she would go to him the next day. That night, they lay together on the bed of soft leaves that he had gathered, her powerful limbs wrapped around his, and cries of delight sprang from both of them. He did not hear her leave, did not know that she was back in the *hale pe'a* before full light. He knew nothing except his want for her, which filled his body and his heart . . .

Whenever I talked that story, Liko lay on his stomach in the sand, his right hand under him, writhing and groaning. Vicky and I looked away, but True did not.

I knew before I opened my eyes that it had returned. The bleakness that filled me, the heaviness that settled into my arms and legs, the awful emptiness.

"Get up, get up, sleepyhead," True chirped, hopping about my bed.

It was too much of an effort to answer her. The words echoed somewhere deep inside me but would not rise. *Go away, leave me be.*

She plumped down on my bed and tickled my chin. "Martha Moonie, you're late, late, late," she teased.

I sighed, it was all I could do, then I turned my face away, not to have to see the expression of alarm that was coming over her face.

"Go away," I managed to get out.

"Go away?" she repeated, as if I had said something she didn't understand. "Are you feeling poorly, Martha? Are you hurting?"

I could not summon the strength to answer.

She put her hand on my forehead, waited for a long moment and then took off, running.

"I thought she was done with that," Aunt Winona said, frowning with irritation. "Seems I was wrong."

"Done with what?" True asked.

"Martha's decided to take herself a little vacation from work," Aunt explained, huffing up. "She used to do it often before you came. I'd hoped she'd grown out of it."

"Grown out of what?" True wanted to know, trying to control her growing impatience.

"Laziness," Aunt answered. "Just that. She has a pure, lazy streak, and she just ups and refuses to work. And poor Mr. Wright will have to take over her classes again, as well as his own. I just hope she comes to her senses in time . . ."

True didn't wait to hear whatever else Aunt had to say, as she was off and running back to our cottage. This time she didn't sit on my bed, as if she understood that any jolt, any physical touch, might be painful to me.

"Martha, can you stand? Can you use the slop jar? I'll carry it out then, and bring a basin of water so you can wash your face."

I wanted her to leave, wanted to close my eyes to the bright light of day, wanted to sink back into the greyness, wanted even to deny the urgencies of my body. But looking into her eyes, seeing something that was akin to panic, I forced myself to nod. She held onto me, helped me hitch up my gown so I wouldn't wet it, held onto me as I squatted. The silence was broken by the sound of my water against the ironstone slop jar. Liko stood in the doorway, watching, but I didn't care.

"Go feed the chickens for me," True told him. "I'll be along in a bit."

"What's wrong?" he ventured.

"Go!" True hissed, and he went.

"He's just worried about you," True said. "Like I am."

I sighed; it was all I could do. It was an extra burden to carry—True and Liko, their concern for me. I would have wished them away, if I could.

I stayed in my bed all that morning while True went off to her chores and Uncle took my classes. At noon, both of them came to the room, with Liko just behind.

"Martha, can you tell us if something is wrong?" True asked timidly.

"She's not lazy!" Liko blurted, and both Uncle and True glowered at him.

"Of course she's not," Uncle said. "Maybe a dose of tonic? Do you think that will help?"

I turned my face away in disgust. Aunt Winona's tonic was foul tasting, and I never saw that it helped one bit.

"No," True said. "But Uncle, if Liko and one of the boys could take over a few of my chores, maybe Martha and I can go for some walks."

To encourage me, she said, "Not long walks, Mooney, just little ones. I think you'll just feel better, if you can be up and moving."

Uncle paused at the door. "Let True help you, Martha. I think she may be right about the walking."

And so we walked . . . at first, ten or fifteen minutes every three hours. Then for twenty minutes every two hours. It got dark and I thought she would leave me be, let me sink back into the greyness, but she didn't. There was a full moon and she pulled me out of the bed. I wanted nothing so much as to close my eyes and disappear into sleep, but she wouldn't let me and I hadn't the strength to fight her.

At daybreak, we were sitting in the damp sand at the edge of the water, our feet covered with sea froth, her hand in mine, tightly, our heads close together.

"What could a tiny baby have done that would cause its mother to send it away, out of her sight forever?" I asked in a coarse whisper. "Why wouldn't she give her baby to an auntie to keep? That's what the Hawaiians always do, they never abandon a child."

"I guess they must, sometimes," True said.

I sighed again—I couldn't help it. "Unless my father was a haole and she hated that part of me that is white."

"Or if she was the haole and couldn't love the part of you that was dark," True finished for me.

"Yes," I said. "Either way, I don't know which part of me is hateful!"

A wave washed in, and we scooted back to keep our nightdresses from getting soaked.

"You could never be hateful," True said as we walked along the beach, watching the sky cast a delicate shade of pink on the waters. "A tiny baby could never be hateful. The person who gave you away was hateful, not you. Or maybe it was something else, something she couldn't help . . ."

"Oh, True, what could it possibly be? I've thought and

thought about it . . . there are times when I think I'll go mad if I don't know . . . I couldn't have come out of thin air, could I? There has to be a mother, doesn't there? And people who are part of me?"

"We'll find out, Martha. Maybe not right now, but some-day. I promise I'll help find your ohana."

As we rounded the point, we saw Liko racing down the beach as fast as his little legs could carry him, his coarse black hair all disheveled from sleep.

"If only he could run on those strong arms of his, he would be here in a minute," True said.

I had to smile at the thought.

She touched the corners of my mouth with the tips of her fingers, looked at me with those solemn blue eyes and then hugged me, hard. "You can't know how good it is to see you smile again," she said.

"You're back, you're back," Liko screamed, flinging him-self into us. True and I dropped to our knees to include him in our embrace and I thought, "This is all the ohana I have, True and Liko and me."

True stood on her tiptoes in the doorway, unable to contain herself.

"What could possibly produce that look of absolute satis-faction?" I asked, laughing.

"Uncle isn't going on the mountain outing!"

"What?" I exclaimed, puzzled. "Then we can't go . . . can we? I mean . . . oh, but we've worked so hard making all the butterfly nets . . . and the little children are so excited . . . what will . . ."

"Listen!" she stopped me, reeling into the room in a spin, smiling a beautiful smile. "Uncle has to go into Honolulu to take care of some *urgent* business with Vicky's pa. Evan came out to tell him . . ."

"Evan is here? Now?"

She twirled around twice and landed on her back on my bed, her arms flung over her head. "He's just left—had to hurry off, but he'll be back tomorrow morning just after daylight . . ."

"Evan is going to take Uncle's place?" I guessed.

"Yes!" she sang out. "Yes, yes, yes . . ."

I remembered then, Evan poring over the butterfly collection Uncle had brought with him from Georgia. Evan had spoken of collecting expeditions with his father on Maui, and it seemed as if Uncle knew something about Evan's father as a collector. Certainly he was impressed with Evan's knowledge. So it made perfect sense—Evan would be the obvious one to take Uncle's place.

Even so, True's boldness embarrassed me. The next morning she was out before anyone else, getting the mounts ready, helping Aunt make certain the cook had packed all the foods we needed, seeing to the proper packing of the equipment. By the time Evan arrived, she had us all out and ready and waiting . . . two of the smallest children had curled up and were sleeping in the wagon.

She spurred her mount into the lead, next to Evan. Four of the bigger boys doubled up on the two horses that followed, and two more drove the wagon with Aunt Winona and the little children and provisions for three days. Liko and I brought up the rear on the ponies.

It was an amazement to see True . . . who was not a chatty sort of girl . . . talking so. I don't know what she was saying, but now and then Evan would say something back, and she would look satisfied.

For about an hour we moved in a long, gradual ascent up the mountain. Then the road became much steeper and only just wide enough for the wagon. The sunshine had turned to mist, the mist to a slow, easy rain, and the roadway turned to mud. Evan dismounted to lead the wagon team.

It was lunchtime when we arrived at our destination, the summerhouse of the Tobin family. It couldn't properly be called a house; in fact, it was a ferry boat that had gone aground on the rocks off Kawaihoa Point. Mrs. Tobin, a bit of an eccentric, had the fine idea to dismantle the beamy old boat and reconstruct it in the cool, high hills behind Honolulu. Mr. Tobin was a practical man; his one weakness, as Vicky's pa put it, was that he could deny his wife not a thing. And so the boat *High Hopes* came to be moored in a mountaintop forest. Tonight, we would sleep in hammocks slung below deck . . . rocked by the mountain winds instead of the ocean waves.

The children swarmed all over the mountain boat, paying no attention at all to the steady drizzle but climbing ladders up and down, having such a fine time that Evan had difficulty calling them together for the demonstration. When there was only an hour or so left of light, the sun broke through, casting long shafts through the trees. "Butterflies love the sunlight," Evan called to us, "and they love sunny pathways. Let's see if we can find one or two . . . I'll show you how to catch them."

"Should we carry our collecting jars?" the little boy Jimmy asked.

"Let's take just one jar, but we won't put the poison in it. Today I'll show you the best way to net a butterfly, and how to get it from the net into the jar without damaging the wings. That is very important, because no one wants a butterfly with a broken wing. Today is for practice . . . we'll release any butterflies we catch."

A collective groan rose from the group. "The children are keen to take specimens back to Uncle," Aunt told him.

Evan nodded. "Just be silent for a moment and look up that pathway there," he said. "Keep looking at one place, and don't make a sound."

A pleasant sort of quiet fell as we concentrated; it was only a few moments before one of the boys whispered urgently, "Look!" And then, as if by magic, we all saw: all kinds of flying insects, mostly small but some larger butterflies and moths, fluttering in the light or sitting, preening on a bush . . . the forest was alive with them.

Evan moved up the path, True was a few paces behind and the rest of us came in order. We saw the net go up, waft gently in the golden light. With a deft flick of his wrist, Evan closed the bag and we all crowded around to see his catch.

"We have here a gossamer-winged butterfly—a Long-tailed Blue, an old fellow, I think, judging by the nicks on his wings," Evan said. "Let's get it in the jar so we can have a closer look."

We crowded in close. "Step back, children, step back," Aunt fussed. "Give Evan room to move."

"Most butterflies fly straight up by instinct. So if I pull the net like this," Evan said, holding it up, "and position the bottle over it like this, we should be able to put this old fellow in the jar without touching him."

"Why can't you touch it?" one of the boys asked.

"Because," Evan said, deftly maneuvering the Long-tailed

Blue into the jar, "you are almost certain to disturb the scales on the wings, even if you don't tear the wing."

Evan held up the bottle with the butterfly inside, and the children cheered.

"How do you know it's a him?" one of the little girls asked.

Evan laughed. "That's another lesson," he told her.

"Let me set it free," True said.

"What?" Evan asked, puzzled.

"I want to set it free," she repeated, this time more urgently.

"No, no," one of the girls shouted, "it's such a pretty one . . . let's take it back to Uncle."

"Mr. Wright wouldn't want this old guy. True's going to release him as soon as everybody's had a chance to see . . . be sure to notice the black spot here on the lower part of the wing."

Evan watched her face as True twisted off the lid of the jar and held it straight out in front of her. "Fly away, fly away," the children began to chant, but the gossamer-winged butterfly did not move. True turned the jar on its side and carefully moved two of her fingers inside, until the creature caught hold. Slowly, carefully she lifted it out and held it up as high as she could. True laughed as the butterfly lifted in the breeze.

As they walked back, Evan asked, "Does it trouble you, the idea of killing the specimens?"

Embarrassed, she looked down. Finally she said, "It seems such a shame, not to leave them as they should be . . . in the sunshine, fluttering about. That's the beauty of it. Not to be pinned in a box."

"That's almost exactly what my father used to say. I always thought it hurt him when he had to take a specimen," Evan told her.

"Why would he have to?" True asked.

"Well, when he discovered a new species, for one thing. He used to correspond with what he called the butterfly people—collectors around the world. There's even one species named for my father—Coulter's Blue. He found it in the uplands of Maui."

"I think I would have liked your father."

"I suppose you would have," he answered.

Evan's organizational abilities became obvious the next morning. He divided us into three groups, each with a leader and a sub-leader. Evan was carrying the tin field box with the cyanide lumps in one corner, tied in gauze. He would rotate among us.

The night before, Evan had put us through a safety drill three times. Each leader carried a poisoning jar with a lump or two of cyanide or potash in the bottom. Each sub-leader had a whistle. One signal would bring Evan to transfer the specimen from the jar to the field box, two blasts would mean an emergency.

True and I were with Aunt Winona and three of the little boys—a six-year-old Hawaiian child with a palate so deformed he could scarcely speak and five-year-old twins found deserted in the cane fields a few months ago. The three had been clinging to our skirts a good part of the morning, afraid of their very shadows, and we had spent so much time convincing them they were safe that we had been unable to net even one butterfly. Aunt managed to get each boy to carry a net, but she could not get them to so much as look up in order to see the flying insects.

"Come along now, children," she said—we could hear the exasperation rising. "We are going up to that ridge there, see it? Walk up here with me, see how easy it is?"

True broke in, "Let me lead the way, Aunt . . . the little boys can be in between us . . ."

Aunt was in no mood to listen. "No, now move on along. Not that path, there, that one . . . Go!"

"Aunt, no," I tried to tell her, "I don't think . . . Evan said we shouldn't leave . . ."

But she was loping on ahead, pushing the boys ahead of her, brushing them on with a little switch she had pulled off a bush.

"Stop!" True shouted, at the same instant that the earth gave way and the little boys and Aunt went tumbling, down and down in a shower of dirt and pebbles and dead leaves, into a ravine that had been hidden by the foliage.

True blew two sharp blasts on the whistle, before she went scrambling over the edge.

"Lie down on your stomach and put your hands over the side," True yelled up at me. "Aunt is right here. I'm going to push her up, you pull . . ."

"Oh, no, no, no . . ." Aunt was wailing, but you could hardly hear for the boys' screams. Over the side I could see them. One was caught on a ledge, another was clinging to a bush and the third was almost at the bottom, partially buried . . .

True and Aunt were only a few feet down. "Take Aunt's hands—but be careful that another piece of the path doesn't cave in," True directed.

Aunt clamped onto my hands so tightly I thought my bones would break; she clambered over the side, shaken and pale. "What can we do? What can we do?" she was saying over and over.

At that moment Evan came crashing through the leaves; he pulled up short. "Oh, Evan, look," Aunt sobbed.

Evan seemed to grow icily calm, even distant. "Can you walk?" he asked Aunt, rather sternly. "Go as fast as you can—but go carefully—to Liko, tell him to bring the heavy rope, the one hanging on the mast. Tell him to hurry, and you stay with his group." He leaned over and simply picked me up. "Martha, you go with Miss Wright."

I hurried her away as fast as I could, wanting to give Evan and True a chance to help the little boys, whose screams ripped the late morning calm of this mountain glade.

True took off her dress, so she could move more easily in her camisole and bloomers, and began to lower herself.

"Wait," Evan ordered. She stopped, looked up at him.

"Liko is smaller and he has strong arms—"

"But that could take time," True told him, "and the twin at the bottom—we need to dig him out fast. I can do it."

He looked at her, then at the children. The boy with the split palate was whimpering like a wounded little animal. "All right," Evan said, taking a rope out of the sack he had carried. "Tie this around your waist. I'll handle it from above, and guide you down."

She did not feel the scratches and pricks of the bushes as she moved, as fast as she dared—and as Evan would allow. She reached the first child, checked to make sure he was secure on the ledge, and went on down.

She pulled the second child, screaming, out of the bush that had caught him and secured him behind a rock. She had to pry his fingers from her arms; he was screaming so hard that she was afraid they might pull another part of the cliff away.

"Let him cry!" Evan shouted from above in a voice strong enough to help her push the boy away.

Her feet touched the bottom; on all fours she made her way to the place where one of the twins was half-buried in debris. Furiously, she began to dig and pull at him to get him free. His head was covered with loose dirt and dead leaves; she reached for his face, turned it to her and was relieved to see two enormous black eyes peering at her.

"It's all right, it's all right," she comforted him and felt a surge of relief as his eyes filled with tears. Suddenly he was clinging to her, wrapping his legs around her waist, holding on so tightly that she had trouble looping the rope around him. "Slowly now, slowly," Evan cautioned as he pulled them slowly up the hill.

True could feel Evan on the other end of the rope, feel the steady strength of him; she took a deep breath, leaned as far back as she dared and walked slowly up the steep dirt embankment, trusting to Evan to catch them if she fell.

As soon as Evan lifted the boy out of her hands she said, "Let me go back. There is plenty of rope. Please, Evan . . ."

Evan's hands were testing the boy's arms and legs. "Lots of cuts and scratches, but no broken bones," he said. Then he looked at her, directly in her eyes as if to gauge something, and said, "One more time, then Liko should be here."

She brought up the next child so quickly that Evan was astonished. A feeling of strength surged through her; she could do anything, she knew it.

The last child, the boy with the cleft lip, had cried so hard that he was shaking all over and rather than clinging to True, as the others had, he pushed her away, fought her. She was hanging precariously, her bare feet clotted with mud, trying to calm the child, to get a firm hold on him, and she was working to keep her balance at the same time.

Liko's head appeared over the edge. "Ossie, behave!" he shouted angrily, and the child went into another paroxysm of fear and anger.

Evan must have pushed Liko back, because now all she heard was his voice, quiet and serious. "Take your time, True. The other boys are going to be fine, only scratches and bruises. We're in no hurry now, so just calm him . . . or, better yet, why don't you come up now that Liko is here, and I'll come down and bring him up."

Hearing this, Ossie threw his arms around True and wouldn't let go, for fear she would leave him again. He was shuddering, and his breathing was coming in short, hard gasps.

Slowly, she worked the rope around them both, and slowly, she began to make her way back up the side of the hill. She could feel Liko's added strength on the rope . . . only a few minutes more.

The leaves of a branch caught the child in the face and he screamed, flailing his hands so that he hit True hard in the face.

"Two more steps. Hold on, True," Evan said, "hold on."

She was leaning back too far, she knew. She stretched hard to try to gain a better footing.

"You're almost here," Evan coaxed, and she could feel the urgency in his voice, the need to have them safe. "You're doing fine, True, you're just amazing, just one more step now . . ."

She pushed her foot against what felt like a root and felt a flash of pain. She loosened the rope and felt it drop away as she pushed the boy Ossie toward Evan. In his panic to be rescued, the child lunged for Evan's arms and kicked so hard at True that she caught the blow in her stomach, lost all balance.

Evan shouted, "The rope . . ." but the rope had fallen away. She went tumbling down and down, clutching at bushes, reaching for clumps of earth that came loose in her hands. She felt like a rag doll, turning and falling. Finally she rolled into a pile of loose soil at the bottom of the ravine.

"True! My God!" Evan cried out in a voice filled with anguish.

And Liko screamed, "Are you all right, True? Please be all right."

Her whole body hurt, but she could move her arms and legs. "Yes," she managed to answer and was surprised at how weak she sounded.

She didn't know how he got to her so fast, but Evan was there, kneeling beside her, his face filled with worry. She tried to smile at him, but the cuts on her body were beginning to smart, and all she could do was grimace.

Evan moved his hands over her legs, working them back and forth, checking the cuts. Next he put his attention to her arms, sliding his hands expertly over them, turning her over gently, asking if this hurt, or this, if she could move that. True had never seen this Evan, filled with worry yet able to work.

With one hand under her neck, he used the other to brush the hair back from her eyes. "You have a dirty face," he said, trying to smile.

Laughter hurt, so she grimaced again and whispered, "I'm sorry."

He looked up to the sky and shook his head. "My God, True, that's what I should be saying to you. But we won't say anything right now. We've got a strong rope, Liko can handle it from above . . . I don't think anything is broken, but I know you must be sore all over. If you can stand to be moved, I'm going to take you up."

His words went flooding through her, filling her with peace. Evan was here beside her, and she didn't have to worry now. She was safe. Her body ached and smarted but her mind was effused with a golden light, and she knew what it was to be happy. Completely, finally happy.

"You're going to sit on my legs as if they were a chair, can you do that?"

She told her legs to move, but they wouldn't. Evan saw and told her, "Don't worry, you've just run out of steam, that's all. You've had the breath knocked out of you. But we can't stay down here in this damp ravine until you get it back, so we'll have to do it another way."

"I'm not wearing my dress," True said.

Evan laughed out loud. "Now I know you are all right. Your dress is on top, don't worry. What we have to do is find a way for you to hold onto me so I can get you up."

A shaft of sun cut through the dark green and fell on True's hair, lighting it. She felt the warmth of it and closed her eyes to catch the sun on her face.

Liko called from above, "Hey, these Keikis they move around too much. I take 'em back."

Evan was kneeling beside True. She could feel his mind racing, trying to figure a way to bring her up. "Maybe I should rig a stretcher, just in case . . ."

"No," True said in a whisper. "If I can just rest a few minutes, I'll be able to move. I know it."

He began to massage her arms, his hands moving expertly over the muscles. Turning her gently, he kneaded her back, working his fingers into the tight muscles. She welcomed his touch through the thin muslin of her camisole.

"You're cold," he said, quickly stripping off his shirt and helping her into it. She took a deep breath, to breathe in the smell of him.

His chest was covered with fine, tightly curled hair. His muscles were long and lean, not bulky but taut. She had never seen him without his shirt; she had a terrible wish to put her hand over his heart, but she knew she should not . . . and she knew the effort was beyond her.

They could hear Liko returning; there was no other sound quite like his short legs running through the forest. "All right now," Evan said. "This is how we are going to do it. All you have to do is be as quiet as you can, and let me and Liko do the work. You're going to have to sit on my lap, facing me . . ."

It took him a while to lift her onto him and to get the rope tied around them.

"Ready?" Liko called. "I tie to tree like you say."

True lay against him, her face tucked against his neck, her chest pressed into his. She felt like a rag doll, unable even to move her legs, which dangled loose on either side. She lay into him and felt his muscles moving for them both.

Safe, she knew she was safe. "Slow, slow," Liko murmured from above, coaxing them on. "No hurry, Evan . . ."

She could feel Evan's muscles flexing, hard and even, his legs between hers pushing. She listened to his breathing and paced her own to it. A flush of heat flickered from some deep place in her; she felt as if a lump of amber had melted and was spreading. She heard herself moan and was surprised at the sound. Then she felt Evan rising hard against her and was suffused with a feeling of gold and shadows; she did not know where he ended and she began. She felt what was in his mind; she felt she was walking around in his body. His neck was hot against her lips. She wrapped her legs closer around him, rolled gently to get deeper into him.

"True, don't . . ." he said.

She stopped. He was so close. She had never felt such a great wanting, but he had said no, don't . . .

She started crying then, soft sad tears. Evan was angry. She knew that she should not have given in to the warm amber wanting that had spread through her, she should not have let herself see and feel what was inside of him.

Liko reached for her, lifted her easily, rocked her in his strong arms. Evan turned away, leaving Liko to tend to her.

Although no one was badly hurt, Evan decided to end the outing a day early. By working feverishly, he had us packed and down the mountain before sundown. True was made to ride in the wagon with the children while Aunt rode alongside Evan. It was hard to say which of our little group was most miserable.

4

Vicky's pa thought True and me to be good for his wee girl, as he called her—though she was not wee at all. She was slender and as tall as True. In the weeks that followed what Uncle called "the Great Butterfly Debacle" we spent much of our time at Ainahau. True had always chafed under the oppressive attention of Vicky's mother and her governess, but now she seemed happy to go to Ainahau because she thought she might see Evan there.

Three weeks had passed, and he had not been out to our end of Waikiki. True was filled with remorse for whatever she had done to make him turn away from her. She felt it must be something to do with what had happened when he was carrying her back up from the ravine. She was about ready to spin apart, wanting so to put things right between them.

Miss Gardiner, Vicky's young governess, insisted we should undertake to learn some ladies' arts. We submitted to one afternoon each week on the lanai at Ainahau, becoming proficient in the intricacies of embroidery and crocheting and sewing a fine hem. Early on one of those mornings I found True riffling through a box of things which normally gathered dust on top of our cupboard. She emerged with perhaps a dozen small wooden spools of linen thread, a packet of tiny pins and what appeared to be a large pincushion.

"What is it?" I asked.

"You'll see," was all True would say, clearly enjoying my puzzlement. That day she amazed us all when she placed the pins in several rows on the cushion and in twisting and twining the threads began to make what looked like a wide border of fine linen lace.

"It is called 'knyppla,'" she answered Miss Gardiner's

question. "It is Swedish; my mother taught me." Knyppla was more elaborate than any of us, including Miss Gardiner, could manage, and sometimes we simply stood and watched True's fingers fly, weaving the thin strands of linen in and out. I loved to watch her, bent over the work, stray hairs falling forward on her smooth cheeks, her concentration complete.

When Evan finally did appear, True was at the far end of the lanai, facing the sea, working on the lace. He stood rather awkwardly, observing her for a time before she looked up. When she did, two bright pink splotches appeared on her cheeks—but her hands never stopped.

She wanted to say something, but the words flew out of her head.

"The scratches and cuts have healed?" he asked. She nodded—I could see a flush of red move up her neck—and still she did not speak, but only smiled at him.

Evan cleared his throat. "I wanted to tell you . . . what I wanted to say was what a good job you did, getting the little boys out of the ravine, I mean. It was heroic . . ." He cleared his throat and continued, "I should have told you at the time." He was uncomfortable, you could see.

"I thought you might be angry with me," True was finally able to say, adding lamely, "but I didn't know why."

It was Evan's turn to blush. He shrugged and told her rather stiffly how lucky they were that someone hadn't been badly hurt. He said he was sorry if he was rude to her, and that if he was mad at anyone it was at himself for letting them all get into that predicament. He leaned against the bannister, his hand shielding his eyes from the sun, and suddenly he seemed to be at ease again. He said, "Sometimes I think what could have happened . . ."

"But nothing bad did happen," she reminded him. "Except we didn't get to bring back many poisoned butterflies."

A wry grin spread across his face. "What makes me think you don't regret that much?" he asked. Then he repeated, rather formally, as if the point had to be made again: "What you did was a brave thing, and I'm not sure how things might have turned out if you hadn't moved so quickly."

"It was the only thing to do, and I just did it, that's all."

I glanced around; Jenny had turned the corner and was approaching. I could tell by her small, quick steps and the set of her mouth that she was not pleased to find him with True.

"Can you come please, Evan?" she said tersely. It was not a request, but a command.

As he rose to leave, True asked, "We're still friends, then?"

Evan smiled back and answered, "That hasn't changed."

"What hasn't changed?" Jenny asked as they walked off together.

Evan answered, "Nothing ever changes around here. Haven't you noticed, Jen?"

After that, Evan started coming back to our hale with Vicky's pa; they had discovered that Uncle Jameson was both knowledgeable and astute on the subject of politics, American and Hawaiian. They had also discovered that he almost never left our beach, so if they wanted to talk politics with him, they had to come out. Sometimes Vicky came along, leading the way on Fairy. Liko seemed to sense when she was in the area; invariably he announced her arrival before she turned the last corner.

Uncle and Archie Cleghorn would settle down on the lanai, sheltered under a grape arbor that Uncle was training. Aunt would come running with a pitcher of lemonade, and when she left the men to talk, Uncle would bring out a bottle of the apple brandy he kept tucked away in the back of his cupboard, behind his volumes on horse breeding in the Americas. (Liko told us this; Liko seemed to know what was in every cupboard in every cottage.)

Evan would come with Vicky to find us and visit for a time; then he would join the men. Sometimes she would tug at him to stay and play with us, and he would tug back to tease her, and say that she should be listening to Uncle if she wanted to grow up to be a real queen. That always got Vicky, somehow. Now and then we would sit on the edge of the lanai, especially when the men's talk got furious and argumentative.

"Forgive me for impuning your brother-in-law the King," Uncle said to Vicky's pa on one of these visits, "but he is acting the fool with Claus Spreckels."

Vicky's pa looked surprised. "David sometimes acts the fool, I won't disagree with you there—but I would have thought you would agree with his decision to pay off Claus and get him out of Hawaiian politics—right now half of the

national debt is owed him. It seems to me we have to get free
of him. People call him the 'sugar king' and I don't think
there is any question but that he sees himself as more powerful than David."

"Spreckels amazes me," Evan put in. "Did you know he
talked Toby Wakefield into putting in sugarcane at Mau'-
loa? Spreckels is financing the mill, of course, and he has
convinced Toby that it will make his fortune."

"That wouldn't be hard to do," Archie Cleghorn offered
dryly. "I mean convince Toby—he is long on charm and
short on applying himself to any kind of labor."

"If Spreckels runs true to form," Uncle said, "the Colonel
will end up without a mill to process his sugar and deep in
debt—to Claus Spreckels. But let's get back to King Kalakaua and this big new loan his British agent is floating in
London to pay off Spreckels. You're in on that, aren't you,
Evan?"

"I'm on the advisory committee, yes. I have to admit that
when the move for a new loan came up in this session of the
legislature, I agreed with Spreckels. He said it was time for
the government to cut back, to practice a little economy for
a change. I don't think he counted on the British coming in
so quickly with an offer to float a new bond issue in England—and giving the King a way to buy his freedom from
Claus, with enough money left over to run the Kingdom the
way he wants, for a while, at least."

"I know how everyone feels about Spreckels," Uncle put
in, "but I can't but wonder if the King isn't exchanging one
evil for another, perhaps worse one . . ."

Vicky's pa pulled on his beard. "What do you mean by
'evil'?" he asked, a bit too formally.

Uncle answered with a small smile. "I'm afraid I apply
that term to moneylenders as a group. Perhaps I should tell
you that my own father made his fortune that way—by
financing, among other things, slave ships to the Americas.
Now, at least, his money is financing this children's home."

"Yes, well, I see what you mean," Archie Cleghorn said.
"But to get back to the British financial syndicate that is
offering a loan—why would it be better to borrow from
Spreckels and give him even more power than he already
has?"

"Why borrow at all?" Uncle asked calmly.

Archie looked as if surely Uncle must be joking and seemed surprised when Evan put in, "That's what I've been arguing in the committee . . . a period of economy, to pay off Claus as fast as possible and lessen his influence."

"It won't happen," Archie Cleghorn said. "It simply cannot. David has too many grand ideas. He sees himself as King of the whole bloody Pacific. His famous Polynesian Confederacy, you know—with himself as King-Emperor."

"Well, why not?" Uncle asked half seriously. "The Brits didn't invent Empire, though you practice it more thoroughly than most." It was the first time Archie Cleghorn's Scots background had been mentioned.

"When you think about it," he responded in the spirit of the debate, "the British have as good a claim to these islands as the Americans do—after all, it was 'our' Captain Cook who discovered Hawaii in the first place, and Vancouver was a great friend of Kamehameha's, some time before your missionaries arrived."

"But it was the missionaries who came to stay, to live and work and teach . . ." Evan put in, playing the devil's advocate, knowing it would rile Uncle. "They didn't come to conquer."

"Didn't they now?" Uncle asked, rising to the bait.

We all knew how Uncle could get worked up over the missionaries. He thought they had simply substituted their God for those the Hawaiians had voluntarily given up. Worse than that, he felt the missionaries had imposed their narrow, New England puritanical standards on a native population that had a highly developed economy and a rich cultural history. It disgusted him that the native dance, the hula, had been banned as "decadent and degenerate."

"The missionaries," Uncle liked to say, "taught the Hawaiians to read, to cover their bodies and feel guilt, but they could not teach them to be mean." Still, the original missionaries practiced what they preached, someone would say in their defense. And someone else would add that the old ways were doomed with the first ship from the outside world. And still another party would counter that it wasn't the missionaries so much as their children—usually referred to as "the Mission Boys"—who made themselves rich at the expense of the natives. What rankled Uncle and Archie Cleghorn the most was how the Mission Boys seemed to think they should decide what kind of government was correct for the Islands.

"One of the peculiar things about this," Uncle said, "is how these same men—born here—consider themselves to be Americans first, citizens of Hawaii second."

"Evan," Vicky's pa broke in, "your father came here from the States—where is your allegiance—to Hawaii or to the States?"

"Here," Evan said without hesitating. "My father came from California and before that Massachusetts, but he called Hawaii 'Paradise Discovered,' and he thought a man would have to be mad to want to live anyplace else. I feel that way too—I'm not looking forward to leaving next week. But before we lose the point, I think it's important to remember that while the Mission Boys are hell-bent on annexing Hawaii to the States, neither the U.S. President nor the Congress thinks much of the idea. In fact, time and again the U.S. has turned down the annexationists."

"That's true for now," Uncle said, "but I wouldn't count on it forever." He believes we are in an era of colonial expansionism and that if the Americans—suddenly no longer smitten with the notion of Manifest Destiny—back off too far, the French or the Germans will come poking their warships in Honolulu harbor, and then of course the British would have a historical imperative to look into the situation. Uncle says there is a certain breed of man who believes he has been chosen by divine intervention to go out and save the savage populations of the world.

Archie Cleghorn looked glum, and we all knew why. He feels it is his duty to protect Vicky's future, to see to it that the throne is preserved so that when her time comes she can ascend it.

After a long moment, Uncle turned to Evan and asked, "So, do you agree with Archie that it is a mistake for King Kalakaua to borrow two million dollars from the British?"

Evan stretched his long, lean frame, tucked his arms behind his head and answered carefully, "I don't think anybody has worked out just how much this money is going to cost in the long run. I tried sifting through all the papers, but the terms are complicated. For example, I know that some of the bonds will be discounted at two percent, but I can't get anybody to tell me how many. The syndicate is taking a commission of five percent, and then we'll have to pay interest on top of that. It looks to me as if we could spend a quarter of a million or even more to get two million, but the fever to get rid of Spreckels by paying him off is running so high I can't get anybody to sit down and study the details of the bond plan."

Uncle looked thoughtfully at Evan. "You won't last in this government, son. You've too much common sense."

"But you'll be needed one day," Vicky's pa put in quickly. "Probably it's a good thing you'll be off to study the law for a time. I'm glad you took old Eli Barrows' offer. He's a tough old bird, outspoken and crude, I'm afraid. But he's always been an excellent judge of men, you have to give him that. It's how he's done so well with the slaughterhouse— hired good men and paid them a fair wage."

A puzzled look spread over True's face. It was the first we had heard that Jenny's father had anything to do with Evan going to Yale.

It took a few days, but Vicky found out for us. Eli Barrows had offered to loan Evan the money if he would then agree to work at the Barrows firm for at least two years, and to pay him back in six. Some town gossips, Vicky told us, are saying that what Eli is really buying himself is a son-in-law, but Vicky's pa told her that was nonsense, that Evan would be paying enough interest to make the loan a good business transaction for Eli Barrows and Company, not to mention acquiring Evan's services for a two-year period.

"But Pa did say he knows old Eli would be mightily pleased to have Evan as a son-in-law."

Early one morning a gardener from Ainahau arrived with some new plantings for Uncle, and an invitation for "the two young misses" to join Vicky as guests of her uncle and aunt, the King and Queen, that same night. There was to be an entertainment on an American ship then in port, with the ship's doctor giving a demonstration of mesmerism.

"I think it sounds jolly," Aunt said, "so long as you get all of your chores finished." The King and Queen of Heaven might invite us out, and Aunt would insist we do our chores first.

As we made our way on board the USS *Jefferson* as part of the royal party, which included some European visitors, the people stood and made way for us. I felt a thrill in my chest that I had never felt before. All the white people were standing to salute our King and Queen, and us.

Hawaii's most prominent citizens sat on chairs provided in the main salon. I saw Evan and poked True; he was with Jenny and her parents. Eli Barrows was a large man with a red face and a barrel chest. He filled his own chair and lapped over into his wife's, a poor little grey thing who looked like a sparrow with a moulting coat.

Vicky whispered in my ear, "That's Alec Marston sitting two over from Evan—he's already getting bald, what a perfectly silly man. He seems to be a leader of the Mission Boys. I suppose he despises me. I wish Evan wouldn't sit so near him."

"Don't be a goose," I said, a bit too loud.

The King turned around to look at us. A wave of mortification was about to wash over me when he smiled, and his handsome dark face was alive with light.

Just then, a slight man of middle age with long, blond hair and a drooping moustache came to stand just in front of us, his hand slightly raised for silence.

He seemed overwhelmed by the size of the audience, and especially with the royal guests. He began, "I want to tell you at the very start . . ." His voice was soft and quiet, and those in the back of the salon shouted, "Speak up, speak up." He cleared his throat and began again, louder this time: "I want to begin by saying that I am not used to doing this little exercise in front of such a large and illustrious audience. I'm afraid that what you are about to see is perhaps more of an entertainment than a serious scientific study, though someday the workings of the human mind will be known, and we will understand much more than we do today."

He clasped his hands together and asked if he might have a volunteer, "someone to help us with our little presentation."

Marston stood; a small murmur rustled through the audience.

"Come up here, sir," the doctor said and held out a comfortable chair.

"Alec always knows how to get the best seat in the house," someone called out, and there was polite laughter.

"Now, sir," the doctor explained, "I want you to make

yourself very comfortable . . . are you comfortable? Yes, then. Now, if everyone in the audience will be very quiet. That is extremely important, now . . ."

He went on to explain that Mr. Marston would have to concentrate on a shining object that the doctor held in his hand. He began to move it this way and that. "Watch carefully," the doctor said in his soft voice, "back and forth, just watch now. Don't take your eyes off of the wand. If you begin to feel drowsy, don't worry, just concentrate, yes, that is right . . . watch carefully . . . I am going to start counting slowly, very slowly . . ."

Listening to his droning voice, I felt my eyelids grow heavy. True reached over to pinch me. I jerked awake and noticed that Marston was sitting with his eyes closed, his thin lips slightly open.

"Can you hear me, Mr. Marston?" the doctor asked.

"Yes," he answered, sounding like a ghost.

A rustle of wonder rippled through the audience. The doctor paused and frowned slightly.

"I want to ask you some questions, sir," the doctor went on. "You have no need to worry. These are just simple questions . . . take as much time as you wish. Perhaps you can tell us what you had for dinner this evening?"

In trembling tones, Alec Marston repeated his dinner menu in perfect detail, mentioning to his wife's obvious embarrassment that the mutton was not prepared as his mother made it, which was the way he prefers.

The doctor seemed to hesitate, but then he said, "Perhaps you could give us your children's names and their ages."

Marston answered a few more questions; he seemed more at ease than the doctor. Finally he said, "I'm going to count to ten and clap my hands, and you will wake up, sir, and you will not remember anything that was said."

When the doctor clapped his hands, Marston jerked awake, his eyes wide.

"What?" he said, full of surprise. "Where am I?"

A look of chagrin passed over the doctor's face. "Can you tell us, sir," he said to his subject, "what you remember of the past ten minutes?"

"Everything!" Marston crowed. "I was only pretending to be in a trance . . . to show this for the foolishness it is. Mesmerize, you say! It is all a trick . . ." He raised his hands over his head and strutted around as if he had just won a boxing match.

The doctor's face turned a bright, angry red. "If I may say, sir," he spoke up, his voice rising in controlled anger, "I did not ask for you to pretend. Certainly, I did not want it. I guessed that you were not responding honestly . . ."

Marston shouted, "Honesty! You're the one who is being dishonest with this business . . ."

A voice louder than any other burst through the noise. "Sit down, Marston, and quit making a jackass out of yourself," Eli Barrows thundered. "Man, you haven't the brains of an ox if you can't see what a stupid thing it is you've done. Get on out of here. Where's his wife? Take him home, girl, and make him eat that mutton he made such a fuss over. Take the fool home."

The crowd dispersed quickly. I was behind the King, who asked to see the doctor. "I'm sorry, sir," the King said. "I'm afraid we can be hopelessly provincial."

The discussion in the carriage on the way home was lively, with some of the royal group claiming to be more embarrassed by Eli Barrows than by Alec Marston.

"Poor Jenny was furious with her father," one of the women in our carriage said, and someone else added, "She is always furious with her father. She thinks him a dolt."

"I wonder what Evan Coulter thinks of Eli Barrows," the first speaker came back.

"I wonder what he thinks of Jenny Barrows," the other said, the last word on the subject.

"I think what your father said tonight was fair enough," Evan tried to tell Jenny. "Marston was making a fool of himself. He managed to ruin what might have been an interesting experiment, and to embarrass the poor doctor and the ship's officers who arranged the evening. None of them could call Marston out for his bad behavior. Look at it that way, and your father did us all a service."

Jenny whirled around to face him, the expression on her face furious. "If you think it was the right thing to do, why didn't you stand up and call Alec Marston a fool in front of just about every important person in Honolulu?"

Evan frowned. "Are you saying . . ."

"I'm saying that Alec may be a fool, but he is a powerful

fool and it would be well not to make an enemy of him. Father is incapable of . . ." The puzzled look on Evan's face stopped her.

"I like your father, Jenny," Evan told her. "And I think there is something to be said for speaking out without always thinking of the consequences."

Tears sprang to Jenny's eyes. "It is humiliating, Evan," she said. "To me and to Mother."

The tears stopped him from saying what sprang into his head: that Alec Marston's wife had more to be humiliated about than Jenny. He had not seen Jenny in this mood before. She was irritated and angry; he felt himself pulling back from her. He recognized the feeling; his mother had been dead for three years now, and he had almost forgotten . . .

"I want to talk about something else," Jenny said, lifting her chin with determination. "I think that you are going to have to do something about True Lindstrom."

Evan felt as if he had been in the line of fire and had taken a direct hit. Remembering the ravine, he flushed and turned away.

Furious that he would turn his back on her, Jenny lashed out, "She is so smitten with you, Evan—and I do wish you wouldn't encourage her as you do. You just have to wonder what in the world the Wrights are doing, allowing those two orphan girls to spend so much time with Kaiulani and the royals. I mean, they should be thinking of those poor girls and how hard it will be on them when they have to settle for so much less in life. They can't expect . . ."

"I don't know what you are talking about," Evan said, his voice flat and hard. "I can tell you that Archie feels lucky to have found two such good friends for Kaiulani. She has been stronger and happier since she met them, and Archie says it is because of those two 'poor orphan girls,' as you call them. As for True being 'smitten' with me—I'll just remind you that she is only fourteen. I am twelve years older—and you are fourteen. I would like to think that we are both old enough for a little charity."

He watched the effect of his anger, saw her face register shock, then fear. He knew she did not like to be reminded that she was older than he. She knew she had gone too far, and now she was going to back off as his mother had used to back off. A familiar old weariness settled into him; he guessed it must always be this way with women, them pushing and pulling and crying, if need be.

"Evan!" Jenny said, suddenly smiling through her tears, "I honestly believe we are having our very first argument—and over something so silly. I don't know what comes over me . . . Papa, well, he just has a way of getting me off my feed. If I've been silly, I am sorry. I truly am. I suppose this must be some kind of milestone . . . our argument, I mean. Don't you think?"

If he had been Eli Barrows, and if there hadn't been that business with True at the ravine, he might have told her what he was thinking.

He did not bend to give her his usual good night kiss, and Jenny knew for certain that it was True Lindstrom's fault.

5

My major fascination at this time was a small girl named Amalie Garnier. The First Mate of the French ship *Clarion* had brought her to the Sisters at the Convent of the Holy Names. Her mother, her father and her baby brother had died at sea of a fever that swept through the ship, en route from Cochin China to the western coast of Canada, claiming the lives of half of those aboard. When the First Mate—who had taken command when the Captain expired—put in at Hawaii he left the child with the Sisters until relatives could be contacted in France.

After many letters over the course of many months, the Sisters discovered that none of the French relatives was willing to send for the child.

Had Amalie been docile, the Sisters might have kept her on. But she spoke no English and flew into a rage when she could not make herself understood. Sometimes she hurt herself; sometimes she hurt others.

Jenny Barrows brought her out to us. "I tried to explain to Sister Catherine Joseph that my French is hardly fluent, but at least we can comment on the weather and the scenery . . ." Jenny smiled prettily at the child and said to me in the sweetest of tones: "Pity she's such a plain little thing. If she were pretty, people might be more tolerant of her bad temper." Without another word, Jenny went tripping off to find Aunt Winona—she came out from town often enough these days, bringing this and that for Aunt—some honey, a book, some plantings from her mother's garden. Jenny is courting Aunt for a friend, and I cannot but wonder to what end. Amalie is a pale child, and not in the least pretty as you think of little French girls—though I hated having Jenny say it out loud like that, as if the child were not there.

Her hair is long and fair and unkempt. I suppose her

mama brushed it for her, because it has not been properly brushed for many weeks. And her face is too white, the features all too large except for the mouth, which is small and hard.

"Bonjour, Amalie," I said. When I offered my hand, she put both of hers behind her, defiantly. Uncle had been giving us French lessons for only a few weeks, but I had a few phrases ready: "I hope you will teach me to speak French," I said as well as I could. "And I would like to teach you to speak English."

She looked at the ground.

At first, she would not speak at all. When she discovered that Uncle could converse with her in French, she simply refused to speak to any of the rest of us or to try to learn English.

One afternoon soon after Amalie's arrival, I went looking for Uncle and found him on his lanai, reading.

"We must do something about Amalie," I told him, sitting down on the step.

He closed his book regretfully, and I knew he would have liked for the problem to resolve itself without him.

"Do you have something in mind?" he asked.

"As a matter of fact, I do," I answered. "I think you must withdraw completely from her instruction. As long as she has someone to translate for her, she will never learn English, and she must."

Uncle's face clouded over; we had all seen Amalie's tantrums, and we knew full well that this would cause a spectacular explosion.

I went on: "She must be made to understand that the key to her survival here is learning, and that I am the one who will provide that learning but only with her cooperation. You are going to have to be harsh, Uncle, if we are going to help her."

He looked out to sea for a long time, and then he nodded before returning to his book. I felt a small rush of pleasure, followed quickly by a foreboding. The next days and weeks would not be easy.

In fact, they were a preview of hell. Amalie's stamina was remarkable, her stubbornness monumental, her temper terrible. My shins turned black and blue from her kicks, her arms were covered with red marks where True and Liko and

I grasped them to keep her from hitting out. She screamed and spat and threw herself on the floor, kicking.

As soon as the violence subsided and they felt I was no longer in danger, True and Liko and everyone else gave her wide range, but I could not, because I knew—I could see it in her eyes—that she was trapped inside of herself, that the only way she could free herself was to learn to speak. When she had spent herself, I would lead her out with me to the beach—as True would lead me whenever the gloom descended on me—and I would repeat to her the names of everything we saw: the sea, *la mer;* the cloud, *le nuage;* the woods, *le bois;* the bird, *l'oiseau.*

Wonder of wonders, because she insisted on speaking to me in torrents of French, I discovered that I was learning her language much more rapidly than she was learning mine. Although I would have liked to practice the pronunciation . . . the lovely, singing rivulets of French that pour out like perfume . . . I did not. Not yet, I told myself. First I must make her speak to me in English.

The tantrums decreased exactly as her command of English increased. She did not smile, and she frequently spat at me or shouted an epithet that I felt grateful not to understand. But she stopped hitting me almost altogether, and my shins and her arms looked the better for it.

One Monday evening as we all sat down at the long table on the lanai for our supper, I rang the small china bell for attention. "Tonight, Amalie has asked if she can give the blessing."

Everyone became very quiet; by then, almost all of the children had experienced her wrath, and I could see that they were worried.

"Thank you, my Lord in Heaven," Amalie began in English, "for this food that we will eat. And thank you for good people here with good hearts who have given me into their home. In the name of the Father and the Son and the Holy Ghost, Amen." She crossed herself then, picked up her fork and started to eat.

Everyone sat, stunned. I smiled, picked up my fork and joined her.

Liko started it. Clapping, at first. Then smiling his big, jolly smile. True joined in, and everyone else—even Uncle and Aunt—all of them clapping and smiling at Amalie.

She stopped eating, looked around from child to child. "Brava, Amalie," Uncle said, and each of the children picked it up. "Brava, Amalie . . ."

The smile started at her chin, it seemed, and spread up into her mouth and eyes. She put her hands up to her face, as if to say she couldn't believe their cheers.

From that day forward, Amalie became my best student, my stalwart little friend. Soon enough she was reading easily in English. When I was certain that she was proficient, I asked her to speak to me one hour each day—usually in the evening, before bedtime—in French.

These hours became a cherished time for both of us. I was learning a whole new beautiful language, and Amalie felt, she told me, "so much less lonely" when she could speak her mother tongue.

Most important for me, I learned how essential it is to look at each student carefully, to try to understand what each needs. With the students in our home, each of them scarred in some way, it was all the more necessary. After Amalie, I was ready to take on all challenges. And what was even better, she became ready to take them on with me.

It was Amalie who was first to realize that young Ossie with the fearful split lip and palate would always copy some of his figures backwards—e's and c's and d's all reversed. "Perhaps that is why he cannot learn to read," she said. "Because in his mind, he sees it backwards."

Uncle thought it a fanciful idea but he admitted he didn't have a better one. "Experiment," he said.

It was my idea to have Ossie trace the letters of the alphabet in the sand. "If he can figure out that he is reversing them, then maybe he can reverse them back again in his mind."

Amalie sat with the child, tracing over and over again the letters that he turned around. I suppose we will never know what did it, but slowly, very slowly, Ossie learned the alphabet. And then, even more slowly, he learned to read from the simple readers. His pace was far behind what it should have been for his age. "But he is catching up," Amalie pointed out to me. I hugged her to me for her optimism. Ordinarily she did not like to be touched, but on this day she put her arms around me, very gingerly I must admit. It was a small token of how far she had come. How far we both had come, to be jubilant over the slow progress of a poor little boy with a twisted mouth.

Aunt Winona was sometimes included in our invitations to Ainahau. We knew—because Vicky told us—that her mother found Aunt Winona "fussy and far too talkative," but Vicky's Aunt Liliuokalani—who was next in line to the throne—had taken a fancy to the Southern spinster who ran a home for orphans at the far end of Waikiki beach.

Aunt Liliu, as Vicky called her, had a summer place at Waikiki. Like her sister, she had married a haole—his name was John Dominis and he was the Governor of our island, Oahu. In town, they lived in a big house called Washington Place, which they shared with his mother, whom Vicky said was "horribly nasty to poor Aunt Liliu."

Waikiki turned out to be Princess Liliuokalani's reprieve, and Aunt Winona's as well, since Uncle, who did not take part in social gatherings and almost never left the hale, urged her to join in. The Hawaiian *alii*—or royalty—had always considered it appropriate for a high chiefess to have a place apart from her husband. Together on the beach at Waikiki the alii could relax in the old ways—with luaus and dancing and music. The King had a home near his two sisters—Vicky's mother and Liliuokalani. That summer, the three of us scouted every leafy corner of the three big estates; all were staffed with Hawaiians, and they all loved Vicky, last in a long line and their queen-to-be, and since we were her friends, nothing was denied us.

Ainahau was given to Vicky by her godmother, Princess Ruth, a great, glowering old woman with a face like a frog's. Vicky's pa, a talented horticulturist, turned it into a huge, wonderful garden—the house itself was modest, with a long leafy lanai where everyone gathered.

One day we arrived to find Vicky tearing apart a package wrapped in ti leaves, her mother looking on, both of them excited.

"It's from Mama Nui," Vicky told us, meaning Princess Ruth. "She's coming for my party today. I can't imagine why she would send . . ."

"Hurry," Vicky's mama interrupted, laughing and caught up in the excitement of the present.

"I am hurrying," Vicky said, lifting a small circlet of

flowers out of the box. All of us caught our breath at the exquisite arrangement of tiny mountain flowers of purples and pinks and blues.

"Oh, how beautiful," Princess Likelike exclaimed. "I do believe this is the most beautiful haku lei I've ever in my life seen." She placed it on her head as she would a crown and asked us, coquettishly, "Does it suit me, girls?"

We had never seen Vicky's mama so happy and laughing before; she seemed a different person altogether. "Oh yes," we said, almost in unison.

"No!" Vicky raised her voice to be heard, but she was smiling. "Don't forget, Mama, this was Mama Nui's gift to me. And it's my party—tell me why I should let you wear my beautiful haku lei?"

"Sweet girl," the Princess came back, her voice caressing, "because you are so young and beautiful—you don't need flowers to draw all eyes to you. But your poor Mama is so old and withered. Who will look at her?"

Vicky put her arms around her and bent to lay her nose against her mother's in the old, Hawaiian gesture of affection. "You aren't in the least old, Mama," she scolded, "Papa says you are still a girl at thirty-five. Think of him! He is fifty-four."

"Your father is ageless, and he's a haole," the mother answered.

That evening, Princess Likelike appeared wearing the haku lei nestled in her dark hair, and smiling at us as if we were conspirators. Vicky glowed with pleasure. She whispered to us, "You finally get to see Mama at one of the good times."

We were to have danced that night for the first time, Vicky and True and I. A *kumu hula*—a dance master—had been giving us lessons, and Vicky chose this party, when she knew she would be surrounded by her close ohana, to make our surprise debut.

Luck was with me. As we ran across the lawn in our skirts of ti leaves I stepped in a hole and wrenched my ankle. I could scarcely walk, much less dance. Vicky's mama insisted I sit next to her, while Vicky and True carried on with the performance. True glared at me as if she thought I'd twisted my ankle on purpose, because she knew how I dreaded the idea of dancing, especially in front of the alii. I couldn't resist smiling back at her.

As soon as the drums started, as soon as the chanters lifted their voices, True's frown vanished. From that point, the two tall girls moved and turned, their arms lifting in exquisite counterpoint, their slender young bodies swaying in perfect rhythm. Now and again they called out the responses to the chants, they caught and changed moods, laughing together now, sad again with the music washing over them, catching us up. The ohana sat motionless, caught by the beauty of two graceful young girls, one as breathcatching as the other.

"The dark and the light," Vicky's mama said in a strange, strangled voice. "The gods must see them."

As Evan Coulter leaned against a palm tree, studying the young dancers, he felt a strong, almost physical throb of dread. *This is what I am going to miss,* he told himself, *the music, and the dancing and the laughter . . .* He closed his eyes to let the memory of it wrap around him, and when he opened them again Jenny was standing in front of him, frowning.

6

A kona wind had been blowing for two days, making us hot and testy. Vicky lay in the hammock, her eyes almost closed; Liko sprawled against a tree, a perfect reflection of Vicky's listlessness.

"Let's swim," True urged, action always the answer by her way of thinking. But the sun was too bright, the air too heavy, pressing down, even True could not get us moving.

"Tell us a story, Martha Moon," Vicky demanded, as if it were her last wish on earth.

"Too hot for stories," I tried, feeling listless.

"About Kaahumanu after she became King Kamehameha's favorite queen," Liko coaxed, adding, "If you talk a story, I'll fan you," and with a lauhala mat he stirred the air around us.

"What a good friend you are," Vicky said, trailing her arm in Liko's general direction.

"What a goosey grin you have," True said to him, mocking Vicky's tone.

Without opening her eyes, Vicky let escape a small, trilling laugh which made all of us smile. True looked pleased with herself for bringing us out of the doldrums, if only for a moment.

Now it was my turn. I began:

The year was 1795, on the island of Hawaii, at the place Kamehameha loved best on the warm southern shore. Kaahumanu was in the King's great hale, with its high, pitched roof, pushing her feet back and forth over the smooth rocks that covered the coral stone floor, not looking at him as he spoke to her.

"I say no," the King said.

"I hear you say no," she answered before his words were out, still not looking at him.

"You hear but you do not heed," he said.

"All I hear is no for woman," she answered. "No bananas, no shark meat, no pig for woman . . . no man eats with woman, no woman in temple, no no no all kapu. Woman is no better than dogs, and you say so. You, the King god."

The giant man's face twisted into an ugly scowl. "I am King, with the gods I say what is kapu, and you will hear me."

"I do hear you," she answered, spitting out the words.

He met her anger: "You will not lay with any other, only with me. From now I put a kapu on your body."

She looked at him, eyes raging. "And you—who have twenty wives and more—who will you lay with?"

"I am King," he shouted, so that all outside heard him, and moved away, fearful that he step out and in his anger punish them.

Kaahumanu stood, drawing herself to her full height, and looked at him, as a woman does who knows the source of her power.

"I want you here, with me, when I am here," he said, his voice almost even.

"And here I am," she answered.

"There are those who say I should throw you to the sharks, for the trouble you bring me."

She looked at him from the corner of her eye. "If you did, you would worry that I might take a bite of the shark, and you say the meat of the shark is kapu for woman."

She braced herself not to cower, for she believed he would strike her, but he broke out in a great loud laugh that sounded throughout the village, so that all who heard came out of hiding and went about their work.

"You will not lay with the young chief Kaiana," he said with such quiet that she did not hear until he continued. "He is comely and strong and young, yes. I see how you look at him, but no more."

She turned and walked slowly out of the hale, bending through the doorway so he could see the fine curve of her body as she left.

She swam to the place of the rock shaped like a turtle between two palm trees, but she did not shout out to him. Instead she waited until she was in his arms to tell him, "We must not meet here again. Others know of this place, and he is having me followed, yes."

Kaahumanu ran her fingers along the tattoos that ran down Kaiana's beautiful face and neck and onto his chest, and she told him, "He has put a kapu on my body."

The young chief groaned. "He will kill us. He will have to kill us."

"No. He goes soon, and we can meet then."

Kaiana kept his hands on her shoulders. He could not be with her and fail to touch her. In the village, when she sat in the favored position, he felt pain when the King put his hand on her arm or touched her leg.

She looked into his eyes and saw, in the depths of refracted light, the tenderness that she knew would cause his death.

"When did you lay with me, the first time?" she asked quietly.

"Long ago," he answered.

"We were children still, yes," she went on, and then she asked, "Is it time for us to part?"

"No," he cried, burying his face in her neck. "No . . ."

When he could speak, he told her, "I go with the King when he sails to take the island of Maui. He says my warriors are needed. It has been decided."

She took a deep breath. Kaiana was to be part of the war party, then, and the King, her husband, who kept her counsel, had not told her. She knew that if Kamehameha were victorious on Maui he would move across the channel to take Molokai, and then he would turn his war canoes toward Oahu, to take over Honolulu and the deep water bay where foreign ships were beginning to appear. Then he would be King of all the islands save Kauai, and that would fall soon.

Kaahumanu rested her forehead against Kaiana's, and touched her nose to his as tears streamed down their faces. *Aloha nui loa,* he whispered. *Aloha nui loa,* she answered.

And then she warned, "Watch for the spear at your back. Run when you must."

He stood on the shore and watched her swim away, watched until she was no more than a leaf upon the water. And as he stood, he felt the earth lift and roll and quake beneath his feet.

"Pele is angry," the King said to Kaahumanu. "She has sent fire shooting into the sky, and the red akule fish are

swimming in her waters. The priests have read the omens—
Pele demands the death of an alii."

He heard a pleading in her voice that had never been there
before: "I ask you," she said, "do not leave for Maui.
Change the war plan."

He looked into her face. He looked for a long time before
he turned away and with a voice as hard as ice from the
mountaintop, he said, "We go."

Kamehameha's army in war canoes sailed for Maui, the
young chief Kaiana and his men with them. The invasion
was swift, the battle fierce. Maui was theirs and very soon
the great army took to the sea again, to cross the channel to
conquer Molokai.

Molokai fell to the invaders; nothing could stem
Kamehameha's tide, it was said; only the chief of Oahu stood
in his way. On Molokai, Kaiana stood with his men, waiting
for the King to call him to the council of war. He was certain
the King would sail for Oahu, there to meet his last resistance.
Kamehameha's power was great; the white man had brought
him guns, and he had used them well. He should move quickly
now, Kaiana knew. His men were in good spirits, ready to
follow Kamehameha and his chiefs. Kaiana talked and
laughed with them, as if all was well, but he was watching now.

He watched as one chief went into the wood, toward the
temple where the councils of war were held; he walked down
the beach, where some of the warriors fished, and could find
no other chief. Soon he came upon a man who had been a
friend of his childhood, and he could see that the friend did
not want to speak to him.

"What is it?" he asked. "Tell me."

His friend looked away. "The council of war, you are not
to come."

"Does the High Chief Kamehameha say it?" Kaiana
asked, and his friend looked down.

Kaiana was filled with fury and fear. Kaahumanu had
warned him, and it was so, he could feel it in his stomach, in
his chest, in the sound of the sea. Kamehameha's chiefs were
plotting to kill him.

He told his plan to those of his men he knew he could trust
with his life. They filled three canoes, and when the great war
fleet gathered to make the crossing to Oahu, Kaiana and his
chosen men sailed away with them. Once they found them-

selves in open sea they turned to the windward side of the island. There they joined the Oahu chief in his stand against Kamehameha.

"Follow me," the warrior chief of Oahu said, and Kaiana and his men followed them through Nuuanu valley, climbing to the high ground. They could see the forces of Kamehameha gather far below, could watch as the full tide of his army washed into the valley and up the steep walls toward them.

At their backs, the Nuuanu Pali dropped for a thousand sheer feet; there could be no retreat. The warriors of Kamehameha came up the valley, swirled around them, guns pouring smoke, spears raining down. The Oahu warriors broke and ran; they fell screaming to their deaths, over the Pali. But Kaiana did not run; he faced the great wave of warriors, his spear raised. He was killed as he stood, facing his enemies, who once had been his friends.

Kamehameha was now King of all the Islands, save Kauai, and soon the King of Kauai would bow to him.

When the great King returned to the island of Hawaii, a crowd gathered to meet him and cover him with flowers, but Kaahumanu was not there. He sent to her father's house, but her father said she had gone on a journey to the other side of the island. The King sent runners to bring her back. He wanted to see her, to tell her of his triumph, to tell her of his plans.

Waiting to receive him was his sacred wife, who had delivered him of two sons and a daughter from the royal blood line, children who were descended from the gods. Waiting were other children from other wives. The wives and the children gathered round, but they were not enough. Kaahumanu was not a wife for breeding. She was a wife for wanting and talking to and—he thought—a wife for vexation and trouble.

He wanted to tell her about Kaiana, how the young chief had deserted and then stood a traitor against his King. He wanted to tell her himself, but it was too late. She knew. If he could find who had brought the news ahead of him, he would have his tongue cut out, his eyes ripped from their sockets. He wanted her to know that it was Kaiana who had chosen to fight against his brothers, and he had paid with his life for the treachery.

He knew she would not believe him. That woman, he moaned to himself, why had the gods afflicted him with that woman.

After the sun had fallen into the ocean six times, Kaahumanu returned.

He said to her, "The volcano and the red akule fish . . . the kahunas said an alii must die. It was Kaiana's life that Pele demanded . . ."

She put her hand on his mouth, and in a voice crushed with sorrow she said, "It is done."

The King turned away from her, and when he turned back his big head fell forward. "I am weary of war, Kaahumanu. The killing days are done. Now is a time for peace in these islands."

"Yes," she said to him, sighing, "the people need time to plant, the plants need time to grow, no boy child should be reared for battle." Because the King wanted it, it was. Peace would reign from that day, and from that day, too, neither would speak of the young warrior Kaiana.

For many years after, there were those who came to Nuuanu to see where Kamehameha had fought his last great battle. And always they would stand in the place—in the very steps—where Kaiana had met his death, and then they would go to the base of the cliff to walk among the bleached bones of the defeated warriors who had fallen from the high Pali . . .

At the end of a story there was always a long, quiet pause. On this day, the only sound was the soft grind of the hammock as Vicky rocked back and forth in the stifling heat.

Finally Liko ventured, "We could ride over to Nuuanu. There are bones there, even now—we could find the footsteps."

"No," Vicky and True cried out with such vehemence that I thought for a moment poor Liko would cry.

"Not today," I told him.

"I don't mean today," he said and pouted.

"Never," Vicky answered. "It's too awful, what they did in the old days. Pa says they are superstitions, that's all . . ."

"You mean about Pele calling for the death of Kaiana?" True said. "But don't you see—it wasn't Pele that killed him—it was Kamehameha."

"No," I put in. "It was Kaiana who killed himself, because he chose the wrong side to fight on."

"But he had no choice," True argued. "The King forced him to change sides by leaving him out of his councils of war. That could mean only that the King planned to kill him."

I countered, "It was because Kaahumanu had warned him. It might not have been so."

Vicky spoke for the first time: "I think it was so, because when the King told her of the death of Kaiana, he said Pele the goddess of the volcano had wished it . . . as if it had been predestined."

With that, Vicky burst into tears. Pulling her knees to her chin she lay in the hammock, and only the sound of her wracking sobs broke the sullen quiet of the day.

Evan came to say good-bye on a day when True was away exercising the horses. I stood by, fretting for fear he would leave before she returned, madly trying to think of a way to hold him.

"It was good of you to come," Uncle ventured. "The girls have grown fond of you—and I must say, bringing Princess Kaiulani into our lives has been a special favor."

Evan laughed easily. "I should tell you that Archie said the same thing to me—for bringing all of you to them. Kaiulani has always been frail, or so he thought until he saw her racing down the beach with True and Martha, and Liko has her swimming like a fish." He crossed the lanai and looked out over the ocean and his mood changed. "Princess Likelike is not well," he said. "That's why Archie didn't come with me today, and why Kaiulani hasn't been over since last week."

"What is it?"

"Nothing the doctors can find. That's what is so aggravating. She has simply taken to her bed, and she has to be coaxed to eat."

"No symptoms? Pain, fever. . .?"

"None. When I stopped by today the King was there. He came out onto the lanai scolding Archie for pampering his sister. He said he didn't want to hear any more of her superstitious nonsense."

"What superstitious nonsense?" Uncle asked.

Evan paused and then said, "She believes a kahuna is praying her to death."

Uncle's face clouded. "I know the old alii believed they could not let so much as a fingernail fall into the hands of a hostile kahuna, or he could use it to pray them to death. But—I didn't know any of those beliefs persist."

"Many of them do," Evan told him. "More than you could believe, even with Christians like the Princess. When you have lived in these islands all your life, you learn there are not always answers. You learn not to be surprised."

"At what happens or what people believe?"

"Both," Evan admitted. "But I'm counting on Archie to prevail. It isn't easy for him, balancing between two worlds—the Hawaiian alii class and his own very rational Scots background."

I heard the familiar thudding trot of Liko's pony and, racing around the corner, sent him scurrying down the beach to find True and bring her back. For once he did not ask why; he had only to look at my face to see the urgency.

When I returned to my listening post, Evan was saying to Uncle, "That time I met her father when he asked me to bring her the letter . . . I didn't . . . you see, I knew what had happened to True's mother. People on Maui talked about her. I even knew the Hawaiian luna who killed her. I remember being surprised about that—he was one of the hardest-working men I'd ever known, and kindly too, or so I thought. But you see, I didn't even try to talk to her father, to see what he planned to do about True, and I've been thinking ever since that I should have done more for her, when I had the chance."

Uncle twisted one of his hands in the other, as he did when he was thinking. "Of course, you didn't know True when you met her father. You could have had no idea. It is always hard to know about True," he went on, shifting the subject slightly. "I mean, what anyone can do for her . . . what she will allow you to do for her. She never speaks of her mother, not to us at least and I think not to the others. She gave me a draft for fifty dollars which her father sent with you, and told me to apply it to her keep. I put it in the bank in her name. If he should send more, perhaps one day she can go off to school, too."

Evan frowned. "What will happen to her and to Martha and the others, I mean—they're still children now, but when they grow up?"

Uncle pretended to examine his specs. "I'm not certain they were ever really children, they've had to endure so much. But I suppose the girls will marry, and the boys will find work. That's what usually happens, isn't it?" It was not Uncle's favorite subject, so he changed it. "When do you leave, Evan?"

"Tomorrow, early." But he could not seem to shake off the subject. "I don't think I've ever known anyone with as much spirit as True . . ."

Uncle was finished. "I shall miss our talks."

"I more than you, but I figure Archie will carry on. He likes your company, and he trusts you. These are hard times for men like Archie—devoted monarchists, insiders yet outsiders as well, because of their color."

"You don't consider yourself one of them?"

Evan shook his head. "Not one of them. I'm sympathetic, but I don't think we can go back to the old ways, and I don't think the Americans are going to stay out of it all that much longer. Whatever changes take place, I'd like to help it happen without doing damage to the old order."

Uncle pointed down the beach. True was galloping the horse through the hard sand of the surf, water splashing all about. "Look at that girl ride," Evan said admiringly. "With that white hair flying, you could take her for an apparition."

"Maybe she is one of your Hawaiian goddesses," Uncle said.

He walked with her down the beach, True leading the horse back to the stable: Evan straight and slender, his long stride shortened to match hers, the wind tousling his thick hair and sending True's flying in ribbons of white. She scarcely reached his shoulder now, but she was growing. When he returned she would be tall enough.

"I've been thinking," Evan began, then stopped and started over again. "That time I met your father, I wish now I had gone after him, asked more questions. I've heard he is working in the timber country not far from Seattle. I thought I could make some inquiries when I get to San Francisco . . ."

"No," True said.

"No?" he asked.

"My father knows where I am. He didn't come when

. . . he didn't come . . ." She stopped and, as if to finish the subject, said, "I do not want you to ask about my father. But I would like it if you would write to me."

Surprised, he asked, "And will you write me back?"

"Yes, I will," she answered readily. "I thought I could send you the news of the Islands. Uncle takes all the papers, and I can write you what he and Vicky's pa talk about."

"And will you write me about yourself?"

She blushed then; a pretty pink flush spread up her neck and to her cheeks.

"Yes, I will," she said.

"Then I will write you back, though I think I won't have much to say—I expect to be studying all the time, and it is a while since I have opened a book. I'm still surprised that Yale took me. Do you think they expect me to be a native with tattoos on my face?"

She wanted to say that they were right to take him, that he was smart and kind and fair. She wanted to tell him how safe she felt when he was near her, how he made her remember what it was to be happy. But she could not without scaring him away. All she could do was wait. All she could say was, "I have something to tell you."

He waited, raising his eyebrows in expectation.

"When you come back," she said, slowly, as if to make a point, "everything will be different."

"I expect it will," he answered, so quickly she knew he didn't understand.

"I don't know if you expect the difference, but it will happen," she said, feeling as if she were speaking in some foreign language. At that moment Jenny Barrows' voice could be heard, calling him. She stood waiting for him, hands on her hips, and shouted, "Come right now or you will miss your going-away party."

Evan's departure marked the end of that sweet summer. Vicky no longer came to our hale but sent for us to come to Ainahau, because she wanted to stay close to her mother. When we were there we had to stay nearby, most often on the wide lanai with its mottled shade.

Nothing was the same; where before there were always people around, laughing and jolly and easy, now they came and were silent. We spoke in low voices; sometimes Vicky's

pa would come out and ask us to take a stroll through the
gardens, to see the mangos or the hibiscus or to pick some
flowers for the house. His eyes—so kindly, and now so sad—
made us feel even worse. A pall had settled over Ainahau,
and after a time I no longer wanted to go there.

"You must," True said.

"Why?" I asked. "I know you hate it too, sitting there
with Vicky, it is so awful . . . waiting . . ."

"We have to go," was all True would say, her mouth set
so that I knew it was no good to argue.

Christmas came and went. We gave Vicky a book of
pressed mountain wildflowers which Uncle Jameson had
helped us gather and catalogue. I wrote verses for several of
them, and True made a lace bookmark of such delicate
beauty that it quite took Vicky's breath away. She gave us
beautiful tortoiseshell combs for our hair, which made us
look, we thought, very grown-up.

January seemed to us to be almost achingly beautiful—the
sea a sharp turquoise, the sand smooth and gold, the great
billowing clouds that filled the sky in the afternoons as if to
set the stage for sunsets of such wild flamboyance that even
the oldest of the natives would stand and watch.

On the last days of the month, Mauna Loa erupted with
a vengeance, spewing ash and smoke into the air, bringing
thunder and lightning to the Big Island. Fire rained from the
sky and a great flow of molten lava began to snake down the
mountain, burning everything in its path.

When we arrived at Ainahau that morning, Vicky met us
at the gate; her hair was uncombed, her clothes were rum-
pled and her eyes were red with crying. "Now Mama says
that Pele of the Volcano calls for the death of an alii, and she
says she knows she must die. She won't eat, not anything,
and she is so terribly weak she can hardly speak. Uncle
David has been here and he's furious with her, and Papa
pleads with her, but it doesn't do any good, none at all.
What am I to do, can you tell me, True?"

Pain flickered across True's face; she closed her eyes and
put her arms around Vicky and held her so tightly that it
must have hurt, had Vicky not already been in so much pain.
I put my hand on Vicky's back, needing to touch my poor
friend.

A strange, lowing noise made me turn to look down the

road. A procession of Hawaiians was coming, old men and old women mostly, one or two of them chanting a mele, the ancient genealogies passed from generation to generation in the form of a chant; along the side, walking in her old, lopsided way, was Auntie Momi. Tears were streaming down her face, but she was making no sound at all.

The others passed on by us and settled themselves along the palm-lined avenue that led to Ainahau. Vicky looked at us, as if she were drowning and we could save her.

Auntie Momi started up the path. "What is it?" I asked under my breath.

"The red akule fish are swimming in Pele's waters," she told me. "Always, when they come they bring with them the death of an alii. The Princess Likelike is pau."

With my fingers I traced the tears that washed down her old, lined cheeks. "Is there nothing we can do, Auntie?" I asked, surprised at the weakness of my own voice.

Auntie didn't answer, but began the chant that would trace the line of Kaahumanu, through the generations, back through all the years to when the first men stepped off their canoes in the time so distant that only their names remained, saved in the long lists committed to memory by each new generation.

The chanting began then, the sounds lifting and rising in terrible rhythms, surrounding us, filling the air all about us, catching on the afternoon breeze and gaining in mesmerizing volume as the day went slowly by.

On the lanai, True sat very straight, holding tight to Vicky's hand. Miss Gardiner stayed close to us, never saying a word, but wringing a handkerchief so hard that it seemed it must tear.

"Your mama wants to see you now," Vicky's pa whispered in her ear. She looked up at him, her eyes wild with fear. "I'll be with you," he told her. "I'll be there."

He had to pry her hand from True's, so tightly was Vicky holding on. She approached her mother's bed, but now the woman lying there did not look like her mama at all, but like someone else, someone she didn't know. Her father had gently to push Vicky to touch her hand.

"Come close," her mother said, and in a voice that seemed to come from someplace else, she told Vicky in slow and measured tones, "I have seen the future, and I can tell you

this, my sweet Princess Victoria Kaiulani. You will leave
Hawaii-nei. You will be away for a very long time, until you
are grown and a woman. You will not marry. You will never
be queen."

Vicky broke and ran, stumbling and sobbing. Miss Gardiner caught her, and True moved to take her other arm;
together they all but carried her down the path to one of the
grass huts by the sea.

As we sat, trying to calm Vicky from her convulsive sobbing, the chanting seemed to rise and hold, one long loud
moan from the throats of a hundred or more Hawaiians who
now lined all the walkways. And then there was silence,
sudden and absolute, with only Vicky's anguished sobs to
mark her mother's death.

7

"How long has Vicky's pa been talking about sending her to school in England?" True wanted to know.

"Oh, for quite a long while now," Miss Gardiner answered, placing her teacup precisely in its saucer.

"Since before her mother died?"

"Oh my, yes," she said. "The Princess Likelike was against it, very much against it, you know." She looked inquisitively at True.

"Well, I know she was sometimes angry . . ." True ventured.

Aunt Winona, impatient to be part of the conversation, broke in, "I understand she once took her riding whip to a poor man who didn't polish her buggy to her liking . . ."

A look of disapproval passed over Miss Gardiner's face. "She could be imperious, yes, but she could also be quite loving and sweet."

True rubbed Aunt Winona's arm, a tactic she had discovered would silence her.

"I wonder," she began. "Did the Princess ever talk to you about the monarchy—what she thought might happen?"

"Oh, not really . . . I mean, we spoke about Princess Kaiulani. At first, she said I had no right to discipline a royal princess. She wanted her treated with the respect accorded royalty . . ."

"But did she think the monarchy would last?" True persisted.

"My impression was that she did not," the governess said carefully. "I overheard her say that to the King once, but it might just be that she was vexed with him at the time, as she often was."

Aunt Winona shifted the conversation and soon the two were talking about the King's successful campaign to revive

some of the old customs, and especially the hula, despite the
missionaries' insistence that the dance was lascivious and
lewd and should be abolished.

That evening True found Uncle Jameson reading in his
study. "I have noticed," he told her, marking his page, "that
when you pull your left ear, you are trying to piece together
some errant bits of information."

In fact, his sister had already told him of the teatime
conversation.

"I can figure how the Princess knew that Vicky would be
going far away for a long time, and how she could say that
Vicky would never be queen. But how could she know—and
how could she say—that Vicky will never get married?"

"You sound as if you believe Princess Likelike's presenti-
ment."

"Vicky believes it . . . that's the problem."

"I see," Uncle said. "Well, I don't happen to think anyone
can know the future, just as I don't believe it is possible for
any of us to escape death."

"Then why did she say it?"

Uncle sighed. "You would think she . . . I don't know. But
let's try to deduce what she might have meant. You have
already figured out two of the predictions. You know that
the Princess' father has been talking about sending her to
school in England for some time, to prepare her for her royal
duties. I can see why he might be even more determined to
send her away now, so that she doesn't become afflicted with
what he calls the 'native predisposition to the spirit world.'

"As for the other prediction, that Kaiulani will not
marry—if you look at the blood lines, which are very important to the Hawaiian alii class, there are very few men here
who qualify to marry a future queen. The Hawaiian royal
line is carried through the women, remember. A high chief
or a king could marry many classes lower than himself, but
for a woman of a high chiefly family, that was not possible.
She could marry one class below, sometimes perhaps two.
But never any more than that. In old times babies of those
unsanctioned unions were put to death, their necks wrung.
Of course, King Kalakaua—and the last two Kamehame-
has, as well—sees himself in a larger world, and feels a
special kin to other monarchies. I have heard that King

Kalakaua even wrote letters about arranging a marriage for Kaiulani with a Japanese prince. Now, that would create an alliance between Japan and Hawaii that would certainly give the Missionary Boys cause for alarm."

He went on: "Perhaps it occurred to Kaiulani's mother that the few men considered of high enough birth would not be acceptable to her daughter, perhaps it was her way of saying that Kaiulani need not be a pawn, and if need be could choose not to marry at all."

True pulled on her ear. "But if Vicky is the last of the royal line, wouldn't she be expected to marry to give the kingdom an heir?"

"Expected, yes. But forced—I don't think so. That doesn't seem to be in the Hawaiian character."

Again True was silent for a time. "So if her mother predicts she won't marry, and Vicky is told to marry someone she doesn't want, she can tell about what her mother said when she was dying, and she won't have to marry?"

"What do you think?"

"Maybe," True said. "But what if she does meet someone she wants to marry, and what if everybody agrees?"

"Then the old prediction can be put to rest, and Kaiulani can marry and live happily ever after."

She looked at him, her eyes suddenly fierce. "That doesn't happen very often, does it?" she whispered, as if she were afraid to say it out loud.

"Perhaps more often than we know," he said gently, and she looked at him like he'd given her something small and sweet to hold onto. She turned to leave. Then she stopped and said, "But what if Vicky believes she can't ever marry, because of what her mother said?"

"Well, maybe there will be someone to talk with her about what her mother might have meant."

"Yes," True said, thinking so hard she left without remembering to say good night.

In the weeks following Princess Likelike's death, Vicky's pa made a habit of riding over at about sunset, bringing along a bottle of good brandy which he and Uncle would consume as they sat on the lanai of Uncle's cottage and talked into the night. Sometimes Vicky would come along and stay the night because her father left so very late.

During this time one of the little boys became sick with the measles, and the two cottages at the far end of the beach were quarantined. Aunt Winona stayed with them, and True and I were in charge of the other children.

The outbreak prevented Vicky from coming but not her pa. He continued his almost nightly discussions, after which Uncle slept long into the morning, while we prepared breakfast and attempted to teach his classes.

On one of these nights, our room was too stifling for sleep. "We could go for a swim," True offered, adding, "or we could go hear what Uncle and Vicky's pa are talking about."

"You mean under the lanai? We're much too old for that," I began, laughing.

We slipped under the porch, only a few feet from where the two men sat across from each other at the game table, the bottle between them, and held our hands over our mouths to keep from giving ourselves away.

"You can imagine—I was a big, strapping lad of sixteen when we came here," Archie Cleghorn was saying. "And you remember how it is when you are young, a big raw boy with all the juices rising, and landing up in this place where the women—ah, the Hawaiian women—they wanted it just as much you wanted it, no pretending, just go off into the bushes, and she'd unbutton you and take your pants off for you and lay down on top of you, laughing and happy and you'd have it.

"You'd see the girl later, and she'd smile and laugh and tell you how good you were, no guilt. None at all. It was paradise for a boy . . ."

"Why just for the boy?" Uncle wanted to know. "Wasn't it paradise for the girl, too? I'd always heard that with native women . . ."

"Oh, well, the missionaries were strong then, they let the Hawaiians know right away that their old, happy, easy ways about sex were wicked. Did you know that in the old days, I mean before the missionaries, the Hawaiians encouraged their young people to have it with each other—as much as they wanted—though later on they expected them to settle into what we would call a marriage. Even then, the woman or the man was allowed to have sex with others. And the alii class could have more than one wife, of course. Kamehameha had as many as twenty, and plenty of children. Though only one wife—the sacred wife—could produce heirs to the throne."

"They mated brother and sister, I heard that," Uncle said, his voice thick. "Put a bed up for them in the town square and everyone came and looked on to make sure he planted the seed right. Jesus! Poor buggared Christians, they just weren't up to a seed-planting ceremony like that, so they let Mary do it all by herself."

The two men choked with laughter, and then it was quiet while one or the other poured a drink.

"Sex with someone just for the pleasure of it," Uncle said. "What harm could it do?"

Archie mumbled, "When the white man came—the sailors first—the wives and daughters swam out to the boats and opened their legs to the sex-starved men."

"And in return, the sailors gave them venereal disease," Uncle said. "That's what harm it could do to a people who knew no disease. The first step in the eventual eradication of the Hawaiians."

"Don't say that," Vicky's pa cried out, and Uncle shuffled over to pat him on the back and tell him, awkwardly, that he was sorry, and to pour another drink for both of them.

"Many white men left their children behind. But some of us didn't. I did as the Hawaiians. When I was young, I played as they played, I lay with more girls than I can count. My God, it was good, Jameson. But as I grew older, I stayed with one . . . Lapeka. She is mother to Helen and Rose and Annie, you know. I've kept them near me. I need to have them close."

"But you married the Princess Likelike . . ." Uncle said, leaving whatever question he had in mind unasked.

Vicky's pa sighed and said, *"Na Lani Eha.* It means The Four Sacred Ones. That's what the Hawaiians called them: Likelike, Liliuokalani and the two brothers—Kalakaua and Leleiohuku. Their ancestor was a cousin to Kamehemaha I, a high chief. Miriam was nineteen when we married. She chose me, I don't know why . . . I was almost twice her age, but it seemed to me then that she was giving me a chance to help. Now all that is left are King Kalakaua, who has no children, Liliuokalani, who is forty and without children, and my little Kaiulani.

"It's true," Archie Cleghorn went on. "They are dying

out, the Hawaiians. They look so big and stalwart—those great brown bodies—but there is something soft in the center. Sometimes I think it is that sweet goodness, that easy spirit. And *mana*—you know about mana?"

"The life force, the power that is in all things," Uncle answered, like an altar boy answering the priest's ritual questions.

"Aye, and I believe in it," Vicky's pa mumbled.

Uncle asked, "Is that why you're sending Kaiulani away?"

We could hear the big man shift in his chair, and when he spoke his voice was thick and tortured: "Vicky's blood lines give her exceptional mana, and I've come to believe it is her only hope. If she goes away, she can accept her strength . . . I know she has it! You saw her with the children here, running and swimming like any normal child. She has my stamina in her. But they won't let her. If she stays here, the softness inside will take her away. Her mother . . ." He stopped then and sat in silence for a long time. Uncle waited. Under the porch, we shifted and leaned against each other. We had intruded; we should not have been listening. I knew that True wanted to be away as much as I did, safe back in our beds, not hearing any more. We put our hands over our ears, but it didn't help. We heard anyway, words we could never take away.

Vicky's pa went on in that awful, choked voice, "Before she died, she was trying to tell me something. It seemed as if—I hope I am wrong, dear God—but I believe what she was trying to tell me was that our Kaiulani would not live past her twenty-fifth year."

We bit our lips and buried our faces in the sand and tried not to breathe; we held each other, our rough sandy cheeks pressed together, too terrified even to cry.

8

"Come meet Colonel Toby," Vicky called to us from across the palm grove, her voice high and false, a voice for strangers. "Everyone in the world needs to know Colonel Toby."

I did not look at True, but I knew she would be frowning. In the six months since her mother's death, Vicky alternated between being morose and falsely gay; from day to day we never knew which it was to be. Tears came easily, so did wild laughter; usually, one followed the other.

"Colonel Wakefield," Vicky went on with mock seriousness, pulling each of us to her, "these are my wonderful friends." The Colonel, taking the cue, bowed low and said how perfectly charmed he was to be making our acquaintances. He was tall and thick, with a wavy crown of sandy-colored hair streaked now with grey, nicely trimmed whiskers, an important way of holding himself and a rakish air. He also had a laugh that said he was bound to enjoy whatever you had to say to him. You could not help but smile back.

"Be nice to the Colonel," Vicky admonished us like a schoolteacher, "and he may invite us all to his big cattle ranch, Mau'loa. You remember Evan talking about Mau'loa?" she added, to make certain she had True's attention.

But the Colonel did not take the hint. Instead, he turned to me and said, "Miss Martha Moon, now there's a name that just suits a little girl with such bright eyes. Come be my dinner partner, Miss Martha."

I was beside myself, to be singled out by Colonel Toby. He had the nicest, kindliest manners and a way of looking at you that made you feel he just couldn't wait to hear what you had to say.

By the time the eating was done and the singing started, I had discovered why he wanted to talk to me. He needed a teacher for his school at Mau'loa. He knew that my Hawaiian was better than passing good and he had been told, as he put it, that I had a way with children. I took a sip of water and swallowed hard to hide my embarrassment. It had dawned on me how stupidly silly it was to think he chose me because of my big bright eyes. All he needed was a teacher for the pokey little school he ran for his ranchhands' children. Words were flying around in my head, and I tried to pull them out and put them together in the right sequence, but before I could, two young girls flung themselves on Colonel Toby, and he had his hands full trying to handle them both.

"This one is my ragtag Rachel," he said, ruffling the mass of black curls that crinkled around the face of a girl of about ten years, so that she dissolved in giggles, "and this one is awful Etta," he said of the other, about a year younger, "and they are my two curious little monkey girls," he added with a father's pride. The girls giggled and wiggled and wheedled until they got their father to agree to allow them to go on an excursion with the Wilder children and, having got what they came for, they were off with a whoop. I watched and smiled hard and tried not to look forlorn; I wouldn't want it known how I envied those girls, running up like that and flinging their arms about this kindly man and knowing he wouldn't mind a bit.

By the time they left I had the words straight: "Thank you, sir, but I'm afraid I can't accept your kind offer. I have promised the Wrights I will stay and teach the youngest children at Hale Mana'olana."

He patted my hand in a fatherly way and told me he understood but that he hoped, someday, I would change my mind. These last words he said distractedly, because he was watching the approach of a woman as tall as he, with a lift of the chin and the carriage that would have told me she was alii, even if I hadn't already known.

I did know, of course; everybody in Hawaii knew that Laiana Wakefield was descended from a high chief of Maui. She was firmly fleshed with a full, dark face and eyes that seemed not to blink; if she wore a feathered cape instead of the tight-fitting, high-necked European dress, she would look every bit a chiefess. There were those who figured that she had married beneath her, even if Colonel Toby was

related to Kamehameha the Great. His great-grandfather
was the first Tobias Wakefield, who had married a granddaughter of Kamehameha's. Still, she hadn't been an important granddaughter, her bloodline was not so good as
Laiana's ancestors, according to old Auntie Momi, who
knows about such things.

The Colonel attempted to introduce us, but his wife was
so intent on what she had to say that she scarcely took note
of me. "Jared has had . . ." she started, then started over
again, "Jared is feeling poorly," she told her husband, her
face dark with worry. "I am taking him home."

"But it's so early, we can't . . ." the Colonel tried, but her
look said there was to be no argument. He sighed, then
seemed to pull himself up and, turning to me said, "Good
night, Little Miss Martha Moon. I've enjoyed our visit, and
I hope you'll remember our school, if ever you should want
to travel to another island."

I found True and Vicky hiding behind a lantana tree,
trying to stifle the sort of mad laughter that once loose, can
never be stopped.

"Whatever made you say such a thing to poor Jared?"
Vicky gasped, holding both hands over her mouth to keep
from laughing.

Coming up for breath, True managed, "I don't know. He
just seemed to need a needle stuck in him . . ." and they were
off again, laughing so hard they had to gasp for air.

I frowned at True; she knew that Vicky would soon be in
tears. "What happened?" I wanted to know, trying to sober
them up. They took deep breaths to keep quiet as Mrs.
Wakefield walked by, holding hard to the arm of a tall,
beautiful boy with a look of resignation in his dark eyes.
Mother and son made a point of not paying us any attention; I glanced at True and Vicky and found them studying
the ground as if they hoped it might open up and swallow
them.

"Oh, heavens," Vicky whispered when they were out of
hearing, and she repeated, "Oh, heavens, we have been
bad." She was chagrined and, at the same time, caught in the
madness of the laughter.

I was beginning to think they'd never be able to tell me,
when finally True blurted, gasping between words, "I was
simply trying to make conversation. I asked if he could

explain to me about . . . *gelding* . . . he should know, growing up on a cattle ranch. You would think . . ."

"Unfortunately," she began again, "I asked him just as he was swallowing, and he came near choking to death on a piece of fish—his face turned a terrible dark red, and his mother came bearing down on him, giving him such a thump that the fish went flying out of his mouth onto the table. His poor back is probably bruised."

Vicky's laughter dissolved into tears, the tears into hiccoughs, and it took us a good while to calm her down. Finally she said, "I doubt that Jared has ever even seen a castration. He's so sickly. For as long as I've known him, he's never been able to play with the rest of us. Until you said so today, True, I'd not thought of him as a good-looking boy—only a puny one."

"He's about the most beautiful boy I think I've ever seen," True said, matter-of-factly. "Too bad he hasn't a lick of sense."

"You don't know that," I told her. "Because he's sickly doesn't mean he's empty-headed."

Vicky, sensing an argument brewing, broke in, "It is too bad he hasn't any of his pa's fun or fancy."

"His mama scares me something fierce," I admitted, not really wanting to fight with True. "Maybe what he needs is somebody like Liko and us."

True and Vicky looked at each other in a superior way. "Dear Missy Moon," Vicky said, making a joke of being condescending, "you do just want to save all the sorry people in the world, don't you?"

I only wanted to save our small band—True and Vicky, Liko and me. I wanted to keep us as we were, and I knew it wasn't possible; even then, we were already spinning apart.

"I will not say good-bye," Vicky sobbed, holding us close, her great, brown nearsighted eyes filled with tears that mixed with our own, wetting our faces as we clung together. The flower leis piled around her neck added a sweet, sad scent to our good-byes. True and I watched as she climbed up the ramp of the SS *Umatilla* beside her pa and her half-sister Annie, and we waited, feeling empty and lonely already, as the band played "Hawaii Pono," and our eyes filled with tears again when the whistle blasted and the ship pulled away from the dock. She did not stay at the railing with the others, and we were not surprised. She loved her father too much to tell him how frightened and sad she felt, how afraid of the future in a cold, distant land. True and I were the only ones who knew and, like Vicky, we could do nothing about it.

It was May 10, 1889; the midday sun was hot and half of Oahu had gathered to see the Princess Kaiulani off to England, where she would go to school at Great Harrowden Hall in Northamptonshire and get the education expected of a queen. The Hawaiians had come to say good-bye, hundreds of them. Some of them had started walking at first light. They sang and they cried their alohas and waved until the big ship was only a small mark on the horizon and then no mark at all. Vicky's pa would go with her as far as San Francisco; she and her half-sister Annie would continue on to England with the British Vice-Consul and his wife as their escorts.

We did not know when Vicky would return or when we might see her again. True and I promised ourselves that we would never breathe a word of her mother's terrible prophecy, not even to each other, nor would we allow it to enter our thoughts.

Still, it pursued us in our dreams; True would sit upright in her bed, shivering over a dream that had her trying to swim out to sea, to where Vicky was calling for help, and have wave after giant wave wash her back to shore. In my dream, I would be all alone in a street in a strange big city, looking for Vicky. The day that she sailed for England, all we knew for certain was that when the sun rose again, Hawaii would not be the same.

August 1889

Our Dearest Vicky:

True and I are sitting side by side at our writing desks, scribbling away as fast as we can—me to you, True to Evan—to send the startling news right off. You have missed such fireworks! Finally Robert Wilcox got his revolution under way. He passed out red Garibaldi shirts to his eighty followers, most of them hapa haoles like Wilcox himself (and me and thee!). He led his men down to the palace, carrying a newly drawn constitution which would restore all of the royal powers that the 1887 constitution took away. He meant for the King to sign it!

I am sorry to report that not one of the revolutionaries had thought to see if the King was of a mind to sign it, or even if he was going to be at the palace, and it turns out he was not—on both counts.

Once King Kalakaua heard what was going on, he took off for his boat house and would not see Wilcox or any of his messengers. The militia was called out, and they managed to run the red-shirted Wilcox band into the large bungalow on the palace grounds. Not a very good position, because the militia took up posts high up in the surrounding buildings, encircling them. Throughout the long night the two groups simply looked at each other, and there was hope that it might all end peacefully. Then, for no reason anyone seems to know, a shot was fired, and soon enough everyone was shooting every which way. It was like the popping of fire-crackers on Chinese New Year. The government boys, perched in the opera house, could fire down on the bungalow at will.

Poor Wilcox, he was in a sorry fix. Pretty soon someone thought to have two of the baseball team's best pitchers toss sticks of dynamite down on the bungalow, tearing off the top story, creating a terrible din and causing such fire and smoke and commotion that finally the revolutionaries surrendered.

In the end, seven of Wilcox's men were dead and twice that number wounded. Nevertheless, Wilcox is considered to be quite a hero by the Hawaiians; Uncle says no jury will ever convict him. I hope not, but I have to say that I also hope he won't be leading any more young men into battle. In the end, the revolution meant to return power to the King came to nothing . . . except for those hapa haole families who today must bury their dead.

We heard much of this from Jenny Barrows, who came out the next day to see Aunt. I think you will be amazed to learn that the two have become fast friends, with Jenny making the long drive out and back at least once each week. She comes to give the little children drawing lessons, but I believe she has given up on that almost entirely. "They sim-ply will not follow directions," she told Aunt. (In the children's defense, I must say that Jenny lacks patience.) She and Aunt must be thirty years apart in age, yet they chatter the afternoon away on the lanai. You know how Aunt does love to talk.

True sends her love, and so does your faithful friend, Martha.

In her letter to Evan, True gave her version of the failed revolution, with her own conclusion: "It is hard to imagine stupidity in a more concentrated form than that of Robert Wilcox, Hawaii's own comic opera Garibaldi. He can do nothing but damage to the monarchy, as Uncle says the King quite obviously understands."

She paused, her pen poised over the letter, then added, "Martha says to send you her best wishes." She hesitated again, her lips pressed firmly together, then signed off with a flourish: *Me ke aloha pumehana,* True.

She looked at the words. *With warm affection.* Maybe it was too forward—what if it scared him off and he quit writing to her altogether? As it was, she heard from him no more than once every six, and sometimes eight, weeks, though she herself wrote him every Tuesday, to be included in the weekly sailing of one ship or another. Lately she had taken to waiting until the last minute to send her letter, because Jenny had been offering to carry their mail with her back to Honolulu. "No letter, True?" Jenny had said the other day. "I hear you are a fine little correspondent." True hadn't answered.

Me ke aloha pumehana. She closed her eyes and ran her hand over her breasts. She smiled; they were growing. Sometimes at night she pushed them together and imagined him looking at them, touching them. She would press her mouth hard against her arm and let her hand move to her stomach, to the place between her legs that flushed warm and moist . . . if only Evan would wait for her.

Evan Coulter gave himself over to the rocking of the train as it picked up speed and rattled through the Pennsylvania countryside. In two years at Yale, this was the first time he had left Connecticut. He looked out at the winter landscape, at the lifeless trees and the dark, foreboding woods. Winter here seemed so filled with death. He tried to imagine it in the summer, soft and green and warm.

He wondered if he would ever feel warm again. He looked at his hands, soft and sallow, and he thought about the sundown light on the beach at Waikiki, and the scent of pikaki, and the next thing he felt was a familiar stab of homesickness. *Damnation,* he said to himself, then he decided not to fight it, but to allow his thoughts to drift to home. He felt in his pocket, brought out a cellophane packet and breathed deeply of the jasmine True had sent in her last letter.

Strange that it was True who sent him pressed flowers, and not Jenny. Yet it was Jenny who wrote long, romantic letters, light and entertaining and warm. True's letters were factual discourses, filled with data and other people's opinions. At times he felt she must be copying directly from the newspaper. Still, in a peculiar way, they gave him a better sense of the Islands than Jenny's letters.

Me ke aloha pumehana True had taken to signing her letters. He smiled. The train rattled through a tunnel and out over an embankment which looked down into a deep ravine. He thought of True again, of the day she carried the three little boys out of the ravine, and then he carried her out. He shifted uncomfortably in his seat and made himself think of something else.

In Pittsburgh he walked from the station to the Carnegie Museum. "Sit down over there, please," the secretary commanded, looking at him over her spectacles, as if he might be a new specimen to be pinned to the walls. He was settling in for a long wait when the secretary came bustling out of the inner office, telling him to hang his coat there and leave his case there and to come follow her.

Dr. Holland strode across the room, grasped his hand and pumped it hard. "My boy, I cannot tell you how delighted I am . . . how absolutely delighted . . ." he said, pumping his arm some more, "to be meeting the son of Frederic Coulter. An amazing scholar, your father—what a pleasure, what a real pleasure."

William Holland was a small, pink man of large enthusiasms, first among them the collecting and cataloguing of the world's butterflies. The collection he had amassed for the museum was one of the world's finest. He had corresponded with Evan's father for almost a decade. "It's a great pleasure for me, too, sir," Evan said. "My father shared your letters with me."

"I hope he also shared his love of collecting," Holland said. "And I do hope you know what a great, great contribution he made to our science! I would have given anything to go out into the field with him. His notes were . . . well, simply superb. But you know all that, of course you do," he finished, calling for the secretary.

"What?" she said rather crossly.

"Tea, tea, Blanche. With some cookies, if you please. Don't fuss at us, we're going to settle into some serious butterfly talk, and you mustn't scowl and carry on."

The woman scowled nonetheless, and for a moment Evan thought she might tell him to come out and put on his coat and leave at once, but she only closed the door behind her, harder than was necessary.

"Don't mind Blanche," Holland said airily. "She could run the office by herself, and I keep telling her so, but she thinks I'm impudent. Oh, but I have so much to ask you . . . so many questions about your father, about his marvelous, marvelous work . . ." Then he said again how much he admired Frederic Coulter, and Evan could feel something warm expanding inside of him.

They spent the afternoon talking about the butterflies of the Pacific Islands and about the body of work Evan's father had contributed to the world's knowledge of lepidopterology. Before he left, Evan presented Dr. Holland with the case he had brought along, containing his father's last field notes and a few fine specimens—including Kamehameha, *Vanessa tameamea Eschscholtz* and a Blackburn's Blue *Vaga blackburni.* It was all he had been able to salvage from the shed his father had used as an office and laboratory, before his mother had it destroyed.

For a moment, Evan had the uncomfortable feeling that the good doctor was about to burst into tears. Then he clapped his hands together like a delighted child and pored over the material right then and there, as if it could not possibly wait. "Marvelous, marvelous," he kept murmuring.

Evan could not stop smiling; all the way back to Connecticut, he could feel the warmth rising in him, the pride. To his wife and neighbors, Fred Coulter had been an eccentric, a failure. But to Dr. William Holland, director of the Carnegie Museum, Frederic Coulter was a contributor to the world's store of knowledge.

Late that afternoon, Evan returned to the house in New Haven where he had taken a room. For an instant he considered passing it by, walking over to the campus, delaying his return. He would have liked to hold onto the warmth of his visit for another hour or so.

Instead he let himself into the front hallway, where on the long refectory table he found two letters waiting for him. One from Jenny, and the other was an envelope from Davis and Gathers, the law firm that handled Eli Barrows' affairs.

Jenny's perfect penmanship was marred, the lines slanting down the page. "Dearest Evan," she began, "I feel as if I must write you immediately to tell you that Papa has died this morning, just one hour ago. He went off to work as usual, so early that neither Mama nor I were up, though sometimes we do get up to see him off. He keeps such awfully early hours. At eleven o'clock, a supervisor at the meatpacking plant appeared to tell us that Papa had fallen over, just as suddenly as that, and before they could get the doctor he was gone. His heart gave out, the doctor said.

"Mama is just wandering around, wringing her hands, not knowing what to do. And I don't know either—oh, Evan, I wish you were here! He loved you as a son, I am sure you know that. But I will pull together, and do what needs to be done. Papa would have wanted me to, though I know he was counting on you to be back to help. Oh, don't listen to me now, Evan. I am just so filled with grief for my poor father. I do know that you liked him for his good qualities, which were many, and I comfort myself with that. I am giving this letter to Mr. Davis, Papa's lawyer who is here now, and who says that he will be writing you as well.

"Your loving Jenny"

Evan sank into a chair and let his arms drop. Eli Barrows dead. Big, fat, loud Eli. Blunt, honest, fair Eli. Kind and loyal Eli. He ran his hands through his hair and wished that he had been able to see him again, one more time, just to say good-bye and to tell him . . . tell him what? That he liked him and that he was sorry . . . sorry for what? Why should he have felt sorry for Eli, who was shrewd and successful?

Evan thought of his own father, who had been neither shrewd nor successful, but quiet and eccentric, fascinated with the small, winged creatures of the forest.

He did not open the lawyer's letter that night. He left it on his desk, walked around it, wished that he did not have to read it at all. The next morning he woke with a sense of dread. All of the warmth, all the good feeling from the trip to Pittsburgh was gone. Eli was dead, had been dead for more than a month now . . . that was how long it took a letter to get to him. He tried to think what might be happening in Honolulu, what Jenny and her mother would be doing.

He opened the envelope from Davis and Gathers as he might have opened a summons to an execution. Two letters were inside. One, from Henry Davis, told him of Eli Barrows' death and the instructions he left to deliver the other letter to Evan "in the event of my client's untimely death." It was a sealed envelope with "For Evan Coulter" scrawled across the front in a rough hand.

"If you are reading this I am dead," Eli Barrows wrote. "I wisht it weren't so, because I would have liked to be here when you got back to see how that Yale law education fits you. I'll admit this much too—I wanted to see you married to my Jenny. She has her sights set on you, I don't have to tell you, and she's made a good choice. She and her mother are well taken care of, I've seen to that. If I could think of anything to say to convince you to marry Jenny, I'd say it. But that's your decision, son. I am going to urge you to stay until you're done there at Yale. It won't do you or my girls no good if you come back without finishing. I am directing Henry Davis to forgive the loan I made to you. I'm also releasing you from the pledge to work for Barrows and Company, since it will be sold upon my death. In return, I'll ask you to look after Jenny's and her ma's affairs. I mean, look after the lawyers and bankers who are handling the inheritance, and make sure they are doing right. I've left instructions that you will have the 'paramount word.' Keep them honest.

"You're a decent man, Evan. There aren't many of them around. I'm counting on you to do the decent thing."

Evan put on his coat, wrapped a long scarf around his neck and walked out into a freezing February rain.

9

Archibald Cleghorn was not at all partial to poker, but he was very good at it. David Kalakaua discovered this aptitude and insisted that his brother-in-law should be one of the regulars at the King's famous—or infamous, depending on who was winning or losing—boat house poker games.

Archie Cleghorn could never deny the King (he was known to feel that David Kalakaua had reaped the lion's share of charm in the family). So he played poker, and with a certain regularity would take home a tidy sum from his winnings. He won most often from his brother-in-law, from whom he refused to collect, putting him off with "we'll settle up later" or "I'd rather you'd keep it on account—don't want to get in trouble with your sister."

Early in November of 1890, when the King was preparing to leave for San Francisco, he called his brother-in-law to the palace and ushered him solemnly into the room he used as a private office.

Seated behind his ornate desk, the King had said, frowning, "Archie, old friend, it is time to settle up. I hope you've kept track of how much I owe you over the years . . . I'm afraid it's going to bankrupt the kingdom."

"You called me up here for this?" Cleghorn guffawed (at the same time feeling, as he would confess later on, infinitely relieved). "I haven't the slightest idea what the figure is, David, and even if I did, it wouldn't matter. It's a game, all in the family, I don't want a cent."

A large, sweet smile spread over David Kalakaua's handsome face, and Cleghorn thought once more, as he had so often in the past few years, how intensely likeable he was. He believed that if it hadn't been for David, the monarchy might have collapsed by now. Of course, David had made mistakes—he had the Hawaiian predilection for pomp and high living. There were those, including his sister Liliuokalani, who scarcely veiled their contempt for David for signing the Reform Constitution back in '87, which stripped the monarchy of so much of its power. The "bayonet" constitution, Liliu had dubbed it. But Cleghorn was a realist; he knew the King had little choice, and he admired his brother-in-law for keeping the Reformers off balance.

"Archie," the King had said, his voice husky with affection. "Do you think I'm the sort who would back off from gambling debts? For shame, brother." He gave way to a fit of coughing. "There has to be an accommodation, Archie," he was finally able to get out.

"We'll talk about it when you return," Cleghorn had said.

"No, now," David Kalakaua insisted. "You don't leave this room without telling me what I owe. My honor's at stake, Arch." For dramatic effect he had put his hand on one of the ceremonial swords that hung on the wall behind him. Archie Cleghorn shook his head and grinned; still, it worried him; it wasn't like David to be so dogged.

"All right then. If I know you at all, your majesty, you'll spend some time while you're in California looking over horseflesh. I've had it in mind for a while now to find myself a stallion that can beat Toby Wakefield's big grey. If you should happen to see such an animal, I'd be willing to call in all my markers. How's that?"

"Done," David Kalakaua had said, and the two men had embraced upon taking leave of each other.

Three months later, David Kalakaua was dead in California. Liliuokani was Queen, and Kaiulani was Crown Princess. And eleven days after the funeral Archibald Cleghorn received notice of the arrival, on the ship *Sharon* out of San Francisco, of a bay stallion purchased from the Galway Ranch in Merced, California.

True was rubbing the bay's foreleg when she noticed a flash of blue cambric out of the corner of her eye and glanced up to see Jenny Barrows swinging down the path that led to the stables, walking directly toward her. A small, electric warning pulse ran up True's spine. She was hot and dirty from the day's work in the stable; she knew she smelled of sweat and horse, knew her hair was whisping out of the dusty old bandana around her head. She felt hot and ugly and large compared to the woman dancing down the path, crisp in her delicate cotton dress and with a fresh face. True did not want to see Jenny; she did not want to talk to Jenny; she wished with all her heart that Jenny Barrows would drop off the face of the earth.

"Hello, True," Jenny called out, as if they were friends.

True tried to force a smile but it must have seemed a grimace because Jenny said, laughing, "Don't look so downcast! I decided to come and hear it from the horse's mouth, but don't worry—I promise to keep your secret." She paused only to take a breath. "Everyone's talking about this horse." She stood for a minute, her eyes scanning the big bay. "Oh, my," she said, her voice filled with awe, "he is a lovely animal." When she reached to touch the bay, he quivered and turned to rub against True.

"Shh, boy," True murmured, running her hand over the smooth neck.

Jenny spoke rapidly. "You know I suppose that all of Honolulu plans to go to the race next week, everybody's just aching to see *True's Surprise.*"

"True's Surprise?" True asked, baffled.

Jenny's laugh spilled over. "So you didn't know! I thought as much. In fact, I told Mother that you were far too modest a girl to let them name the horse after you—but that is exactly what Mr. Cleghorn did. It's General Jackson running against True's Surprise here," she reached to stroke the bay, "and absolutely everybody is talking about the race. You know what friendly rivals Colonel Toby and Mr. Cleghorn are, have been for ages—I don't know when there's been such excitement—and with a week yet to go. I hate to tell you how much money is changing hands. General Jackson is the big favorite, of course, because he's never been beaten and because your stallion is an unknown. To tell you the truth, some folks don't even think he exists. They think dear Mr. Cleghorn and Mr. Wright are planning a practical joke."

She moved in to caress the bay, and to True's annoyance, the stallion nuzzled Jenny.

"We've been keeping out of sight on purpose," True told her, though she hadn't meant to, and was instantly angry with herself.

"I think you're saying I shouldn't be here?" Jenny said

with a little, pouting pretty smile. "To be honest, I suspected as much—but I thought you wouldn't mind." She hesitated for the slightest second, then continued, "Because Evan asked me to come. He writes that you've been such a fine correspondent, sending him all the news and clippings from the papers and all—the whole time he's been in New Haven. And he says you've told him all about the race."

A trace of bile backed into True's throat; she swallowed and the taste was so bitter she thought for a minute she was going to have to spit it up. She tugged too hard at the lead rope, and the bay moved sideways, pushing her against the stall door. "Back, boy," she said, slapping him with a gentle roughness on his flank, "go on there, move back, move back now."

"Be careful," Jenny said, a trace of alarm in her voice. "Can you hold him, True?"

"Of course I can," True snapped. "What do you think I've been doing all these months? I suggest you put some money on True's Surprise. And tell Evan we're going to win."

Jenny stepped back, stung. "You can tell him yourself," she said in a tightly controlled voice. "Evan is coming home. I thought you would want to know—" She hesitated, then added, "I guess I also thought that you and I, well, that we might be friends."

"He's coming home? When? How can that be?" True asked.

Jenny answered patiently, "Perhaps he'll be here for the race. He's on his way now. Somehow—I think by working himself almost to death—he managed to finish early . . . I guess he just wanted to come home." This last she said with a small, secret smile, as if she knew something that True should be able to guess.

True was not interested in guessing; she had not planned on Evan this early. She was not ready, not yet. She frowned.

"Did you hear what I said about our being friends?" Jenny pushed.

"Yes, I heard," True answered.

"And . . . ?" Jenny coaxed.

"Don't you think I'm too young to be your friend?"

"No," Jenny answered warily, "I don't."

"But that's the way you've always treated me—like I was one of the children." Her voice had an edge of spite in it. She was taunting Jenny, because she had taken her by surprise. She did not want to talk to Jenny about Evan.

"I don't understand," Jenny came back, annoyance creeping into her voice.

"You want to be my friend now, because Evan is coming home."

Jenny leaned against a post and effected a small, exasperated smile. "Perhaps you're right," she said. "Certainly Evan is fond of you. He is grateful for all the letters. Goodness, True—you've written him almost as often as I have. He tells me that he thinks of you as an interesting young girl. And naturally, he feels sorry . . . for your situation."

"He asked me to write him," True said, holding ground.

"I'm sure he did," Jenny answered. "Evan is a very courteous, very kind man. He would never hurt anyone's feelings if he could help it. But I don't think he counted on you writing quite so much, or quite so often."

"Did he tell you that or is it what you think?" True demanded.

Jenny looked hard at True, a trace of contempt flashing out of eyes that had suddenly turned hard and dark. Her mouth tightened into one sharp line as she said, "I hope you aren't going to do something to embarrass yourself—or to embarrass Evan. You may remember that I was with Evan when we first met you; by then, we had been seeing each for some months. I have seen no one else in all that time and neither has Evan."

"Has he asked you to marry him?"

A bright pink flush appeared on Jenny's neck; she raised her hand, as if to cover it. "I hardly think that is a question you should be asking."

"You said you wanted to be my friend," True countered.

Jenny's fury surfaced in her voice: "You are simply a girl who has taken a fancy to a grown man. It happens quite often, and it really is absurd, you know. Evan thinks you are harmless, that you will soon 'grow out of' any attachment you might have to him."

"But you don't think so?" True shot back.

It was plain to see what Jenny thought: that True was a threat, that True could ruin her last chance, her future, that True must not be allowed to get in the way.

Jenny took a deep breath to compose herself and changed

the subject abruptly. "Did you know the Baumgartner family when you lived on Maui with your family? I understand they were one of your neighbors. They've asked Mother to help them find a housekeeper—they can't seem to keep their girls, I don't quite know why. Maybe it is all those children, five or six, I believe. Usually they get a girl from the reform school, but when they heard of the Wrights' good work at Hale Mana'olana, well they thought they should help out by giving them a try. I believe Mother intends to mention this position to Miss Winona . . ." Before she walked quickly back up the path, she said, "Naturally, if your name comes up, we would recommend you."

When Jenny was out of sight, True allowed herself to collapse against the bay. She knew the animal could feel her heart beating. *Don't think about it,* she told herself. The familiar, musty smells of the stable steadied her. *Think about Evan coming home, Evan being on his way right now, this minute.* He had not asked Jenny to marry him, not yet. She could feel it, just as she could feel Jenny's fear. *Jenny was trying to have her sent away, back to Maui, where her mother had died. Please don't let that happen,* she prayed. True laid her cheek against the horse's powerful neck and told him she could not go back to Maui, not ever. She smoothed her hand over his sleek coat to calm herself. It was too much to think about now, too much—Evan's return and Jenny's threat. First she had to think about the race . . . about True's Surprise winning.

Race day dawned bright and hot; high clouds stretched across the white blue of the sky. Even the great expanse of the ocean was still, as if the world had ceased to breathe. Uncle was up and out at first light, walking nervously along the beachfront by the stables, struggling with the discontent of facing a day outside of routine. He found Liko asleep in a corner of the stall.

"I didn't want anything to spook him, not the night before the race," Liko explained, as if he expected Uncle to be displeased.

"Good, good," Uncle said distractedly and did not seem to hear Liko's sigh of relief. Had he not been so absorbed in the race, Uncle would have noticed how fitful Liko had become, how afraid. Each month seemed to bring a new child to the hale; the cottages were crowded, and Liko knew better than anyone how strongly Aunt was pressing to send the older children "out into the world."

He had taken to hiding under the lanai each evening to listen to Aunt and Uncle discuss the day, as was their habit. He started this practice after one of Jenny's visits, when Aunt had seemed more agitated than usual. He had come upon her muttering out loud to herself—one of Aunt Winona's peculiarities—"We either stop taking in new children or let go of some of the older ones," she was saying. "We cannot afford to build more cottages or pay to feed more children. It is that simple, and I have got to make him understand."

She repeated this ultimatum to Uncle at the end of the day, as they sat together on the lanai. His response was soft, reasoning: "Where will they go?"

Aunt answered with exasperation, "We'll find them places. They are good workers—Liko is a strong boy, he can work in a stables or do field work just like anybody else. True is perfectly capable of running a household, helping with children and cooking. I heard today about a German family on Maui who need a housekeeper . . ."

"A housekeeper? And on Maui?" Uncle's tone was sharper. "True's trouble happened on Maui, have you forgotten?"

"Brother, now listen to me. This family—the Baumgartners I believe is their name—they know about True's mother and they are willing to take her anyway. Their farm is at the opposite end of . . ."

"Stop it, Winona. Right now. I don't want to hear any more about this. It would upset True, and she is working night and day to get the bay ready for the race."

"The race!" Aunt spat out angrily. "That's what you care about, not the children and what's to become of them."

Liko, under the floor, felt suddenly cold. She had gone too far. Uncle allowed the silence to grow. Finally he said, very carefully, "I do know that the children must go out into the world, but I won't send them until they are ready, and until there is a place for them where they will have the opportunity to thrive."

When Aunt finally answered, it was in a meek voice. "But what shall I tell Jenny? She and her mother have gone to such a lot of trouble to find a place for True. You know it isn't easy with the murder and her mother's reputation and all."

Uncle stood, walked to the railing and looked out to sea, as if to find an answer there. "I suppose True is going to have to live with that," he said with a sigh. "People are cruel, even unto the little children . . ."

"She is not a child, Jameson," Aunt countered. "She is almost seventeen, and she is, well . . . She has become a young lady."

Jameson Wright turned and looked at his sister. "You are right, of course she is . . . a pretty young lady, at that. And I suppose I have taken advantage of her skills with the animals, with the bay especially. You know, of course, that if we win this race, the school will have enough to pay for several years of True's keep and it will ease our financial worries as well."

Aunt snapped back, "I don't think we should be counting on gambling money."

Uncle answered in a tired voice: "You can tell Jenny that we will inform True of the offer, and that it will be her decision."

"But you will tell her after the race," Aunt said, to be conciliatory.

"After the race," Uncle agreed.

True dressed with uncommon care, pulling on her cotton undergarments, smoothing them over her slender thighs and, for such a slight girl, her surprisingly full breasts. In the years that Evan had been away, True's figure had filled out—and yet her body was hard and firm. Aunt was fond of saying what a beauty True could be, if only she would stay out of the sun and put on a little bit of flesh to soften her out.

I recognized in Aunt's voice the tremor of regret that comes of never having been a pretty young woman—not with her nose and big teeth and low-slung jaw. I also thought I heard a shrill note of warning: True could not stay with the Wrights much longer and neither could Liko. Unlike me, they had no skills that were needed. From Liko's reports, I recognized that Jenny's campaign to send True into exile could well succeed.

True's answer to her future was Evan Coulter, and it

worried me no end. She pulled on the divided skirt I had
sewn for her, then the freshly laundered blue-sprigged blouse
and a soft leather weskit—I had made the costume from a
picture I saw in one of uncle's equestrian magazines. She
pulled her hair back in a single, thick braid and put on one
of Vicky's old left-behind straw hats "for luck." Exposure to
the sun had made her skin glow like a ripe peach, and her
blue-green eyes shone with a radiance that startled. She was
not so much beautiful as astonishing-looking; there were
times when she seemed luminous, as if her long, thin bones
were sculpted of silver that came shining through.

But she wasn't thinking about how she looked—she was
thinking about the race. "What worries me," she said,
speaking slowly as she sometimes did, when she was trying
to think something through, "is the jockey they've hired.
Uncle thinks he will do fine, and the few times he's been on
the bay I suppose it has been all right, but I don't know—
something isn't quite right. He hasn't had many rides, I'm
not sure he knows . . ."

I waited, and when she didn't say anything, I asked,
"Knows what?"

"I'm not sure he knows how to *feel* when the bay is ready
to go full-out. I don't know if the bay will . . . tell him
. . ."

"You expect that stallion to speak right up?" I asked, so
seriously that True would have to laugh, and she did.

The race track, laid out over a half mile in a wide field in
Waikiki halfway between our place and Honolulu, was a
bustle of activity when we arrived. There was nothing fine or
polished about the place; there were no seats or boxes, only
a rough oval track of red tropical earth, newly raked for the
day's races, and an expanse of greensward where townsfolk
could watch.

Buggies and wagons and horses began arriving early; ladies lifted parasols against the sun, men removed jackets and
squinted in the midday glare. Aunt and I brought the children in the buckboard and spread a picnic on the green. It
was while I was retrieving one of the little boys that I ran into
Evan Coulter and Jenny Barrows.

"Martha Moon," he called out to me, and at first I didn't
recognize him at all. I remembered Evan as squarely built,

with a boy's big hands and a slow, easy smile. This Evan seemed taller, *finer* in a white summer suit, puzzling. I couldn't think what to say to him; he saw and, smiling his old, slow smile, said, "Jenny told me you had managed to grow up while I was away, but she didn't tell me just how well it suited you. What a fine-looking somebody you've become, Martha."

I could feel myself flushing with pleasure; I took the hands he held out to me and studied him: He had thinned, all the rough boy-corners had been smoothed off, but his eyes still had a glint of humor. I'd expected True to change, but I'd thought Evan would stay the same. He hadn't. This Evan was different from the one who'd gone away, though I couldn't say how.

"Are you glad to be home?" was all I could think to ask.

Jenny Barrows answered for him: "If he isn't, he wasted all those pounds he managed to lose in that cold little room, studying night and day to finish law school ahead of time, and with honors, of course." Jenny's face was flushed with light; I had to admit she looked prettier than I'd ever seen her.

"Yes, I'm glad to be home," he answered, embarrassed at Jenny's effusion. "And the best of it is, I seem to have come just in time for our friend's big moment."

I squeezed his hands and dropped them, saying, "If True wins, be sure to come back to the paddock after the race."

"I'll come no matter what," he called after me, adding, "but I'm betting on True's Surprise."

My face was burning—from delight at seeing Evan again, for the thrill of telling True, and from fear for what was to happen. I collected my errant little boy, and headed for the paddock where True would be waiting to warn her.

By one-thirty the track was surrounded by a crowd packed ten deep, haoles up front, dressed in their Sunday best and calling out to each other in high good spirits. Japanese and Chinese men in dark shirts and loose trousers filled in the spaces, talking to each other in rapid-fire bursts of speech, while the Hawaiians, big and bright and brown, walked easy in the sun, laughing and visiting, their children dancing in and out.

No one on earth, I thought, knows how to enjoy themselves quite like the Hawaiians; other people know how to work, but the Hawaiians know how to play. A game, a race—this race, any race—was cause for celebration. Old Auntie Momi had arrived in a wheelbarrow which one of her nephews had fitted out with a big red umbrella to shade her. She waved at me, and when I ran to press my nose against hers, she told me she had bet three of her best pullets on True's Surprise.

The match race was set for two o'clock. Colonel Toby was strutting around the royal enclosure, where a tent had been raised for the Queen and her husband, Governor John Dominis and the court. There was much laughing and joking and calling out to their friends, Archie Cleghorn and his group, who were ensconced just next to the royal enclosure.

Two o'clock was fast approaching. I was watching Vicky's pa, who would be giving the signal for Uncle and True to bring the bay to the starting gate. My heart began to beat more rapidly, my throat felt dry. With only a minute or so to go, a man wearing a suit with a thick sweat stain on the back came and squatted on his haunches next to Mr. Cleghorn. For a few moments they were deep in talk; then they called over to Colonel Toby, and the three men left, heading for the holding area behind the starting gate, where they joined Uncle.

"We've got ourselves a problem," Uncle came to tell True. "Seems there's some folks out there who think we are pulling a funny one on them, and they say we can't use our jockey. There's some rumor going around that he's been brought in to fix the race . . ."

"How? Why?" True said, her eyes blazing with indignation. "It doesn't make sense . . ."

"It doesn't matter," Uncle said, his eyes flickering back and forth as if he would like nothing so much as to be away from it all. "What matters is the race, getting it started and done with. There isn't time to argue, we've got to go now or not at all. Do you think Liko can ride for us?"

True looked stunned. "Liko? No. He hasn't been up at all, he doesn't know the bay . . ."

"Then it has to be you."

"Me?" she said, dumbfounded. "Me?"

"There's nothing in the club rules that says a girl can't

ride. And Colonel Wakefield agrees. You're wearing your boots, I see; can you get into the silks?"

Archie Cleghorn was clenching and unclenching his big hands. "True's going to ride," Uncle told him firmly. "She should have been the one all along."

"Yes," True told him, her voice suddenly sure. "Uncle is right . . . right . . . perfectly right!" she called back as she ran for the wagon where the jockey waited in the purple and white silks she hoped would fit across her chest.

There was no time for word to reach the crowd; the man with the sweat stain and a few Chinese standing close by were told that "a stablehand" would ride the bay.

"I think it's a jolly idea for the girl to ride," Colonel Toby said to his son. "Besides, it can't but give us an edge—why don't you put another twenty or so on General Jackson?"

Jared Wakefield remembered True all too well from the luau; whenever he thought about that meeting he felt a fresh wave of embarrassment. One day he planned to give the white-haired True the straight answer he should have given her that night, instead of going into a choking fit that caused his mother to haul him off like he was a three-year-old. His face flushed with the old mortification; he got up and made his way to the back, in the embracing shade of a big banyan tree where the betting was going on, and put twenty dollars on True's Surprise.

The crowd shuffled and called out as the horses nervously danced around the starting gate. Mounted on the big grey was a well-known forty-year-old jockey called Timmy, but all eyes were on the bay. When it had first come into view a moan swept through the crowd, a kind of exclamation of surprise and wonder, as if to give the big bay its due. True was having a hard time holding him; the stallion danced sideways, tensed and nervous in this strange new place with all of its peculiar noises.

True leaned forward to touch his neck; he was wet with sweat. She stroked him, talking all the while, but the noise was too much. His neck arched, his eyes widened. She murmured, "It's me, old boy, just me and you. Stay with me, just stay. I'm right here, right here . . . and we're going to give them a race they'll never forget." Her cap was pulled so tight to hold in her hair that it sent sharp pains through her head. She couldn't think of that—she couldn't think about Evan. She could think only of getting the bay into the gate.

"That's it, that's it," she said, as they edged into the enclosure. "Just the way we practiced it." The bay was tense, but collected now. They waited, poised, for the crack of the starter's gun.

The grey shot out of the box in a perfect start; the bay reared, stunned by the roar of the crowd.

True's knees clamped into him, she threw herself forward and told him, "Go, go, go . . ." He reared again.

"It's all right," True told herself, relaxing her grip. "It's all right," she said out loud, and her body translated the words to the stallion, for he plunged through the gate and was off, running as he'd always run for her, as if it was what he knew and what he was certain of in the world. And she, sitting high on the massive stallion, felt it too: the certainty, the sure sweet thundering rhythm of the race. She felt him get his stride, felt the wind at her face, saw the blur of people crowded against the fence, saw the trees and the sky and the whole world, sailing by. She wanted to scream with the pleasure of it, but she knew any sound she would make would be lost in the thunder of the crowd and the roar of the track. The bay was running now, running at the top of his form—and Evan was there to see it; Evan was watching. *This is what it is all about,* she said to herself. *Running the race is the answer and it doesn't matter that we can't win.*

The grey was a good eight lengths ahead, a formidable lead, an impossible lead. Several men tore up their tickets and let them drift to the ground. The grey was too good a horse, and Timmy too good a rider to get careless. The race was over before it had begun. "All but the shouting," a squat Irishman said in obvious disgust.

"Hey, that's one good-lookin' horse," a massive Hawaiian said to Evan, who had found himself a place on the fence, "but he's no more chance for win this race."

"You never know," Evan told him, grinning. "Maybe True's Surprise has got some magic working for him. You ever think of that?"

The Hawaiian clamped Evan on the shoulder with a big hand and laughed as if it was the funniest thing anyone had ever said to him. Uncle watched, feeling the old sink of defeat rising from the pit of his stomach, the old despair coming back to wrap around him. He should never have agreed to do this, he told himself; Winona was right. He should have left all of this behind in Georgia. He watched True and wondered how he could have allowed her to get up on the massive stallion, to risk so much . . . He dropped his face into his hands just as the crowd caught its collective breath in a sound that came out as a rolling gasp.

The bay was gathering momentum, was running full-out, his great galloping legs striding wide, his feet scarcely touching the ground. True felt the wind stinging her face, her eyes were streaming tears, and she knew from somewhere inside her that the bay could produce the burst of speed it would take to catch the grey. She knew she could ask for it, and he would give it. She believed, at that moment, that if she asked him to fly, he would. The wind whipped at her and tore away her cap, but she didn't feel it; her hair flew out, a flash of white like a flag, caught by the sun; the crowd saw and screamed. And the Hawaiian standing next to Evan said, "Hey, look that wahine!"

Evan answered, "My God, it's True," and his face took on an expression of such amazement that the Hawaiian clapped him on the back, as if to share his wonder.

The roar of the crowd told the grey's jockey that something was happening; he ducked his head under his arm to look back. The bay was there. Right there. It couldn't be, but it was. Jesus God. He laid on the whip. The crowd screamed, and the noise rose and wrapped round the moment when the horses crossed the finish line in what seemed the same instant. No one knew what had happened.

The silence was sudden and seemed to expand. No one could believe their eyes. They had never seen such a horse, such a burst of speed—it couldn't be.

A man with a megaphone walked onto the track, lifted it, put it down as if to clear his throat, then lifted it again. The air was heavy with expectation. "It's General Jackson by a nose."

A Chinese began screaming wildly, a signal which caused the rest of the crowd to explode in pandemonium.

The grey was named the winner, but it was the bay that everyone was talking about. "One more minute," someone said. "Just one more minute . . ." And someone else answered, "Hell, just another second would have done it. That bay was moving like a locomotive . . ."

There was confusion in the winner's circle. Archie Cleghorn was pounding Uncle on the back, and men crowded around them, as if they were the winners. Colonel Toby stood by, without the usual bonhomie. He was not a popular winner, and for Toby, being popular was all important. The Queen was there, ready to put a big double lei of tuberoses and orchids around the winner's neck, but she didn't seem quite to know which horse should get it. The bay was getting all the attention. There was some confusion among the judges as well, one of the three seemed to be changing his mind. Colonel Toby was the first to regain his composure, taking up the megaphone to say to the throng, "Races don't come more exciting than this one, folks; we'll be talking about it for years, and we'll all be able to say we were here. I say it was fairly run and fairly won, but I'll tell you this, I want to thank True's Surprise for his slow start. Otherwise, the General here wouldn't have had a chance in the world. And I take my hat off to pretty little True Lindstrom, one mighty fine rider!"

Two Hawaiians hefted her on their shoulders, high above the crowd, and bobbled her up and down. She threw back her head and laughed, drunk with the joy of the incredible ride. Evan stood on the edge of the crowd that had gathered around True, watching. Jenny Barrows observed from a small, nearby knoll which gave her the height she needed to see all that was going on, even if she couldn't hear Evan as he faced True for the first time in three years.

True saw him, called out to him and the Hawaiians tossed her gently into Evan's arms. He caught her and the crowd, watching True's face, roared its pleasure. "How is it that every time I come back to the Islands you've just managed to accomplish some impossible feat?" he asked, holding her up high. "Is there anything you can't do?" Her eyes filled with tears, as she groped for the right words and could not find them; happiness flooded her face. *Nothing,* she wanted to shout, *there's nothing I can't do.* Uncle and Vicky's pa surrounded them then, and Jenny could only catch glimpses of True's face, luminous in victory—shining out at them all, blinding them with her radiance. Jenny shuddered. She would have to act quickly, or she would lose Evan Coulter.

10

True was crazy to go, and nothing would do but that I go with her. I did not want to make the trip to Mau'loa, I cannot say why. It would be my first sea journey, my first visit to another island. How to explain my reticence? I told Aunt Winona it was because I didn't like leaving the children for so long; in truth, I am worried that they will find they can do without me. But that is not the whole of it. Evan and Jenny were to be part of the group invited for a week of riding and hunting and picnics and parties—one of Colonel Wakefield's famous house parties—and I know that was why True was determined to go. Evan has come to visit twice since his return, but always in the company of others—once with Jenny—and True has not had a chance to speak to him alone.

I cannot talk to her about Evan; she does not want to hear what I have to say, does not want to be told what is obvious: that Evan is doing everything he can in the kindest possible way to discourage her. True and I speak to each other carefully, avoiding what needs to be said, because it is not to her liking.

The journey did not begin well. Uncle called us to hurry along, lest we be late for the ferry. True reached to pull her hat off the peg, picked up our valise and we shouted good-bye across the way to Liko, who had been lounging around the school cottage, watching us.

"Good-bye," he called back and burst into tears, his great, shaggy head waving from side to side.

We stopped short. Then both of us moved toward him, stumbling into each other awkwardly.

"What is it?" True demanded, worry like a shadow on her face. "What's wrong, Liko?"

He turned away.

"What?" I demanded, suddenly frightened, "Tell us!"

He coughed it out: "I leave end of week—same day you come back. I go work at Rose Plantation on Maui."

True stared, first at Liko and then at me.

"Why were you going to let us leave without telling us?" I asked, feeling a hard knot in my stomach.

"I work in the stables, with horses. Cleaning up. Whatever they say I do, I do it," he said with a pretense of cheerfulness, but all we heard was the fear. Liko could almost never be coaxed to leave the hale, not even to go to Vicky's. Now he would have to go to another island, all by himself. "Aunt say I no ruin your holiday," he whimpered, sniffling.

"I can't leave," I told True.

She ignored me and spoke to Liko as if she were giving him directions, "We have to go. But we will try to come back early, to ride into town with you. And I'll come to Rose Plantation to see you. I promise, Liko, as soon as I can, I'm going to find a way for all of us to be together again."

At first I thought she had lost her mind, to make such a promise, and then I figured she was saying it only to calm Liko and to convince me to go with her to Mau'loa. I was furious with her. And myself more, because I knew I would go.

Colonel Toby had invited True, and he had asked that she bring "the little teacher" along. Uncle felt we should be obliging to the Colonel, who had been such a good sport about the race—not pressing for the money Uncle owed him.

True was convinced that Evan had asked for us to be included in the weekend party; I tried to point out to her that it made no sense. She closed her eyes and ears and went blindly on her way, and I went with her, an ache in the pit of my stomach at the thought of leaving Liko alone and miserable.

The steamer *Kilauea* rolled in the deep troughs, draining all color from the faces of at least half of the passengers and throwing stomachs into torments of upheaval. True was terribly ill; I was sick at heart. *Serves her right,* I said under my breath, *for giving Liko false hopes.* I applied a wet cloth to her head and washed off the streaks of vomit that splashed on the front of her dress.

In a weak voice she pleaded with me to understand: "If I

don't warn Evan, if I am silent now, I will regret it all my life—and so will he, I know it."

I made myself ask, "Do you honestly believe that he will listen?"

She clamped her handkerchief over her mouth and slowly shook her head.

"No?" I said, confused.

"I don't know," she answered, muffled. "He thinks of me as a child. But I know what he wants, better than he does, Martha, I promise you."

"How can you know that—how can you promise?" I asked, exasperated. "Sometimes you make these pronouncements, as if you have secret powers, like telling Liko we will all be together. It is cruel, True—how can you raise his hopes so?"

She leaned out over the rail and lifted her face to catch the sea spray. "I will do something so we can be together, the three of us," she said again.

"Right now," I told her, unable to swallow my rising anger, "the school may have to close because Uncle lost so much on the race. I may have to leave, Liko is going and you don't have the slightest idea where you'll be living two months from now."

"I do," she told me calmly. "I'll be on Maui."

I stared at her in stunned amazement. "You can't. I thought Uncle promised you wouldn't have to go to the Baumgartners'. I thought because of your mother and what happened . . ."

"Rose Plantation is scarcely an hour's ride from the Baumgartner farm."

Then I understood. "You would go there just to be near Liko?" I asked. "You would do that?"

"Of course," she said, surprised at my surprise, and I threw my arms around her and held on tight, though she complained that I shouldn't because she smelled so sour.

The day was sharply clear but the seas were heavy; the beamy old steamer wallowed in deep troughs, down a long shute and then up, up and out again in a shower of sea spray. We stayed on deck, shielded by an old oilskin we had found tucked in an open cabinet, preferring the fresh air to the closeness below deck. True leaned against me, weak and drowsy and in no mood to talk. I found myself thinking about some historical papers Uncle had given me to read, a

monograph sent to him from England, about the explorer
George Vancouver, who had been with Captain James Cook
when he discovered the Islands in 1778. Vancouver had
returned three times between the years 1792 and 1794, and
had become a friend of the first King Kamehameha.

Some of the information in the monograph seemed to fit
with a story old Auntie Momi had told me only a few days
before, having appeared early one morning. She knew that
I would be going to Mau'loa, and she said she had come to
tell me a story about the wild cattle on that island.

September 1798, Kealakekua, Island of Hawaii, Uncle's
historical paper was dated. Auntie's stories had no dates, but
I knew hers was simply another version, from another view-
point. As the *Kilauea* made its way from Oahu to the Big
Island, I occupied myself with putting the stories together in
my own version.

Captain George Vancouver felt the prickling heat of vermin
crawling around his waistband and scratched through the
wool of his uniform. It's the bloody cows, he thought; the
whole of his ship was crawling with fleas, the stink of it was
more than even he could take and the Hawaiian King stub-
bornly refused to allow them to come ashore. He sat in the
bow of the longboat, squinting toward the royal enclosure
and the King's house; as they drew closer to shore he saw the
massive figure of Kamehameha. Surely he would give him
permission to bring the cattle on shore today; he had already
lost two cows, which left three cows and a bull, and he didn't
think the bull would last another day without some pasture
and sweet water soon.

"Sir," he said, bowing low before the giant figure of the
aging man. Yesterday, the King had been in full regalia—
western suit with a shirt and a tie, a silver sword and boots
that pinched his huge feet. Today he wore only a loin cloth
and a look of exasperated despair.

Queen Kaahumanu had not been with him yesterday;
Vancouver had missed the giant woman with her great
breasts and lusty laugh. The fights between the King and this
Queen were legendary. Vancouver would never understand
how the two of them had gotten on for so long, but now he
was convinced it was Kaahumanu who was on the King's
mind, keeping him from thinking about the cattle.

He dropped his chin and the reek of the barnyard lifted from the damp wool of his uniform. Still, he did not bring up the subject of the cattle right away; Vancouver trusted his second sense, and it told him to proceed with caution.

"I should like to pay my respects to the Queen Kaahumanu," he said instead, probing. Kamehameha grunted; in late middle age, he was still a powerful figure. He shifted, the loin cloth slipped and the British captain could see the old man's privates, hanging loose, big and dusky grey. That pipe has gone ramming aplenty in its time, the Englishman thought to himself. He would have liked to smile in admiration, but he did not allow his face to register any mood. One had to be careful with the old bull of a man.

"Gone," the King said, raising a hand theatrically. "Three moons on the sea."

Vancouver caught a glimmer of agony in the great man's voice. He knew he couldn't get the King's mind on the cows until the trouble with his favorite wife was settled.

"Is the Queen visiting at her father's house?" he asked.

No answer. Vancouver nodded, as if to say he understood. "May I have your permission to visit the Queen at her father's hale?" he ventured, then added, "And might I tell her that it is my opinion that your house is empty without her?"

The old man shrugged. Yes, it meant yes. Vancouver knew full well that the King could say no, and often enough bellowed it out. "Then I will see her now," he said, watching the king's face to make certain he wasn't making a mistake. The King waved him away.

The captain walked through a dusty grove of palms, wishing more than anything for a drink of cool water and knowing there was nothing but tepid, foul stuff on this arid side of the island. As soon as he could, he meant to send a detachment of men up into the mountains with the cattle to find some fresh grass and a cool stream to replenish the ship's store of water. He had spent all of his time trying to convince the King to let him bring the cattle ashore before they all died. He passed a covey of girls who fell back, watching him and giggling, speaking to each other in high, happy talk. These women are not the same species as those at home, Vancouver thought once again. They walk around, bare-breasted with only a tapa cloth wrapped around their waist, seemingly happy to share their food, their laughter, their bodies. They swam out to his ship each night, naked and wet, they crawled into the bunks with the men, and opened their legs, riding the waves of men, all night long.

When he first came here with Cook, twenty years before, they had been the first white men these islanders had ever seen. The natives had taken Cook for a God and had killed him when they discovered he was not. In some ways, he thought, Cook had tried to play God—he had not wanted the men to fornicate with the women. He knew what diseases the seamen carried, and what it would do if it spread to the native women. But the Hawaiian women could not be stopped. They loved it too much, and their husbands and fathers and brothers bedecked them with flowers and paddled them out to the ships, asking in return a few nails, a pair of scissors, a piece of cloth. Cook had failed in that too. The Islands were rife with venereal disease—you could see it.

Kaahumanu bent low to come through the door of her father's house. He thought, as he always thought when he saw her, of Juno. Big—she was well over six feet tall—and graceful, with the most enormous breasts he had ever seen— full and erect. He tried to imagine the two giants—the king and this queen—coupling. He could feel himself stir and looked away to calm himself before she might take notice and point and laugh at him, as she had once before.

She was not in a mood to laugh this morning; her face wore a sullen, stubborn expression.

"Good morning, dear Queen," he said to her, bowing low enough to give her a view of the top of his head, with its thinning crown. "I have been to see the King this morning. He sits alone in his house, with no one to speak to."

She said nothing, but continued to stare at him. He could continue to speak.

"You see, I have brought some cattle, three cows and a bull—large animals with horns on their heads—strange, big creatures such as you have never seen before. It is a gift from the King of England, you see . . . to the King of Hawaii and his Queen . . ." this last he added in a burst of inspiration.

"You stinking too much," she said, wrinkling her nose.

He laughed. "I know—I haven't had a chance to bathe yet. As soon as we get the cattle ashore, I plan to spend half a day in one of the pools down here."

"You stinking coat," she added.

"Yes," he agreed, "that too. If you would like to come back to the King's hale with me, I can present the creatures to you and the King today. Then I will be free to get clean again, and I will be grateful to you, madam, more than you can ever know." Probably she did not understand this last, but he said it with a flourish which he guessed she would appreciate.

"I come to see cow and bull," she said, with a shrewd glint in her eye that told him she understood it all.

She walked into the royal enclosure as if she had never left, and Kamehameha took no more notice of her than if she had been there all along.

"Have I your permission to bring the cattle ashore?" Vancouver asked, formally.

"Bring them now," the King said.

The bull snorted and stumbled as his feet touched ground for the first time in many months; the whole of the village had gathered to watch, and pressed close in. The bull was weak and terrified, and charged one small cluster of natives, lowering his horns as if to impale them. They scattered, screaming, and the bull turned and ran, wobbling, toward the King.

The great man fell back, alarmed—the animal was bigger than any he had ever seen. Vancouver, standing next to him, fell back as well, not to embarrass the King, and called out to two seamen to grab the bull's horns. Kamehameha recovered rapidly, laughing at himself and his fear. Soon the cows were attempting to take their first steps on land, lowing loudly, and the crowd took it up—moooo, moooo. Moooo, laughed Kaahumanu, the first of the natives to walk down to the cow. She leaned over and touched its teats, pulling hard on the udder and everyone laughed. Soon, the children were leading the cows around, laughing as the poor creatures kept slipping in the sand, trying to get their shorelegs after months aboard ship.

Vancouver ate that night in the King's eating hut, feasting on roast dog and bananas and poi. "If you come to visit in my country," he said, as he had practised, "and you eat with my King, he will have his cooks make for you meat from animals such as I have brought to you today. It is good, as good as pig, as good as this dog. Very good, and much more from each animal than from pig or dog. Your people will have much to eat."

The King looked interested, so he continued. "The animals I brought this day are very weak, the bull may not live. But two of the cows are with calf, and one of the calves may be a bull. You must tell your people not to harm these animals. They must be allowed to go into the pastures on the mountain slopes, where there is grass for them to eat and water aplenty. They will multiply, to make more cows and more bulls. The people must not kill them now, not for many years. If they do not, you will have a new source of food that will feed your people well."

"How many years?"

Vancouver thought. "Ten," he said, knowing little about animal husbandry.

"I put a kapu on the animals," the King said. "For ten years whoever kills animal will die."

His words were repeated around the room, one man to another. Then the word went out to the people of the island, and soon everyone knew: The beasts that came ashore today, and all their progeny, must not be harmed or slaughtered. They were kapu. The King had ruled it; the King ruled by kapu; no man could deny him.

The landing had come too late for the bull; it died on the walk into the mountains. A month later, the cows calved within three days of each other, and both of the calves were bulls. Within a year, they were joined by a black bull and two cows from Spanish California, fierce and hardy animals. The gentle, tall grass of the uplands and the protection of the kapu would make the cattle thrive.

The wild herds multiplied until you could see them by the thousands from the sea, roaming the gentle slopes of the island. George Vancouver and Kamehameha the Great had created the cattle industry in Hawaii.

All at once the seas seemed to calm, the spray to subside. We lifted the oilskin and looked: Rising out of a clear aquamarine sea was the Big Island, the tropical green wall of its pali rising in sharp relief, glowing green in the midday sun. It seemed to have lifted out of the sea, soft and rolling, its mountains crowned by a blaze of snow caught in the sunlight, its long green meadows sweeping down from the mountains, rolling in iridescent greens all the way to the edge of the black-sand beaches.

11

Longboats carried us from the steamer to the black-sand beach at Pa'ele, where Jared was waiting with a wagon and a sturdy team of horses. "I must say you look a bit green about the gills, True," he told her, managing to combine both sympathy and a good-natured laugh. When she groaned, he said, "You don't have to tell me. The worst hours of my life have been spent on that rolling tub, going back and forth between islands." He placed our cases very carefully in the back of the wagon, then ceremoniously helped each of us onto the seat.

"In an hour we will be upcountry where it is cool, and by then you'll be feeling just fine," he told True, smiling one of his sweet smiles. Something about how beautiful he was made me want to cry. Jared was scarcely fourteen, an age when most boys are gangly and awkward, but he wasn't. Not on the outside, at least—he was tall and delicate and, on this day, eager to please.

"If you don't keep your promise," True said to him in a growl, "I promise to shoot you in the foot."

Jared Wakefield laughed so hard I thought he might lose his balance and fall off the wagon. True must have thought so too, for she looped her arm in his to keep him steady, and the wagon began the long, lumbering climb up the grade to the mountain meadow and to Kolonahe, the Wakefields' Mau'loa home.

Jared was right; True perked up as soon as our wagon left the arid shore and climbed into the cool reaches where pastures began to stretch out in thick waves of grass, whispering in the winds. "Who is at the house now?" True asked, as if she were just making conversation. Jared could hardly remember, and I could just feel True squirm. It took him a full five minutes to think of Judge Sawyer's daughter's name. It was Mary. We had lumbered on over the rough road with its deep mud grooves for another twenty minutes, with some careful prompting by True, before he remembered Evan and Jenny.

"Do you know them?" Jared asked, and when she murmured yes, we did, he said, "Well, it's supposed to be a secret, but since you know them I'll tell you—they're going to announce their engagement at dinner tonight. Pa had me put champagne in the coolhouse for a celebration."

Jared, usually silent in the company of his parents and their friends, grew expansive at the reins of a wagon, in charge of two young women not all that much older than he. Looking ahead, driving the team, he did not see the look that came over True's face, did not sense her body grow tense. The road took a long, sweeping turn and then began a steep climb; rocks had been set to keep the roadway from washing out. One of the horses stumbled and almost went down. Instead of giving him slack to recover, Jared jerked the reins and the wagon heaved and lurched.

"Give me them," True demanded, her voice hard and angry. "You're going to get us all dumped out." He handed over the reins, then sat silently as she steadied the team and pulled it to a halt.

She tried to return the reins, but he wouldn't take them.

"Jared," True said, exasperated, "please take them back."

Jared, it would appear, could be stubborn. He shook his head. "I'm not very good with horses, and you are," he said. "If you wouldn't mind, I'd like you to drive the rest of the way—it's only a few more miles."

True turned to look him full in the face. "That was awful of me," she said, as contrite as I've ever seen her. "It could have happened to anybody, and I had no right to take the reins from you. It was mean of me, and if I could cut my hands off right now to show how sorry I am, I would."

Jared looked at her in amazement and laughed. "You do speak your mind, True. I noticed that about you . . . that's why I asked Pa to invite you two for the party. I'm so tired of trying to figure out what grown-ups mean. They say one thing and mean something else—I figure I won't have that problem with you."

Poor True, I thought. First she finds out that Evan is going to marry Jenny, and now she's told that it was Jared

who had wanted her here, not Evan. Just sickly, beautiful
Jared.

True didn't flinch, she picked up the reins and snapped
them gently. The team—sensing her will—began to move
smartly, in step, so that the jostling stopped and we rode
along the dirt road, with green pasture on either side for as
far as we could see, and here and there a herd of cattle,
almost black in color and with great long horns.

Soon enough we came to a tunnel of ironwood trees,
arching high overhead. The road was level here, and the
wagon rode smoothly as the trees cast feathery shadows over
us; I felt lightheaded, giddy. I closed my eyes for a moment
and when I opened them I saw old Auntie Momi, standing
by the side of the road. She was carrying something, holding
it close to her chest. The ironwood rustled in the breeze high
over my head and I heard the call of a seabird; I glanced up
and when I looked again, Auntie was gone. At the end of the
road was Kolonahe. "It means 'gentle, pleasant breeze,'"
Jared told us, and then in self-mocking tones, "Welcome to
Mau'loa."

Jenny stood close by to the doorway leading onto the big
lanai, listening to Rachel Wakefield chatter on, but I could
see that her eyes were on True. She watched her approach
Evan and a white-haired gentleman.

Evan introduced them, explaining to True that the
man—a Mr. Scott—was the owner of a ranch in California,
here to try to interest the Colonel in improving the herd by
buying some breeding stock.

"I didn't notice any fences on the ride in," True said.
"Wouldn't it be hard to improve the herd without being able
to separate them?"

The man looked at Evan and raised his eyebrows.

"Right you are," Evan answered, grinning now at True.
"I should warn you, sir, Miss True Lindstrom here is right
about a lot of things. Ask her to tell you about the match
race last month."

"True's Surprise," Mr. Scott said, looking at her with new
respect. "So you are that True!" When he started plying her
with questions, Evan quietly disengaged himself and joined
Jenny and Rachel.

He was smiling as he came up to us, but the smile vanished

when Jenny could not keep herself from saying, "I see you eluded your ardent young pursuer."

"Jenny," he said, warning.

"I know, I'm sorry," she told him, tucking her arm in his as they walked away, but flashing a smile back to let Rachel—and me—know she wasn't.

My face burned, feeling what True would feel if she had heard. Rachel looked at me, and said: "Mama says that Jenny's been set on Evan so long she's lost any other chances she might have, and now she's just outright scared, that's why she's so testy. Mama says it's a shame, when a girl gets worried like that, how it makes her behave. Jenny practically made Pa promise he'd announce their engagement. Pa says that Evan's just got a bad case of the balks. He says not everybody wants to marry so bad they'd dive off the Pali for it, like he would've to marry Mama, if he'd had to. At first, Grandmama wouldn't let them, you know." I didn't know, but Rachel didn't seem to mind. She talked as if she couldn't stop. "Marry, I mean. She said Mama and Pa could never see each other again, she didn't think Pa was anywhere good enough for Mama, and she sent him packing . . . but Mama cried and cried. She cried for so long that Grandmama finally had to give in and let her marry Papa. And it's a good thing too, or else I wouldn't be here, or Jared or any of us . . ."

Rachel rattled on: "Mama says Jenny is clever, all right, because she knows that giving Pa a reason to celebrate is like giving catnip to a cat. There is champagne and there's going to be toasts, and singing and dancing and too much drinking. Papa does love a party."

"Let's take a walk," Evan said, guiding Jenny across the front lawn.

The lights from the house, and the noise of the party made him feel lonely. He had thought about this island, this place, almost every night for the three years he was away, and now he was back and he felt lonely. How could that be?

"When did we decide to announce our engagement tonight?" he asked, his voice stiff.

She waited a moment, then spoke softly. "I know, Evan—it all seems so backward. And I'm afraid I did have something to do with the confusion. But when I arrived—before you got here—the Colonel asked me when we were going to tie the knot. I suppose I was a little embarrassed, to be asked outright like that and not know what to say—because we haven't really, well—so I said something kind of breezy like, 'Oh, any day now . . .' And you know the Colonel, how he loves to celebrate, and pretty soon he just took it over and I didn't know what to say."

"You could have said you would have to talk it over with me."

"Oh?" Jenny asked, walking away and turning her back to him. "And what would you have said?" Evan touched her shoulder, pulled her around to look at him. "I would have said that I'd like to wait for a while, at least until I get myself established."

"You have been offered a position at Davis and Gathers."

"We've gone through this before. Your father asked me to watch out for your inheritance, yours and your mother's. He asked me to keep his lawyers 'honest.' I don't think it would be entirely proper to join the firm."

"How better to keep them honest?" Jenny asked. "I know what Papa would say—he would say you can do a better job from the inside than from outside. And there wouldn't be anything wrong in it. You'd only be making certain they do what they are supposed to be doing."

"What if I don't want to join Davis and Gathers?" he asked.

She looked at him quizzically. "Why wouldn't you? It's the best law firm in Honolulu. Why did you spend three years at Yale if you didn't want to practice law?" She paused, then added in a calculating tone, "I'm not asking that we be married before you have decided what you will do. I'm only asking that we announce our intention to marry . . ."

She slipped her arms around his neck and pulled him to her, opening her mouth to his with a passion he had discovered in her since his return. She took the lobe of his ear into her mouth, he could feel her tongue on it. He pulled her hard against him, his hands moving to her breasts. The sound of laughter came drifting out from the house. "Not here," she whispered in his ear. "Not now, but soon."

Jared gave True the excuse she needed to avoid the engagement party. "He asked if we want to go meet his Uncle Eben and Aunt Maile, the ones who run the ranch," she told me, her voice dull with the pain of disappointment. "They live farther up the mountain in the old Home Place—the one built by the first Tobias Wakefield way back when. Jared seems real fond of the old couple. They don't have any children of their own, so they pretty much raised him."

"I'll stay, you go," I told her, wanting to help but not knowing how.

Jared and True rode steadily for something more than an hour, the first half in complete silence, the only sound the high cracking of a tree branch or the hoot of a *pueo*. That True was miserable was apparent to Jared. Possibly he had said something he shouldn't have, though try as he might he couldn't think what it might be. It was like that with his sisters. They were always crying at the oddest moments when he thought everything was fine. He hoped that True was different from his sisters. He would have liked to tell her that, but he didn't want to risk it. Better just to wait and see, but he did hope she said something before they got to Uncle Eben's. He didn't like to bring any upset into Uncle's house.

As if she could read his thoughts (he jumped when she said it, wondering if she had), True suggested, "Tell me about your Uncle and Aunt."

He was happy to oblige: "Uncle was the only son of Pa's uncle; now there's just the two of them. Uncle and Aunt never had any children. I heard Pa say once, when he'd had too much to drink and got to talking when he shouldn't that Wakefields hadn't wanted Uncle Eben to marry Aunt Maile, she being the daughter of slaves. All the Hawaiians were against it, not just Grandmother. But Uncle meant to marry Auntie—he wouldn't have it any other way. Then the kahunas said that they would never have a child, and they never did. They seemed to want to have me with them. Mama and Pa were always travelling, and they had my older brother, Toby. I think Aunt and Uncle took me because I was the runt of the litter."

True looked at him, surprised. He laughed. "It's no secret. My brother Toby was the one who was supposed to take over the ranch. I mean, he wanted to—he was always out with the hands, in the middle of everything. He rode before he walked, that's what they say, anyhow. But he died in an accident. They were shipping cattle to Oahu, riding them out to the steamer, you know—the cowboys swim them out into the surf and lash them to a longboat, about six to a boat, three on each side. Then they have to get a belly-band around each steer and swing it up on board the steamer. It's hard work. One of the hands is always getting himself ripped by a horn, or kicked or something. My brother talked Pa into letting him go on the longboat, the sea was pretty heavy that day, and they were trying to keep it close to the steamer when a cross wave rolled by, sending the steamer up and the longboat down. When the steamer came back down, it sliced right through the longboat. Toby was crushed under the bow."

"How awful," she said, looking at Jared to see what he thought.

His voice cracked. "It was. I remember that day all right. Pa just sort of stood in the corner and stared. You know how he likes to make people happy—he just doesn't know what to do when things get bad. He surely didn't know what to do with Mother. I thought she had gone crazy, wailing and crying and tearing at her hair. I'd never seen anything like it until then, but I've seen it since . . . how Hawaiians mourn for the dead. I've even felt like doing it myself, a couple of times." He grinned, and she managed to smile back.

Relief flooded into him, and he began to talk again, as he had on the trip up, before she took over the reins. "I want to warn you about something. My Uncle Eben, well, he's kind of like some of the other old ranchers around here. What he thinks about are the cattle, and the work that needs to be done. He and Aunt Maile live a simple life. My parents . . . are different. Mama is alii, you know, and Aunt Maile coming from slaves and all—I know Mama feels that Aunt is a good woman, and she's always been happy to have me visit with them, but Mama isn't used to being around Hawaiians like Aunt Maile. Anyway, she would rather stay at our house in Honolulu, since most of her friends are there and we go to school there. So Mama and Aunt Maile don't have much to say to each other."

"Still, they are related."

Jared grinned. "I doubt they'd agree with you. Auntie Maile's never expected my mother to have anything to do with her."

"You sound like Uncle Jameson," she said and laughed. "He's fascinated by Hawaiian class distinctions. Do you know about the *kauwa*—the outcasts? They called them 'corpses.' Was that the same as slaves, do you think? Uncle said that if a kauwa married anybody but another kauwa, their children were strangled. Kaiulani writes us about the English. She seems to be caught up in European royalty, who is important and who is not. One month a German count is 'desperately' interested in her, and the next month she has moved on to the house of a Bourbon Del Monte."

The subject, she could see, made him uneasy. "I'm not fascinated by any of them," Jared told her. "They just are. Pa went to school with the King. They were all friends, Mama, David Kalakaua and his sisters. Uncle didn't know any of them. All he ever wanted to do was run the ranch, so he didn't even go away to school. Grandfather started a little school here on the ranch, mainly for Uncle, but he opened it to the ranch hands' children too. The first teacher was from Wales. You ought to hear Uncle sing some of the songs . . ."

"So it's your uncle who runs the ranch?"

"Pa helps out, when he's around," he said, seemingly worried that she might think badly of his father, she thought. "And he handles shipping with the meat-packers on Oahu. He's been busy lately trying to handle the problems caused by the men who bought Eli Barrows' meat-packing company. They've been raising prices on us." There was a long pause, as if Jared was considering telling her something. Finally he said, "You will probably hear some grumbling from Uncle. He gets testy when Pa brings so many guests to the island. It means the hands have to stop their work and do this and that—and it also means taking horses away from their chores when we don't have any to spare. And there are the cattle we always slaughter. Uncle counts it all up—he thinks Pa is too high-handed. Says he's going to put us all in the poorhouse."

"Is that right?" she asked.

"Oh, I don't think so," Jared told her, knowing he shouldn't be talking about these things. "Pa says Uncle is tightfisted."

There was no dramatic avenue of ironwood trees leading to the old Home Place, only a grove of eucalyptus trees

brought from Australia years ago. The house was plain and
made entirely of local wood.

Aunt Maile was a large woman with wavy iron-grey hair;
her face grew round with pleasure when she saw Jared.
Uncle limped out of the house behind her, moving slowly
with the help of a staff.

Jared kissed them both, tenderly, on each cheek before
turning to introduce True.

"Welcome, welcome," the old man said in a voice that
cracked with age and effort. And then, as if he had only so
much patience, "Come in, come in, I've just hotted up the
old firetub and we're about to roast some peanuts. Cold
enough tonight, wouldn't you think? My boy, it's good to
see you. Come in, young lady, don't worry about your
mount . . . Kekoa here will take it, that's right."

Aunt Maile touched True's hair, holding out a strand to
be caught by the last of the sun. "Like gold," she said, with
such pure delight that True felt for a moment she was going
to cry, and she had to bite her lip to keep the tears from
flowing.

The greeting at Kolonahe had been elaborate; all the right
words had been said, and still she had not felt welcome.
Now, at this simple country place, an old couple made her
feel as if she were coming home.

Colonel Toby built Kolonahe just outside the upcountry
town of Napua. It was the island's showplace, with elaborate
gardens and grass tennis courts and a show ring for horses.
It was not just one house, but a collection of long, low
buildings, the rooms letting out onto a central courtyard. Set
apart, the family home was a high-gabled New England
house with long porches all around. Guest rooms were in the
low buildings; meals were served on a big, central lanai
shaded by massive jacaranda trees. Formal dinners were
held in the big house, where the dining room could seat
forty; if more were on hand, tables could be set in the ball-
room.

Beyond the main houses were several smaller buildings for
servants, a cookhouse and a barn. Farther down the lane,
but within sight, was a tiny school which doubled, on Sundays, as a church. Great banks of *ohai-ula*—flame trees—
grew around all the buildings, interspersed with hibiscus and

plumeria and Christmasberry bushes, and in the woods were tiny wild orchids.

The next morning, young Rachel agreed to go for a walk to show me the schoolhouse. We picked our way down the lane, stepping aside to avoid cow patties and horse droppings. She was a large, gangly girl, not nearly so beautiful as her taller sister and brother, with a skin that was closer to the warm brown of her mother than her light-skinned father.

It was interesting to observe these children whose mother was a full-blood native and whose father was a hapa haole with definite European features—a straight nose and precise lips and light hazel eyes. Each child seemed to be a different combination of the parents: Jared's dark hair and hazel eyes, his smooth tan skin and his regal bearing blended the handsome best of both. Like his mother, he carried himself as if the world were meant to watch. Rachel, on the other hand, had inherited her mother's size without her grace, her mother's burnished color and her flat forehead and large lips as well, which did not go at all with her father's chiseled chin.

"Do you think you will come to Mau'loa one day to teach in our school?" Rachel asked, hurrying on to add, "Papa says you are a teacher. I couldn't bear to be a teacher—I hate so to do my lessons. I'd far rather be out riding with Pa and the cowboys."

I laughed, and said teasingly, "Well, perhaps someday I *will* come teach here, just to show you how interesting my classes can be. We study all manner of things—like mushrooms—and we go looking for field flowers, and we study the stars."

"The stars?" Rachel said, stopping short. "How do you study the stars?"

"We take a telescope out at night, and train it on the moon and all of the constellations. We can see so many of them from Hawaii, you know. Even the Southern Cross, at some times of the year."

"Pa says the best place to see the stars is on top of Mauna Kea, though it gets awfully cold up there at night."

We turned to peer up to the great mountaintop, its peak crowned now by a white wisp of a cloud. "I think that would make a wonderful school outing."

"We could ask him to take us," Rachel offered, suddenly growing excited about the prospect of an outing. "We could put up a tent and take heavy blanket rolls and plenty of tea."

"That surely would be an adventure," I answered. "I'm beginning to think I should have agreed to come teach you . . ."

Rachel looked at me, astonished. "But we would never be allowed to go to this school," she said, as if I should have known. "Mama is taking us to England to school. She says there are no schools good enough for us in Hawaii."

I felt my face go hot. "Perhaps you will see the Princess Kaiulani," I said, and before I could stop myself, I added, "She is a very good friend of mine, you know." Immediately, I was furious with myself for needing to prove my importance to this child—and for using Vicky to do it.

For some time that morning I wandered about aimlessly; no one thought to speak to me, and I was just as glad. The women were busy with their own friends, either visiting or helping organize the afternoon's outings. I felt awkward, out of place. Remembering that I had seen some interesting-looking volumes in the library of the big house, I made my way up the steps and slipped into the pretty room with its dark carpets, heavy Victorian settees and carved tables.

An album lay on top of one of the tables, and I began to turn its pages, stopping at a sepia-tinted photo of a large, white frame house, New England style, almost hidden by a great banyan tree. Posing on the porch was a group of girls in pretty white dresses, behind them their mothers and grandmothers in holokus, to the side several nursemaids holding infants. Native women were fitted out in their Sunday finery while the girls might have been languishing on a fine haole lanai in Honolulu. Their white dresses gleamed and shimmered bright, as if to set off the dark faces of the fashionable young women. Their hair was drawn back in the latest style; they might have been well-bred girls from the Mainland. All that gave them away was the dark Hawaiian faces, the black wavy hair that could scarcely be contained, and the nursemaids who stood awkward before the camera, barefoot. I looked at the photo for a long time, studying the faces. So engrossed was I that I didn't hear Mrs. Wakefield until she said, "I get homesick every time I look at that old book—that is my father's house in Lahaina, Maui. We were all dressed up for a church service, a baptism. There I am, right in the middle. I was about fourteen years then. It was a baptism for my little cousin Bernie—there, in the nurse's arms. Auntie Momi."

"My nurse was named Momi too," I told her.

Laiana Wakefield smiled absentmindedly. "It means 'pearl,' did you know that? So many of the old aunties were called 'Momi.' "

"My Auntie Momi is very old—she lives on Oahu."

Laiana Wakefield sighed. "This one died long ago, dear soul—soon after the fever took little Bernie. I still dream about her now and then . . ."

Jenny came running down the stairs, saw us and stopped. She was flushed with her victory of the night before. Mrs. Wakefield joined her, leaving me alone once again.

Evan was one of the few people I knew well enough to approach, so I set out to find him. It would, at least, give me a purpose for a few minutes. I tracked him down in the barn, in the tack room getting ready to set out on a ride. The light was filtering in through one window. He squinted, then smiled when he saw it was me. "Miss Moon," he said. "Just what are you about, Martha?"

"Nothing, really. True is off with Jared visiting his uncle and aunt, and I'm at loose ends."

"Is that where she was last night?" he asked, keeping his eyes on the tack he was straightening.

"She didn't want to celebrate your engagement," I said, "that was all."

He looked up at me, his eyes steady and serious. "I didn't know that you and True would be here," he said.

Why I said what I said then, I'll never know. I suppose his words made me angry, though why they should I couldn't say—or maybe I was feeling generally out of sorts. But what I said was: "It sounds to me like there's plenty you don't know, and some you don't want to know. True has something to say to you. Even if you think she's a child, even if you think she doesn't know about anything at all, you ought to hear her out."

The muscles in his jaw seemed to clench, but he just kept on with his work. He lifted the saddle, then he stood for a long minute, thinking.

Finally he said, "When is she coming back?"

"By noon. They should be heading out about now."

He walked the horse out of the barn, swung easily into the

saddle, tapped his hat slightly to me and set off at a trot, in the direction of the old Wakefield homestead.

True recognized him from a distance, and without even stopping to think she said to Jared, "That's Evan Coulter, come to meet us. He's an old friend. I expect he's coming to tell me some news. I wonder if you'd mind going on to let Martha know where I am. She doesn't really know anybody much, and we've left her alone a long time . . . I'd be awfully glad if you'd keep her company 'til I get back."

Jared was happy to oblige. As soon as Evan reached them, Jared told him, "I was going to show True the Kala Heiau, but I need to get back. Why don't the two of you ride on over? It's no more than half an hour. Skirt the cane field down there, then follow the line of boulders that leads up the meadow; when you get to the biggest one—on top—you'll be able to look down and see it. The kahunas say it's the most powerful temple in the Islands. Very strong mana up there. Go and you'll see."

Evan set the pace at a slow trot; she matched her horse's gait to his, and they moved together across the field, the sun warming their faces, the fresh, open smell of the range wrapping around them.

On a hillock overlooking the cane field, he stopped; the cane was blowing, the sound of the rustle of the leaves lifted to them. A misty rain had swept down from the mountains to collide with the sun, forming a great arc of a rainbow which hovered over the blowing green cane field.

"This must be what you meant," she said to him, "that first time you came to Mana'olana. You said then that you couldn't explain how you felt about this island."

He looked at her but said nothing.

"The cane field may look beautiful," she went on, "but Mr. Eben Wakefield says it is going to be the ruin of the ranch. Seems like Mr. Claus Spreckels talked Colonel Toby into planting sugar cane, promising that he would have a sugar mill built on the island by the time the cane was ready to harvest. The Colonel borrowed heavily to finance the cane; now it is ready, but there is no mill. That means that the cane will rot in the fields. Did you know that?"

"Yes," he said. "Some of us tried to warn Toby. Your uncle told Archie this was going to happen before any cane was planted, and Archie told Toby, but he was so certain it would make him a rich man."

"Why doesn't he take better care of the ranch, if he wants to be rich?"

"I don't know," he answered. "I've asked myself that question . . . and in a way, that's why I'm here this week. Toby has asked for my help, but I'm not sure there's any advice I can give him that he is likely to take." He paused, looked out over the valley and added, "Whenever I got homesick for Hawaii, this was what I thought of—this island, those mountains, the feeling you get here of being between heaven and earth."

They did not speak again until they pulled up short at the very top, near the big rock, and stood looking out: to a wide, green promontory just below them, piled high with the rocks of an ancient temple—called a *heiau*—and beyond that the endless blue of the sea, marked on the horizon by the vague black shape of Maui.

She would remember the moment for the rest of her life as a great, soaring swelling inside of her, a feeling of standing on the edge of the world, within reaching distance of the sky.

She threw her head back and took a deep breath; he looked at her and smiled.

"Mana," she said to him. "Don't you feel it?"

He turned to look again, out over the ancient heiau, to the vast ocean beyond. "This place, right here . . ." he tried to say.

"This place, right here," she repeated, "Power. Mana."

"Yes," he answered, and they dismounted and walked their horses down the long, sloping hill to the heiau below. For a time they simply wandered along the outer edge of the ancient structure, looking up at the great wall of massive stones carried for many miles long centuries ago and piled, one on another to form the great outer wall. Then they climbed inside, tracing the altars, the places where sacrifices were once made. Where slaves—men called kauwa—were gutted and spread out on the altar stones as offerings to impatient gods.

That morning, Maile Wakefield had lifted a lei of wild orchids over True's head and kissed her good-bye. Now True placed the flowers on the altar stone. "To make certain the gods know we are kindly spirits," she said, smiling up at him.

"We are kindly spirits," Evan replied. "Even kindred spirits, I think. Kind friends." Standing before the altar, he smiled easily and said, "I'll never, if I live to be a hundred, forget the first time I laid eyes on you. You were diving into the ocean, bare as the day you were born, and I swear I thought you were a mermaid."

Her eyes opened wide. "I always thought maybe you had seen me that day, but I could never work up the courage to ask."

"What you did was dangerous, and for a long time after whenever I would think about it I would be angry, for what could have happened—and if it had, I'd never have forgiven myself. But there was something so powerfully brave about it too—as if you had to challenge the world, to show people something. I could never figure out just what it was that you had to show them, but I knew you had to."

She lifted her shoulders in a gesture of mild confusion. "I'd only been with the Wrights for a short time. I was very young and terribly afraid. Things had happened to me . . . and I suppose I needed to prove that I wasn't afraid, that I could take care of myself. In a way," she said, smiling to show she wasn't serious, "I was flinging myself on the altar of the gods, as they used to do here in this old temple. Testing my magic. I'm not so foolish anymore."

He looked at her, grinning. "Is that why you rode the bay in the race?"

She raised her hand to her hair to brush it back in a delicately feminine gesture of embarrassment. "That wasn't my choice—it was Uncle's and Vicky's pa's. And they only wanted to win."

"You didn't want to win?" he asked, teasing.

"I did win," she answered.

And he blurted, "You certainly were omnipotent that day—God!"

All this while it seemed that a magnetic field lay about them; they fell silent, listening to the whistling of the breeze as it clattered through the long grasses and around the rocks. A solitary frigate bird sailed above them, sliding sideways on the wind.

Afraid to look at her, he looked away; finally he made

himself say, "Martha said you had something to say to me, something I needed to hear. That's why I came looking for you this morning."

She could feel her heart swelling inside her chest, and she wasn't sure that it would leave her enough air to speak. "Are you . . ." she began, "going to . . ."

"Jenny and I are going to be married in two months," he answered, his eyes following the flight of the bird.

"It is wrong," she said, her voice low and urgent. "You are making a terrible mistake. Don't marry Jenny Barrows. Please don't do it."

He looked at her, his eyes troubled.

"Jenny and I," he started, then stopped and said, "I've promised, I've given my word. It is time for me . . . for Jenny and me . . . to marry. It is . . . was . . . decided . . . a long time ago."

"It is a bad promise—break it," she said, her voice suddenly strong.

She saw the turmoil in his eyes, the cross currents of anger and confusion. And the resolve.

"If you had stayed away just one more year . . ." she tried to tell him. "In another year you will know what I already know. You don't want the life Jenny has planned out for you . . . the life she wants. It isn't going to be enough . . ."

His face clouded over, a hard cord of vein gripped his neck. "That's enough, True. Don't say any more or you are going to cause problems that can't be fixed. You don't know. I've done a great deal more thinking about my life than you know. There are . . ." he started to say "complications," but instead he said, "I'm sorry that I disappoint you, I am. But plans have been made. A good many other people are involved, and there is no chance that I am going to change them. I want you to try to understand. We have been friends for a long time. I would like . . ."

In an attempt to stop the tears, she had lifted her head and turned it from him. The effect was to show her in profile with the sun behind her, catching her in the light. For the first time he saw the woman that the girl would become, and he felt a cold, hard hand clamp onto his chest.

Defeat seeped into her, pressed down deep, so that all she could feel was the agony of loss; standing on the ancient altar, the stones uncompromising, she began to understand the futility of sacrifice.

Her body convulsed with sobs; he wanted to reach out to comfort her, but he knew he could not. He looked up, to the hill above them where they had been standing only a short time before, and wondered what would happen if an earthquake should shake this promontory loose and send them, adrift, out to sea.

12

Rose Plantation
Ulupalakua, Maui
April 1893

My sweet Martha,

I rode up here this morning to see Liko, as I usually do each Sunday, and he was not here as he always is, but off gathering up some cows which managed to break through a fence sometime last night. Dear, thoughtful Mr. Mackey insisted I should not turn around and take the long ride back to the Baumgartners, but wait for Liko an hour or so in the arbor of his rose garden, with a tall cool glass of punch by my side. I could not resist; I believe the kind gentleman might even have kept me company, if I had not asked for some paper and a pencil to write to you.

It is thanks to Mr. Mackey that my employer has agreed to allow me to ride one of his horses to Rose Plantation each Sunday so I can visit with Liko. When Mr. Baumgartner refused my request for a horse that first Sunday, I'm quite sure he was certain I'd change my mind and go to church with the family. He pointed out that although it had been agreed that Sunday was to be my day of rest, it would be very difficult for his wife to care for all of the children at church. I politely suggested that he should take charge of the three older boys, and his wife could surely handle the three little ones. Believing that God helps those who help themselves, I left early in the morning to walk up the mountain to Rose Plantation, arriving by noon. Mr. Mackey insisted on sending me back on one of his good saddle horses, with Liko to keep me company and return the horse. I do believe Mr. Mackey shamed Baumgartner, for he grumbles still

137

about my use of the horse, but he doesn't forbid it because he knows now that I will walk if I must. So here I am, the sweet scent of roses all round me, knowing you must be waiting to hear what I have to say about the amazing events of these past few days.

There is so much to tell. Where to start? It was late Thursday morning, and I was going through what has become a thrice weekly ritual: Mrs. Baumgartner appeared at the door to the pantry, where I was taking stock of the week's supplies, to tell me I simply had to speak to Kuulei.

"Why should I speak to Kuulei?" I asked in my ritual opening.

"She won't do as I wish."

"What do you wish her to do?"

"She does not fold the bedsheets as I like."

"I shall tell her, once again."

"She did not come when Little Miss called her."

"Kuulei would prefer to play with Little Miss than do her chores," I explained, as I have explained so many times before. "I have told her that she must complete her chores first."

"When I asked her to polish Grandmother's silver, she said you had told her to scrub the kitchen floor, and she wouldn't mind me."

And that, of course, is the real problem. Her help has never minded her—which is why this house was in such a state of chaos when I arrived—and they do mind me. The Hawaiians who have worked for her are neither mean nor lazy, as she has accused them. They simply could not abide being told to do one thing only to have her change her mind two minutes later, and told to do something else, with the children pulling in six different directions. They also could not abide her complaining nature, which is curiously (and not very pleasantly) combined with her husband's loud contrariness. How this cold, sallow couple ever landed up in this warm, brown country I'll never understand. What I do understand is how I am able to bring some order into their chaos. I am firm and I am white. The B's (and the Hawaiians know this) have a disdain for sweet tempers and dark skins.

As I was saying . . . on Thursday last I was listening to the usual list of infractions, and when it was finished, Mrs. B says, more petulantly than usual, "You have a guest waiting to see you in the parlor. Mr. Baumgartner is with him now, and I've said you'll be along just as soon as you speak to Kuulei."

I was, in fact, in no great hurry to find out who was calling. There have been several unpleasant inquiries about my family, as well as several men—some young, others not—who have been riding out from Lahaina to "take stock of me" as it is said. There is, I suppose, a shortage of marriageable haole women on this island, but I do not much like being looked over like a piece of horseflesh. (Though, considering my own mistress, perhaps there is something to be said for looking over the property before attempting to acquire it.)

I should have known that Mr. B would not have wasted his time on troublemakers or marriage-seekers. He was in fact beside himself (I could tell by his bright red cheeks) at the arrival of Judge Evan Coulter, a man of some importance in the islands, and of especial importance right now on Maui, where property rights are being contested.

Evan stood and smiled as I came in, and said something miraculous like, "Hello, True."

I thought my heart would stop at the surprise. I couldn't find words, so I only smiled.

"Where's your tongue, girl? Say hello to Judge Coulter," Baumgartner barked, as he likes to do before strangers.

Evan's natural good manners failed him. He looked at Baumgartner as if he were some very small insect he would as well step on. "Miss Lindstrom and I are old friends," he said in a voice verging on violence. "I have news for her from mutual friends in Honolulu, and I would like to speak to her alone."

"From what friends?" Baumgartner had the temerity to ask, missing Evan's anger altogether.

If I hadn't laughed then, I think Evan might have exploded.

"Please, Mr. B," I said to my employer. "Your good wife is having a bit of a problem, and she would like you to help her."

"It's your job to help with her problems," he answered petulantly, like a big baby with several thick red rings of fat around its neck.

"I know," I coaxed, "but in this case I think you can do it."

When Mr. B left, Evan just shook his head and said, "So that's how it is? Even with that tightfisted bastard, you're still in charge. I shouldn't have worried."

"Were you worried?" I asked.

He sat down on the horse-hair sofa and I took a chair close by; the light filtered in from the high window to the east and lit his eyes, as beautiful and, now, as sad as any I've ever seen. It was the sadness that brought tears to my own eyes, and gladness too for seeing him again, and it was my tears that made him reach for my hands, and we sat there looking at each other and holding on.

After a few minutes, Mrs. B came to the door and began to whine at me to come help her with one of the babies.

"Wait here," I told him, taking my hands away so she could not see us touching. "I will take care of this, and then we can take a walk—we'll have no peace here."

We walked a long distance that afternoon, through a gully covered by a canopy of trees high above, all the way to a small waterfall and pool I have discovered. I think of it as my secret pool. Sometimes, when I've had enough of babies and too much bickering from the B's, I go there alone and take off all my clothes and lie back in the cool water, letting it splash over me. Evan and I sat next to the pool and talked—about his work, about all that is happening in Honolulu, about the so-called Provisional Government.

We talked on and on . . . about Liliuokalani's abdication and the U.S. government's hesitation about annexing Hawaii and what it means, about Vicky's trip to Washington to try to convince President Cleveland to restore the monarchy, about her pa being appointed Governor of Oahu.

Evan believes, as I do, that the Monarchy is finished. He doesn't like it, and he worries a great deal about Governor Cleghorn and Vicky. But in the end, he says, if Hawaii's destiny does lie with the United States—and he believe it does, whether we want it or not—there can be no monarchy, not even a monarch that is largely ceremonial, which the Governor seems to favor. Certainly not the one envisioned by Liliuokalani, with all powers returned to the crown. Evan thinks a monarchy is simply not compatible with the American spirit. Even so, the great American passion for equality does not extend to dark-skinned people, he says, and most of our natives are dark. Evan doesn't think Americans will ever accept the Hawaiians—or any of the Asian races that are so prevalent in the Islands—as equal, and that is why he is against annexation. If he had his choice, he says he would prefer to remain a republic, retaining certain economic ties to the United States.

The Governor is bitter, Evan says, because he believes the Queen made it easy for the Missionary Boys to take over; he thinks she threw the monarchy away and with it Kaiulani's future. Evan says the Queen simply hastened the inevitable by forcing the issue. But he knows, too, that for the Hawaiians, who want to keep their Queen and as many of their Island ways as they can, it is a terrible blow.

Evan will be coming to Maui each second month, when the circuit court sits in Lahaina. He told me, as he was leaving, what I already knew from you: that Jenny is expecting their first child. He spoke of Jenny only to answer my questions, which were few. I dare not ask if he is happy, as he so clearly is not.

It has nothing to do with me, I am certain—otherwise, he would not have come to visit me. Jenny wants him to be content as other men are content with a life that has been patterned by others and made to fit him. Except it doesn't fit.

Evan spent his boyhood near Hana, did you know that? His father had a little grocery store, but his real loves were butterflies and transcribing the old Hawaiian meles and legends. He learned to speak Hawaiian—not the pidgin that so many haole shopkeepers get by with. Sometimes he took Evan with him into the mountains, their butterfly nets always ready, and often they went to talk to Hawaiian storytellers.

Evan's mother did not approve of either of these pursuits—I gather she did not approve of his father, either. Gradually, she took over the store, keeping Evan close by as her helper, and his father was gone for longer and longer periods in the mountains. One day, after a bad storm he did not come home at all. Evan went looking for him and found him lying under a tree, drenched and feverish. Three days later he was dead; three weeks later, Evan and his mother were on the boat to Honolulu. She was so angry with his father that she would never speak of him, except to tell Evan that she was not going to let what happened to his father happen to him. She died believing she was right.

She was wrong, though who can say what forms Evan's butterflies and ancient legends will take? Whatever they are, Jenny will hate them and, like his mother, will probably die believing she was right.

Jared writes that he is coming to Lahaina next week to visit his cousins and (I suspect this is the real reason) see a doctor who combines hot mud baths with massage, said to be good for the muscle aches to which Jared is prone. When he gets here I plan to take him up to Rose Plantation and get Liko to give him swimming lessons.

Jared finally admitted to me that the reason he will never go swimming with us is because he never learned how to swim properly. Can you imagine that? But Liko can teach him in a small, protected beach we have found only a short ride from here. Then I'm going to give Jared some riding instructions—he never learned to ride properly either. With just the two of us on the trail together, he won't have a chance to be embarrassed. That's what I must talk to Liko about today, and figure out how we can find the time from our chores. It won't be all that hard for Liko—he is everybody's pet around here, especially Mr. Mackey's, who calls him out to sing and play the ukelele for his guests. He even had a pair of leather chaps made for Liko, and a paniolo hat, the kind the Spanish cowboys wear, and a red-and-white-checkered shirt.

This has turned out to be a happy place for our Liko. Mr. Mackey has created a beautiful ranch, with many guest houses which he likes to keep filled, and all manner of wonderful occupations for guests—there is even a bowling alley, and little native boys to mind the pins. I have been invited several times for house parties (again, a lack of young single women is the reason) but of course the B's won't hear of it—except for one time when Mr. Mackey came to fetch me himself and wouldn't take a no from my Teutonic master. It riles the B's that their hired help is invited and they are not. Liko and I can scarcely wait until you can come.

Evan asked if I had thought about visiting my old home, the farm here on Maui. It is on the other end of the island, and I have not been there. One of the natives, who remembered me as a child, told me that the forest is taking back the house, that vines are coming in through the little glass windows that my mother polished until they gleamed. He said that nobody goes near the house. He also told me that he himself had seen a figure of a woman, "all laughter and sunlight," floating about the old house.

That is how I remember her, sometimes. Pure sunlight, clear full laughter. I try not to think of other times. A day or so ago a few lines of a song she used to sing came sailing into my head. Perhaps I'll remember more of the nice times, sometimes I hope so.

Evan is making inquiries about what happened. I would like to stop him, but he seems to think he must.

If ever I go back to that house, it will be with Evan. I feel that. But I think I will not, I hope I need not.

Liko is coming now! He has just called to me from the corral. Thank you for sending Evan to me, Martha Moonie. I am not certain that he would have come, had you not asked him to deliver the beautiful holoku. (How can I possibly thank you and Aunt Winona for sewing such dear things for me? What would I be wearing if you didn't keep me in pretty dresses?) But especially, you have my enduring gratitude for understanding that anything that could ever be between Evan and me will be right and good.

Thank you too for sending along Vicky's letter with Evan. All my love to Aunt and Uncle, and most especially to my Moonie little friend,

                                                                    True.

March 8, 1893
The Arlington Hotel
Washington, D.C. USA

Dearest Martha and True,

I am in Washington after all—I had to come. Else perhaps someday the Hawaiians will say that Kaiulani could have saved us but she didn't even try. Mr. and Mrs. Davies are with me. We have met with the new President Cleveland, who was entertaining, and his young bride, who is dear and beautiful.

Alec Marston is here; having overthrown the monarchy, now he is pleading the cause of Annexation. Oh, but I want so to come home, to be done with this exile, to be with Papa at Ainahau and swim in the sea with you again. You will not know me, I think. I am no longer the schoolgirl who left Honolulu. Just listen to what the American newspapers say about me: "The Princess is a tall beautiful young woman of sweet face and slender figure." And this: "She has a delicate, exquisite beauty; she is a finished musician, an artist, a linguist and her gentle manners are those of a born aristocrat." You must not laugh! (It is I who must remember to laugh.)

Laughter is not easy these days. Do you realize that I have spent the whole of my life preparing for a race that will never be run?

We go from here back to England. I do not know when I will be allowed to come home. I want so much to see you both.

She signed her letter, as she had taken to doing since Kalakaua's death made her the Crown Princess, "Kaiulani of Hawaii."

Honolulu
Hale Mana'olana

Dear True:

Evan came today to see Uncle Jameson—he has been helping with some bank loans; I know because Aunt let it slip when we were sewing. Uncle hasn't been away since the day of the race, and Aunt says it is just as well, if he can't control his urge to gamble.

When my classes were done, I found Evan waiting for me and I knew he had come to tell me about his visit with you.

I did not admit that I had already received a long account from you; nor did I allow him to see my shock when he told me some important news which he brought you, and which you left out of your letter altogether.

Why couldn't you tell me that Evan had made inquiries and had discovered that your father died seven months ago? Have you pushed it out of your mind? Or have you buried it deep inside of you, where you think it cannot hurt? It worries me, dear friend, that you never speak of your father. I am so very afraid that it means you are pained, still, by his abandonment of you. When I asked Evan what you said when he told you, his answer was, "Nothing. She didn't speak at all for a time, and when she did it was about something else."

Evan said that the authorities in Oregon wrote that your father died of blood poisoning, after being punctured by a nail while working as a ship's carpenter. He also told me, as I know he told you, that he had corresponded with the priest who gave your father last rites; at the end, your father asked for "the forgiveness of my daughter, True." Perhaps, dearest friend, if you can find it in your heart to grant him this forgiveness, your own burden will feel lighter. I tell you this, at the same time knowing that I need to grant my own unknown mother and father that same forgiveness, if I am to live with my own abandonment.

I preach! Forgive me. Now I will tell you more of what Evan said about you (should you have any interest in this subject!). He corroborated my impression that the Baumgartners are impossible, but that you have taken over with "a firm hand and a lot of good humor." He said you have a real affection for the children and for the Hawaiians who work on the ranch. He also reports that Mr. James Mackey is smitten with you . . . and that whenever you come onto his ranch, he can scarcely keep the hands at work, they stare so. Evan says that they are all fond of Liko and treat him like a pet.

Evan is worried, I can tell, about the bad feeling that exists on Maui—about the murder. He says no one will go near the house where it happened, and that the Hawaiians who live nearby believe your mother's spirit lives there. Evan says the family of the luna who killed her has suffered—it plagues them yet, the murder of a white woman by a native. They have come to Evan because of his position. "A terrible discontent" is the way he describes the situation. He asked me if I knew that some people believe you saw what happened that night. It is said that you did not speak at all for days after, and then all you seemed able to do was describe your mother, the awful scene after it was done.

You were a child when you left Maui, and now you've returned a grown woman—one who, Evan was told, looks very like her mother. So your return has caused a new wave of rumors and troubles. Evan tells me that some of the luna's family came to ask you about that night, but that Mr. Baumgartner intervened, and made matters worse.

Why haven't you written me about any of this? Don't try to shelter me, True. I am your friend, you mean more to me than anyone on this earth, and you must let me help you, in whatever way I can.

I asked Evan if you could be in any danger, and he said he didn't think so. He says you scarcely ever leave the farm, except to go up to Rose Plantation to see Liko.

One odd thing: I told Evan that you hadn't wanted to return to Maui, and he said that he didn't think you should have returned either. He said he knew, a long time ago, about "the mystery" surrounding the murder.

"What mystery?" I asked.

He answered that there seems to be some question about the murder, about there being some others who might have done it—haoles. He said at the time the local authorities thought it best for everybody just to accept things as they seemed, with the two deaths, and close the case and hope it would be forgotten. But he says it hasn't been forgotten, not by the luna's ohana.

Evan thinks you can't bear to think about it, even, and he said no little girl should have to endure what you had to endure. He sounded very tender. He wanted to know if you had told me anything about that night, and I had to say no, which is the truth.

All the while I was talking to Evan, something was at the back edge of my mind, nibbling at me. Then I had it. I blurted, "You say you didn't want True to go to Maui, but it was Jenny and her mother who arranged it with the Baumgartners."

He stared at me. A small frowning crease appeared between his eyes; he pinched it with his fingers.

Realizing my blunder, I apologized and told him that I had thought he knew.

I asked after Jenny, and he said she is feeling a bit seedy and isn't up to visitors. The ladies' club version is somewhat less considerate—they say you'd think she was Eve and having the world's first baby.

In her defense, however (not that I am above being a gossip), I did see her one day last week when Aunt and I were in town and had to deliver some papers to Evan. She had dark circles under her eyes, and her color was bad. I do believe she is having a difficult time.

With much love I am your,
Martha

13

January 1896

Silver sheets of rain blew in billowing gusts as the *Kinau* approached the wharf at Lahaina, Maui; the opaque green surface of the ocean was riddled with drops. It was a warm rain, the kind that True and I once would have raised our faces to, and allowed to soak through our dresses.

I lifted my shawl over my head and ran down the gangway; despite the rain, the usual crowd had gathered to see the steamer dock. Friends stood waiting with flower leis and welcome-home smiles for the travellers, and I almost collided with True before I realized she was lifting a ginger lei over my head. The delicious strong scent of it caught at my breath.

"True! At last, at last . . ." I said, holding her tight as the rain coursed over us.

She answered, laughing, "It's taken you three long years to get here. Did you think I wouldn't come to meet you . . . ?"

We stood together in the rain, and the Hawaiians who had come to watch the steamer arrive watched us, but without the usual smiles and murmurs and alohas. I wondered how long True had been standing there, surrounded by a hostility I could almost feel, waiting for me. She hurried me into a covered buggy and we were off without delay.

The rain continued to pour from the heavens in great, shining sheets; I was glad for the rainstorm, glad for the privacy it gave us, closing us in together after so long a time.

I could not quit looking at her. She was the same and yet changed—in the sound of her voice, which is lower now and more vibrant, in the way she holds herself, in her laugh, which seems to spill out more easily. She has experienced a metamorphosis, has become a beautiful butterfly.

147

"Look at you," she said to me. "You aren't my goosey little girl friend anymore. You're all grown up!" I held onto her arm and started laughing then, and she did too—at what had happened to us in the past three years and because we had one whole month together, starting at that moment.

"I'm almost sorry I won't get to meet the Baumgartner family," I told her, as she guided the horse over roads that rushed with water.

"No, you aren't," she answered. "They take awful advantage of sweet and agreeable people like you. Be glad they have returned to their native land for six months. We are, though I do miss the little girls. The boys, I'm sorry to say, have managed to acquire the worst tendencies of both parents and I'm glad to be shut of them."

She smiled over at me, brushing back a strand of wet hair, then patting my hand. "Peace and quiet and a nice, long visit with you is what I've been looking forward to—and for the three of us to be together again. We've waited so long. Now you're here. You are actually here and I can hardly believe it."

"Here" was a farm perched part way up the mountain just behind a giant monkeypod tree; the house was white with a green trim, wonderfully neat and pretty with a long lanai around two sides, open to the air.

In the kitchen, the cook—a big, brown woman in a bright yellow muumuu—was taking bread from the oven.

"That smells like heaven, Ipo," True told her.

Ipo exploded into laughter; it rippled through her large body and made her dress tremble. "Come have two big bites of heaven, then, or as many as you can, with some sweet butter and honey. And coffee, yes my poor little all bones wahines, coffee here."

"Oh, Ipo," True said, putting her arm around the big woman, "just look—my Martha is finally here."

"I see, I see," Ipo said. "Friend John come by, say Liko on his way soon as storm gets by. This be a happy place, I say so." The laughter rippled on out as we sat in the kitchen, eating fresh hot bread from the oven and basking in the glory of being together again.

Liko came before the rain had fully stopped. He ran up the path, as wet as could be, and flung himself at me, tucking his big head into my waist. I put my hands on his face and felt the scratch of whiskers. My throat went dry, then a lump formed and I felt myself crying. Liko—sturdy little dwarf— had grown up too.

The three of us sat on the lanai until the sun went down and the mosquitoes came out, then we moved into the old parlor. There was too much to say, words came tumbling out—of the details you do not say in letters, all the answers you cannot make. When it became too dark to see we lit oil lamps, and Liko laughed and said, "Old Baumgartner would have a chest spasm if he could see us using up his precious oil!"

"How would you like to use up some of his homemade wine?" True asked, and she and Liko laughed outright at the look of surprise on my face.

And so we sipped wine and chattered on into the night. They wanted to hear the latest news from Honolulu, and I told how, on New Year's Day, all of the revolutionists had finally been released from jail, all except Queen Liliuokalani, who was still under house arrest in Iolani Palace, but it seems it will not be long before she is released as well.

We were irate about the banning, once again, of the hula as "lewd," and how anyone wanting to vote must not only swear allegiance to the Republic, they must disavow the monarchy.

True said she was most furious with the United States Congress, and with President Cleveland—who admits that the Queen could not have been deposed without the threat of U.S. warships in the harbor—yet refuses to take action to restore the throne. "Hypocrites, all of them and especially the mighty United States of America, in which we all put our trust," she said, waving her glass in the air as if she were waving a flag. "Well, yes," I said, trying not to get splashed, "but there was that business about the Queen talking about beheading some of the Missionary Boys."

Liko roared, "Slice off heads, smash 'em all, tear out guts . . ."

"Good grief, Liko," I put in. "I'd almost forgotten how gruesome you can be."

True opened another bottle of wine. I thought perhaps I shouldn't have any more, but when she filled my glass I didn't stop her.

Concentrating hard, I tried to inject a sober note into the

conversation: "Uncle believes," I said, enunciating carefully, "Uncle believes that the Americans are going to agree to annexation because they think Hawaii will be a key position of power in the Pacific. The Americans are watching Japan." Proud of myself for finishing this speech, I sat smiling.

"I met President Dole," Liko blurted, as if we had just been talking about the president of the Republic. "He came up to Lahaina, up to Rose Plantation. What he said was good. I cheered like all of them."

"He is the enemy," True growled.

"Uncle says," I began again, slowly as the walls seemed to move at the edges of my vision, "that Sanford Dole is an honest man. Did you know that once, back when all of this was starting, he wanted to bring Vicky back to take over the crown from Liliuokalani?"

"Oh," True said, looking at Liko, who had fallen asleep on the floor and was snoring.

"Evan," she said then. "What about Evan?"

"Oh, Evan," I said, losing my train of thought entirely. "Evan is going to be President of the Republic one day."

"No!" True said, astonished. "He didn't tell me that."

"Maybe he doesn't know," I offered, taking another sip of wine to stop the whirling inside my head. "But that's what Uncle says—that Evan can be whatever he wants to be, because both sides trust him. And Aunt says that Jenny wants him to be President and talks about it all the time. But Evan says that is foolish talk."

"What's foolish?" she asked, leaning in front of me to look into my face.

I tried to think about it. "I don't know," I finally answered and burst into laughter.

She looped her arm around my neck and started laughing too. Liko heard us and woke up. His hair was tousled, and in the flickering light he looked like a cherub. In a woosy voice he said, "You promise we be together, and here it is."

True stood, smoothed her skirt with her hands, and in a voice as prickly as a blackberry vine, told us, "I meant together, not just for now, I meant . . ." The laughter had stopped, and just as suddenly, I had to rush outside to empty my stomach.

*   *   *

When I woke the next morning it was full light. I had a terrible taste in my mouth, and I heard True scream "Get away! Don't touch me!" I groped my way to the window and looked down to the grassy lawn. Three large Hawaiian men were moving around True, in a circle. From behind the house Liko in his underpants came bolting at them, brandishing a pitchfork, heading straight for the biggest of the three. Ipo was right behind him, waving a frying pan over her head and shouting, *uoki!* One Hawaiian moved behind Liko, picked him up with one hand, plucked the pitchfork from him with another and held him in the air, sputtering. I was suddenly embarrassed at seeing the great bulge of Liko's underpants—another sign of change. Ipo stopped short and the Hawaiians were talking to her, so quietly I could not hear. By the time I reached the yard, the Hawaiians were gone.

"They say they come talk to you. Why you not talk?" Ipo asked True.

True looked up at her, anger spilling out. "Because I have nothing to say to them. I've told them everything I know. Why don't they believe me? Why must they go on and on about evil signs and bad dreams? My mother is dead, why can't they let her be?"

"The kahunas want you to come to that place," Ipo said.

True's face went white. "I will not," she said. "I will not." And then, softly, "I cannot."

I slipped my arm in hers and led her back to the kitchen. Soon enough Liko came in, dressed in his bright red shirt to give him courage. "I'm going to go talk with Mr. Mackey about those Hawaiians. He'll know what to do," he said, swaggering a bit to hide his discomfort with the pitchfork episode.

"Thank you for helping me, Liko," True said. "It was brave—there were three of them and only one of you. But I'd rather you didn't say anything to Mr. Mackey. It is all so long ago, and sometimes people get strange ideas about things like that, so please, let's just forget about what happened this morning. Can we?"

Liko nodded, and soon after breakfast we waved him off, promising to see him on Friday, when we would be riding to Rose Plantation for a weekend house party.

"Dear little Liko," I said as he rode off.

"Not so little anymore, didn't you notice?" True said, giving me a sly sidelong glance.

I giggled. "Yes, I did. My goodness, True, I've never seen anything so . . . big. Whatever happened?"

"I suppose he just got riled, charging in like that. Maybe that's what happens with men. Liko's head is normal size and so is his *ule.*"

I almost choked, and she had to thump me on the back. "That's what the Hawaiians call it—I'd suppose you would know," True said, laughing at me. "Perfectly good word, perfectly good tool—I've seen all kinds of animals use it— horses and bulls. And even . . ."

We were walking out to a pasture where two orphaned calves had been penned.

"Even what?" I probed.

"Oh, I don't know if I should . . ."

"Then tell me, and let me decide if you should," I said, knowing if she'd gone this far she wanted to tell me.

She pushed open the gate just enough to let us through, and the calves came rushing up to her, bawling. "Remember I told you that I was going to have Liko teach Jared how to swim?"

"That was almost two years ago," I reminded her. "You said he was not a very apt pupil."

"Yes, well . . . in fact, Liko did teach him to swim. I didn't know what to make of it. They seemed to have such a good time, splashing and cavorting about in the water. Neither of them had ever really had a friend . . . a boy friend . . . and I was so pleased to see them having fun. But pretty soon it was clear that Jared could swim just fine, but he said no— and Liko said no, they would need more lessons. I couldn't get Jared to come riding with me. He just wanted to be with Liko."

We were busy now, feeding the baby calves with big bottles, laughing at the slurping and sucking noises. "Here we are, mothers to babies after all," I said. "Would you say that is natural or unnatural?"

"That is the question," True answered solemnly.

Puzzled, I looked at her. "What do you mean?"

"I mean Jared and Liko . . ." Her voice became hesitant. "Once, when they came out of the water, they were both . . . big."

"Big?" I said.

She looked at me, wanting me to know what she meant, and when she could see that I didn't, she said in a low voice, "Their *ules.*"

I stopped feeding my calf and stared at her.

She shook her head. "I shouldn't have said anything. Forget it, please, Martha. It isn't important, really."

Walking back to the house, I broke the silence. "But what does it mean, True?"

She smiled in an embarrassed way. "I think it means they love each other. You should see them together—they are absolutely giddy."

"I don't understand," I said. "I still don't know what it means."

"I'm not certain I do either, and I've wanted so to talk to someone about this, and there was absolutely no one I could trust. Not even Evan, because he doesn't know Liko and Jared the way we do. When I look at Liko and Jared, all I see are two sweet friends who will never be quite like other people—poor little Liko, and poor beautiful Jared. And suddenly they are happy, just being together. Didn't you notice how Liko glowed last night, talking about Jared?"

"I didn't," I said, adding ruefully, "one glass of wine and I didn't notice much of anything. I guess it seemed natural—since you took Jared under your wing, that he and Liko be friends. Liko and I have always followed after you."

"I know," she said, "and that's why I'm so worried; I feel as if I have to protect them."

"Do you mean they love each other as men and women love? How is that possible? How do they . . ."

"I'm not certain. They kiss, and do other things."

Amazed, I blurted, "What other things?"

"I went looking for them one day. The B's had said I couldn't go, but then they changed their minds and said I could. I figured Liko and Jared would be at the beach, so I headed there straight off and I just happened onto them . . ." she said, shyly. "I left before they saw me," she finished.

"Does anyone else know?" I asked, but she didn't answer, not then.

We walked back to the house and settled on the lanai; she put her feet up on a wicker stool and lay her head back on the chair. "Too much wine last night," she murmured.

"Here it is only midday and I'm feeling spent." Then she went on, "I am pretty certain that Mr. Mackey suspects. He is good friends with Colonel Toby—the family comes to visit about twice a year, and Jared is there much more often now. Mr. Mackey is terribly fond of both of them, but he told Liko that he was neglecting his chores when Jared was around, and that the two of them shouldn't be spending so much time together."

"Liko told you that . . . ?" I asked.

She nodded. "He was angry with Mr. Mackey, which can be dangerous for Liko, but he doesn't seem to be able to help himself. I'm afraid. I want to talk to Evan about it. I feel he might be able to help, but I don't think I'll have a chance to talk to him on this trip, and I'm worried too—about what he will think of it all, if it will change his feelings."

"And you? Does it change your feelings?"

She looked at me, her beautiful steady look. "My mother told me once that love was never ugly. I try to remember that."

"Your mother sounds very wise."

"No. No, she wasn't . . . wise. But she did love—she loved me, first of all. She always said that, that I was first. After me . . . all the others."

"The others?"

"The men. The ones who came when my father was away at sea. She said they came to her to warm their hands, and she loved them all."

She lay back in the chair and closed her eyes; her chin was quivering. I could see that she was clamping her teeth tight, and that she was breathing deeply.

After a time she seemed to get peaceful. I began to hum an old song and she sang the words, quietly.

"I see Evan each time he comes to Maui. We ride together, and talk."

"About what?" I asked, carefully.

"About everything. His work, mine . . ." She laughed. "I don't know how it happened, but as you can see, I am perfectly capable of running this farm. As soon as Mrs. B realized I could—and she was the first to admit it—she got after the Mr. to take her back to Austria for a visit. To be honest, I was amazed that he would go off and leave me in charge. Even with Pono to help."

"Who is Pono?" I asked.

"Pono Rourke, about the best hand you could hope for—I think he must talk to the cows, because he doesn't talk to people."

"I'm not surprised they left you in charge," I said.

"Evan said so too," she laughed.

"We're back to Evan," I told her, looking at her for the truth.

"I suppose you could say that Evan has come to me to warm his hands," she said, adding, "but always from across the room. That's all. He doesn't talk to me about Jenny, and I'm almost positive he doesn't talk to Jenny about me. He scarcely ever touches me—to answer the question you haven't asked—and I'd be willing to bet he doesn't touch her, either. From everything you've told me she has turned into a complaining woman. If only she could have married someone ordinary, she might have been happy."

I puzzled over that for a time and was about to ask her to tell me what it was, ordinary love, when she went on: "Evan does talk about little Harry. At first the talk was happy, but lately he seems to be worried about the child. I gather Jenny keeps him close."

"I've never thought of Evan as being without spine," I said. "Surely he has some say."

"I don't think he insists on much of anything with Jenny," she said. "I believe both Jenny and little Harry will be with Evan this weekend, at Rose Plantation. The guest list must have tempted Jenny, I would imagine. The last time I saw her was at Mau'loa. Four years ago."

"You'll find her much changed," I told her. And I couldn't help but think: She'll find you even more changed. Jenny's soft loveliness had hardened, the pink had become a sallow ivory while True is in her first, fresh bloom—tall and slender and sunlit, a rare pale blossom just unfurling, exotic on these tropical shores.

"Ordinary love," I repeated, "you make it sound sad. But your mother told you that . . ."

"Love was never ugly," she finished for me. "But she also taught me that some people aren't very good at loving—she said it was like swimming or fishing or cooking, or riding a horse or dancing or picking a bouquet of flowers, or even laughing or making a dress or a speech. Some people do it well, are wonderfully talented and inventive, while others have no imagination at all—just give them a recipe or a pattern, and they are satisfied. They want all kinds of limits. She used to say that loving took the most imagination of all."

"And marriage?" I had been wanting to bring up the subject. "What did your mother have to say about love and marriage?"

True crossed her arms, holding her elbows in her hands, and leaned forward, wincing as if her stomach ached. "Ah," she said, "well."

"Ah, well?" I prodded, and she smiled.

"She said that marriage hadn't anything to do with love, that marriage was what you did to survive if you were a woman. But she said that after a terrible row with my father."

"Did she love your father?"

She looked past me, toward the mountain. "I don't know. I never did know."

I came right out with it: "Has anyone here asked you to marry them?"

She burst into laughter. "So that's what you are getting at! You're afraid I'm going to be left at the gate. Well what about you, has anyone asked you for your hand in marriage?"

Her words riled me. "No," I said. "Who'd ask me? Who'd even know I was out there at the end of the beach, with an old maid and her bachelor brother?"

"Who—ee, Martha Moonie is mad, mad, mad," she teased. "And I do believe she wants to find a man."

"I don't!" I spat at her. "Stop teasing, True. It doesn't matter about me, but it does about you. Why aren't you seeing any of the men who come calling?"

At that moment True noticed a short, wiry man standing at the edge of the yard. "Pono," she called out and got up to go speak to him. When she came back she explained, "I'd be surprised if Pono Rourke has uttered more than forty-seven words in his life, and him from a big Irish family. There's no better cowhand alive, and he's a hard worker, but he certainly isn't a talker. You practically have to be a mind reader to hold a conversation with him. He wanted me to know he was off to ride fences . . ."

She was talking about Pono Rourke to avoid my question. The look on my face must have convinced her it would not work, for she said, "I send away the men who come calling, because I don't want to see any of them. Mr. and Mrs. B are happy to discourage them as well, because they need my services. To tell the truth, if it could be like this all the time—with the family away, I think I'd be happy enough just to stay and run the farm."

"What about Evan?" I reminded her. "Could you do without Evan's coming to call so regularly?"

She looked away, and when she looked back her eyes were close to tears but her voice was steady.

"The trouble with Evan," she said, "is that everyone else thinks he is wonderfully successful, when in fact he is bored. Challenge is the one thing that fascinates him . . . that and Mau'loa. Maybe it goes back to his own father, how much he loved the land and the Hawaiian lore."

"His father was out of the pattern, for a haole," I had to agree.

"Yes," True said, "and it killed him. I won't let that happen to Evan."

The determination in her voice frightened me; I did not want to know, yet, what she was thinking about Evan.

She was not expecting my next question: "Do you believe that Liko and Jared . . . that they should belong together?"

She thought about it, and finally she said, "I don't know."

I did not sleep well that night; thoughts came flying into my mind, as the breeze stirred the curtains at my window and sent the branches of the monkeypod tree scraping against the wall. True's words echoed into my dreams, where Liko and Jared laughed as the surf sprayed up all around them, and Evan and Aunt Winona stood on the shore, waving and calling to them to come in, come quickly, trying to make them see a great wall of water, a rogue wave, that was washing in to drown us all.

14

Crosscurrents were in play the night of the party at Rose Plantation. Auntie Momi had talked of them, of how wild forces come together, spinning and mixing and churning in every direction until a path is cut, and you must go with that path.

We were late arriving, what with the milking to finish before we set out and having to bathe—and of course we primped some, braiding our hair with ribbons and flowers—and putting on the new holokus I'd brought for us: True's a mossy green cotton sprigged with stripes of delicate little pink and white flowers; mine a dark blue, with a white collar edged in lace.

I knew True was nervous because she sat so straight, even while leaning out to hold the horse when it shied away from the fire wielded by torch bearers, young Hawaiians with glistening dark bodies which seemed to reflect the fire— strong bodies and quiet faces. I envied them their repose, their calm, their ease in movement.

Liko must have been waiting for us, for he darted out to take the horse, and I heard him whisper to True that Jared needed to see her, right now. I'd never heard Liko speak with such urgency, and it frightened me. Before he could say more, Mr. Mackey was greeting us, and behind him Colonel Toby was smiling broadly, as if he was just ever so happy to see me again.

I thought later that it was something like a play, and our entrance had been perfectly timed—arriving just as Mr. Mackey and the Colonel had all but finished greeting guests. And since we were the last to arrive, they escorted us in to the big room where everyone had gathered—True on Mr. Mackey's arm, me on Colonel Toby's. The two girls from Mana'olana made an entrance which did not go unnoticed.

Evan saw, and so did Jenny, standing beside him, her sharp little chin lifted in defiance. Colonel Toby's wife saw and frowned—not at me, but at True.

"Let's go say hello to Miss Laiana," the Colonel said, steering me towards her. She dismissed me with a quick "oh yes," before she asked the Colonel to go fetch Jared.

"I've been looking for Jared, too," I told her. "I haven't seen him now for six months—since the luau at Ainahau. And it is nice to see you again, Mrs. Wakefield."

But Laiana Wakefield was not in a mood to visit with a schoolteacher from an orphanage. "Excuse me, dear," she murmured, without looking at me, and moved purposefully through the crowd, tall and stately, hips swaying, the orchid in her hair trembling. She made me feel small, so very small. I had no right, no right at all to be here, I thought, and looked quickly around the room for True.

She was talking to Evan and Jenny. "Here you are, Martha," Jenny greeted me, as if we were the best of friends. "I have so wanted to come see you, but young Harry keeps me busy; I scarcely get any peace at all."

"Where is Harry?" I asked, grateful for Jenny's kindness.

"He's gone to bed," True spoke up, disappointed. "I was afraid we'd be too late."

"He'll be up bright and early, if you'd like to make an appointment—at, say, six?" Evan laughed.

Jenny pretended he wasn't joking. "Don't be silly, Evan. The girls will be dancing until the wee hours." To us, she added in a confidential stage whisper, "Evan can't remember what it was like to be young and going to these parties. The Judge is much too serious, don't you agree?"

True laughed politely, but I could only look away. Laiana Wakefield had shown me how insignificant I was, and the idea of dancing defeated me. I coughed to keep from crying.

"Well," True said ruefully, "Jared's asked for my first dance, and Mr. Mackey's promised me the second—so I know I'll be dancing the first two."

Jenny's words came out falsely gay: "Oh, I suspect you'll be dancing more than two dances, True . . . many more. Don't you think so, Evan? A pretty thing like True."

Evan would not let himself be drawn in. "I'm doing as well as True. My first dance is with Miss Belle Winfreed, who is seventy-nine years old today and who took care of me, she tells me, for three weeks before I was a year old. The next is with Miss Martha Moon, standing right here beside me." He tucked his arm in mine. "After that, wife, I'm planning to dance with whatever lady I can talk into taking to the floor with me . . . just to prove how serious I can be."

Jenny laughed. "Then I suppose I'll just have to get in line."

Jared appeared in the far doorway at the end of the large room. Whenever I saw him after a lapse of time, I was struck again by his beauty: tall, with shining dark hair and a sultry, sulky look about him. (How sad, people said, that the Wakefield boys were so handsome and the girls so plain.) True excused herself and started for him.

"Jared Wakefield?" Jenny asked me, her eyebrows arched.

Her insinuation was clear enough to make me cut her off by answering, "Yes, that's Jared all right. I thought you knew him."

Liko was with the musicians, playing a gourd-shaped instrument. He rolled his eyes at me, and I knew that meant he was close to tears. I leaned down to whisper, "Can you get away long enough to tell me what is wrong?"

He shook his head vigorously; my presence unnerved him. I turned away, to find young Rachel Wakefield waiting to speak to me.

"Glory!" I said, both pleased and startled. "I thought you would be in England at school."

"We should be," she told me. "Except Mama can't leave right now." She lowered her voice, "She won't leave Jared."

"Why not?" I asked.

"She's worried that he's going to do something foolish," she said coquettishly.

"Jared hasn't a foolish bone in his body," I said and laughed. "What could he possibly do?"

"Take up with somebody he shouldn't," she answered in a low voice.

My throat constricted, and I couldn't trust myself to speak. *Oh God,* I thought, *how could she possibly know?*

"Are you all right?" Rachel asked, touching my arm as if to steady me.

I was trying to think what to say when Rachel whispered in my ear, "I know she's your best friend, but Mama thinks she's unsuitable for Jared."

"True?" I murmured in amazement, relief flooding through me. She nodded yes. It took all my self-control to keep from bolting to warn True about this curious turn of events. "Your mama is mistaken," I told Rachel, knowing she would repeat what I said. "True and Jared are simply the best of friends, no more."

"If you said that to Mama," the girl said deliberately, "she would tell you that you were under True's spell, too. She believes True is *kahuna 'ana 'ana* . . ."

"She can't," I said, shocked at the notion that anyone could believe True to be a sorcerer, that she practises black magic.

Colonel Toby whirled by, dancing with one of the Wilder girls. Mr. Mackey and True followed their lead, and couple after couple took to the big dance floor that had been laid out on the grassy lawn, under a spreading kiawe tree.

Evan touched my shoulder and said, "Care to dance with a serious old man?"

I held onto his arm as if the currents were pulling me under.

"I have the oddest feeling," I told him as we made our way to the dance floor. "It seems like bad things are happening, just out there past the circle of light."

He smiled his slow smile as we circled the floor and he said, "I've just been telling Harry that there's nothing to fear of the dark, Martha. That's what most people don't know— the biggest, most exciting part of the world exists beyond the circle of light . . ."

"True says so too," I said.

"I'm not surprised," he replied.

The next time I saw True she was standing next to Jared, standing very close so she could hear what he was saying. She listened so intently, and Jared was speaking with such obvious emotion, that I could see how his mother, or Jenny Coulter, might suppose they were taking up with each other.

In fact, Jared was sick at heart. "I don't know why he did it," he told True. "I haven't any idea why Uncle Eben has suddenly decided to leave his half of the farm to me instead of to Pa, but it's made Mama and Pa terrible mad. They were counting on having the whole thing. Uncle's been ill for so long—they say they never doubted that one day the ranch would be theirs, and now they think Uncle has talked me into something. They say he's set me against them, but I never asked for it, True. I never even thought about it. I don't know anything much . . ."

True cut in: "Did your Uncle Eben say why he decided to leave his half of the ranch to you?"

Jared rested his hand on her shoulder and bent his head to hers. *His mother watched, Jenny watched, Liko watched.* Then he said, "Because he believes Pa will end up selling it off, piece by piece, for cash. He thinks maybe I will be able to hold onto some of it. I don't know. I've told Mama and Pa that they don't need to worry . . ."

"Why not just refuse to take it, then?"

Jared lowered his voice. "Mama says I have to take it, because if I don't Uncle might just leave it to somebody else outside of the family. That's when she started talking about it being time for me to get married."

True looked at him, startled. "Married? Who does she want you to marry?"

"Some puly girl who lives over in Hilo. I've hardly even talked to her."

"But why? You're scarcely even twenty, what is this about?"

Jenny Coulter wanted to know what it was about as well. When she could, she placed herself next to Laiana Wakefield and, after some polite conversation, Jenny found a way to ask, "Can we be expecting a Wakefield wedding soon?"

Laiana Wakefield looked at her with regal disapproval, and Jenny became flustered. "I thought . . ." she began. "I noticed that Jared and True Lindstrom . . ."

"No," Jared's mother said firmly. "They are friends, no more—but if rumors are starting, and it seems they are, I suppose it's best that they don't see each other. I thank you for telling me, Jenny."

Jenny's face burned—to have Laiana Wakefield accuse her of spreading rumors was bad enough—but what was worse was realizing how much she wanted True to be safely married.

She excused herself to go look for Evan. *Why can't he stay with me at these parties,* she wondered, feeling the anger rising, *can't he see how hard it is for me to be alone?* She scanned the dance floor, looking for True. She saw her bright hair flashing as she twirled around, and Jenny felt her stomach constrict, until she noted that True's partner was a full-bearded ship's captain from Australia.

By the time Jenny found Evan at the far end of the lanai, deep into conversation with two ranchers from Kauai, the bubble of anger inside of her was ready to burst. "So here you are," she accused him. The ranchers, recognizing trouble, excused themselves.

"What is it?" Evan asked; experience had taught him to keep his voice low.

"I just want you to know that I'm going up to bed."

"It's still early, Jen. Are you worried about Harry? I checked him ten minutes ago, and he is fine. He's sleeping soundly."

"I have a headache, and I'm very tired."

"I'll come with you . . ." he started.

But she stopped him with a cold "No. You stay and enjoy yourself."

She turned and moved quickly away, her fury leaving small ripples in the air. Evan felt the familiar rush of regret and desolation; it happened like this, without warning. He was about to follow her when James Mackey put his hand on his arm.

"Join me for a brandy and a cigar, Evan," he said. "I need a respite from women."

Mackey's study was a sanctuary; it smelled of leather, cigars and men. Evan breathed deeply and took refuge in it. He swirled the brandy in the glass and took a sip. "I can see why some men take to this stuff," he told Mackey. "It goes down warm and easy."

"That it does," Mackey agreed. "Being an old bachelor and having no one to keep count, I've promised myself I'll never drink alone."

"So that's why you shanghaied me just now—you needed a drink," Evan said.

"No, I shanghaied you because I thought you needed one."

Evan frowned and stared into the brandy glass.

"I feel my status of bachelor emeritus gives me certain privileges," Mackey went on in a light tone. "One of these is to offer brandy and a modicum of sympathy when I notice a husband-in-distress."

Evan sat forward, careful now. "In this case I'm afraid it's the wife who deserves the sympathy," he told the older man. "I got to talking to the Kurz brothers about their cattle operation on Kauai, and I forgot where I was and what I was supposed to be doing . . ."

"Yes, yes, that is what husbands do, isn't it? Drift off into fascinating discussions about cows and manure and such and leave their ladies unattended. I suppose that is why I've never married, all those fascinating discussions I might have missed . . ."

Evan sank back in the chair, took a deep draw on his cigar and exhaled a cloud of smoke that circled his head. "Haven't you ever been tempted?" Evan asked.

"Tempted many times, married never," Mackey answered. "Still am, tempted that is, but it's much too late for marriage . . . too late now. A good marriage is rare. I suppose I've only witnessed two or three truly good ones in my lifetime. I'm a gambler, as you know—but with those odds . . . Still, when I see a woman I consider to be a likely candidate . . ."

Evan, surprised at the older man's intimate revelations, could only think to reply with a joking question, "Any of those here tonight?"

"If I were twenty, or even ten, years younger, I'd be thinking hard about Miss True Lindstrom," Mackey confessed, pouring them both another brandy. "She's an interesting mix, those long bones and that luminous skin. A Valkyrie, our True. But the part I like best is that she breaks rules. You've known her for many years, I believe?"

"I first met True when she was twelve or thirteen, I suppose," Evan told him. "I'll never forget it. She was standing on a rock at the edge of the ocean, at a place where the water rushed in with tremendous force. She dived in before I could call out to her. It was dangerous, Christ—challenging the sea like that—but she did it. She won, and I have to say it was something to witness . . ."

"I can see how it would be," James Mackey said.

They sat in an easy silence for a time. And then Mackey leaned forward and quietly asked, "Why did you marry her, son?"

Evan was caught off guard. He stood, very carefully put down the brandy glass and thrust his hands in his pockets.

It was a question he might have expected from tough, blunt Eli Barrows, but not from a sophisticated man like James Mackey.

He decided to give the answer he would have given to Eli. "It seemed to me that Jenny had a clear idea of her place in the world—what she wanted, what should be, how it all worked. She offered me a chance to be part of that world, part of a family, a history. It isn't Jenny's fault that I still have no idea of where I fit, or that I can't seem to stop questioning how things work and that causes problems." He rose and began to pace, putting in sardonically, "I left Davis and Gathers, those good Christian men, because of a foreclosure. An old Hawaiian was about to lose his land—not a lot of land—because he was ten days overdue on a loan. He asked for thirty days more and I gave it to him. I was reprimanded, and the case was taken from me. The old man missed the next payment and lost his land and it was all perfectly legal." He shook his head, as if to clear it.

"My boy," Mackey said, rising to leave with Evan. "Why do you suppose I make my life on this mountaintop?"

Later that night, long after the dancing was done, I told True about my conversation with Rachel.

"Me?" she said, incredulous. "Mrs. Wakefield thinks . . . Jared and me. . . ?" She started laughing, not a real laugh but the kind that is instead of crying.

"Oh, Lord," she finally said, "I see now why . . . how confused things get. How are we ever going to sort them out?"

True was up and dressed for riding early the next morning, with not a sign that she had slept for only a few hours. She looked fresh and happy. "Auntie True is going to give Harry Coulter his first ride," she said. "I can hardly wait to get my arms around his sweet little body."

I lay in bed and looked at her and teased: "Laiana Wakefield thinks you're after her Jared, and Jenny Coulter thinks you're after her Evan, but the sweet little body you want to squeeze belongs to three-year-old Harry!"

She grinned. "He makes Evan's eyes light up, just to talk about him, so how can I not adore little Harry?" She thumbed her nose at me in parting and skipped out the door as excited as if she were going to a fair.

Half an hour later she came back in, her eyes dark as rain clouds and her shoulders slumped in dejection.

"Jenny?" I guessed.

"Oh yes," she said. "Oh yes. Jenny Coulter just threw a royal fit in front of everyone—the hands, Evan, Mr. Mackey, everyone. I was simply sitting on the horse with the child in front of me, not even moving, just sitting. Three-quarters of the people on this island were put on a horse before they were three—all alone! The boys were cheering us on. Harry was making happy noises and Evan was grinning from ear to ear. I was only going to walk around the ring with him, that's all. What is wrong with that woman?"

Jenny appeared in the doorway, her face mottled with anger. "The question you should be asking is what is wrong with you," she said, furious. "You can't seem to leave us alone. Stay away from us, True Lindstrom. Do you hear me? They are mine. Stay away."

She wheeled and left, and True collapsed on my bed, her eyes closed against everything that had gone awry.

Two months later, a week after I had returned to Waikiki and while the Baumgartners were still in Austria, Evan made his scheduled trip to Maui. He had thought he would stay in Lahaina, would not go out to the farm to see True, but in the end he did go. It was important, he told himself, not to let Jenny's accusations infect him. If he did not go to see True, it would be the same as admitting that something improper existed between them.

"Did you go to visit True?" Jenny would ask, her voice high and arch.

"No," he would say.

"I don't believe you," she would answer, or "Is that right?" which meant she did not believe him.

When he arrived at the farm, True was in the corral examining one of the horses' hooves. Her face was sweaty and streaked with dirt. "Somehow, I wasn't really expecting you," she told him as she splashed her face with cold water he pumped for her from the cistern, "not after my fiasco with Harry and Jenny."

"It wasn't your fiasco," he told her, and then he admitted, "I thought about not coming, but then I remembered that the Baumgartners were away and that I might be able to talk you into taking a ride with me. I've an awful urge to get out into the country."

She smiled. "I'll just need to talk to Pono for a minute and saddle up. Let's get you a better mount, too, if we're going to do some real riding."

He interrupted, "James Mackey sent a message into town, asking me to come up for the night. Think you might be able to stay over as well? That way, we can swing around and end our ride there at about sundown."

She thought about it for a moment. "I'd have to be back early in the morning, but yes, I want to see Liko anyway. Mr. Mackey says I'm always welcome, so I guess I'll just test him."

Evan smiled, remembering what Mackey had said about True.

"Why are you grinning?" she asked, then answered by saying, "I hope it's because you are just plumb happy to get off a judge's bench and onto a horse." Within half an hour, she had them saddled up and ready to leave.

"Follow me," True said, setting off at a trot. "I'm going to show you some countryside that will make you cry, it's so beautiful."

They rode without speaking for an hour, she a few paces ahead of him. He allowed himself to feel the roll of the land, the sharp bright green of it. He breathed it in through his nostrils, his pores; he could raise his head into the clouds that billowed and shifted in the sky. He matched his horse's gait to hers, their bodies rose and fell in rhythm. He studied her straight back, the strong thin rise of her neck, the ease of her shoulders. When he looked at her even now, he could see a child standing on a rock at the edge of the ocean, filled with resolve, a child who rejected pity. He tried to see her as James Mackey saw her, but he could not. He had known her too long, had thought of her as a younger sister. No, that wasn't right, not as a sister. He thought of her with the same fascination he had seen in his father when he was tracking a remarkable new species of butterfly. As they climbed higher and the sun slanted low, the land and the sky merged and enclosed and claimed him. True was right; he wanted to cry, it was so beautiful.

* * *

"I believe in God again," James Mackey told them. "Two of my favorite people, in my hour of need. It can get to be bloody boring on this mountaintop, if all you have to talk to are the cows."

Dinner was animated; Evan caught them up on political events in Honolulu, and True and Mackey talked about the current drought and how it was going to affect the herds. The three of them vied to hold the floor, spoke over each other, laughed and apologized and said, "You first." When the clock struck ten, True gasped. "I had no idea. That's what happens when I get drunk with good company. Good night, good night, dear gentlemen. I must be up with the dawn. No, no, stay and finish your coffee. Have a cigar, do what men do when the ladies leave. Someday, when I'm not so sleepy, I'm going to ask to join you in that inner sanctum. Evan, if I don't see you tomorrow . . ."

"I've some business with James in the morning, but I'll stop by for my horse about midday."

"Yes, good. And thank you, dear Mr. Mackey, for taking me in." He stood to take both of her hands in his, his grasp telling her how happy he was to have her. She kissed him on one cheek and then the other and touched Evan's shoulder as she left the room.

The men sat in silence, as if True's departure had drained them, left them empty. Finally the older man spoke, his voice echoing with discovery: "How long have you loved her?"

A full six months after my return to Waikiki, Jenny finally accepted one of Aunt Winona's invitations to tea. Their friendship had waned after Jenny's marriage. Aunt had never been invited to the big new home they had moved into on Beretania Street, with quarters for Jenny's mother, and her feelings were hurt, though she would not admit it.

Aunt greeted Jenny with a rush of words, about how grateful we all were to Evan for helping Mana'olana through a difficult time, about how much she had hoped Jenny would bring little Harry along, and what a pity he couldn't come— she hoped Jenny wasn't still worried that he might catch something from the children—how well Jenny was looking, though in fact she had an unhealthy pallor to her skin.

Jenny sighed and sank into a chair on the lanai. "Ten

years," she said. "I was thinking about that the other day. It's been ten—almost eleven—years since we came out here, Evan and Kaiulani and I. It seems like another lifetime."

"It was, in a way," I spoke for the first time. "Certainly for Vicky it was. She is coming home now to a different world . . ."

"And no kingdom—poor Kaiulani."

She seemed so downcast that I felt a surge of pity for Jenny Coulter. I thought of what Evan had said about the circle of light and what lay beyond it; Evan must have understood that Jenny could not go there, that she never would.

"We've just heard that Kaiulani will be home before Christmas," I said, though I hadn't intended to, since the governor had just that day told us. "Her pa has almost finished the new house at Ainahau as a coming-home surprise—it's very grand, don't you think?"

"Kaiulani was always very grand, compared to the rest of us. Papa was always having to give them money for this and that. He was very generous to the monarchy, even when they were frivolous . . ." Jenny said, and I wanted to bite my tongue for having confided in her. She went on, "She's going to have to learn to live without those pretensions."

"She wasn't pretending," I said tartly, allowing my anger to surface. "To the Hawaiians she will always be royalty; nothing can change that."

"She always was very much the little princess," Aunt Winona put in, wanting to make Jenny feel better and at the same time not say anything against Vicky.

"I know," Jenny went on in her tired voice. "The Hawaiians call her their 'last hope.' How awful to be anyone's last hope! It doesn't really matter how well meaning we are, don't you see?" Jenny came back, "White men have always triumphed over dark men. It's no different here than anyplace else. White men take the land and rule, no matter the right or wrong of it, no matter what. It's a fact of life, a force of nature. We can't stop it, so why shouldn't we try to work to make that takeover as nice as possible, instead of flinging ourselves against the winds and the ocean tides and trying to stop what can't be stopped? The monarchy is done; it is all over."

"Is this what Evan believes?" Aunt asked, timidly.

"Oh, Evan." Jenny threw up her hands, sending a spoon

whirling on her saucer. "I've stopped trying to make sense of what Evan believes."

Evan's work load at the court in Lahaina had been lighter than usual, and for that he was sorry. Had it been heavy, he could have avoided going out to the Baumgartner farm, and he did not want to go. Still, he had the better part of the day free, and he had promised Toby, and he had promised the luna's ohana. God, he said to himself, he hated this. She didn't deserve this kind of anguish. But he had to do it, not for them but for True. Somebody had to tell her, to make her understand; somebody had to protect her, and he knew no one else he could trust.

He hired a horse and rode out to the Baumgartner farm, arriving late in the morning. To his relief, he found True alone on the lanai. She did not rise to meet him; instead she wrapped her arms around herself and called out, "I knew if I sat here and concentrated hard enough, I could make you appear."

"Ah ah!" he laughed, awkwardly. "Watch what you say. I could be called as a witness if you are ever prosecuted for practising black magic."

She winced. "Ouch," she said, "you've been talking to Mrs. Wakefield. She's convinced I'm about to steal away her baby boy. She's been keeping Jared so close we haven't even heard from him in months . . ."

For a minute, Evan could not think what to say. Finally he settled for a weak question, "Who is we?"

"Liko and me. Jared writes to us both, usually every week—but not at all lately. I can't help but think something is going on, but there's no way to find out."

"Something is going on. That's why I'm here, one of the reasons. Colonel Toby came to talk to me about his brother's will," Evan offered.

"I know about the will," she said.

"That's what I understand," he came back.

She looked at him sharply. He wanted to be straightforward. Toby had put him in an awkward position, more awkward than he could know. "Did you know that Eben Wakefield died ten days ago? And that the Wakefields *are* afraid of you?"

She frowned. "No, I had not heard and I'm sorry. I liked

Uncle Eben, he was kind to me. But afraid? What do you mean?"

"Toby came to talk to me, and asked me to talk to you. Jared now owns half of Mau'loa, at least by law. You're right. They do think you have designs on Jared. But what really worries them—Laiana, mostly, I believe—is that if you should marry Jared, you might not be willing to defer to them," he told her. "You seem to have made an impression on Uncle Eben when Jared took you there. The story is that you asked so many questions about the ranch that Uncle ran out of answers."

"Whose story?"

"Eben's and Jared's."

She thought about that for a while. "What did you tell the Colonel?"

She could see how uncomfortable he was. "No, wait," she said, stopping him. "First maybe I should ask you why you agreed to plead their case with me."

"I am not pleading their case," he answered. "I told Toby that I would prefer not to become involved in this kind of discussion. But at the same time, if somebody is to do it, I want it to be someone with your best interests in mind."

"What makes them think I would have the slightest interest in marrying Jared?"

Evan looked away. "I don't know, but they do seem to think so. They've been trying to get Jared interested in a girl in Hilo—and he won't have anything to do with her because, Toby says, it's clear Jared has taken up with somebody here on Maui."

"And they think it must be me?" she asked. "What do you think about me and Jared?"

Evan frowned; he clasped his hands, then unclasped them. "I think you would be the best thing that could happen to just about any man . . . and to Mau'loa."

She stared at him until he looked at her. Then she smiled. "Thank you," she said, wanting to touch him so badly she had to clasp her own hands together. "Thank you very much for that, Evan." She could feel her throat closing. She coughed to clear it, stood, and walked away from him.

He stood as well, moving beside her to look out on the broad lawn, leaving an arm's space between them. *Maintain a distance,* he told himself. "I told the Colonel that it didn't seem to me that Jared was ready for marriage."

"What made you say that?" she came back, so quickly that Evan heard the worry in her voice, and began to sense a pattern to her questions.

He had to think. "I don't know. He just seems like a boy, like the kind of boy who may not . . . I can't say why, but there is something about Jared that isn't . . ."

"You are full right," she broke in, trying to keep her voice steady. "Jared doesn't want to marry anyone, ever, but his parents were right about one thing—he *is* taken with someone on this island."

Evan looked at her, puzzled. He didn't know what she was trying to tell him.

She took a deep breath. "He loves Liko. I wanted to tell you, to ask for your help."

"Liko . . . Liko?" was all he could manage.

She turned away from him.

"God, True," he said and began to pace, running his hands through his thick hair, now and then stopping to look out to the woods, though she knew he wasn't looking outward at all, but thinking. She waited and watched. His absorption pleased her; she could study him all she wanted—the way his shirt clung to the small of his back, the fine blond hair on his forearms, how he put his hands on his hips while he thought—more like a cowboy, she thought, than a judge—a man for the outdoors, trapped inside.

"Let's go for a ride," she said, suddenly. "I need to talk to you, to ask for your help. Liko can't stay at Rose Plantation much longer. Mr. Mackey has told him he will have to leave. I've been going wild trying to think what to do."

"True, I don't know what to say. I don't. I can go have a talk with James Mackey, if you think . . ."

Mackey's words flashed into his mind then: *How long have you loved her?* But he had been wrong, it wasn't love Evan felt for True. It was something else, and he couldn't name it any more than he could name the surge of power he had felt when he saw her that first time, arched over the water, or in the race on True's Surprise, her hair flying out from her cap.

"No," she said. "No. Don't talk to Mr. Mackey. There's nothing to be done. I guess I knew that all along. It just seemed like . . ."

He shook his head. "I'm sorry," he said. "For you, and for Liko and Jared, I wish it wasn't like that . . ."

"They aren't 'like' anything except themselves," she said with an edge of anger in her voice. "Just please forget I ever told you. You will forget?"

"I won't forget," he said, "but I won't say anything. I wouldn't hurt them, True."

She nodded and reached to touch his arm. "I know that. I do."

They stood side by side without saying anything for a time. The breeze shifted, tossing the branches of the plumeria tree until the blossoms covered a large patch of green lawn. One blew against Evan; he picked it up and studied the glossy white petals, the pale yellow center. He leaned against the railing, locked in thought. Finally he turned, as if he had made a decision.

"You said something about taking a ride. This seems to be a day for hard issues. There was another reason I came out to see you today. The man who was accused of your mother's murder, the luna," he began slowly, speaking carefully, as if he were presenting a client's case, "his wife and his son and daughter have been coming to see me. They come every time I'm on the island, I am sure because they know I see you. You know how that is, everybody knows where everybody else is, it seems like."

He cleared his throat, and then he said, "They have brought me such convincing evidence that I am inclined to agree with them that the case should be reopened."

She began, slowly, to shake her head. No. No. No. She closed her eyes.

"Listen to me, True. They want to clear his name. It was a bad thing that happened, and they seem to be paying for it just like you. They can't find work."

"Is that my fault?" she snapped, not wanting to talk, wanting him to stop.

"Of course it isn't your fault. You've been hurt and they know that. But they are convinced that you saw the man who did kill your mother, and that makes you—in their eyes—the one person who can clear their father." He paused, shook his head. "They also think their father's spirit cannot rest."

"I suppose they are good Christians?" she mocked.

He didn't answer, but said instead, "Three Hawaiians saw you standing in the doorway of the little house. They say you were talking to someone. No one saw who it was. They only saw you. If you can tell us who it was, it will clear their father."

"I don't remember, Evan, why can't you believe me when I say I cannot remember?"

"I believe you, True. I've told the family that I believe you. But they think," he pressed on, "that if you come, go through the house, see it again with the kahunas that you might be able to remember."

"No," she said, "oh, no, no."

"True," he said, "I wouldn't ask you to do this if I didn't think court action would be more painful for you. I can't deny them a hearing. They understand how hurt you have been by this, but they are hurt, too. Remember, they lost their father."

"He killed himself, after he killed my mother," she tried, but her voice was weak.

He told her, "I don't think you believe that." He waited a minute, then he added, "My appointment on this court is almost finished, and I won't renew it. That means I will be making only one more trip, and I want to be the one to do this with you, True."

Now she looked out to the woods, breathed deeply of the eucalyptus. "Do you know how long I've been trying to erase the memory of my mother . . . in her bed . . . all the blood . . ." She took a deep breath; he could see the rise of her breasts under the fabric of her dress. "But the luna was good to me, and so was his wife. I played with Loki and Kaeo. They were my friends. Sometimes I stayed with them, when someone came to be with Mama . . ."

"Was someone there that night, True?"

He leaned forward, looking so directly into her eyes that she could not look away.

She took a long time to answer, and when she spoke, her words were scarcely a whisper.

"Sometimes I think so, but I can't be sure, and I don't know who . . . in my dreams . . ." She gave in: "Can we do it now? Right now?"

"Yes," he said, "we can go now."

* * *

They rode in silence. He looked at her long slender fingers, rough from hard work and the sun. She had been a fierce girl, and she had become an amazing woman. She was not afraid. But what then kept her from the house where her mother was murdered? Bad dreams, was that it? When Harry had bad dreams, the child would creep quietly past his mother's bed, to come into the room where Evan slept alone. Jenny didn't like it, when Harry came into bed with him. "I won't allow him to come into my bed," she had said, "and you shouldn't either." He wondered if Harry had gone to her bed first, had been turned away. Like father, like son, he thought; he shifted in his saddle to rid himself of the thoughts. Jared and Liko moved into his mind and he shut them out. No, he told himself. He wouldn't allow Harry to come into his bed again. Jenny was right.

They rode another hour, across wide green pastures, along narrow paths that looked far out to the sea, through a stand of eucalyptus trees where they stopped to breathe in the sharp air. By the time they arrived at what once had been a clearing around the farmhouse, the luna's ohana had gathered and were waiting. Loki and Kaeo and their mother stood apart from the others, solemn, sad.

Evan dismounted, but True did not. He saw that her eyes were wild—in a moment she would spur the horse and be off. He put both hands up to her, she looked at them for a long moment, as if trying to understand what he wanted her to do. She allowed him to lift her off the horse. He kept his arm around her waist for support, not so much worried that she would fall but that she would bolt. They had come too far to go back; he counted on her to realize it.

She steadied herself, moved away from him. She tried to smile at Loki. "She's grown up," she whispered to Evan.

"So are you. See how they look at you? They can't believe you, either." Her breathing was shallow, coming in little gasps. The Hawaiians, silent, cleared a path for them to the old house, empty now for a dozen years. Morning glory vines trailed over what had been the lawn; they strangled the lanai and were creeping into the house itself. The woods were taking back the old place; soon it would tumble and return to the land.

A woman's voice lifted in resonant, melodic Hawaiian: the luna's wife, chanting. True felt cold, but she could not turn back. She had come and now she must finish it. What could it matter? she had asked herself a thousand times. What could possibly happen if she came here, did what they asked? They took my mother in when the others would have nothing to do with us. Our luna held me above the waves and carried me on his shoulders, and Loki put flowers between my toes and laughed with me . . .

I should not have come, I should not, she told herself, clamping her teeth hard, biting the inside of her mouth so that blood trickled out.

Evan stopped, grimacing in the high sun and the full afternoon heat. He removed a handkerchief from his pocket and dabbed at the blood. When he was done, she clutched the handkerchief in her hand and moved ahead.

The kahunas were waiting, their faces old and wrinkled. She heard their voices lift in the chant. She entered the house by the door they had never used, the parlor door, hanging awry now, perpetually open. The windows were all broken, the pretty little panes her father had fitted in so carefully. The panes she and her mother washed and polished, one of them on either side—a game, follow my hand, round and round—until they gleamed. Shards of glass lay in dust, under the first tendrils of the creeper vines.

They walked carefully, Evan holding her hand. Most of the furniture was gone, even the portrait of her Swedish grandmother, her mother's mother—"mormor"—which had hung on the east wall. Now all she could see was the oval outline of where it had been.

In the dining room, where she had slept on a cot in the corner, she stooped to pick up a piece of blue and white pottery. Evan knelt with her. "My mother's teapot," she whispered, nestling the bit of pottery in her hand. "We had tea together, and pretended it was snowing outside, except I couldn't remember what it was like, snow."

She put her hands over her ears, to shut out the sounds of the chanting. Through the open window she could see Loke, with her thrusting forehead and massive body, covered now by a muumuu. No longer young, never pretty. Poor Loke. *Pretty is as pretty does,* her mother's voice said, so clear she felt her heart lurch inside her.

She stepped into the room where her mother had slept. Her mother and her father, when he was home . . . and the others, who had come to warm their hands in her mother's light.

"I can't," she told him, attempting to turn away, but he was guiding her, his hand on the small of her back, gently, very gently moving her into the room. The bed stood: there was a brown mark on the canvas strips, her mother's blood.

The sound started in the back of her head, roared into the front, like the sound of the waves rushing into the sea caves and out again. Something soft and round began to move inside of her—trees in shadow and light, moonlight, bright. And there looking at her, the knife in his hand and horror on his face. *O gode Gud, forlat me,* he had said in the tongue of his motherland, *O gode Gud, forlat me.* The sound came ripping up through her dry throat, spilled out into the hot and empty room: a scream, one long shrill scream.

The chanting stopped; silence lay over them, thick and suffocating.

She slumped against Evan. "My father . . ." she whispered into his chest. "It was my father . . ."

15

Kaiulani returned on the SS *Australia;* it arrived at Oceanic wharf on the ninth of November 1897, but True and I did not go down to meet it. Everyone else was there—great crowds of Hawaiians waited for hours on the wharf, waiting to see the girl who might have been queen. The Governor asked True and me to stay at Ainahau. He wanted us to be on the lanai to greet her—he wanted this homecoming to be as perfect as he could make it. Poor man. He had built a wonderful new house as a surprise, but it was a sad substitute for the loss of a kingdom. Vicky had been away for nine long years—we had changed, each of us had changed. True and I sat waiting in the big wicker chairs on the lanai, saying little, uneasy.

"I want to see her," True said, as if I had accused her of not wanting to see Vicky.

Irritated, I answered, "And so do I," adding what I knew she was thinking: "Vicky was twenty-two last month. I wish I could stop thinking about it."

We have been testy, True and I, since her arrival from Maui two days ago.

"That was pure foolishness," True said. "Vicky's mother wasn't in her right mind, so she couldn't know . . ." She stood and began to pace. "I wish I could have wrung her neck before she had a chance to say it," she added fiercely.

I sighed. "It is time you told me about the trouble with Liko."

She took so much time to answer that I was about to erupt. Finally she said, "Liko is miserable. He's so frightened he can hardly speak above a whisper."

She moved to a place on the lanai where she had a view of the drive leading into Ainahau and went on, "I don't know what happened . . . maybe nothing. It looks as if Evan has found Liko a place with a family—the Cassidys, who live on a farm out near Hana. They have five daughters, so Liko is needed to help with the chores in return for his keep. There has been some sort of financial settlement made by Mr. Mackey—he is a kind man, but he is also a businessman and a rancher. I suppose he is trying to avert any problems. I know Evan had a talk with him, but I don't know what was said—I haven't seen Evan. I understand he is away now, so we can't ask him. I'm not sure he would tell me, anyway. I do know that the Cassidys are supposed to be a lively family, and that it should be a happy place for Liko, though it is isolated and harder for me to get to. But the Cassidys say they will let Liko come stay with me once a month."

"And Jared—have you spoken to him?"

"No, his mother makes sure of that. Once he wrote and asked if he could visit me. The B's were happy to receive him—a Wakefield in their home, you know—but then he wrote and said he couldn't come after all. I suppose his mother said no."

"All the Wakefields should be here this week, to welcome Vicky," I said.

"Maybe I'll have a chance to speak to him. Liko gets letters, but he thinks Jared is afraid his mother reads them, they say so little," she answered, rising, her voice quickening with excitement. "Here comes the first of them. There's the carriage with Vicky. Oh, Martha, there she is, look at her . . . let's go see our girl."

Her eyes were huge and dark and flickered back and forth, as if trying to take in everything at once. She greeted us with a certain strained formality, but she held hard to our hands, not letting go, as if to say that words didn't matter, not yet. We toured the house with her, and she made appropriate little gasps of pleasure at each new room, still holding so hard that my hand was growing numb.

"Papa says that Fairy is out in the pasture," she told us in a small, breathless voice with an unmistakable English accent, and we followed her out back, where the old white pony was waiting. She slipped onto his back and rode, ever so slowly, around the enclosure.

Vicky had become a tall, wistful woman with dark eyes too large for her face. She was as fragile as the rare and beautiful night-blooming flowers that her father grew. Her homecoming dress was of delicate white linen batiste with a high collar trimmed in French lace.

When she clammered off of Fairy's back, the old Hawaiian who tends the horses was so overcome that he bowed so low I thought for a moment he intended to prostrate himself. In a queenly gesture, Vicky touched his shoulder and said a few quiet words, and the man rose with a beatific smile on his face.

We had not altogether understood the affection the Hawaiians held for their royals, or the burden it imposed on them. But Vicky had known from the beginning, and she knew it now. The weight of it sank heavy on her, you could see. The fact that the Mission Boys and their Republic and the United States of America did not recognize her kingdom did not erase it.

That afternoon Vicky moved among the hundreds of old friends who had gathered on the lawn at Ainahau. Now and then she would look for us, and smile, and raise her hand as if to say, "Just wait."

When she was finally able to get away, she told us, "I brought an English saddle with me—I've become oh, so proper, you know," she said and laughed at herself. "Will you go riding with me on the beach? I've dreamed of that all these years—of galloping down the beach, water flying every which way like we used to do."

True laughed. "Will you insist on winning?" she asked.

"No longer," Vicky said. "What a horrid little thing I must have been—how did you ever abide me?"

"We didn't," True told her, for the first time slipping her arm around Vicky's waist. "You thought it was England that turned you into a lady, when really it was us. Martha and Liko and me."

"Couldn't Liko come?" she said. "He used to be so fond of me. I thought he would be here."

True didn't look at me. "He couldn't get away from work. Working people are poor, you know."

"Not only working people," she said and sighed. "I had to plead to get Aunt Liliuokalani to give Pa the job of Governor; otherwise we couldn't have made ends meet. I'm glad to be home, so he doesn't have to go begging to the Treasury to keep me in England."

"We're glad you've come home, too," I told her. "You're badly needed, you know."

"Needed?" she said, for the first time allowing the sadness we sensed in her to surface. "I think not. No. Too late for that, for need. There's nothing I can do now. Sometimes I think I was born for mourning."

"Born for morning?" True said deliberately. "For galloping down the beach at sunup, you mean?"

Vicky laughed. "I should have remembered what little patience you have for pathos."

True stayed on at Ainahau for one month, her first time away from the Baumgartner ranch in the four years she had been there. I spent as much time as I could with them, but in a way I was relieved that it was True who was with Vicky constantly that first month. Perhaps it was the color of my skin, perhaps it was Auntie Momi's stories, but something deep and sad in Kaiulani seemed to seep inside of me, and there were times when I felt I could not bear it.

In those weeks, True and Vicky took off for long rides together, packing along a picnic as we used to do, and soon enough talk came easy to them. One day, on a ride into the mountains, they stopped at an abandoned cabin and spread their lunch on a table left behind, under an ohia tree. Perhaps it was the cabin that brought it all back so vividly, but True found herself telling Vicky about the day Evan had taken her to her old home, to discover her mother's murderer.

"Your father?" Vicky said, her eyes wide.

"No one knew he was in the Islands," True explained. "He was supposed to be on a lumber schooner on the Oregon coast. I waited for him to come for me. I knew it would take time. I waited and waited, but he didn't come back. An older Christian couple in Lahaina had taken me in. One night I heard them arguing. I remember the man saying that my father probably wasn't coming back because my mother had been a profligate woman. And his wife said that maybe he wasn't coming back, because I wasn't his child."

Vicky did not know what to say, so she pressed her forehead against True's cheek.

"The world is so sad," Vicky said. "Do you see how poor the natives look? They were so tall and beautiful, and now they seem so destitute. And Aunt is off to Washington to beg from white men who know nothing about us, nothing at all. We've made such a mess of it."

"Who has made a mess of it—who are you talking about?"

"All of us—from Kaahumanu on . . ." suddenly Vicky blurted. "Can't I please be honest with you, at least? Mama said once I wouldn't marry. I don't know how she knew, but she was right. Having children does not in the least interest me. The only thing that interests me is what I was trained to do. I think I might have been an effective queen. I might have given our people a voice in the future of the Islands, but of course that's no longer a possibility."

They rode home in silence, stopping now and then to look out over the land, over the cane fields green and blowing, to the far distance where rain fell, casting ribbons of color high in the sky. Vicky offered, "The only thing that hasn't changed is the land, the awful beauty of this place."

"Come," she called, spurring her horse, "I'll race you to the road!"

"Wait, stop," True called, laughing. "It's too rough, you could fall."

But Vicky was already crashing down the path, throwing up dust, and as True slapped her mount into action, she felt a well of excitement rising in her.

There is a sameness to our days, to the weeks and months and years; the ocean waves roll into the shores, the trade winds blow, the palm trees sway, the sun shines, and the rain falls in timeless, lulling patterns. Over the centuries, the islands have lifted from the ocean floor, have known nature's change, but the change is slow to come, and we do not see it.

Until the mountain erupts, throwing fire into the sky, turning night into day. Or the ocean empties our shores, as if the tide has gone out and out and out, leaving fishes flopping on the dry sea bed. And then it comes rushing in again with a sound and a fury you will never forget, a massive wall of water, in and in and in, the ocean rushing up into the streets of the towns, washing away all before it, dragging it out to sea. Or the winds come, not the gentle trades but fearsome winds, shrieking and snapping the tops from the coco palms, blowing so hard it lifts the natives' huts

and scatters the pili grass over the island, so hard the steeple
topples from the church, the roof is ripped from the stable
and the rain slashes in, with the wind fierce in its fury.

In the spring and summer of the year 1898, the lulling
rhythms of our days would be interrupted and our Islands
changed forever, not by any violent act of nature, but by a
series of acts of man—violent in their way, which would
reverberate into all of our futures.

In March, the Committee on Foreign Relations of the
U.S. Senate reported favorably on the resolution to annex
Hawaii. On May 17, the House of Representatives agreed.
For the first time, it seemed that the United States was
willing to accept the Islands so long thrust at it by the
Mission Boys.

There was a reason for this sudden, major shift in opinion.
In April, the United States had declared war on Spain. On
the first of May, while the attention of the citizens of the U.S.
was trained on Theodore Roosevelt and his Rough Riders in
Cuba, Admiral Dewey was sinking the Spanish fleet in Manila harbor, and the Philippines came under the flag of the
United States of America.

Suddenly, Honolulu must have seemed the perfect stepping stone to the Philippines and the South Pacific. On June
1, troop ships carrying American soldiers to the Philippines
arrived at Honolulu. They were welcomed joyfully by all
who had worked and prayed for annexation—not a majority
of the people, almost none of the natives, but most of those
who were allowed to vote in our erstwhile Republic.

On June 15, the U.S. House of Representatives passed the
resolution calling for annexation of the Hawaiian Islands. It
was only a matter of weeks before the Senate would agree,
before it would become law, before the Hawaiian Islands
would become part of the United States of America.

Queen Liliuokalani remained in Washington, waiting and
praying that all her good friends in the Congress would come
to her aid, but her prayers were not to be answered. It was
done; we all knew it. Vicky knew it. She grew irritable with
those who insisted on giving her hope. "There is none," she
would say. She has become increasingly dismayed with
Honolulu, with the arrogance of the faction that rules. She
is restless and is beginning to accept invitations from friends
on the other islands. I cannot but think of Liholiho,

Kamehameha's first son, who wandered from island to island to escape the burden of rule. Kauilani wanders now because she has lost it.

In May, even as Admiral Dewey was dispatching the Spanish armada, Evan Coulter sat in the room that served as court chambers in Lahaina, hearing the last case of the day, which was to be his last case on the island of Maui. When it was done, he signed a large number of documents, said good-bye to the clerk and several officials who had gathered in the crowded chambers, and walked slowly over to the stable, where he would hire a horse to ride out to the Baumgartner place.

"Hear you're leaving us, Judge," the stable boy said as he brought out the grey mare that he knew Evan favored.

"That's right," Evan told him, "and I'm going to miss this old girl. She's given me some good rides."

"I wish all the masters who hire her could ride as good. So does she, I expect."

The mare wanted to leave at a fast trot, but on this day Evan was in no hurry and held her back. He was trying to work it through in his mind, True's place in his life. He had felt responsible for her from the beginning. It was not an unwelcome responsibility, never onerous. She must have sensed that, must have known that he wanted to help her. *Could he have sensed, when he took the letter from her father, that he was becoming a participant in the family's tragic history? In that one moment, could his taking True to her home to name her father as the murderer of her mother and the luna have been preordained?*

He pondered this question as he climbed the green hills; he paused on a rise and looked out at the shimmering sea. He knew that they were intertwined, True and he, caught up together as seaweed can catch you. That wasn't right either—he did not feel caught, or tightly bound. Even as a child, she had fascinated him. He had always been glad to see her, but the idea of not seeing her had never pained him. Until now. He stopped his horse and sat, perfectly still for a long minute. For this past year, at least, he had been measuring time between these visits. He came alive in Lahaina. Correction: He felt alive when he was with True Lindstrom. Jesus God, why hadn't he admitted it?

* * *

Because you are a married man, he answered himself grimly. Because it would mean that Jenny was right, had been right all along. A week ago she had clenched her teeth in the way she did when she was seething with anger—so you knew she would be screaming if she wasn't worried about the servants hearing—and she had accused him of continuing in the position of circuit judge long after it was to his benefit because he wanted to see True Lindstrom. In Jenny's mouth, her name had become a curse.

He had learned not to answer Jenny when she clenched her teeth and screamed at him silently. He knew she would not hear what he had to say. After a time, he admitted, he no longer cared about making her understand. Maybe he was at fault, for not caring, for never caring enough about Jenny to make things right. She had been a soft girl, capable of laughter once. No more: Fear and anger had made her sharp and with a meanness that he did not like to admit. What he wanted now was peace in the house for the boy. Harry had become pale and silent. At times it almost seemed like Harry was frightened of him.

What was closer to the truth was that Harry was afraid of almost everything. Flying bugs, a feisty rooster, the dark. Evan's father had taken him into the thick green woods and made him feel safe, but he had not found a way to do that for his son. Jenny had been furious the few times he had tried. He thought of Harry sitting in front of True on the horse . . . the small, shy smile until his mother appeared, screaming at them. He had been embarrassed for her, more than for himself. He knew that if he continued to give Jenny her way, it would be Harry who suffered. It was that, more than anything, that had made him decide on another course of action. One that would necessarily end these trips to Lahaina.

He stopped at a stand of royal palms, planted long ago to mark the home of an alii, and knelt to drink from a spring that ran in rivulets down to the sea. He held water to his eyes, which burned from a lack of sleep. James Mackey's words surfaced again—he could not seem to keep them buried. *How long have you loved her?* He didn't think he knew what it meant, to love a woman. He had loved his father, and he loved his son. He could look at the boy and feel a sweet tenderness in the center of him, rising to catch in his throat. He had not felt it with Jenny. Maybe she knew, maybe that was how he had failed her. What he felt for True was something else, a fascination or maybe just admiration, in the way she met the challenge. Her banishment to the Baumgartners had been a challenge—flung at her by Jenny, in a spirit of spite. Is that why he had continued to see True? No, he couldn't blame Jenny for that. Had he taken the circuit judge position in part because of True? He didn't think so, but he couldn't be sure.

It didn't matter, because she had met the challenge, had won. His regret at giving up these visits to Maui was more than True. It was being able to get away from Honolulu, the meetings and the talk, the incessant talk, so much of it needless. The petty squabbles and the power lust. He stayed away from the politics of power as much as he could, trying his best to navigate around the edges of it. And that just seemed to make them want to pull him in, as if they couldn't tolerate his standing apart. Out here, riding the slow, easy slopes of Haleakala on a good, strong mare he could breathe easy; he could forget for a time.

He did not want to stop seeing True, but he had to. For her sake and for Harry's. And because he had been waking in the hours before dawn with images flashing on the back of his eyelids: True, astride him as he brought her out of the chasm all those years ago. He felt again the engorged heat of his desire as she moved to position herself over him. His eyelids, hot with memory, flashed to the day he had made her go back to her mother's house. She had held hard to him, her fingers tight on his arm. She had trusted him. Sobbing, the heat of her tears wetting his shirt, her hands trembling in his. He had wanted to draw her into him, to comfort her by absorbing her. He had wanted to gather all her hurt into him from within; the surge of heat he felt was kindled by some glowing coal. He had locked it all away for a long time, had avoided looking at it, admitting it existed—that he wanted to touch her, to hold her. He saw her again, at the heiau on Mau'loa, telling him not to marry Jenny. Anger blew in on him—at her, at himself. He had allowed this to go on too long, he had gone too far, he had to leave. And he had to tell her—he owed her that. God. He owed her more than that, for careening into her life as he had, for allowing them to be caught up together, for not pushing her away when it might have saved them both.

Baumgartner was standing by the gate, his face red in the heat, his shirt splotched with sweat. He squinted up at Evan and directed a stream of chewing tobacco out of the side of his mouth before he spoke. "She's off," he said, his voice thick. "Mad as hell and I don't know to where she's gone. I tell her this is no boarding house, she can't have that dwarf coming here no more every month, another mouth to feed. Let the Irishers feed him. Why should I? She starting to think she runs this place, can bring people in . . ."

Evan only looked at the man, his repulsion so great that he wondered if he could trust himself to speak. "Did she leave the island?" he asked.

She had not left the island, but she had taken off down the road, the man said, walking like she was never going to stop. Evan noted a hint of worry. The bastard knew how much his sorry family needed True.

"You find her, Judge, bring her back," Baumgartner called after him, grudgingly. Evan knew where True would be—they had walked once to a pool created by a small waterfall deep inside an overgrown canyon, where great banyan trees formed a high canopy, and birds flickered through the pale green light. It was where she went, she had told him once, when she needed to get away from everyone. Her safe place, she had said. It took more than an hour to get there on foot; he rode as far as he could, then he tied the mare to a bush and plunged into the thick growth, a canopy of trees covered over with thick-skinned tropical plants and twisting vines. Mosquitoes flew about his head, into his eyes and mouth. He pushed on, hanging onto the vines in places where he slipped on the slick slopes, jumping over small streams until he found the path and heard, for the first time, the sounds of the waterfall.

She was in the pool, screened from him by the fall. He could see her face, shining in the green light. Bird sounds punctuated the quiet, and a tiny yellow bird flickered down and rested on a tree near her, observing. True stared at Evan, but she did not speak. He looked, at her face, at her breasts white in the scattered light, shadows playing on them. She did not change her expression, did not move. She met his eyes and did not turn away.

There was no thought in it, no contemplation. He removed his clothes deliberately, as if that had been the rhythm of it all along, as if the music had been written long ago in preparation. He stepped into the pool, into the water. The cold caught his chest, the spray his face. He swam as if to push the water out of the way, moving to her, never taking his eyes off her. As he crossed under the fall, the water rained down on him, poured onto his face, into his eyes and mouth, and then he was with her, was touching her, holding her, and he gave himself over to an iridescence that exploded in his head—and did not think, because he knew there was never anything he could have done to stop it.

He moved his hands down her thighs, pressed her close, breathed her into him, and she came as if she knew every small corner of his body, every crease and rise of bone, her fingertips on old scars, and on his lips, and in his mouth and her laughter bubbling in his, meshing and holding in tiny gulps, as if they could at last assuage their long hunger. The drought was over; the water splashed down on them, to their core; they opened themselves to it and were revived; they would live and bloom.

She spread her drying sheet, lay down and pulled him onto her. He held her face in his hands and looked into it, and the tenderness came flooding up and out of him and spilled over into a glow so that he felt in his ears and behind his eyes the sweetness of the curve of her back, his tongue on the pink of her breasts, his hand in the warm wetness between her legs. He felt the throb and motion of her . . . the luminosity . . .

She moved to pull him into her, she wanted to feel him hard inside of her again, reaching, reaching for the center. She wanted to explode inside of him once more, to feel all the colors shatter, to know . . .

"I love you, True," he said, breathing the words into her ear. And then he whispered, "I will find a way." She smiled and kissed his lips to silence him; she did not want to speak of the future—now was enough. Right now, here in the green glow of the forest. She wrapped her legs up and around his back, pulling him into her fiercely. He felt them plunging off of the rock together, into the sea, into the maelstrom that swirled around the rocks, plunging into the heart of the sea, shuddering at the sting that raced through him . . . strong and sharp and alive, more alive than ever he had known.

They lay together, came together, exhausted each other, rested. He put his face into her breasts and smelled himself, interwined with her. They bathed together in the pool, and touched each other's bodies and smiled and kissed the small blue marks of love they had left on each other.

"No more a virgin," he whispered into her ear.

She threw her head back and laughed out loud. "I gave you that long ago. Oh lord, I can still feel you."

He moaned. "If you knew the guilt I wallowed in, getting hard on a little girl . . . I felt as if I had violated you . . ."

"I know," she told him, her hands exploring the thickness of his hair, which was wet now and dark. "It took me a long time to realize how bad you must have felt. And even longer to realize what a vixen I had been, for tempting you."

"I never thought about that—about your wanting." He was silent for a moment. He kissed the inside of her wrist and told her, "You cannot stay with these miserable people."

"I know. I have to leave," she agreed softly, forcing herself to speak when she wanted simply to cling to the silence, the warmth that encircled them. Tangling her fingers in the hairs on his chest, she bent to kiss a soft place on his neck.

He pulled her to him again, came into her, breathing to feel the whole of her, knowing now what she had known from that first day. She held his face in her hands and she whispered, "What has happened doesn't matter. All we need to know is that this is right. We are right. As long as we don't forget, we can be together."

He buried his face in her hair and shut out everything but the two of them, alone in the world with only the sound of the waterfall to remind them they were on earth.

By the time Evan reached Lahaina that night, he had a plan. It would take time—perhaps as much as six months. The hardest part was Harry, making certain he could see him. But it would work; it would have to work; he would make it work.

16

When she saw three chattering red-haired girls tugging at a goat and laughing as if they couldn't stop, True knew she had found the Cassidy place.

Before she could dismount, one of the girls called out, "You must be True," and the other two went screaming off toward the barn, shouting for Liko.

The Cassidys were as rowdy and happy a family as Evan had said they were; they welcomed her to their table and pelted her with questions—all kinds of questions, many of them about the Princess Kaiulani.

"Liko has promised she will come and visit him . . . us . . . do you think she will?" freckle-faced Maggie demanded.

"If she comes to Maui, yes," True said and laughed. "Liko taught Princess Kauilani how to swim—did he tell you that?"

"Oh, yes," the girls chimed. "He's told us everything about the Princess."

One added, "We're glad to hear he wasn't just making up the stories."

The father only sat and smiled, and the mother moved back and forth from the kitchen and the table, not allowing anyone to help her, a homely, jolly woman given to making clucking sounds.

It was late afternoon before True and Liko could be alone.

"They're nice people, the Cassidys," True began.

"Yes, very nice," Liko answered, but there was a hesitation in his voice.

"But it isn't Rose Plantation?"

Liko nodded, swinging his big head in woe. "I miss you coming on Sunday, and I miss Jared. He hasn't been to see me once, and the letters, even the letters don't come so often. I wish I knew if . . ."

"If he's going to get married, like his mama wants?" she finished for him.

Liko hung his head.

"I'm going to find out," she told him. "That's why I came today. I wanted to tell you what I am going to do, and I want you to understand and be patient and wait for me. If it works out like I plan, we can all be together again."

Liko looked confused.

"I'm leaving the Baumgartners," she told him. "Tomorrow I'm taking the boat to Mau'loa to see Jared, to talk to him face to face. His mama can't send me away if I show up at their door, at least not before I have a chance to talk to Jared. I promise to write you before I leave there, to let you know exactly what is happening. Then I'm going to Oahu, and I'll be staying with Aunt and Uncle and Martha at Mana'olana."

Liko was full of questions. She could see the panic swelling in him, his little chest heaving with worry.

"Shhh, shhh," she said to him, holding his hand and insisting he sit down beside her on a log. "Listen to me now. I'm leaving the Baumgartners, because it is time to leave. I've lost all patience with them, and without patience no one can live in that house. I haven't spoken to Evan for two months—he won't be coming to Maui anymore; he's given up his place on the bench."

"Is that why you're leaving, because of Evan?" he blurted.

His words stung her. She closed her eyes, remembering how frightened Liko must be about her leaving. When she spoke again, her voice was calm and even. "You must listen to me, Liko, and trust me. I have something I need to do. It will not be easy, and I have to know that you will be all right, that I can count on you to stay here and do good work for the Cassidys. They are fine people, so do not make them feel that you are unhappy here. I'll write to you each week. I won't forget, I promise."

"I've never seen anybody look so hangdog as you do, Jared Wakefield," she said, frowning at him.

"You'd look hangdog too, if you knew half the things Ma says about you. She just about choked when you turned up. I think she would've sent you away if Pa hadn't been here."

True felt sick. It had been a rough passage. She had lost

everything in her stomach, and now she felt weak. She shook her head to try to get her thoughts in order. They walked away from the house, to the edge of a long meadow where sheep were grazing. For a few moments, True watched a lamb trying to nuzzle its mother.

"I doubt your mama is going to give us much time to ourselves, so I'm going to have to talk fast, Jared, and I want you to listen hard . . . just as hard as you've ever had to listen in your life. Now, tell me this. Are you set to marry somebody?"

Jared raised his chin in a motion True recognized: His one strong trait was stubbornness.

"I'm not going to marry that Hilo girl. She's a puling sort, without one single interesting bone in her body. If Mama told her to go jump in a pile of cow dung, she'd do it. Besides, she makes a funny noise when she breathes. Like this . . ." He made a soft, snorting sound, and True tried to smile.

"What will happen if you say no?" she asked.

Jared shrugged. "Mama will just find somebody else. She won't give up. She's fastened onto this idea that I have to get married, since we need more males in the family and I'm the only son."

True nodded. "You know what that means, don't you?"

"I can't," he said, his handsome face turning red. He began to cough. "I can't do that, I can't."

"And if you marry, you won't get to be with Liko. Have you thought about that?"

He looked at her sullenly, a grey cloud of unhappiness flickering across his mind.

In a voice soft with understanding, she said to him, "I know how you feel about Liko, and how he feels about you. He is miserable now, not being able to be with you. And I think you must be feeling lonely too."

Tears sprang to his eyes. He turned away from her, but she firmly pulled him back. "I believe I have a way to solve your problem, and Liko's—and my own. Listen to me, Jared. Are you listening?"

A small choked sob escaped him, but he nodded. "You know that Liko had to leave Rose Plantation," she said, in a tone thick with innuendo.

Jared nodded again; he closed his eyes tight, and tears dripped off his long, dark lashes.

True did not have time to comfort or reassure him. "I must leave the place where I am staying. The family won't allow Liko to visit me, and it is time for me to go."

A strong metallic taste came into her mouth; she swallowed to keep it down and took a deep breath. "I want you to marry me, Jared," she said quickly, and she watched the shock spread over his face. She began to speak rapidly. "Wait now and listen to me. Your folks already believe I'm the reason you want to go over to Maui all the time. They think you are courting me, and that you are going to want to marry me—that's the real reason your mama wants you safely married off to someone else. So—why not marry me? That way I have a home of my own—your Uncle's old place, the Home Place, I would guess. We could bring Liko and Martha to live with us, the four of us together—our own little ohana. Then you and Liko could be together without anyone saying a word or making any kind of fuss."

Jared was staring at her. "Do you know what you are saying?" he asked. "True . . . I don't know. What about. . . ?"

"What about what?" she said, gulping down the rising impatience she felt. "You'll probably never see Liko again if you don't think about this plan, and God knows what will happen to him. You and I, we've always been friends. Your parents think we are more than that. They may even think we've already been together—physically."

"Wait, whoa," he told her, backing away as if she had threatened him. "No, now. That's . . ."

"What?" True said. "You know what I'm talking about, Jared. I know you know." She could see he was beginning to think about it, to consider, and that was what she wanted.

"You haven't been with me, like a man and a woman, we both know that," her voice was soft now, cajoling. "We know you don't want to be, but other people don't know," she said, "and they don't have to know. But if the Colonel thought you had been, and that there might be an heir . . ."

Jared sat down, hard, and stared at her. "But he would find out. Mama would know."

"That's the one thing you would have to do . . . make a baby with me. Once we do, that part will be over. We'll just be friends like we've always been. Only that, friends living

together with our other good friends and a little one for all
of us to take care of. And no one else would have to know,
ever."

"I don't know if I can . . ."

"You can," she told him firmly. "We can." They saw the
rider at the same time: Laiana Wakefield, cantering out on
a big roan mare to rescue her only son. True and Jared stood
together, watching. True heard the sound of the wind in the
ironwood trees and the bleating of the sheep.

She could feel the resolve welling in Jared; she knew she
had won when he put his arm around her shoulders; they
were going to face his mother together.

"You'll do it?" True asked.

"Yes, I will," Jared answered in a voice that carried out
over the grasslands. "I will." He began to laugh. "Damn yes,
I will."

Uncle helped me move True's bed back into our room, and by
rising at first light I was able to finish the quilt I was making for
her in time for her arrival. It was blue on white, an appliquéd
breadfruit pattern. Vicky said it was the most beautiful Hawaiian quilt she had ever seen. Vicky has been on Kauai—she
can hardly stand to stay here, now especially. The news came
only last week: the Senate has passed the resolution, President
McKinley will sign it and the Territory of Hawaii will be
created. The monarchy will be finished forever.

Ocean voyages had never agreed with True; she was pale
and weak when she arrived, and she stayed in bed all of the
day following her arrival.

Aunt and I were happy to bring her tea and biscuits, but
she could not seem to keep even that down. It was not until
the following day that she felt well enough to sit up and talk.

She waited all that time to tell me of her arrangement with
Jared.

I stared at her. "This can't be," I said. "This isn't what
you want, this shouldn't be. Oh no . . ."

"Listen to me," she came back, as harshly as she could in
her weakness. "This *is* what should be. It is the only way. I'm
going to run that ranch. I'm going to make Mau'loa the
biggest, the best in the islands. That's what I'm going to do,
and I'm going to have a son to pass it on to, or maybe a
daughter, I don't care which."

"You can't mean it," I kept repeating, though I could see that she did.

When True announced her betrothal, Aunt Winona produced a galloping soliloquy about the two young sweethearts, how thrilling it was to see their long friendship blossom into love, how she thought she had seen it from the beginning. Such a sweet, handsome young man he was, so dark against True's lightness, with such a fine Hawaiian-haole background, how beautiful their children would be . . .

Uncle asked if Evan knew.

He noticed that True didn't meet his gaze. "I haven't seen Evan for quite some time, not since he finished his work on Maui," she answered.

"Nobody much has," Uncle told her. "Archie told me the other day that Evan is giving up most of the boards he sits on. He has been offered the post of attorney general, and it looks as if he is going to turn that down as well. We don't know quite what to make of it."

His statement seemed to float in the air, waiting for someone to comment, but no one did. Evan was on Kauai at the moment. Aunt told us, explaining, "I saw Jenny the other day in town. She scarcely spoke to me at all. She's become quite sour of late, everybody has noticed it, but she did tell me that Evan was on Kauai."

Vicky came back late on Thursday, and when her pa told her True's news, she came straight on to Mana'olana. She burst in on us, flinging herself at True, demanding "What is this about?"

"It's about my marrying Jared Wakefield," True said simply.

Vicky stared at her, searching her face for something secret written there. Seeing that True was serious, she wrapped her arms around her and kissed her on both cheeks.

When Vicky had heard all of the details True chose to give her, she declared: "Well then, you will have to be married at Ainahau. You must! We'll have a grand wedding. Oh, it will be just the right thing, to take our minds off all this other dreadful business. Have you chosen a day?"

"Soon," True said, "as soon as possible."

"August 6," Vicky decided. "That gives us three weeks to plan it. Auntie Liliu is on her way back from Washington now.

The transfer will not take place until August 12. We can still fly our flag, we'll sing our songs, and we will have a luau and dancing. Oh, it will be a fine wedding, a Hawaiian wedding."

"The Wakefields don't want Jared to marry True," I spoke up.

"That just shows how stupid and silly they are," Vicky said and sighed, as if it were no impediment at all. "I suppose we've always known that, but don't worry, I know just how to handle the Colonel."

"True and Jared want a simple ceremony," I tried again.

"Nonsense," Vicky said. "If you're going to do it, True, let's have a big celebration. Let everyone know you aren't going to hide in the bushes. Sing it out. The one thing I can still do is gather a crowd. Everyone you want will be there, I promise."

As soon as he returned from Kauai, Evan Coulter appeared at the hale. True would not see him. She said she did not feel well enough.

"This is not like her," I told him. "I don't understand," I said, though I thought I did. In my heart, I believed that True was angry with him for giving up the position that took him to Maui. I suspected that Jenny had given him an ultimatum, had said that he must not see True again, and he had given into it. I couldn't get it out of my head that she would not have gone to Jared, if she could have continued to see Evan. When I said this to her, she told me I was wrong, but that was what I thought.

Evan returned. "She's making a mistake," he told me when it was obvious that she wasn't going to talk to him. His face was grim. "Tell her that, Martha. Tell her not to go through with it, that it is wrong."

I looked at him, and for the first time I felt angry. "That's almost exactly what she said to you, Evan. And you wouldn't listen."

He turned away, his fists clenched. After Evan left that night, Uncle said to me in confidence that he'd never seen him so frayed and that he thought there just might be some truth in the rumors, about Evan acting peculiarly. "I don't think True's forgiven him," Uncle offered. "I mean, that whole thing about making her go back to the house where her mother was murdered, having to admit that it was her father who did it."

"That may be," I said, to keep Uncle from asking any more questions.

True made me promise not to cry on her wedding day. "This is not going to be a sad day," she said. "This is only the beginning. We'll be back in the spring, and by then I am hoping to have things worked out so you can come teach in the schoolhouse on Mau'loa, if you will. Not the Colonel's pokey little one, but a new one next to the Home Place, where we will live. I want you to come live with us—with Liko and Jared and me. We will take care of each other, the four of us. An ohana. You must know that this is best for us all, and you must not cry."

Evan did not come to the wedding; Jenny arrived without him, and those who asked where he was were given the elaborately embroidered excuse she had invented. Colonel Toby was there, as Vicky had said he would be, and so was Laiana Wakefield, though she would not speak to me when I tried to greet her. I watched her, the way she lifted her face so she seemed always to be looking down at you, and I thought: You are a fearsome woman, but you've met your match in True. And I'm going to be standing there, right behind True, and I'm not going to be afraid of you either.

On the green grassy lawn that spread down to the sea, gay Chinese lanterns bobbled in the warm breeze, a group of Hawaiian musicians played the soft, lyric melodies of the Islands, and the father of the groom was coaxed onto the dance floor; he moved into the easy, arm-swaying motions of the dance. Soon there was a chanting . . . *True, True* . . . and a murmuring cheer when she walked to the dance floor. Her bare feet moved on the smooth floor, her dress was long and white, and she wore a lei of maile leaves around her neck. She moved with exquisite grace, raising her arms, swaying with the music.

Then Jared jumped onto the stage, his bare feet planted firmly. A roar went up from the crowd, and the music pounded into strong rhythms. Beautiful Jared moved through the dance as if born to it, tall and lithe, life itself, as True swayed against him, all grace, all beauty. Those who saw them dance that day would remember it ever after;

people would speak of it—were you there when the young Wakefields danced on their wedding day? they would say.

True and Jared said their vows under the spreading banyan tree, the one that had been named for Kaiulani. Jared, twenty years old, looked handsome and pleased with himself; True, twenty-three that day, was triumphant.

All the while, old Auntie Momi's words echoed inside my head: *The path True has chosen up the mountain is a hard path, filled with brambles, not well trod and with no clear view of the top.*

17

A new year, the last of this century. These past months have
seen the end of so much in these Islands.

"Tell our story," True had said to me on her wedding day.
"Tell it outright and honest," she told me. I am not a little
shocked at how well I have followed those orders, perhaps
more than even True might like. I wrote what I saw for myself,
what she and others confided and, now and then, what I
supposed or expected had happened. There are omissions, to
be sure, things I do not know and things True has not yet told
me. Still, I believe that if I am patient, in time I will find out,
will have those missing pieces of the puzzle that will allow me
to finish the story properly so that a reader in the new century
might understand what we cannot at this moment in the old.

Here I sit on this first day of the last year of a century, at
the beginning of one ending, as it were, running my fingertips over the beautiful koa wood journal True gave me on
her wedding day, and which I have filled in the five months
since. I read what I have written and wonder how I could
have been so *outright*. It was not for True, I think, but for
me. Writing these words has made me think, has helped me
to understand, has, in some way I cannot explain, set me
free. Could that be?

I cannot stop writing, nor do I want to. There is such
comfort in looking at the pages filled with words—the tall
loops of the l's, the feathered tails of the y's—I love the very
act of writing, of dipping the pen in the inkbowl, of sliding
it along the page in waltz time, of bowing and curtsying with
the blotter and blowing, ever so softly, to make certain the
page is dry before starting another. I caress the finished page,
read it over and blush at the pleasure it gives me.

True has called me a storyteller, and perhaps she is right. This much I know: the story she urged me to tell is far from finished.

True will not be coming back this spring after all. Instead, I am to go to Mau'loa to be with her when her baby is born; I will make my home there, with True and Liko and Jared and the child. The carpenters are even now building a new schoolhouse with rooms for a teacher in the back; it sits next to the old Wakefield homestead. "It is cool and quiet and lovely in this place, so high on the flank of the mountain that you think yourself in another world altogether," True writes. "There is so much to do, Martha Moon. A ranch to build, children to teach . . . come quick!"

I am to go as soon as I am convinced that little Miss Amalie, for so long my best student, tells me that she is ready to take over my classes. In fact she has been ready for some time, and has only to admit it to herself. By spring, I believe, I will be able to leave, and I will take with me a supply of new journals, nice practical Schoolbook Blueline Brand with speckled black and white covers and pristine empty pages to fill.

January 11, 1899

Governor Cleghorn came by this afternoon to bring me a note that Vicky had tucked into a letter to him. He seemed jovial (I have heard that his Hawaiian wife will soon present him with another child) and even poked a little fun at Vicky for writing that she was "too amused watching the country bumpkins" at a dance she had attended in Waimea.

Vicky has gone to the Big Island—she left before Christmas—to attend Eva Parker's gala wedding and she has stayed on at Mana, the Parker Ranch compound near the town of Waimea. "I expect she's having a good time," the Governor said, laughing, "because she's asking for her money and her holokus, some bromo quinine pills, headache powders and sardines. In between all the send-me's, she managed to tell me she's been riding all over the ranch, jumping logs and pig holes and hanging on by her teeth.

"Kaiulani has been drenched once or twice, but she says a hot bath and warm drink have revived her."

When her pa calls her "Kaiulani," I know he is worried. I am worried, too.

When I last saw her, she spoke bitterly about a group of Americans who had come out to Ainahau, pounded on the door and asked to have their pictures taken with "the ex-princess."

Poor Vicky! One moment she can be bright and laughing, and the next she is wrapped in unutterable sadness. On August 12 the Hawaiian flag in front of Iolani Palace was lowered, the American flag raised. We are now an American territory.

There were Portuguese, Japanese and Chinese at the annexation ceremony at Iolani Palace, but there were no Hawaiians. I went with Vicky to Washington Place, where we gathered around Queen Liliuokalani and waited for the deed to be done, as you would wait for an execution.

"They haven't left me much to live for," Vicky told me, not in anger but with resignation.

Every eligible young man in the Islands, haole and Hawaiian alike, looks at her with longing. She is so very beautiful, and when she chooses she can be charming. There are always rumors about her and her cousin Koa—David Kawananakoa—but I know that her pa thinks him too much of a ladies' man, and much too frivolous for his girl, and Vicky herself called Koa "a goose." A young captain on the troopship *Peru* seemed to catch her fancy—Putnam Strong was his name. He spent all of his days at Ainahau; they swam in the ocean and rode into the mountains. More than once when they were out riding they stopped off to see me, and we had such a good, laughing time together. Putnam is a big man, solid and strong and oh, so certain of himself. When his ship sailed for Manila, I expected Vicky to be sad and moping, but she wasn't. "It was fun for a time," was all she had to say when I asked her. Once out of sight, he seemed completely out of her mind.

Another young man, Andrew Adams, a writer for the Honolulu *Advertiser,* comes and goes. The Governor is fond of him, and for a time we thought Vicky was, too. But when I asked her, she would say only, "We quarrel . . . it is too tiresome."

She is gifted in so many ways—she has given me one of her oil paintings that is breathless in its beauty: hibiscus of the most subtle color of yellow. But at the moment she seems caught up in a restless round of travelling; she simply cannot abide the men who are running the territory and she looks for any excuse to leave Ainahau for the outer islands. And she complains, all the while, of headaches and nervousness and other indispositions.

More than once I have wished True were here to give Vicky a good talking to, to make her think of what she must do. But Mau'loa is a far distance from the Parker Ranch, and Vicky knows if she goes there True will not offer a sympathetic ear. Besides, True is busy, trying to revive a cattle ranch that Colonel Toby seems determined to destroy—to hear True tell it—by draining off profits and refusing to spend anything to make the improvements True says anyone in his right mind can see are necessary.

Her letters are filled with the frustrations she feels. Colonel Toby will not listen to her and neither will Jared. He won't go against his father, True writes, but takes a stance somewhere in between, which of course means that he forfeits any voice he might have in running the ranch, and Colonel Toby wins. Even Liko cannot make Jared see the sense of spending money for such things as fences so they can improve the herd through a breeding program, or finding a way to bring water from the wet side of the island to the dry, to improve the pasturelands and guard against the recurring droughts that decimate the herds.

While other mothers-to-be might be sewing a baby layette, True is immersed in government agricultural pamphlets about grasses and books on cattle breeding. No matter! Aunt and I have started sewing. Vicky has given us some yards of exquisite French lace for trim. By the time the baby joins us, he or she should have an admirable wardrobe.

I feel such great joy at starting my own school—I have some ideas about how the early years should be taught, and I get excited every time I realize that I will be able to try them. It makes me happy as well to think of the baby.

"You did not know your mother, and I lost mine," True writes. "Now the two of us are going to show how happy and strong a child can be with two mothers. I think of the Hawaiian ohanas, and I know that so many of their ways were better than haole ways. This will be your *hanai* child. It will have two mothers and two fathers. Jared and Liko, especially Liko, are as excited as they can be. They sound like two old mother hens, talking about the babe. Liko says, with his usual bluntness, that he hopes it gets Jared's good looks and my strength of character. One thing is certain, this child will never be without a ma or pa. As for me, I hope it gets its Auntie Martha's sweet good nature, not to mention her twinkling laugh, which as a matter of fact I miss a good deal out here on the mountain."

January 19, 1899

Evan. I cannot think of him without remembering his eyes the last time we spoke. Sad, and masked, as if he has shut off some part of himself. I was waiting for Aunt outside the Wilder building, where she had gone to speak to the lawyer who handles the Wrights' affairs, now that Evan has left the firm. Evan came walking out, and I scarcely recognized him—he has grown so brown from the sun, so lean and hard and fit from the outdoors.

"You look like a cowboy!" I blurted, and he managed a grin that said he was glad to see me, too. "I wondered why you didn't come by before you left for Kauai," I told him, and it was more an accusation than I had meant it to be.

He looked away up the street, squinting, but he didn't make any apologies.

"I'm sorry, Evan. I didn't mean to chastise you. It's just that I've missed you, Uncle and Aunt have missed you, and when you decided to leave Honolulu and move to Kauai to manage a ranch—well, we were all just so surprised, and we wondered why . . ."

He touched my arm to guide me to a bench under a spreading monkeypod tree, where we sat side by side.

"I haven't really left Honolulu," he said, looking at the ground. "I come back one week out of four to take care of business, and to see Harry."

I had heard the gossip—that Evan had turned down the position of attorney general offered him by the new territorial government. For Jenny it had been the last straw. When she spoke of Evan's decision to accept an offer to manage a cattle ranch on Kauai, her chin would quiver in rage. She, her mother and Harry have stayed in Honolulu, in the big house on Beretania Street, keeping up the fiction that Evan's stay on Kauai is temporary, and that they have remained behind because of Harry's schooling.

"How is Harry?" I asked.

"Too quiet for a six-year-old," he answered. "Too well behaved, but a good boy . . ."

"Of course he is, Evan—he's your son!" I said. "But why did you do it—go to Kauai, I mean?" I asked, as gently as possible.

He shrugged. "When I was on the circuit court and went to the outer islands, I would always rent a horse and go riding over the rangelands for an afternoon, into the mountain fields and it always made me feel . . . good. Better than I felt in town or in an office. I started looking forward to those times, and after a while when I was out I started to dread coming back. It got to the point where it seemed like I had to make a change. I made the decision to leave Honolulu the day I left Maui . . ." He paused, thinking, and I looked away, to give him time.

He continued in the same low, pained voice. "I had been out riding. I saw True that day . . . and I knew I couldn't come back to this . . ." he spread his hands as if to take in the whole of downtown Honolulu, "so I made a few inquiries, and I heard from Mr. Kurz at Princeville, asking me to manage his ranch."

I bit my lip to keep from saying it, but I couldn't help myself: "All True writes about is cattle and grasslands and breeding stock—imagine the two of you doing the same thing!"

"Imagine," he replied with a hollow laugh, and then he asked, looking at me steadily, "Why did she do it?"

I could not return his gaze. "To give us an ohana," I said, and it came out a whisper. "To give Jared and Liko and me a place where we can be together, and not have to worry about what's to become of us. She always promised us that . . . Liko and me, I mean. And she wants to save Mau'loa, I suppose that's part of it. You know True and how she takes to doing the impossible . . ."

I was trying to work up the courage to tell him about True's baby, trying to find the right words, when Aunt came out of the Wilder building and saw us.

"Evan Coulter!" she shouted out in her big voice and was talking at him as she walked toward us. I could almost feel Evan pulling himself together to make the effort to face her.

On the ride home, Aunt suddenly blurted, "Oh land, I

forgot to tell Evan about True's happy news. I'm certain he would want to know—he was always so fond of her."

It was a hot day, the trades had ceased to blow and we fanned ourselves as we rode and jousled along the rutted old road, but I felt a cold shiver slide up my spine, followed by a sudden feeling of fatigue: as if a disaster had been narrowly averted.

January 24, 1899

Uncle called me from the classroom this morning to show me an article in the *Advertiser:* "Princess Kaiulani is much improved. She and her father, Gov. Cleghorn, and their family physician will return to Honolulu on the next sailing of the *Kinau.*"

I sank with relief into a chair on the lanai and read it again, slowly.

"She's going to be all right," Uncle said to me. "Now you can stop fretting and get some sleep."

I looked at him, surprised.

"It was a full moon last night," he explained. "I saw you pacing on your lanai."

These past few days, since the governor and Dr. Walters sailed to the Big Island to get Vicky, have been more miserable than I can say. How could this happen so suddenly?

February 16, 1899
Ainahau

Vicky is in much pain. She lies in the big four-poster bed, her eyes bright with fever. The doctors say she has inflammatory rheumatism and that it is made worse by a condition they call exophthalmic goiter.

I cannot bear to see her lying there. She seems so all alone in the great bed. Sometimes I long to climb in with her, to hold onto her and not let her go, to scream into her ear to hear me and be well.

Other times I want to leave, but she will not let me. Her eyes hold me, pleading. And the Governor, too. Oh, it is too awful to see her poor, dear pa, his face sad as he sits there, hour after hour.

The rheumatism is moving into her heart, that is what the

doctors say. But what do the doctors know of her heart? How can they know the real affliction?

I have written True to come if she can. The sea voyage will be difficult for her, I know. She is always made so sick by it, and now that she is expecting a child it will be worse, but if she is able . . . Sometimes Vicky forgets, and asks me why True is not here, with us, and once big tears formed in the edges of her eyes and slipped down to the white pillows and when I asked her what it was, to tell me what it was, she said, "True . . . True and Liko and Evan, where are they?"

The *Kinau* leaves today for Kauai and Mau'loa; the Governor sent word to the captain to delay his sailing for an hour, so that he could carry the letters to True and to Evan.

March 1, 1899
Ainahau

Evan is here, sitting beside the bed holding Vicky's hand in one of his, stroking her slim arm, his voice low and teasing. He is talking about the times when she was a little girl, how he would carry her out into the surf on his shoulders, like the Hawaiian warriors of old carried the little sacred princesses, so their precious feet did not touch the earth. Her eyes stay on his face; she smiles. Evan has always been able to make Vicky smile.

Now he is trying to give her strength; he talks to her about the future, about a beautiful beach he has found on Kauai, and a secret cove tucked into the Pali, where he will take her when she is well. And when she sighs and says she doesn't know, Evan says that he knows for both of them and that he is going to take her there, if he has to kidnap her to do it.

"Kidnap," Vicky said, slipping into memory. "True always had to be the captain of the pirates when we played, and I had to be kidnapped."

"Because you were the princess," he told her.

"I was, wasn't I? A real princess then pretending to be kidnapped, but now it's all pretend."

The following day, just as Evan was taking his leave—he was standing in the front parlour, talking to the Governor and me—True came up the stairs, out of the sunlight and into the darkened entryway.

She stood blinking, not seeing us. The Governor moved to

greet her, but Evan stood staring, and so did I. Her body was ponderously large; even the wide muumuu she wore could not disguise the heaviness of the child she carried.

Evan's face froze. I felt a sting of regret. I should have told him. He should not have been surprised like this.

True had come directly from the boat; her face was pale and there were beads of perspiration around her hairline. I wrapped my arms around her as well as I could and kissed her on both cheeks, which were not cool but damp and clammy.

The Governor began to thank her, over and over again, for making the trip in her delicate condition. I could see her take a deep breath, see the heave of her big stomach rise, as she held both of her hands out to Evan.

He did not take them. He looked away from her. True stepped closer and touched his arm. "Can you come with me to see Vicky?" she asked.

He shook his head; he couldn't.

Evan left without saying a word.

The Governor took her arm and consoled her. "You will have to forgive Evan," he said. "He is so upset about Vicky. He lived with us, you know, when he was a boy in school. He was like a brother to her, he came as soon as he could, like you, my dear girl, like you . . ."

March 4, 1899

True's being here has revived Vicky! She has improved steadily all day long. Even the doctors admit it and don't look quite so dour. Vicky joked with True and put her hand on her stomach to see if she could feel the baby.

"I should love to be the first to hold it," Vicky said.

"Then you will be," True promised, adding, "Though I'm selling lottery tickets for that particular part of the program, so you'll have to buy them all."

"You are wicked, True Lindstrom Wakefield. I suppose nothing will do until I get up out of this bed and race you down the beach. I suppose that's why they sent for you."

"That is exactly right," True told her.

"How are you going to race with that big *'opu?*"

"You just come out and watch me. I'll even give you a head start."

"Oh, True." Vicky's laugh turned into a cough. "I suppose you would. I suppose you'd win too."

"Maybe not," True told her. "Maybe you would win, if you tried hard enough."

Vicky didn't answer; she was breathing easily and had slipped off into what seemed to be a peaceful sleep. The doctors registered their approval and sent us, silently, to our beds.

March 6, 1899, five a.m.
Ainahau

All I remember, all I will ever remember is a terrible silence at exactly two o'clock this morning, and then the mad shrieking of the peacocks, the horrid shrill sound of them on the grounds at Ainahau. As if the hateful creatures understood the very moment that she left, understood that Vicky is dead.

18

True sank into the old hammock and raised her feet as high as she could; they were swollen and aching. Her body throbbed, there was a steady pressing pain in the lower part of her back and she felt as if something thick and hard had settled on her chest. It had been that way before, after her mother's death. *Oh, Vicky.* She caught her breath and willed herself not to cry, turning her face to the sea. She did not want to think, she wanted only to rock here in the old hammock, her feet lifted, and not think. She shaded her eyes with her arm and let herself drift, listening to the sounds of the palm fronds tossing in the soft wind and the voices rising from the wide lawns and gardens; the wailing and the chanting had begun.

She wasn't certain how long he had been watching her; she turned her face and he was standing at the foot of the hammock, looking down on her.

She breathed deeply and tried to smile. "Evan."

"I didn't want to wake you. You must be tired . . ." His voice was neutral, controlled.

Tears sprang to her eyes and she tried to blink them away. "I'm sorry," she said, attempting to rise and finding she could not.

"Don't get up," he told her.

"I have to," she said. "I have to."

"Not yet. Rest for a while longer. I'll leave if you want, but you need to rest."

"Don't leave," she said, and she watched as his eyes filled with tears.

Evan turned away from her, he put both hands in front of him on a sago palm, leaned into it and stayed motionless for a long while. Finally he turned back and in a voice that was not quite even told her: "The Governor has asked me to handle the funeral arrangements. It is becoming complicated—the government wants a state funeral. In a few minutes I have to leave to meet Sanford Dole. I came to find you because I want you to promise that you will not go back to Mau'loa without seeing me."

She nodded, making small gasping sounds to keep from crying again.

He came close to the hammock then, and with his fingertips smoothed the strands of hair from her wet face. She took his hand in hers and kissed it. "When will the baby be born?" he asked, his voice hoarse.

"Soon," she whispered.

"Yes," he said.

True closed her eyes. "Don't say any more, not now, Evan. Vicky is gone, and I can't . . ."

He held her hand lightly in his and said, "I know."

Monday, three p.m.

Sanford Dole stood and walked around his desk to greet Evan.

"Sir," said Evan.

"My boy," the older man answered, holding onto his hand longer than need be. "What a sorrow this is, what a terrible loss."

Evan took the chair the former president of the republic, now the governor of the territory, held out for him.

"I have to tell you, Evan, I was relieved when I learned that you would be the intermediary for the family. We know how difficult this is for Archie . . . and what a terrible loss it is for the Hawaiians. We—the government, that is—want to do whatever we can to help in making the arrangements, and of course to assume all expenses."

Evan broke in, "Governor Cleghorn would prefer a private funeral, sir, and one as simple as possible. He has asked me to thank you for your generous offer, and . . ."

Judge Dole broke in, "I understand, I understand. But I'm not certain a private ceremony is possible. Already people are arriving . . . and there will be more. The whole city is in a state of mourning. Thousands will expect to attend this funeral, will want to see their dear little Princess to her last resting place, and I don't believe Archie can handle it without some help. I've asked that the Throne Room of Iolani Palace be made ready for the lying-in-state."

Evan shifted in his seat and leaned forward. "Sir, you are right, Governor Cleghorn is going to need help. The grounds at Ainahau are already filled with Hawaiians who have come to chant the meles. It is clear that he will need assistance in planning the funeral processions, and your offer of having the government assume the expenses will be welcome. I know that you make this offer out of kindness as well as affection for the Princess . . . and her father knows that, too, sir. If I might make a few suggestions . . ."

Sanford Dole sat back in his big chair and began to stroke his long beard, a signal that he was ready to listen.

"Iolani Palace is now so much connected with the fall of the monarchy that I feel certain Governor Cleghorn will reject the idea of having her there. Ainahau is a distance out of town, to be sure. But the road is good, and the house is large enough to allow many hundreds of people to view the body. Also, it has the benefit of being her home, making it seem more a private occasion. As for the public funeral observances, the family feels that Kawaiahao Church would be an appropriate site. It has a long history of serving the Hawaiians . . . though they want Bishop Willis of the Episcopal Church to conduct the service."

The old man nodded solemnly. "There are those of us in this government who were fond of the Princess, and who sincerely admire her father. We should like to show our sympathy by attending the funeral."

Evan was ready with his answer. "Not so very long ago, Kaiulani told me how kind both you and Mrs. Dole have been to her. She has said the same thing to her father, and I know he will be gratified to have you and your wife there. Perhaps you could select a small contingent to represent the government?"

The older man nodded. "I understand. As always, Evan, you've managed to find that narrow ribbon of a path between two rocky chasms. We miss you . . . I miss you. There are too few men willing to listen around here. My offer still stands. When you've had enough time out in the rangelands, let me know."

"Thank you, sir. I appreciate your confidence, but I expect I'll be getting back to Kauai as soon as the funeral is done."

"Yes, well . . ." The Territorial Governor was not finished. "I can't seem to get that dear girl out of my mind. You know, there was a time when I felt that if we could convince the Queen to abdicate in favor of Kaiulani, Hawaii might have had a chance as a constitutional monarchy . . ."

Evan answered, "Yes sir, I know. But the Queen was not of a mind to give up power. She would never have agreed."

Dole sighed and pulled at his beard. "Did you know that Archie went to Alec Marston—who of course was always the principal opponent of the monarchy—and said he thought there might be a justification for dethroning the Queen because of her stand on the new constitution? Archie wanted to know if the Americans might be willing to maintain the monarchy, with Princess Kaiulani as queen, and a regency."

Dole went on: "Of course Marston told Archie that things had gone too far for any such plan, and that it was his purpose to abrogate the monarchy entirely."

Evan shook his head. He hadn't known, and he felt sorrow for his old friend. Suddenly he felt weary. The two men walked to the door, and once again Sanford Dole held onto Evan's hand, as if he were loath to let him go.

"Come back in happier times," the old man said.

Evan left, wondering if there would ever again be a happy time.

March 7, Wednesday

Yesterday we washed her poor, sweet body and prepared her for eternity. I took comfort in brushing her hair; I found the beautiful brush that was a gift of King Kalakaua, and brushed and brushed as we had those long-ago days on the beach at Waikiki when we were children. One of her aunties said that her hair had become lighter, she thought, in the years that she was away in England, but I do not think so. It is the same dark curling mass, the same sweet tangles. *Dear God, how can I tell you the anger I feel for you, for all the gods—Christian and Hawaiian—who would see this happen to my sweet friend?*

I must not think this way, must not let the gall rise in my throat. But oh, how could she be gone? And why were we so helpless to stop it?

True and I have been sleeping here at Ainahau; the Governor has asked us to stay close by, but I feel I will go mad if I can't get away from the wailing and the ancient *meles* and the band playing dirges all day long. I can see that True has had too much of it as well. Evan told me to get her out of here, and I intend to do just that.

Auntie Momi appeared this morning; under the banyan tree, she began to chant a *uwe helu*—a call to the dead that recounts her memories of Vicky. *Auwe, my sweet princess, friend of my daughter Martha. Auwe, hope of our people, who has taken the hidden pathway of Kane.*

I translated Auntie's *uwe helu* for True.

"What is the 'hidden pathway'?" she wanted to know.

"I'm not certain," I told her. "I do know that the spirit— the *uhane*—leaves the body not with the last breath but through the corners of the eyes, like tears, and it makes its way to a particular place overlooking the sea—called *leina,* or leaping place—and along the way it meets an *aumakua,* who leads it safely over the leina."

"Let's go there," True said.

"What? Go where?" I asked.

"To the nearest leina, to say good-bye to Vicky. We are her friends. We should be the ones to help her make the leap . . ."

"But . . ." I began and stopped. "Yes," I said then. "Yes . . . Auntie will be able to tell me where it is, and if it isn't too far, and if there's a passable road—but are you certain you feel well enough to go?"

She didn't hear this last; she was already on the way to the stables to arrange for a carriage. I watched her go, watched the rolling gait that had replaced the old stride.

It was not all that far from Ainahau, but much of the ride was uphill and we had to leave the carriage some distance away and make our way along a narrow path through brambles that pulled at our dresses. "This is too hard for you," I said, listening to her labored breathing. It took too much breath to answer; instead, she pushed on. Finally we came to a small clearing. Below us the waves crashed against the Pali, before us the ocean stretched to infinity.

"A good place to leap to another world," True said, gasping for breath.

"Sit down," I demanded. "Just sit and be quiet."

Silence wrapped around us; only the sounds of the winds stirred above us and the ceaseless rush of the sea below. We sat together, the sun warm on our faces, and waited.

How long we remained so, I do not know. I do know that we felt a different peace there, waiting. "I feel as if any moment she will come pushing in between us, laughing that funny little out-of-breath laugh of hers," True said in a low voice.

We saw it at the same instant and watched it come gliding down to us: a black *mamo* bird with its unmistakable yellow feathers above the tail—feathers gathered in other times to make a king's cape. For a few moments, it sat on the branch of a lehua tree and studied us, cocking its tiny head one way and then another.

I thought my heart would burst.

True moaned, and when I looked at her I could see she was in pain.

"The baby . . ." she gasped.

The mamo bird flew above us, dipped and slid silently against the wind, and then it flew away.

"Good-bye," I called out and wanted to watch the bird fly into the horizon, but I had to concentrate on getting True back to the buggy, back to town.

Saturday

In the old days, when an alii lay dying, the great outrigger canoes would begin to arrive, bearing alii from all the other islands. They would come to wait for the death, and then to grieve and chant and wail before the bones were stripped of flesh and hidden away in a cave, the place forever secret so that no evil spirit could claim them.

Now the boats arrive from the other islands, bringing chiefs and chiefesses and kahunas, and merchants and lawyers and ranchers and politicians, all to bury the Princess Kaiulani, the last hope of the Hawaiians. That is what this funeral is about: the death of a people.

All day today they came—the old Hawaiians on foot, the poor and the lame, they walked down the long palm-shaded drive that leads to Ainahau, entered the house and her bedroom, they filed past the big, four-poster bed where she lies. She looks so small! Tiny orchids and orange blossoms are scattered about the coverlet, entwined in her hair; great baskets of flowers arrive, continue to arrive. The scent overwhelms; it is too much, too much.

And still they come, by the thousands they come. Old and young, rich and poor and all of them come in suffocating sorrow.

Late this afternoon Jared arrived with his parents. Dr. Walters has said that True must stay in bed at the Wakefield house in town. She cannot follow the catafalque to the church tonight, cannot go to the services tomorrow. The doctor says it has been too much for True. A nurse is with her now.

Colonel Toby wept openly; tears washed down Miss Laiana's face. Jared simply seemed stunned. I was greatly surprised when the Colonel embraced me and Miss Laiana bent low to kiss me on one cheek and then the other and to whisper to me words of sorrow. Their pain seemed to shatter something that was caught in my chest, and I found myself weeping quietly in Miss Laiana's strong arms.

It rained all that day, as if the gods were weeping at our loss. That afternoon I returned with Jared to the Wakefield house on King Street. As our carriage pulled up, we saw Dr. Walters enter. True has gone into labor; her face is blotched, her body locked in spasms of pain.

Jared became very agitated, his handsome face dark with fear. "Why is this happening now?" he kept asking. "Why is she in such pain? She should not have gone on that ride yesterday. Why does she always do what she shouldn't?" His mother took him out of the room to quiet him.

In the hallway, the doctor told Miss Laiana that it would likely take a long time, that True's narrow hips would mean a difficult delivery.

Turned on her side, breathing as deeply as she could, she let me put cool cloths on her forehead and dampen her dry mouth. Miss Laiana came to tell her that Jared had one of his headaches, that the doctor had prescribed some sedatives to make him sleep. He wanted True to know why he couldn't be with her.

"He would be no help, none at all," Miss Laiana said with a smile, smoothing the bedclothes and then running her big hands expertly down True's back, massaging and comforting. "I know how it feels," she told True. "But you must be patient; soon enough it will be done, and you will see what a gift you get for all this hurt." The pains continued into the night; she bit down on a wet cloth to keep from screaming. And then, at about three in the morning, they subsided altogether and True fell into a deep sleep.

"Let her rest," Miss Laiana said to me, "and you must rest as well. Remember, the funeral is tomorrow."

"I can't leave True!" I told her.

She looked at me calmly. "True will be here when you return, perhaps with her *hiapo*. Princess Kaiulani is leaving forever. You must go to say good-bye to her, for True and for me. You will go with Jared and his father, for our *ohana*."

Grief and fatigue claimed me; too tired to argue, I fell into a troubled sleep.

Sunday, seven a.m.

I was wakened by one of the housemaids, who told me I must hurry. She had pressed the black dress I had been wearing for four days now; I slipped into it and promised myself that after today I would never wear it again.

This day dawned bright and clear. I went first to True's room, but the door was closed. The doctor was examining her, Colonel Toby told me. He was dressed in formal coat and cravat, and for the first time since I have known him, he did not greet me with a smile. "Mother is with her—she will stay. We must leave now if we are going to take our place in the procession."

"Where is Jared?" I asked.

The Colonel frowned. "The boy has a headache. He says he can't bear the light. We'll have to go without him."

"I want to see True first," I said, and at that moment the door opened and the doctor came out.

"Is she all right?" I blurted.

"She's doing just fine," the doctor said. "She's a strong girl; a first born always takes time."

"Hurry and see her," the Colonel said, giving me permission. "Then we must leave."

True's face was drained of all color and she was breathing in short panting bursts. "Is it awful?" I asked and wished I hadn't.

"No," she lied in a voice beyond weariness. "You'll have to say aloha to Vicky for both of us."

Miss Laiana smiled as if everything were fine. "Now be off, Martha."

It was a stately occasion, a funeral for a queen. Twenty kahili bearers stood around her bier, and 230 Hawaiians were selected to man the long black and white ropes that pulled the catafalque all the way from the Church to the Royal Mausoleum in Nuuanu. King Street to Alakea . . . Emma Street to Vineyard . . . 20,000 people lined the streets and their grief and the sweet scent of flowers thickened the air.

If only Vicky could see, if only she could know how greatly she was loved.

When we returned to the Wakefield place late that afternoon, True was sleeping the sleep of the exhausted, and in the corner, in a white wicker basket, was a tiny pink baby girl with dark blue eyes and a look of utter surprise at the world she had entered.

19

April 2, 1899

Poor Liko. He is so miserable, without any of us on Mau'-
loa. He sends us note after pitiful note, asking when we will
be coming, or if he can come to see us. The business manager
hired by Colonel Toby will not advance the cost of the boat
ticket, and Jared tells True that he is feeling too poorly to
argue with his father.

"It is cruel," True says to Jared. "When I left to be with
Vicky, you told me you would see to it that Liko would
follow me. She asked for him!"

She could see Jared stiffen, see it in the stubborn thrust of
his chin, the way he refused to look at her. She felt a cold,
hard anger rising; in a sharp voice she told him, "Liko loved
Vicky, and she loved him. He should not have been kept
away."

"I wanted him to come," Jared said. "There's no sense in
even talking about it."

She felt the explosion coming, she couldn't stop it: "You
wanted him to come," she mocked. "What did he say when
you told him you wouldn't buy him a ticket?"

A small, blue puff of anger flickered for an instant in his
eyes and she thought: Good! He is going to fight. And she
wanted it—a fight, a good fight. She wanted to scream at
him, pound on his chest with her fists. She wanted to make
him listen to her, hear her.

"He cried, True," Jared said, miserable, "and I felt awful,
but there wasn't anything I could do. I wish you would
believe me and stop being angry. There really wasn't anything I could do."

She slapped the wall, hard. "There was plenty you could
do. You own half of that ranch, Jared. You have a right to

half of whatever there is. You don't have to listen to that jackass your father hired."

Jared assumed his stone face. "You've said all of this before," he told her. "I'm getting another headache, I can feel it coming on . . ."

True turned away. She knew she was really angry with herself; she should have brought Liko with her, but she hadn't thought Vicky would die—she didn't want to believe it could happen. And Jared was right; it was a struggle to get money out of the manager for any of them.

She didn't seem to be able to help these angry outbursts against Jared; it was as if they filled up in her and had to spill out, and it troubled her. She had supposed she could get him to stand up to his parents, but she had been wrong, and getting angry with him wasn't going to make anything right.

The baby pulled hard on her nipple. She laughed and shifted its mouth so it could get a better grip. "Just wait till Liko sees you," she said.

"Won't he be happy?" Jared spoke out. She looked up, surprised to see him standing there, still.

"Of course he'll be happy," she answered. "Maybe that's why I am so sorry he couldn't be here. He didn't get to say good-bye to Vicky, and he wasn't here to welcome Baby. He must be feeling horribly left out."

"I've written him that we'll be back just as soon as the baby is old enough to travel." Jared put out his finger and the tiny girl's hand locked around it. "Look at that!" he said, with such pleasure that True had to smile at him.

"She likes her papa," Laiana Wakefield said, sweeping into the room in that imperious way of hers, along with the baby nurse she had hired. "But off with you, Jared. Baby needs to nap and so does Mother."

Jared left, obediently.

"You can't call her 'Baby' forever," Laiana said as the nurse took the child from True and left. "She needs a name—do you have one?"

True looked carefully at the woman's face; she was beginning to understand her ways.

"I've been thinking of naming her for Vicky," True said.

"You mean to call her Kaiulani?"

"No, Victoria."

"I would like to name her Emma."

"Emma? Why?"

"Because last night I dreamed of Queen Emma. She was standing in the gardens at Ainahau, asking me to help her chase down one of the peacocks—she wanted to pluck a feather. I asked if she wanted it for a hat, and she said no, that she needed it for her new name. I didn't know what she meant, in the dream. But as soon as I woke up this morning I knew. She was asking for the baby to be named for her."

"Emma Victoria Wakefield," True said, as if trying it on.

"That is fine," Laiana said. "It's settled then."

"Shouldn't we ask Jared?" True asked.

Laiana folded her big frame into a rocking chair and studied True.

Here it comes, True thought to herself. *It had to come sooner or later . . .*

"There are those who are counting the months," Laiana Wakefield began. "Those who came to the wedding in August . . . they will say it is March now, not long enough."

"The doctor thinks that the funeral, Vicky's death, the boat ride over here, everything brought it on early," True told her.

Laiana laughed out loud. "Does the doctor know that Jared went to Maui and came back with love in his eyes and made excuses to return, month after month? Does the doctor know how many times you were together, out there on the farm?"

True lowered her eyes, playing her role.

Jared's mother went on, "I understand much now—why you came to Mau'loa to get Jared to marry you, and why he said he would, no matter how we said he should not." She rocked back and forth, two times, three times. "Mothers have no right to stop their children, not when a child is coming. I know how it is . . ." Her voice was surprisingly soft, accepting. Laiana Wakefield sat rocking and thinking, and True said nothing, only waited.

"You gave Jared a child, that is good," Laiana finally said, in her usual brusque tone. "Emma Victoria then. We will call her Emma."

Evan was waiting for us, leaning against the iron fence at the Royal Mausoleum at Nuuanu. We had come alone, True and I, to say good-bye to Vicky.

The hard work of the ranch on Kauai had made Evan lean and hard. His face was bronzed from the sun and his thick hair seemed lighter, shaggier.

I could feel the tension in True; I pulled the carriage to a halt. He walked over and looked up at her, and I had to look away, such was the pain in his face.

While I busied myself with the flowers we had brought, Evan and True settled onto a bench a distance from the mausoleum. No one was about; only the great piles of rotting flowers were left to mark the end of the funeral procession.

A silence welled between them and grew: there was too much to say, too many explanations, and no way to change what had happened.

True cleared her throat.

"Are you well?" he asked awkwardly, flailing out at the silence.

She nodded her head.

"And the baby?" he went on, his voice cracking.

She whispered, "Emma Victoria. I named her for Vicky."

He pressed his lips together and looked off to the rolling hills behind the old mausoleum, where Vicky slept now next to her mother.

"What happened to us, True?" Evan's voice rasped with pain. "How can we live with this?"

His words sent a scatter of electrical shocks through her, alarming her and shaking the words loose: "Evan, please . . . you must try. We have to live with it . . . there is no other way . . ."

"Why wouldn't you see me?"

She reached to touch his sleeve. "If I had seen you, I might not have been able to go through with it. And it was the right thing to do, Evan. It was the only thing I could do."

"The baby . . ." he said. "I didn't know until now, when I saw you at Ainahau. Why didn't you let me decide with you? Did you think I wouldn't . . ." He couldn't go on.

Her voice was low, throaty: "I knew you would," she said, "but I couldn't let you. We might have saved ourselves, but we would have lost so much else. And in the end, I would have been another Jenny—pushing you into a life you did not want. I love you too much to do that." She paused and swallowed to keep the tears at bay, then continued in a determined voice, "The baby is Jared's heir. You must understand that, please. I'm asking you to honor it. I have a home now, and Liko and Martha will be with me. We will all be together. And we'll be safe. It was the only way . . . oh Evan, I need you to help us."

He leaned forward and put his head in his hands. Then he turned to look at her, his eyes fierce with anger and loss. "The child. I want to see her."

"Yes. But not now, not here in Honolulu. Come to Mau'-loa. Come and talk to me about the ranch. Help me with Mau'loa."

"Another challenge?" he asked. "Is that it? Now you have a ranch to run?"

"To save," she told him quietly, "a ranch to save."

BOOK II

Mau'loa

1899–1919

20

Auntie Momi came again this morning. She slipped into the classroom at about ten and took a place at the back, in one of the little chairs meant for the youngest children. She has grown small and soft in her age, swallowed up by the folds of her muumuus, her hair a bright white against the dusty brown of her skin. She comes so often of late that the children scarcely notice; they accept her with equanimity, as they accept the sun and the wind and the sounds of the sea.

Auntie loves to watch me teach, loves to hear me give the lessons. I can feel her eyes on me, her pride swell and enclose me. Sometimes, when this happens, I am suddenly aware that I am speaking in Hawaiian. It is only the children's puzzled looks that tell me of this change.

"Did I catch you?" I will say, so they will think I have done it on purpose. "You must not forget your Hawaiian," I tell them, "and those of you who do not speak it must learn."

I look at Amalie and she smiles; it is a quiet, comforting smile. If she knows my mistake, she does not think it strange. Amalie is my friend. At the end of the lesson, I turn the class over to her and collect Auntie Momi. We will have one, perhaps two hours together before her grandnephew comes to take her home.

They take turns, these big Hawaiian boys, delivering her and picking her up. All smiles, all pleasure. No longer will she stay overnight with me, as she does not like to be away from her little house in the mountains for very long. Her coming on this day is, I know, to say good-bye; I leave next week for Mau'loa.

We sit together in the shade of the coco palms, facing the ocean. Old Auntie's voice carries, as flat and even and full of prophecy as the morning sea, a dry husk echoing like a breeze playing through the cane fields.

"Mau'loa," she began with a quavering sigh. "The goddess Pele is there, she took her fire and lives deep in the mountain." Auntie has long since abandoned any pretense of Christianity; the sisters at Holy Names were not able to infect her as they did me.

I took her hand and rubbed it gently with mine. "I am so sad to leave you, Auntie."

She turned to face me and for a flicker of an instant her old eyes searched my face. "You must go there," she said, her voice rising in a high quiver. "They call you, and now you go."

"Who, Auntie?" I asked, confused and alarmed by this sudden outburst. "Who calls me?"

She threw her arms around me then and began rocking and moaning and crying as she said her good-byes. This was what I had expected; like all Hawaiians, Auntie allows the emotion of sadness to spill out and over us, to wrap around us for this good-bye. I pray it will not be the last good-bye; I do not yet have the courage to face the world without my old Auntie, whose love I never doubt. Such was my sorrow at the parting that I let her strange words *they call you* slip out of my mind.

Jenny Coulter came to say good-bye and brought her son with her.

"Harry," I couldn't help but exclaim, "you look so like your father!"

Jenny lifted her chin. "Actually, he is the image of my mother's second brother, who died in the war between the States. In the Stonewall Brigade. We have a photograph of him when he was going off to war—he and Harry might have been twins. The resemblance is just remarkable. Everyone says so, don't they, Harry?"

The boy looked away, as if the conversation didn't concern him.

Aunt Winona and Jenny launched into torrents of words, and since they seemed to be settling down in the big wicker chairs on the lanai, I asked Harry if he would like for me to show him around the school.

"Oh, no," Jenny answered for him. "Harry has a book which he needs to read—for his school. He can just take a seat over at the table there . . ."

"I would like to see the stables, Mother," Harry spoke up.

Uncle appeared at that moment, greeted Jenny warmly and said to Harry, "Well, son, let's go have a look at the horses."

Harry followed Uncle without even glancing at Jenny. She pressed her lips tight together, but did not stop him. Aunt rose to get the tea, and I made to help her but Jenny said, "Oh do stay and visit with me. You'll be gone soon and who knows when we will have another chance?"

Wary, I took a seat. At that moment I realized Jenny wanted something.

"How is Evan?" I asked, quickly, to ward her off.

"Evan is fine," she said. "But then, I thought you knew that—you did visit with him at the Mausoleum, isn't that right?"

I took a lesson from Harry and did not answer. She stood and began pacing, making short, furious turns. "I know more than you and your good friend think I know. You can tell her that for me." Her face flushed with anger, she took two more quick turns. "Tell me this, Martha, what kind of a woman has a baby after seven months of marriage?"

Aunt Winona came bustling out with the tea tray, talking already and so engrossed in what she was saying that she noticed nothing. I forced myself to remain seated, to appear as unperturbed as possible, but I was seething.

Jenny chattered on as if nothing had been said, but soon enough she brought the talk back to True and the baby.

"Does the little girl—Emma, is it?—look like her daddy?" she asked, feigning innocence and nibbling on a sugar cookie.

Auntie blurted, "Oh, the very image—such a beautiful head, and long fingers, and such big eyes. The Colonel had some photographs of his sisters as babies, and they might have been our Emma! A Wakefield to be proud of, oh yes."

I made myself smile and nod, and I did not point out that the baby had her mother's light skin and blue eyes. When Aunt left again for a few minutes, I turned to Jenny and said, as straight as I could, "Why don't you tell me what's on your mind."

Her anger came welling up again, and I could almost see it take possession of her. "Something is wrong on Mau'loa," she told me. "Something is not right. True Lindstrom has fooled everyone, but I know what she is. Tell her that. Tell her I know."

As the ferry rolled and plunged and bobbed toward the Big Island, taking me to Mau'loa, I found myself alone on deck, the sun on my face and my thoughts—perhaps because my lot had been cast with them—turning to the Wakefields.

Uncle Jameson believes the Wakefields are an example of what he calls "the First Best Solution" when it becomes inevitable that newcomers of a different race must become part of a native society. The original Wakefield ethic, he believes, was built on the idea that because the Yankees know how to work and the Hawaiians know how to live, the two peoples could complement each other if they merged, with each respecting the other's ways.

The first Tobias had set the example when he married Liliha, a granddaughter of Kamehameha the Great. In the generations since, Wakefield men have seemed to prefer to marry native women, and as often as not, Wakefield women have chosen native men. Jared is among the first to break the tradition; I cannot but wonder if True's physical *brightness* does not startle them.

Even so, the haole blood of the founder of the clan is evident: their eyes are a glowing, limitless brown, their noses chiseled, their hair dark and thick but streaked with brown or glints of red.

My mind skips to Colonel Toby and Miss Laiana—both so tall and handsome, the very models of dignity. How to explain that Miss Laiana, for all the purity of her Hawaiian heritage, is more smitten with the ways of Europe than is the Colonel? If the truth be known, Miss Laiana feels even more of a kinship for Queen Victoria than she does for the New England Puritan who was her husband's ancestor.

I lean back against the bulkhead and have to wonder what old Tobias Wakefield would think of all this. It is not all that long since he arrived on the Big Island on the *Emilie K* out of Boston.

King Kamehameha was nearing the end of his long life then; he granted the big, awkward New Englander the right to stay in the islands if he would become a hunter of bullocks.

The cattle brought thirty years before by Vancouver had

wandered off into the mountains and, under protection of the kapu, had proliferated. They were everywhere in the mountains—great black beasts which could rip a man open with their long horns. Because the herds threatened the people and their livelihood, the King enlisted Tobias Wakefield and a few other haoles with muskets to hunt and kill some of the cattle, selling their hides and drying the meat to supply the foreign ships that were, more and more of them, finding their way to Hawaiian shores. It was dangerous business, going out on foot to trap the wild animals and kill them; it was also the only way that the tall, ungainly New Englander would be allowed to stay in the islands.

With his new wife, Tobias Wakefield went to the place called Mau'loa—it means "forever"—on the wide flank of the great mountain, where a small plot of land had been deeded to Liliha. This was to become the heart of the vast ranch and would give it its name.

The sea had calmed enough to allow me to walk, with caution, around the unsteady deck. It also made it possible for some of those who had stayed below to come up for air. Ordinarily I would have joined them for the company, but on this day my thoughts were too much with the Wakefields—past and present.

True had not been interested in the family's history, but Uncle and I had delved into it with the particular relish of a historian and his pupil. Family genealogies have always fascinated me, probably because I have none. My family starts with me and ends with me. The schoolmarm who came from nowhere, but who now has somewhere to go. Children to teach. Good work to do in my time on this earth.

The first Tobias Wakefield—what I would give to have known him and to hear the stories he told, set to paper by his first daughter: The death of King Kamehameha in Kailua and the emergence of Queen Kaahumanu as Kahina Nui, or regent, to share the throne with the new young king. The second Kamehameha had been no match for the powerful woman; soon enough she moved to break the old kapu system, to destroy the old ways, the old gods.

She could not have known how quickly a new god would appear, one who would prove more powerful than all the old gods together: Within months of the great king's death, the missionaries arrived in the islands from Tobias Wakefield's New England home state.

The first Wakefield had made the missionaries welcome at Mau'loa, had lavished on them all of the gracious hospitality of his wife's people. He married his wife in a Christian ceremony and gave her the name Hepzibah. They had already one son, by name Tobias like his father. Soon they would have another, and he would be named Efram.

In her youth, old Auntie had known Efram. When Uncle had questioned her about him, the memory lit some sweet fire in her. "*U'i* that one," she said—meaning beautiful. "Tall and laughing, all the time laughing. The *wahines* came to him like flies to sweet coconut. No stopping him, nobody want to stop him."

Efram had married a *wahine kapu,* a virgin promised to one of the island's great chiefs. Nothing would do but that Efram should have her, and marry her he did. She gave him two children, a girl and a boy, Tobias Three. The present Colonel Toby.

Efram's love match flared white hot while it lasted. Then it happened, as it did often enough on the mountain— Efram's horse fell on him, crushed him, and he was pau. The beautiful *wahine kapu* lay on his grave for three days and three nights, until the old man himself came to lift her off. Leaving her children behind, she took the servants she had brought with her when she came from Maui and set out for that island in an outrigger canoe. She never arrived at her home place. The canoe was never found.

Young Toby Wakefield grew up in the very house where I was now going to live, the old Home Place on the mountain slopes.

What tangled lives, I thought. Eben Wakefield—the only son of the second Tobias—and his cousin Toby had lived to take over the ranch in equal shares. Eben and Maile had been childless—a curse, the kahunas said, for mixing Eben's royal blood with that of a slave. It did not stop them; they became *hanai* parents to many young ones, including Jared Wakefield.

Uncle Jameson, always curious about family ways, had asked Jared why he had gone to live with Eben and Maile, how he had happened to become their hanai son when his own parents were still very much alive. He had answered without hesitation: "Auntie and Uncle wanted me, just as I was."

Before I left Uncle said that I should think of writing the history of the Wakefield family and Mau'loa Ranch, while there were still so many old paniolos around to tell of the early days. For some reason, the suggestion nettled me. If I tell any story, I had said rather sharply, it will be about my own patched-together ohana—the one I am on my way even now to join, as I begin my new life at Mau'loa.

21

Baby Emma cried all night long, little gasping collicky sobs that trembled through her tiny body. We took turns walking her around and around the nursery, True and I. Jared has moved out into the bunk house with the hands, so he can get some sleep—the baby's crying unnerves him so. I must say we are happy to be rid of his complaints.

True has found a wet nurse, so she has bound her breasts to dry up the milk flow. I can tell it is painful, but that isn't the worst of it. She is strung as tight as ever I have seen her.

"Every way I turn, they stop me," she complained as we passed the crying baby back and forth between us. "And whenever I try to get Jared to speak up, he gets a headache and has to go into a darkened room."

"Can't Liko talk to him?"

True sighed. I noticed frown lines between her eyes I hadn't seen before. "Liko has become so cautious. He lives in fear of being sent away. You can't blame him, I suppose—he sees how little influence I have here . . ." Her voice became hard with anger. "Do you know how much it is costing to send Miss Laiana and the girls to England for a year of 'finishing school'? Enough to buy us some good breeding stock, that's how much. And our cowboys don't even have their own string. They scarcely have two mounts each, and have to share horses. When the Colonel"—she said his name with disdain—"brings all his mighty friends up, we have to scramble for horses to work the ranch. And the school, you see what happened with the school . . ."

The baby's crying rose a pitch; True began to jostle her so roughly that I reached for her.

"Go to bed," I told True. "Get some sleep. I have to admit I was disappointed to find the school unfinished, but it won't stop us from starting lessons. We can have classes outside when it is nice enough, and we'll just move them into the parlor when it isn't. Little Emma here will be going to school right from the start, won't you, sweet baby?"

Emma, exhausted, gave a baby sigh and slipped into a sleep that we knew, by now, would last for perhaps an hour, if that long. I lay down on the little cot wedged into a corner of the nursery with the baby cradled in my arms, but I was too troubled to sleep.

We are together, as True had promised we would be, but it is as if a layer of discontent has descended on us, like the mists that come down from the mountain and are as aggravating and as unassuageable as the baby's continual crying. The problems with the ranch, True's disappointments, Liko's fears, Jared's ills are all part of it, but there is more. I cannot name what it is, but it is there, hovering over us. It is the way you feel before a storm, when the skies gather dark and the great clouds roll in, low and threatening. We seem to be living in that still time before the heavens open and rain down on us. I want to talk to True about it, to sort it out but I know I cannot, not yet. She has too much to think about already.

When I arrived the schoolhouse stood half finished, and the damp had done its work. While True and Jared were in Honolulu, the ranch manager had halted all "unnecessary" building. There is more important work to be done, he told them. Many of the ranch families live in an area within a mile of us, but they must walk almost six miles to the school at the Colonel's compound, and back again if they want an education. The girl who teaches the school can scarcely read or write. The Colonel makes light of it. "The girls will marry and produce little cowboys," he would say, "and the boys will always have a job on the ranch, like their daddies before them, whether or not they can read Shakespeare."

Even so, on the day of Vicky's funeral Colonel Toby had asked me rather petulantly why I had agreed to teach in True's school, and not his. He seemed genuinely disappointed, and I was at a loss how to answer him. Colonel Toby counts on charm more than anyone I have ever known. Whenever True complains to him about the ranch manager's high-handed ways, the Colonel always smiles his wide smile and tells her he will have to have a talk with the chap, that perhaps he has gone a little wide of the mark. Of course the Colonel never does talk to him, and the mark is exactly where he has placed it. The miserable hired manager simply does what the Colonel himself hates to do: say no.

Three days ago Emma looked up, smiled a beautiful baby smile, began to eat ravenously at her nurse's breast—slurping and sucking mightily—and almost at once began to sleep through the night.

It has had a marvelous effect on us all—True has lost the dark circles under her eyes, and Jared has moved back into the house and has started to work building a lovely big swan-shaped crib for Emma. Liko joins him to help in the evenings; it is nice to hear them talking and laughing together again. And I have begun to look around me, to see how I can organize my school.

I was sorting through a box of books when True came bursting in with the first full-fledged smile I had seen on her face in a week of Sundays. "Look who is here!" she said and laughed, pulling a small man by the hand.

I tried to recollect where I had seen him. "It's Pono," True reminded me. "Pono Rourke—from the Baumgartners on Maui."

"Yes, of course," I answered, telling him, "True claims you are the best cowboy in the islands . . ."

To my amazement, the man turned a deep, blushing red and could not seem to lift his eyes from his boots.

Dismayed, I looked at True for help but she was too delighted to notice. "Pono is going to work with us," she told me. "Now we'll get something done. Now they won't be able to stop us. Are you going to stay here in the bunkhouse, or with one of your brothers?" she asked him.

Pono Rourke cleared his throat, as if he had to practice before he could speak. "With Pat and his Maude," he said, "over to Taro Falls."

"That's a piece to ride," True told him. "Why don't you stay here? We can move Liko into the house, and you could have his place in the bunkhouse."

Pono did not answer her, which meant that he had made up his mind and wouldn't change it, True told me later. He was one of the seven wild Rourke brothers—half Irish, half Hawaiian and known far and wide for hard drinking, hard working, and inevitable troublemaking. They were big, tall black Irishmen all—except for Pono, who was slight and, although not more than thirty, beginning to lose his hair.

That night at supper Jared repeated what he knew about Pono Rourke: "He's the runt of the litter, the exception in every way. Where his brothers can't stop talking and drinking and carousing, Pono is silent and dry and a little sour. Growing up, those big boys made his life miserable. Now he can work rings around them all—it's said if he takes any one of them on, he can whip them like that."

True spoke up, "Baumgartner must have hated losing him. I've just never seen anyone work as hard as Pono. I always wondered why he would stay there when his family was here."

"Maybe he needed to get away from them," Jared put in sardonically, then asked, "Why do you suppose he came back?"

True coughed and admitted, "I wrote and asked him to come."

Jared stopped chewing. "Did you ask Pa if you could?"

True stood up abruptly, spilling a bowl of potatoes. She raised her voice to him: "You may have to ask your pa permission to go to the outhouse, Jared, but I don't."

Liko slipped off his chair and walked outside without looking back, taking himself out of the fray before anyone could ask him to take sides. I put my hands in my lap and waited. Soon enough True stormed out, sparks flying all about her. Jared did not move. Very slowly, I went down on my hands and knees and began picking up the spilled potatoes.

"I don't know what to do," Jared said.

I hesitated for a moment, wondering if I should talk to him or if, like Liko, I should remove myself.

"You don't know what to do about what?" I asked, taking my seat across from him.

Jared sighed and put his hand on his head in the way he did when a headache was coming on. "Father has said I should leave the ranching to him. He says he will take care of all of us, that all we need to do is tend this property, and one of the cottages on the beach if we want it. The weather is better for me, down there. I'm not much of a rancher, you know. And neither is True."

I smiled to make him feel easier. "Don't tell her she can't do anything she wants to do," I tried to joke, then I said, "The thing True talks to me about is what your Uncle Eben told her. He cared about this ranch, and he thought your pa was going to ruin it. That's why he willed his half to you, and not to your pa."

Jared's eyes grew dark. "I didn't ask him to do that."

"I know that, and so does True. But she feels, well, that your uncle meant for her to speak out. She thinks he was counting on her to do what *he* wanted for the ranch."

Jared shook his head; "It isn't easy for me to say anything to my pa. You know how he is . . ."

"I do know," I said, putting my hand over his and patting it. He looked at me with beautiful, grateful eyes, and asked if I would try to make True understand, and Liko too. About how he was. Because he wasn't strong, and because of the headaches that came on now without warning, sending sharp red pulses into his brain so that he felt like he might split apart.

He said he was going up to see Emma for a bit, then he would work on the crib. Whenever he spoke of the baby, his face softened. "At least I have Emma," he told me. "I'm glad for Emma—she's always happy to see me."

In the nursery he lifted the baby and held her close to his face. He loved the smell of her, the clean sweet-sour smell of warm milk. He rubbed her back until he heard the unmistakeable bubble of air released.

He spoke out loud, as if I weren't there: "Nothing is the same anymore. Liko doesn't understand . . . he probably doesn't trust me, and I suppose he is right not to. I can't seem to do what any of them want me to do . . . nobody but Emma," he said, kissing the baby on her cheek and breathing in her baby smells once more, before gently returning her to her crib.

Pono stayed. There was never any question but that he would be hired, because he was worth any two good men, and some said he was better than all of his brothers put together. True couldn't say why he had agreed to come back. She thought at first it was because she had asked him, but then she heard from some of the other ranch hands that the brother Pono was living with was drinking more than he should and knocking around his wife and children. The brothers had asked Pono for help. Maybe, True thought, he couldn't resist two appeals from home.

True spends her days in the saddle, with notebook and pencil tucked into her saddlebags. She is surveying the ranch, riding from the low dry pasturelands near the beaches all the long, gradual miles up into the mountain pastures. Tracing the waterlines, the lakes and ponds, taking samples of grasses, counting the herd.

Liko is with her much of the time. When the ranch manager objected to her use of this "half-a-hand," as he likes to call him, she told the man to go straight to hell if he thought she was going to give Liko up without a bloody fight. She has spent some time practising with a rifle, shooting away at the cactuses that punctuate the pastureland. Without warning, she raised her rifle and blasted a gull sitting on a fence post. By the time the feathers had settled, the ranch manager had decided Liko wasn't worth a showdown fight.

Still, things are getting better. I may have helped by making True understand that Jared simply cannot stand up to his father and that she is going to have to find another way to save the ranch. She has changed course with amazing ease, it seems to me.

She got Jared to agree to one thing: that no part of the ranch be sold without her written permission, as well as his. She asked him sweetly, as if it wasn't so much, after all. Hadn't his father assured him, time and again, that it wasn't in his mind to sell any of the ranch? The papers were drawn up and signed, and Jared was pleased because suddenly True seemed ever so much happier about things.

She writes Evan every week, letters filled with information about the ranch, and his return letters tell her what to look for in the cattle, how to select the best of them for breeding to improve the herd. Often he sends pamphlets and treatises on grasses and irrigation plans and lists of places to find good breeding stock. Even if she can't do anything about it now, she tells us, she is going to figure out just what it will take to turn this into a fine ranch.

Jared's headaches have returned with a vengeance, and he has developed a cough which worries Liko and me. True scarcely bothers to conceal her impatience; she thinks Jared imagines many of his ills. Colonel Toby was on his way back to Honolulu for the opening of the legislature, so Jared decided to go with him to consult with the doctors who have followed his case through the years. They left yesterday, and Aunt Maile arrived today.

After Uncle Eben died, Aunt Maile went to live with her family on the windward side of the island; she chose this time to come for a visit, and to see the new baby.

Her presence has cast a spell over us; True fell into her arms and kissed both of her cheeks, and even little Emma had only smiles and baby laughs for this big, dear woman. She was sad to have missed Jared and frowned when she learned why he had left.

"When he was a little boy, just growing, I let him swim in the pond," she told us. "The water was too cold, his mother says. But I believe that cold water can make a boy grow strong." She was troubled, you could tell by the quaver in her voice.

True changed the subject, launching into a diatribe about all that was wrong with the farm, ending with her usual complaints about Colonel Toby's spending habits.

"You sound like my Eben, just so," Aunt chuckled. "He would get angry, like you. It made him so angry that he couldn't think anymore, couldn't remember. He started to hide money. He wrapped it all up careful, put it in big Chinese jars and buried them, then he forgot where."

She laughed out loud at the expression on our faces.

"Did you ever find them?" True wanted to know.

Aunt Maile rocked the baby and cooed, "No, no. He hid them too good, never found them at all."

True and I exchanged glances. "Who knows?" we asked, almost in unison.

"I know," Aunt Maile said, "and now you know. And I say, if you find the money it is yours to keep. But how to find it, I don't know. Eben said he made a mark, all the same for every one. Four, maybe five in all. But he couldn't remember what the mark was."

When Aunt had gone, True and I called Pono and Liko and, after swearing them to secrecy, proposed a treasure hunt. We sat at the long table on the lanai and plotted out how we would proceed.

"Old Mr. Wakefield was too sick to ride," Pono said.

Liko chirped, "So it has to be around the Home Place, where he could walk."

Pono drew a rough map of the grounds and divided it into four quarters. Each of us took one, and set out to note anything out of the ordinary, Uncle Eben's "mark."

Every evening all that week we were out, making long lists of anything that could conceivably be a mark. Then we gathered at the table, where I wrote down each item. It would be dark by the time we finished; finally, we had something like three hundred listings of such things as: fence post near corral chipped; ahu covered with honeycreeper near horse barn; one yellow rose bush in middle of reds; red stain near foundation of stone cool house; small stone ahu next to vegetable garden; birdhouse in apple orchard.

On the sixth evening, we stopped just before the sun dropped into the sea. Pono sat at the table, listening, as I read off the list. He looked at his own crudely drawn map of the area, then walked away without a word. We watched him, knowing something was happening. When he returned, his bright Irish eyes were shining. "Come," he said, and we followed him, excitement rising.

"Look closely," he told us, leading us first to the horse barn, then diagonally across the lawn to the vegetable garden, then walking us in a straight line to the little stone cooling shed and again, an equal distance, to the edge of the orchard. When we had covered this territory, he looked at us expectantly.

What had I seen? It came to me suddenly. Of course! The ahu—a boundary marker of small stones piled one on another, like the Scots' cairns. "Five ahus have a black stone second from the top," I gasped.

Pono beamed, and I could feel myself flushing with pleasure. True and Liko whooped; Pono was already on his way to the shed for shovels.

We started digging just as the sun was dropping into the Pacific. "Soft earth here," Pono said, and not another word until the shovel hit crockery. All of us dropped to our knees beside the hole, and waited as Liko's strong arms lifted out an old Chinese jar.

The top had become encrusted with dirt and had to be pried off. "Oh, Lord," True murmured when she saw what was inside: a pile of coins, glinting in the last rays of the sun.

It was dark by the time we found the last jar. We lit a lamp and crowded around the table—all of our faces and hands smudged with mud by now, and none of us caring in the least.

True counted. Three hundred five-dollar gold pieces in all.

"Enough to buy some breeding stock," True said, her voice filled with joy.

Pono slapped his hands against the table, as if to say, "Let's go!" I clapped my hands and Liko did a little two-step jig around us all. True simply beamed. "Thank you, Uncle Eben," she said, clasping her hands together as if in prayer and laughing, too. "And thank you, Aunt Maile, and thank you, Martha and Liko and Pono . . . thank you all!"

Liko frowned. "Is it a secret?" he asked.

True bit her lip. "For a while, yes."

"But not from Jared?" Liko added.

After a pause, True said, "No, not from Jared."

When Jared returned two weeks later, the Colonel was with him and all puffed up with anger. As soon as they rode in, Jared pleaded exhaustion from the long trip and went straight up to his bed, stopping only long enough to see baby Emma.

The Colonel poured himself a measure of Scotch whiskey and settled in the parlor to wait for True to return from her late afternoon ride. I stood in the doorway, not certain if I should enter and try to make conversation or not, and the Colonel was not in a mood to help me. He downed one quick drink and poured himself another, but before he could drink it we heard the approach of a horse. The Colonel strode out, taking the stairs in wide strides and before True could dismount, he was at her, his face flushed red from the drink and his anger.

"I want to know just who you think you are, young lady, getting my son to sign a paper that says I have to get your permission before I do anything on this ranch. My wife doesn't have that privilege, neither do my sisters. But you— the daughter of a *wahine laikini*—you think you can come in here and take over."

True simply sat on her horse and listened. She did not

look away; her face was deadly calm, as if she had been expecting this.

Colonel Toby wasn't through with her. "I am telling you right now, Miss, that you are going to have to change your ways. This ranch does not belong to you, and you have nothing to say about how it is run. I am leaving behind the legal papers that rescind those that give you the right to say when I can sell my land. I urge you to sign it now, before I leave, and we will end this nonsense at once."

True dismounted, swinging easily down. She was almost as tall as the Colonel, and she looked him squarely in the eyes when she said, "No." Then, in case he hadn't heard, she repeated, calmly, "No."

I thought the Colonel might burst. He stamped around, the Scotch sloshing out of his glass. Then he drained it in one gulp and told True, "You can continue to live here, because you are my son's wife and the mother of his child. But do not expect to get one penny from me, not one. And tell your husband that until he convinces you to sign this paper, I have no intention of releasing any ranch fees to pay his personal bills, including his doctors' charges. If he is going to be a man, it's time he start acting like one."

When True did not answer, the Colonel turned on his heel and walked away.

True called after him, "How did you find out?"

The Colonel stopped but did not turn around. True answered for him, "You meant to sell off a piece of the ranch, that's how you found out. You told Jared you'd never sell. You'd never have known if you didn't plan to sell."

Colonel Toby turned back; his face was a bruised, blotched purple. He seemed suddenly to notice me, and as if he couldn't think of anything else he said, "I'm not paying for a teacher, and none of the ranch hands will be allowed to send their children to school here. And I'm not paying to keep the dwarf, either." With that, he left.

True and I sat on the lanai in the long dusk, silent, waiting for the dark to enclose us. I do not know how long we had been there before I became aware of Pono, standing motionless at the far end of the lanai, listening, waiting in the twilight. It seemed right that he should be there, witness to our disappointment; I took comfort from his presence. Pono had cast his lot with us, for what reason I could not be sure, but I was glad for it. His strength seemed to radiate out into the soft and silent night to give us courage.

Darkness was settling in when Liko came to join us. He cleared his throat. "I've been up talking to Jared," he said.

We waited.

"He needs to go back to the doctors. He needs treatments for his lungs . . ."

The silence lay over us, filled now with dread.

Liko's voice trembled. "His father won't send him unless you sign."

True took a deep breath; I could hear the air move into her lungs, and in the darkness I could see the clear white skin on the inner part of her arm. In a low voice she said, "I won't sign."

Liko knew what the Colonel said about him; he had been listening, just out of sight. I was glad it was too dark now for me to see his face, which would have been filled with fear. Everything would have told him to bolt, to run away; his love for Jared won out over his fear.

"I told Jared about the money," he said.

22

Living in these cool uplands is like living somewhere between heaven and earth—the rolling green grasses, waving mile after mile toward the mountains, the morning mists, the winds that moan around the houses and barns like some living thing. And the rank growth all around, bright bowers of flame trees and poinsettias, wild ginger everywhere, orchids climbing every tall tree.

Several buildings are scattered about the original home place, a two-story saltbox built by the first Tobias so many years ago. Every New Englander who sees the old house with its little square-paned windows is reminded of home; only the warmth of the koa wood inside gives them pause. All of the furniture is koa as well, even the nails that hold the house together. It seems almost the perfect blend of haole and Hawaiian: at once spartan simplicity and lavish Hawaiian warmth.

Behind the house are the servants' quarters and vegetable gardens. Across the way is a bunkhouse and next to it a small barn used to store saddles and tack, and a shed for the farm plows and bullock wagons. Out front, in the clearing, is a small stone cool house for storing meat and the cisterns, where water is stored. The pens and corrals are down a ways, near a small dairy barn and a shed used for slaughtering. Beyond that is a peach orchard of some fifty trees.

Aunt Maile had not been much for flowers. With Liko's help I have put in one bed of pansies, and another of impatiens. Even Jared helped me plant some plumeria and jasmine, because he loves their sweet scent. Everything seems to thrive in this lush climate. Except for Jared, who is so thin his clothes hang on him.

Cook tries to tempt him with his favorite Hawaiian foods, but I can see that it is difficult for him to swallow. True is

worried. She never chastises him anymore about staying in
bed so late or tells him to "go climb on a horse and have a
good gallop to knock the skitters out of you."

Today they left for the little beach house for a few days—
True, Jared, Liko and the baby. I have begged off. Uncle
Jameson has sent me a box of books, and I have been look-
ing for a quiet time to sit and read. I can't let on how much
I miss my classes, how much I want to be able to teach. The
days are so terribly long, and so empty of a feeling of worth.
The Colonel has stymied us all.

Nothing has been said of the gold coins. Jared will not
ask, I think. But it is becoming clear to all of us that he needs
medical care. I know True is hoping that the warm, dry air
and the heat of the beach will bring Jared back to health. I
do so hope that she is right.

For some reason I woke just as the sky was growing gray
this morning. For a moment I lay in my bed, and then I
remembered that everyone was away, except for the servants
who work in the house and the vegetable gardens.

"Things aren't so bad as they may seem," True had announced after the Colonel cut us off without funds. "We
have a roof over our head and plenty to eat, and we can
barter for those few things we need." I did not need to point
out that we could not barter for the kind of medical care
Jared needs. To True, the found treasure seemed a gift from
the gods, meant to save the ranch. She knows that Jared
must be saved first, but she is not quite ready to give in.

I pulled on a wrapper, made my way downstairs and into
the kitchen. I looked across to the cookhouse, to see if cook
had started the fire. No smoke and no smell of burning
wood—it was too early. Then I saw them, sitting close together on a low wall—Pono in the middle, a child on either
side. Each was wrapped in a blanket, and he was holding
hard to them.

"Whatever in the world . . ." I murmured to myself,
moving as fast as I could across the circle of wet grass,
forgetting I was in my nightgown, forgetting my hair was
hanging down my back.

The little girl's eyes were swollen from crying, and one of the
boy's eyes was black and blue and his nose had been bleeding.
I looked at Pono for an explanation, but he looked away. His
lip was split and his knuckles, I noticed, were raw . . .

"Bring them in," I told him. "Let's get that eye taken care of and feed these young ones. Then things will look a little better."

"They need schooling," Pono said. He looked at me then, a steady, purposeful look. Certain of me, certain that I could do what he asked of me. A look that flooded me with confusion and confidence.

"First they need comfort and rest. Can they stay here with me for a few days?"

Pono looked away, then turned back. "Two nights."

I nodded, knowing—I can't say how—that whatever he said was right, and possible.

The boy was, perhaps, eight, the girl no more than six. I washed their faces, checked their bruises and sent Pono to the coolhouse to get them some milk. "School it is, then, little ones. But first we have to make you strong enough to study, so I'm going to put you to bed for a little sleep. When you wake up, we'll have breakfast and then we will begin."

They had been frightened and exhausted; now they were simply exhausted. I took them to a bedroom and tucked them in.

Pono was waiting for me in the kitchen. I blurted: "I think I know what happened. Your brother Patrick went on a rampage and hit the children. Is his wife—Maude, I think?— is she all right?"

He nodded.

"And your brother? Did you teach him a lesson? Shouldn't we tend to your bruised hands?"

He turned his eyes on me again, and I felt a sudden flash of heat, as if they had the power to ignite. Dismay and sorrow flooded through me. To protect the children, he had hurt his brother and the pain was there to see, in his eyes. "I'm so sorry, Pono," I told him.

He turned away. "The children need school," he said. "You need school. Start with these. I will bring them every morning, take them home at night."

It was the longest speech I had ever heard him make. "Thank you," I said very quietly. He turned to look at me, puzzled. "Thank you for knowing I missed my teaching," I explained.

He looked at me steadily; it was at that moment that I first realized what a fine, intelligent face he has, strong and kind at the same time. Standing there in my nightdress, I felt the warm sting of embarrassment. At my dishabille, at where my thoughts were taking me.

What a wonderful week this has been! The children, Nancy and James, are bright and lively and hungry to learn. The boy knows his letters and his numbers—as much as his mother knows, I gather—and he wants so desperately to read that I think he would work around the clock, if I allowed it. And the girl, with her beautiful black curls and big blue eyes—whatever bad things happen to them at home, I have to believe that good things happen too, because they are such happy, lively children.

Until now, I had not realized how much more effort goes into teaching damaged youngsters. At Hale Mana'olana, it took us weeks just to get the child's attention, and often they could not concentrate for more than short bursts of time. But these two, oh my! They are like little sponges, just soaking up everything. They want me to go faster, faster. I can't begin to say how exhilarating it is to be teaching such imps.

Pono brings them before first light, since he must be at work by dawn. He has made them a bed in the back of a wagon, and they sleep along the way. He comes for them when his day is done, which often is long after the sun has set. The children chatter at him like birds, telling him all they have done during the day. And I chatter too. Poor Pono is assaulted by all our talk!

I am so glad to have this time alone with the children, to be able to spend all of my day with them, to give them full attention. In the afternoons they work with me in the vegetable garden and with the flowers, and they insist we spell out everything we see.

I am glad to have Pono come in the evening to sit with us in the kitchen, eat his supper (I have insisted that he eat with us) and listen to us tell all that we have done during the day.

He enjoys it, I am almost certain. Often now, I find him looking at me and when our eyes meet I think I can see what he is thinking. I believe, I am almost certain, that he understands how much I have to give, how much I need to give. But what do I understand about him?

* * *

True and Jared and Liko are back, and nothing is changed. If anything, Jared seems paler, even more frail. The cottage is on a perfect little stretch of beach protected from the surf by a reef. "Did you swim?" I asked Jared, and Liko behind him shook his head at me.

"He is too weak to swim," Liko told me after Jared had gone up to bed and True had left for the corral. "He can scarcely dress himself. True will tell you when she settles down—I think she just had to get out for a while now. She's been so cooped up with the baby and Jared and all. She is giving him the money for the doctors."

"When will they leave?" I asked.

Liko looked at me strangely. "True wants you to go with us."

"You're going?" I asked.

"Jared wants me," he answered, his chin thrust out, "and baby Emma. He won't go without her."

"All of us?" I asked, incredulous.

Liko shrugged. He looked so dejected I put my arm around him, and to my surprise he pushed me away.

"What is it," I asked. "What is wrong?"

He covered his eyes so I could not see the tears squeezing out. "I think it must be my fault, Martha. If I had been normal, like others. Maybe the gods are punishing me for my love by hurting him . . ."

I took both of his hands in mine. "You cannot think that way," I told him. "Not if you are going to help Jared. He needs you now, more than ever. Can't you see that? He told me how he feels—he feels weak, and he thinks that you don't trust him because of it. Liko, think how much alike you are, the two of you. Jared is tall and as handsome as anyone I know. And yet inside, he feels weak and small. And you are small, but strong inside, much stronger than Jared in every way. So it is you who must help him; right now, I think you are the only person who can."

He cocked his head to one side and stared at me, aghast. "He thinks I don't trust him?"

"That's what he told me. You must prove to him that you do."

Liko nodded. "I will," he said, his voice low and resonant. "I will."

* * *

I did not go with them to Honolulu. Perhaps it was wrong of me, but I persuaded True that one of us needed to stay behind to watch over the Home Place and keep an eye on what was going on with the ranch.

It was dishonest, I admit, but the idea of living in the Colonel's house, with him in residence during the session of the territorial congress, was not to my liking. Not after he has forbidden me to start my school.

True was no more eager to be thrown together with the Colonel, but she had another reason for wanting to return to Honolulu. Evan has resigned his position on the ranch in Princeville, and is returning to become assistant attorney general of the territorial government. His terse note to True, explaining this unexpected move, said only that Harry was having some difficulties which required him to return.

Aunt Winona, who writes much as she talks—like a waterfall, words spraying out from the pages—gave her version, filtered through one of Jenny's sporadic visits.

"My dear girls," Aunt wrote. "It has been such a day, such a crowded day filled with all the usual busyness and distractions. One of the new boys stepped on a sharp piece of coral and his foot was bleeding profusely before Amalie was able to doctor him, Brother being away in the new pineapple grove.

"This afternoon, as we were settling down to a cool glass of passion fruitade (Amalie's invention), Jenny Coulter came riding up, all smiles and good cheer and wearing a pretty-as-you-please new dress, white with sweet little green dots and a green sash to match, very stylish indeed and like one I saw in. . . ."

I glanced down the page, looking for the message Jenny had come to plant in Aunt's profuse letter-growing garden. "Jenny is as happy as she can be, she says, because Evan has finally found out how lonesome it is without his family, and he is coming back to take a high position in the government. Jenny is having the house redecorated, as she expects she will be doing quite a bit of entertaining, and she is tired of the old-fashioned furniture her father bought when he built the house. Everything is going to be wonderful, Jenny says, now that Evan knows how foolish it would be to waste the wonderful education which her father helped pay for, after all."

Jenny has become prone to mentioning how much different people, and organizations, owe to her father's largesse. She is particularly fond of pointing this out to the remaining members of the royal family, none of whom think the better of her for it.

Governor Cleghorn, who always errs on the side of kindness, told Uncle, "Jenny Coulter has become *pa'akiki*—difficult." In one way she is becoming more like her father: She has taken to speaking bluntly, to saying whatever is on her mind, no matter the consequences.

I do not believe Jenny's explanation about Evan's return to Oahu. There is more to it, I am certain. And I wonder why Evan has not come to Mau'loa, as he said he would.

True wonders as well, though we do not talk about it.

In fact, True talks very little these days; her terrible need to work this ranch seems to consume her. The ideas scattering in her brain, I am almost certain, have to do with cattle and grasses and water rights. It has become a consuming passion. You need only to see her mounted on her big chestnut mare, wearing the leather chaps and weskit and an old straw hat with a band of dried flowers, to know how much she feels for this green island ranchland. Sometimes I fancy that the passion she feels for Evan, so long compressed inside of her, has burst out full-blown in her love for this land, this great flowing country, this mountaintop thrust up from the ocean depths.

True looped her arm around Jared's waist to help him up the stairs at the Wakefield house in Honolulu. The Colonel, standing at the top of the stairs, seemed frozen by shock.

"My God, boy, what's happened to you?" he blurted.

Jared went straight to his old room with its narrow bed, Liko directly behind him with his bags.

In the parlor, the Colonel seemed unable to frame the right question. True, seeing how shaken he was, decided to help him. "We went to the beach, to see if the change of climate would help but it didn't," she told him. "He just kept getting weaker and weaker, until it seemed like the only answer was to bring him here to the doctors."

The Colonel sat down and covered his face with his hands. "I didn't mean it, when I said I wouldn't pay."

True stood very still. "We have some money. Uncle Eben

had buried it in the yard at the Home Place, and then forgot where he had hidden it. Aunt Maile told us about it, and we searched for it and found it. It's enough for whatever Jared needs."

The Colonel looked up at her now, his eyes not quite focused, trying to understand what she was saying.

"Eben? Why would he . . ." Suddenly, he understood. "I see," he said. "Yes. Well, it is ranch money he buried, of course. But you are right to use it for Jared, even though I would have . . . Yes. I see."

True turned away, in case she had not been able to keep all traces of disappointment from her face.

"We will have to do everything possible for him," the Colonel said, regaining his old optimistic momentum. "I must write his mother . . ." he added, uncertain again. And then, "But the doctors will pull him out of it. They always have. Several times while he was growing up. Always poorly, the boy. Comes from when he was staying with Eben and Maile, they let him swim in a pond where the water was chilled. His constitution was never strong after that. You could say that Eben hiding away the gold pieces . . . it is gold that he hid?"

True nodded.

The Colonel finished with a flourish, "You could say it is ironic justice, that gold paying for the medical attention Jared needs now."

True smiled wanly and repeated what she had said to Jared, "What is important is to get him well again."

"I'm glad you've come to your senses, young lady," the Colonel remarked.

"Jared's well-being has always come first," she lashed back at him. "If the money hadn't been needed for this, I would have urged Jared to use it to buy breeding stock."

The Colonel took a step back, removing himself from the wrath he sensed about to pour out. "We can talk about that some other time," he said, in an effort to be conciliatory. "Now I believe we are in agreement about the need to help our boy. Let us join hands, True, and show him we are working together in this."

She took the hand he offered. Jared would be disturbed if she argued with his father; she clamped her teeth tight together so that her jaw jutted out.

"I want you to know, True," the Colonel said then, "that I am thinking about the ranch, what needs to be done. You are correct about the need to improve our breeding stock, and I intend to do something about it. As a matter of fact, I've got an appointment to see Evan Coulter—did you know he has left the Princeville ranch? He did an amazing job there—it was failing and now it's flourishing. I'm going to see if he can't do something for us as well."

True stared at him. *Be careful,* she said to herself, *go slowly.* She wanted to know what the Colonel had in mind. Would he ask Evan to manage Mau'loa? Finally she gave the Colonel one of her radiant smiles and said, "Fine idea, Father Wakefield."

The Colonel glowed back at her, happy to have done something to please her. "Now I am off. Time to campaign for the legislature, you know. We've planned a little ride through town . . ."

She watched him skip down the stairs, his tall figure imposing and full of swagger in his immaculate white linen suit. He mounted a stallion with a shiny black coat and rode off, the very picture of success. At the end of the drive he turned and waved to her, and she waved back, thinking to herself how strangely the world sometimes works, imagining the Colonel approaching Evan to come to Mau'loa.

That afternoon Governor Cleghorn paid a visit, giving her a fatherly hug and shedding a few unabashed tears in memory of Kaiulani. "I'll never be able to see you or Martha without seeing the three of you together—my Vicky in the middle, laughing and happy."

"I know," True whispered as she reached to kiss his cheek. "I miss her terribly, too."

Near the end of the visit, the Governor cleared his throat as if to make an announcement. "This is for you," he said, handing her an envelope with "True" written on it; she felt a sudden catch in her chest as she recognized Evan's handwriting.

If the Governor noticed the pink flush that spread up her neck, he did not let on but continued in the same, kindly voice, asking, "Can you come out to Ainahau for a visit while you're in Honolulu? It's so much closer to Winona and Jameson than the Colonel's house is. I know you will want to be seeing them, and they have so many children now that everyone is doubling up, so perhaps you would be more comfortable with us?"

"Jared won't be able to come," True told him. "He is undergoing so many different treatments, the doctors come every day. But he does seem to be getting stronger, so if he feels he can do without Emma and me, we will come out for a few days. It would be lovely to be back on Waikiki beach for a spell."

He patted her hand and his eyes brimmed with tears. "Come if you feel you can," he said when he left.

She ripped open the envelope. Evan wrote: "Can you meet me at three on Thursday afternoon at the old summerhouse on the beach at Ainahau? Send a message to room twenty-three at the State House."

She arrived at Ainahau before lunch on Thursday, got the nurse and Emma settled in one of the back rooms and joined Governor Cleghorn on the lanai for a bowl of cold cucumber soup.

True laughed. "I haven't had this since before Vicky went to England. I remember her mother, the Princess, telling us it was good for our complexions, and Vicky asking if it would be all right to wash our faces in it rather than eat it."

The Governor chuckled, happy for the remembrances. A small boy came toddling up and climbed into his lap. "This is my son," he told True, "and he is as good a boy as you'll find in the islands." The child's dark eyes sparkled.

"I'm afraid I have to go back into town this afternoon," the Governor said, rising to leave. "You know your way around, my dear . . . make yourself at home."

She stood in the center of the little summerhouse and allowed the memories to flood in. Vicky had loved this place, which was open to the air yet shut off from view by creeper vines and jasmine bushes and cooled by the breeze off the water. Out of habit, she slipped out of her shoes to feel the soft, grassy floor against her feet. She hadn't realized that Evan knew about this place; her stomach tightened as she thought of him, her face grew hot, time constricted. It was early yet; she had not been able to stay in her room, waiting. Her throat felt dry. She rubbed her palms on the folds of her muumuu and studied her hands, which were shaking.

She saw him riding down the beach, his horse trotting easily. She moved out so he could see her and waved to him. He lifted his hat. His hair, streaked by the sun, was caught and tousled by the wind. The sight of him made her feel buoyant, as if she could float in the air. She watched as he dismounted, watched as he walked toward her, watched as his face registered all of the longing she felt.

He opened his arms and she moved into them; they stood clinging to each other, holding hard in a long embrace. Finally he cradled the back of her neck in his hand and held her so he could look into her face.

"Dear God, I've missed you," he said with a deep sigh.

"Yes," she managed to whisper, reaching to touch his lips with the tips of her fingers. "Oh, yes."

"I have to tell you . . . there is so much we need to talk about."

She pulled him into the summerhouse, close to her on the bench and held hard to his hand.

He studied her hand in his, lifted it to his lips. "I have plenty of regrets," he began. "I've made so many mistakes . . ."

She closed her eyes and rested her head on his shoulder for a moment. He lay his cheek against her hair and went on, speaking low and urgently.

"I had to come back. Harry . . . only six years old, poor little fellow. For so long he has simply done what his mother wanted him to do. He was such a well-behaved little boy, never complaining. I could see what was happening, but I didn't fight her. Instead I deserted him when I went off to Kauai, to the ranch. About three months ago, Harry started running away. One time I came back on my usual visit, and he was nowhere to be found. Jenny was out looking for him, and so was old Kemo, who has been with the family for so long, and every other servant. We finally found him in one of the boat sheds about two miles down the beach, hiding in a far corner. Kemo somehow knew he was there. I guess Harry had been asking some questions about it. He'd covered himself over with old palm fronds to try to keep us from finding him.

"I tried to talk to him, but he wouldn't answer. Jenny went between tears and rage, and you could see the boy go into himself, moving away from both of us. Jenny says that if I had been here, it wouldn't have happened. Old Kemo told me Harry has run away three other times, and that each time he goes a little farther. When I asked Kemo what he thought, he gave me one of those sharp side-glances, which means it is my business to figure it out."

"I kept Harry with me all of that week—I even took him to business meetings."

"Jenny didn't object?" True asked.

Evan shrugged and True's head moved with his shoulder. "She is feeling pretty worried, I suppose. She objected some, not much."

"And Harry? Did he go with you willingly?"

"Oh yes," he said. "He scarcely said a word, but he stayed close by my side. I tried to do some things that would give him pleasure, but he doesn't ride very well, and he can hardly swim. We spent some time hiking in the mountains."

He paused, turned to look into her eyes and smiled. "I needed to see you," he said, his voice low and hoarse.

"I know," she answered, pressing close, rising to take him in her arms. He touched his lips to her neck, and she kissed the thick sunburned hair on the top of his head.

He started talking again, more quickly now. "I'd been back on Kauai no more than a week, when Harry showed up. He'd stowed away on one of the cattle boats. He said he had come to stay with me, and if I wouldn't let him, he'd run away again and we'd never find him."

True exhaled. "I thought it must be something like that," she said. "Poor little Harry. And yet, at the same time, I have to admire him."

He smiled at her. "Somehow, I knew you would say that—*good for Harry for standing up.*"

"Most children are too timid," she said, "or they don't have the kind of pa they can run to. He wouldn't come back without you," she said. "You had no choice."

"Jenny has agreed to let me have a free hand with Harry, so long as I am discreet—about his problems, and ours."

"Does she want . . . is she . . ." True tried to ask.

He pulled her to him and held her close. "No," he said. Then he released her and asked, "Is Emma here with you?"

"Yes," she told him. "You must see her, but she was napping when I came down and won't be awake for a time, and there is so much we need to talk about. Colonel Toby told me that he plans to ask you to help with Mau'loa."

Evan nodded. "He wants me to come in, take over and make it profitable . . . like I did at Princeville."

"But . . . ?" True prompted.

"When I asked if that meant control of the finances, he began to hem and haw. The Wakefield ranch's long decline won't be stopped until somebody besides Toby gets control of the purse strings."

True sank against him. "I know, and it isn't going to be Jared. Especially not now, when he is so ill again." She told him about Uncle Eben's gold coins and about the documents that say Toby cannot sell any ranch land without her approval.

Evan shook his head. "I'm not sure that was a wise move, True," he told her. "Toby shouldn't have much trouble getting it overturned; he knows all of the judges. I wish . . ."

She slipped onto his lap and curled into his arms, her face lifted to his; they touched lips together, softly at first, holding, pressing. Their bodies arched and angled against each other; he ran his hand up her dress, and found her hot and moist against him. She moaned as they slipped onto the grassy floor of the summer place and he lifted her dress and looked at her.

"When this happened before," he began, his hands moving around her breasts. "When I loved you like this . . ."

"I know, but nothing can happen now . . . not today . . ."

He moved his hand in long, circling motions over her stomach and leaned to kiss it, pressing his tongue into her navel. She spread open her legs; he kissed her knees, the soft inside of her thighs; with his hands he spread her apart and touched the bright pink center of her with his tongue, sending small sharp shocks up into her stomach and heart and lungs. She thought she might burst.

"Oh God, Evan, love me," she whispered, desperation sweeping into her voice. "Please, please love me."

He removed his clothes slowly, rising to his knees to take

off his shirt. She looked at his chest, tightly muscled and hard.

His skin felt smooth against her body. She slid her hands down his spine, pushing him into her. He entered, full and hard and promising.

Now, she thought, and began to make soft, crying sounds as he lifted, gently rolling, and she pushed, rising in rhythms that matched. The sun penetrated the vines and scattered points of light around them, and the world exploded in all the far reaches of their bodies entwined. She pressed her ear to his chest, heard the hard beating of his heart and understood.

They lay together then, listening to the sounds of the waves breaking on the shore and the call of the seabirds. He brushed a small, bright insect from her hair, and she touched her tongue to the tip of his chin, where a single, salty drop of perspiration stood.

They dressed then, and before they left the summerhouse he pulled her to him again in a gathering embrace. She leaned back to look him full in the face. "We each of us have our responsibilities," she told him, "and we can honor them, so long as we never doubt that this is right."

He smoothed her hair around her face and kissed her softly . . . one lip and then the other. "Looking at you," he told her, "is like looking into a calm, perfectly clear, aquamarine ocean . . . like looking into the depths where the bright fish move, all that color and excitement and beauty . . . all that wonder under the smooth surface . . ."

He followed her up the path, concentrating on the long, sweeping curve of her back, feeling a mist of sadness floating down to wrap around them.

The baby was sleeping still, curled in her basket, her pink mouth spouting bubbles. He looked down on her, his fingers poised on the edge of the basket. She sighed a little baby sigh and moved her hands, but she did not waken.

True motioned for the nurse to leave, then she stood next to him, her hand tucked into his arm. Still, he stood looking.

"Let me wake her," True whispered, but he held his hand up to stop her.

Finally he turned to True and took her chin in her hand, so she would have to look at him. "She is mine," he said.

True closed her eyes and whispered, "She is *keiki a ka*

pueo." A child of the owl, begotten on the wayside, father unknown.

He released her and turned back to the baby, his hands grazing the edge of the basket, as if they could not stay still.

And then he said, "Emma is beautiful, like her mother."

23

Mau'loa

Cattle are being shipped today and tomorrow, which means that Pono cannot bring the children and I am beside myself with loneliness. I am happy so long as my two ravenous young students are here. In the six weeks that True has been away, I have been able to do an extraordinary amount of teaching. We are actually doing some basic geometry; what is just as amazing, to me, is that when the children undertook to explain the geometry to Pono, he grasped the concept immediately. If I didn't know better (and I do), I would almost think that he had been schooled in it already. Pono may not talk, but I am becoming more and more aware that his mind is skimming along like a racer.

Working with the two Rourke children has set me to thinking about what the best class size should be. Ten, I suppose, enough to stimulate each other, with the brightest students setting the pace, and yet few enough for the teacher to give each some time.

On Sunday last, I rode over to the town of Lolia for services. The little community sits nestled in cane fields for as far as the eye can see; riding through them with the wind soughing softly made me feel as if I had entered a world of green, with only a high blue sky scattered with clouds above me. After services, I decided to pay a visit to the plantation camp where so many of the workers and their families live.

I almost wish I had not gone, then I would not know how they live, crowded into awful little huts, dogs and flies and filth all around. And I would not know about all of those children standing about, ill clothed and ill fed, with nothing to do until they are of an age to be put in the fields. Most are Japanese, though I did notice one or two Hawaiians, and I think a few Portuguese families. One little boy of perhaps eight years stood staring at me, his nose running. He asked me something in Japanese, and I was sorry that I could not answer him. All the long ride home I thought about those children, wasting away out in those horrible little cramped huts with no books, no school, no teacher. Further isolated by their language. Perhaps someday, some way . . .

As an amusement I started giving the Rourke children French lessons. A few days later I received a rough-scrawled note from their father which said, simply: NO FRINCH. I decided not to show it to Pono; I figure he has his hands full with Patrick already, and the children have plenty of time, and little need, to learn *Frinch*. Now if I could teach them Japanese. Or better still, if I could teach the Japanese children English.

This morning I was in the strawberry patch, picking as fast as I could. Such a big harvest this year, and so few of us here to eat the berries. Suddenly it occurred to me that if the Rourke children had come today, as they should have, I would have sent a bucket home with them. So I saddled up and set out to deliver the berries.

It would be a chance, I told myself, to meet the mother, whom the children speak of adoringly. The wild Patrick, I assumed, would be with the rest of the hands, wrestling the cattle through the surf and into the transport boats.

The day was sunny and clear, and the ride along the old road with its eucalyptus windbreak invigorated me. I thought: *Why haven't I done this before?* I said to myself: *You must get out and about more.* My euphoria was short-lived.

The signs were all there, if only I had seen them and turned back in time. The children did not come rushing out to greet me, as I had expected them to; they did not move from a sideyard, where they seemed to be puzzling over an old wagon wheel.

When I called to them, they looked at me but did not move. I tied my horse to the gate and was taking the bucket of strawberries from where I'd tied it on my saddle when the mother came out of the house. She is a pretty woman, tall and with dark hair straggled around her face; her eyes told me right off that she had more than a little Hawaiian blood in her. She walked toward me a bit unsteadily, and then I noticed a fresh, raw bruise on her cheek.

"Miss Moon," she said in a soft, troubled voice, "I'm so sorry but . . ."

She hadn't a chance to say more. The door of the small cabin was filled with the presence of Patrick Rourke, big and handsome with a wild crown of black hair and an insolent grin on his face. To keep his balance, he was holding to the top of the door.

"So there she is, the fantastical teacher we all hear so much about, the famous Miss Martha Moon. Pono's little number up there in the big house. He didn't tell us she was just a little brown girl, did he, Maude? Nobody thought to mention that, but then you know about Pono, don't you, Miss? Can't talk, but as our sainted mother used to say, still waters run deep. Little bastard . . . must be a bastard; that runt. So what are you doing here, miss, come to bring some charity? A bucket full of charity from a little brown girl, now don't that beat all?"

The children had moved a few steps away, as if ready to break and run, their eyes filled with shame and fear. The mother kept twisting the belt to her dress; her eyes begged me to understand. "I will come and see you," she told me in a low voice.

"Speak up, Maude," Patrick boomed, almost falling out of the door. "We can't hear you up here."

"Go inside, Patrick, and say no more," his wife told him, her mouth set.

"Oh, it's 'go inside, Patrick' now, after you've just told me to go outside and keep going. I suppose you think little brother Pono will take care of you, is that it?"

"Mr. Rourke," I made a feeble effort to explain, "I only rode over to bring some strawberries. The children helped me grow them."

He reeled back inside, out of sight, and Maude, his wife, came closer. "He only gets this way when things go wrong at work. The new ranch manager . . ." She stopped in mid-sentence, as if there was too much to say to go on.

I handed her the bucket. "Your face . . ." I said.

She touched the bruise. "My pride, more than anything. He'll sleep for a time, and when he wakes up he'll be sick with himself for this."

I nodded. "Come to visit with me whenever you can. I want to talk to you about the children. They are so bright and nice, and they are doing so well."

The three of them stood together and watched me leave. All the way home I debated about how much of a mistake I had made. Finally I decided that it would depend on Pono.

The next day I received a letter from True, written from Ainahau: "I am staying at Ainahau several days each week. The Governor seems to like to have us, and from here I can more easily visit Uncle and Aunt.

"Jared is perhaps a bit better; certainly he is not any worse. He is not yet twenty-one, though sometimes when I look at him he seems worn as an old man.

"You asked me to describe the political picture in Honolulu, now that the dust seems to be settling. The Mission Boys have all flocked to the Republican Party, the Hawaiians to the Home Rule Party and all the rest to the Democratic Party. The Home Rulers' slogan is "Nana i ka ili"—or, vote the color of your skin. The Hawaiians may be dying out, but they still command a majority in this country, so they almost certainly will control the first territorial legislature. The Mission Boys, who so desperately wanted annexation and American citizenship for themselves, have tried to limit voting rights for the dark races, but the American Congress is having none of that, so it is one vote for each male citizen of age.

"All the talk is about the Japanese—how they are coming into the islands in such great numbers to work on the sugar plantations, and how they aren't content to stay in the fields. Everybody is worried about what will happen when those Japanese who are born here begin to vote in numbers large enough to make a difference.

"Colonel Toby is campaigning on the Republican ticket! Perhaps that is the Colonel's great talent—vote gathering. Popularity is his strength. If only you could see him, prancing around town in that fanciful white suit on his coal black charger . . . he cuts quite the elegant figure.

"He has written Miss Laiana about Jared's poor health. If she gets the letter in good time, she should be packing to come home about now, only a few weeks earlier than planned. I suppose that in some ways I will feel relieved. I hope she can guide Jared back to health.

"A judge has said that my signature is not required for the sale of any ranch property. So nothing came of that except ill will between the Colonel and me, and I suppose when Miss Laiana hears of it I will be thoroughly out of favor. Evan warned me it would happen, and so it has.

"He spends much of his time with young Harry. Aunt Winona, who has kept company with Jenny and the child over the past several years, says there is a world of change in the boy. 'I think I've never heard Harry laugh out loud before,' she told me.

"On one of the days when Jared had his medicinal massages, Liko and I rode up into the mountains to visit Auntie Momi, as you asked. She was happy to see us, and her ohana made a big luau in our honor. I can't tell you how she knew we were coming, but the kalua pig was in the ground for half a day by the time we arrived.

"Evan and Harry had been hiking in the vicinity and turned up at Auntie's—yes, I did have something to do with this. They were invited to the luau. Evan thought it would make them too late returning home, but Harry begged to stay. He was so excited, and kept saying that he had never seen a *real* luau, so Evan gave in.

"There are several lovely young dancers being trained by the *kumu hula* and they performed in the old way—wearing only skirts made of banana leaves, their breasts bare. I can't but wonder what Harry will tell his mother. I do manage to see Evan now and then. He has agreed to give the Colonel advice on the ranch.

"We miss you, though from your letter it sounds as if the wild Rourkes are keeping you more than busy. Still, Pono is worth the trouble the rest of that clan manages to make. Ask him please to keep an eye out for that black bull that hides out up near Hokupa falls. If we're going to have to work with the stock we've got, we have to separate out the best.

"Jared sends his love; Liko does as well. Emma sends lots of tiny baby kisses to her Auntie Martha. We all miss you. Aloha nui loa, True."

Three days passed with no children, no Pono. I felt I was going to burst with worry. Going back to the Rourke home was not possible, I knew that, so instead I went to find Pono. My plan was to be waiting for him at the crossroad to the horse corral; he was always there before the others, so I knew he would be riding alone. It was dark when I set out, but the moon was full and my little mare knows the road.

Wrapped warmly in my shawl, I settled in to wait, feeling alone and strange in the night world, and foolish as well. What would he think, my coming here to waylay him? Why had I done such a silly thing? What would I say to him?

He was there before I had time to answer any of the questions welling in me. He had been trotting along and pulled up short only a few feet away. It was too dark to see his face, and I was glad because I did not want him to see mine.

"I'm sorry to startle you like this," I croaked and cleared my voice. "If you are angry with me, I'm sorry. I wanted to tell you that I should not have gone to your brother's house but I had the strawberries . . ." I forced myself to stop. I was rattling on like Aunt Winona, and Pono was the last person who could deal with such a rush of words.

He moved his horse closer, but he would not look me in the face. I took a deep breath. "I'm sorry if I made you angry, Pono. But please don't take the children from me. I want them to return. I want to teach them."

Still he did not speak, nor would he look at me.

"Pono, please . . . I didn't mean to make you angry with me."

He was shaking his head, looking at me now and shaking his head.

"No," he said, "No. It's not for you to be sorry. It's for him, Patrick . . . he shouldn't have spoken so, not to you."

He was ashamed. It had not entered my mind.

"Why?" I said. "You mean because he called me 'a little brown girl'?" I could feel him stiffen.

More quietly I said, "You mean because he called me *your* little brown girl? I didn't mind that, Pono. I didn't."

He ran his hand over his forehead, as if to clear his vision.

I plunged ahead: "I've been so lonely these last few days— for the children, but for you, too."

He looked at me now, and I felt that same warm igniting I had felt before. "We'll come tomorrow," he told me, then kicked his horse and left abruptly.

The next letter from Honolulu was in Liko's cramped little hand. "True says it is my turn to write, she and Jared being

off to talk to Evan and Colonel Wakefield. Jared says he is
ready to stand up to his pa, and True is running around like
a firecracker, about to explode.

Jared is getting stronger, and we are happy for it. His
mother should be arriving soon and nobody wanted her to
see him without meat on his bones. Last evening we missed
you, Martha, because we were all out in the back playing
with the baby—Jared and True and me—and having such a
good time together. Baby Emma went to sleep in Jared's
arms. He was humming to her, and then he started just
talking kind of low and nice to us. He said how grateful he
is that True was willing to use the money we found for
doctors when he knew how badly she wanted to put it in the
ranch. And how happy he has been to be with me and have
Baby Emma close by, and how much aloha he has for us all.
Then he said it was time he kept his part of the bargain. He
says he knows True is right about building the ranch up, and
that they have to do it for Baby Emma. True took his hand
and squeezed it so hard he had to yelp, and then we all
laughed and hugged each other."

The letter ended rather plaintively: "I hope he can do it.
Liko."

Pono is bringing the children every day again. On Saturday,
when he came to pick them up again, he stood in front of me
and cleared his throat in the way that meant he had something to say.

"Yes," I smiled to encourage him.

"Tomorrow we will come to build the school."

I raised my eyebrows in astonishment. "Who? Why? I
don't understand."

He shoved his hands in his pockets and seemed about to
turn away. He thought better then, and turned back. "My
brothers. We're going to finish the school."

"But Colonel Wakefield said I couldn't have a school."

Pono's eyes met mine and I felt the quick surge of heat.
"He didn't say we couldn't finish the school on our time."

I wrapped my arms around myself and began to laugh for
the sheer pleasure of it. "No, he didn't, Pono—you are right,
absolutely right. Oh my, the school, my school . . ."

He smiled then. A beautiful, clear, fine smile. I wanted to
put my arms around him to thank him, but I knew I couldn't

or he might never find the nerve to speak to me again. "Thank you, Pono," I said.

As usual, he said nothing but only took the children and lifted them into his wagon to drive them home. Still, he had smiled at me. And I know that precious few people on this fine earth have ever seen such a beautiful smile.

24

Ainahau was once again to be the scene of a festive luau. Governor Cleghorn, it seemed, was in a mood to bring all his many friends together.

Long lauhala mats were spread on the ground; ten kalua pigs were roasting all day in pits; great mounds of fruit and fish and fresh poi and vegetables were spread out for the hundred or more who came. Only Archie Cleghorn could have drawn together such a group: Hawaiian royalty and Mission Boys, High Court Justices and Asian businessmen, chanters and American military officers and their families, children included.

The best dancers on the island were to perform, the most renowned musicians, singers with incredible soaring ranges. All the lanterns would be lit, torches would blaze to light the night sky. It was the talk of Honolulu. The Colonel fretted that his move to the Republican Party might cause him some embarrassment but he needn't have worried. For this occasion, politics would be set aside.

For the first time in many weeks, Jared felt like dressing up, and he took great pleasure in overseeing the dressing of the others as well. He outfitted himself in trim white pants and a white shirt, open at the throat so he could sport a bright blue silk scarf which he had found in his mother's dressing cabinet. He looked at himself in the mirror and smiled approvingly. Then nothing would do but that Liko wear his paniola costume, with the red checked shirt and leather chaps—and take along his ukelele in case he should be asked to perform. (Jared confided to True that he felt certain this would please Liko.)

But it was True's costume over which Jared fussed most. She would have worn her green-sprigged hokolu, but Jared wouldn't hear of it. Invading his sister Rachel's clothes cabinet, he found a blue silk gown that matched his own scarf. After much coaxing, True agreed at least to try it on. She was amused by Jared's interest in her wardrobe and made uncomfortable by it at the same time. She could not bathe without seeing Evan's hands on her breasts, on her stomach; in these few weeks in Honolulu her body had filled out, softened, glowed. There were times when she thought it must be visible, what love had done to her.

She banished Liko and Jared from the room and breathed deeply of the smell of the crisp blue silk as she stepped into the dress with its fashionable low neckline, its fitted bodice and long loose skirt. She remembered the dress; on Rachel, who had spurted in growth in the past two years, it had seemed loose and chaste. On her the fit was snug; it took a long while to button all the buttons, only then did she look into the mirror and blush at what she saw.

"Come out, come out," Liko and Jared coaxed.

"I can't," she replied. "Don't come in."

But they did come in, both of them, and they gasped in unison.

"Great God, True—look at you," Jared burst out. "You're beautiful!"

Liko, dumbstruck, echoed, "Look at you!"

"I cannot wear this. I won't. Rachel wouldn't."

"Rachel would die of envy if she saw you, but she won't. And you are going to wear it," Jared said, the old stubborn determination returning to his face.

A mix of feelings flooded her. She was grateful to Jared for taking her side on the ranch and speaking up to his father for the first time. And she was glad to see him returning to his old self again, though he was still too thin and prone to headaches; she wanted to please him, but she could not appear in public in such a dress.

"But, Jared, it is too revealing," she said, putting a hand over her breasts.

"Nonsense, you only see a bit of them, where they come together. We can put a flower here . . ." He touched her breasts with such innocence she had to smile.

Jared stood back to look at her. "We're going to let your hair down, and decorate you with red flowers, only red . . ."

"She'll look like the American flag, all red white and blue," Liko piped in.

"Humm," Jared said. "Then maybe pink flowers. We need some color for your hair . . ."

True tried another tack. "I can't wear Rachel's dress without her permission. It wouldn't be right."

Jared didn't seem to hear. Instead he said, "We are all going to make a grand entrance. Give them all something to remember."

At that moment the Colonel returned home; they could hear him at the front door. True moved back as if to hide, but Jared called him in. One look and the Colonel, known for his appreciation of feminine beauty, seemed to forget how annoyed he was with her. "Great galloping ghosts, girl, that dress must have been waiting for you."

That was when True knew she couldn't resist wearing the dress. It was the price they were exacting, Jared and the Colonel, and she had to pay it, no matter how much of a spectacle she made of herself.

On the night of the luau, Jared fussed with her hair until she wanted to scream. She had pulled her hair back and twisted it into a braid as usual, but Jared wouldn't have it. He had made her wash her hair that morning, and he brushed it dry in the sun so that it was full and shiny and hung about her shoulders. A bright pink hibiscus was tucked behind her ear, and a cluster of tuberose was poised provocatively in the place between her breasts.

"You look like a goddess of love," Liko told her, and she groaned.

"What's wrong with that?" Jared wanted to know. "Everybody always thinks of you as being kind of feisty and contrary, let them see you like this."

"I can't go," True announced.

But now the Colonel was in league with his son, and the two of them simply swept her into the carriage, with Liko joining them. He played his ukelele all the way to Ainahau; the father and son were having a good time together, joshing True about her reticence. The two of them were delighted with themselves for bringing a big surprise to the gathering.

Most surprised of all was Jenny Coulter—plump now, and with eyes that had become increasingly small and hard in the past several years. She had been watching for True and was among the first to see the three of them walk across the wide lawn together—the dignified father and the beautiful son in white on either side of an astonishing True. A murmur of welcome went up; the Governor moved to them, held True out at arm's length for all to see.

Jenny shifted her gaze to watch her husband. "Look at that," she said, her voice filled with disgust.

"At what, Mama?" Harry asked.

When his mother didn't answer, he followed her gaze.

"That's Mrs. Wakefield," Harry said, helpfully. "She looks different, doesn't she, Pa?"

Jenny saw the fixed look come over Evan's face. Her voice tightening, she said, "I didn't know you had met Mrs. Wakefield, Harry. When was that?"

"On one of our walks into the mountains. We met her and the little man, the one there in the cowboy suit."

"Is that right?" Jenny asked, looking at Evan in a way that made him know there would be hell to pay tonight. For the moment, however, it was all he could do to keep his eyes from wandering to True.

"Her dress leaves little to the imagination," Jenny went on. "But it does explain some things." Evan was silent; he knew he would hear sooner or later a variation on one of Jenny's favorite themes: True as a seductress.

True stayed close to Jared, holding onto his arm, smiling at him with affection, and everyone looked at the handsome, happy young couple and approved. She caught a glimpse of Evan, but she did not even nod at him. Jenny would be smouldering; she could tell from the frozen look on Evan's face.

The Royal Hawaiian Band gave way to the native musicians with their drums, and the Hawaiians took over. Some of the best dancers in the island jumped onto the stage and began the playful, throbbing, sensual movements of the hula. The mood grew bright, friends called out to each other and then it began: The dancers pulled someone from the audience to the stage to dance, and then someone else.

Jared's face was flushed with pleasure; he stood, and some who had been at his wedding remembered and called for the young Wakefields to dance. "No," True whispered urgently. "Jared, I can't, not in this dress . . . I don't want to make any more of a spectacle of myself, please . . ." But Jared let out a yelp and jumped to the stage and the crowd roared its approval and began to call for her . . . *True, True, True*.

She was pulled and shoved to the stage; the music had started, a soft, languid hula. She smiled with a certain wry resignation and lifted her arms and those gathered howled with pleasure. They danced together then, True and Jared, not the riotous, pounding dance of their wedding day but a tender, softly swaying hula, graceful and warm with a wry affection between them that caused those gathered to smile.

Jenny slipped her hand in Evan's arm and whispered, "The very picture of wedded bliss, wouldn't you say?"

Evan removed her hand carefully and told her he was going to find Harry and take him home. She could come if she wished, he said, or she could stay on and he would send the carriage back for her. He knew she would feel pulled between wanting to stay and add fuel to her already burning resentments or to come home and pour her anger out on him. As he walked across the wide lawn, Harry came bounding toward him, chased by two other boys. His son crashed into him and swung Evan around, placing him between himself and the boys. All were out of breath and laughing.

"No fair," a tall red-haired boy said, grabbing playfully for Harry's arm. "You were supposed to run to the beach."

Evan ruffled his son's hair and felt a sudden rush of pleasure. It was the first time he had seen Harry with other boys on equal terms, playing and having a good time. Maybe it was working, he told himself. With a little encouragement, Harry was moving out into the world.

He did not hear Jenny until she said, angrily, "Were these boys chasing you, Harry?"

The boys scattered and left, and Harry stood looking at his mother with distress and frustration on his face.

Evan interceded, as he had so many times in the past weeks. "They were playing, Jenny, it was a game. They were just having fun."

"It didn't look like fun to me," she protested.

She was about to say more when Harry screeched at her, "That's because you don't know what fun is," shocking all three of them.

On Mau'loa, not long after sunup on Sunday, the very next day after my conversation with Pono, the Rourkes began to arrive. I was dressed and ready to receive them, but I had no idea at all what to expect.

A wild yelping was my warning; they came in wagons pulled by mules and filled with cut boards and children and wives with baskets of food. As they drove into the front drive, I ran out to meet them and was astonished to be swept up by Patrick Rourke, who simply lifted me high and perched me on top of the well wall, then dropped to his knee and sang, in a wonderful rich baritone voice, "Darling Miss Moon, I won't let you down until you say you forgive me. My children love you, my wife adores you and they say they will all leave me unless from your sweet lips comes the answer to my prayers."

I saw Pono in the background, already unloading a wagon. The others crowded around the foolish Patrick and myself, smiling and waiting to see what I would say. Laughter came bubbling out of me.

"Listen to her," Patrick wailed. "Isn't that a proper Irish answer? Yes? You forgive me, do you sweet woman, darling teacher, and will you be a friend of all the mad Rourkes?"

"Yes!" I allowed, feeling full and fine. "A friend forever. Now let me down from here so we can build a school for these children."

He lifted me down and passed me around to the Rourke brothers I hadn't met: Sean and Michael and Thomas. I put both my hands out to Maude, who kissed me warmly on my cheek before introducing me to Moira and Sally and Lina and their children, seven of them altogether, all younger than my two prize students.

"There is a method to our madness," Lina, who was carrying a newborn, told her. "We dearly need a school closer to us, and we need a good teacher, so you see . . ."

Just to watch the brothers work together was a pleasure—such laughing and teasing, with the silent Pono in the middle of it all, giving a direction now and then, setting a hard pace.

"Slow down, Desmond, you're working us all to death," called Michael.

"They call him 'Desmond' when he pushes them too hard," Maude explained. "It was his Hawaiian mother who named him 'Pono.' It means 'The good one,' you know. He was her favorite." Maude shook her head and sighed. "He is good, I tell you, Miss Moon. He keeps his high-spirited

brothers in check. When he was away on Maui things got
out of hand a bit. Now see how he has found you and the
school? Pono takes care of all of us—I daren't think what we
would do without him."

For some reason I did not want to hear any more about
how dependent they all were on Pono, so I interrupted to say
she should call me Martha. Then we organized the children
to pick strawberries and to make a trip to the orchard for
peaches.

Now and then through the long day I paused to watch the
four tall, dark handsome Rourke brothers and their small
brother work together. It seemed as if they were dancing, as
they sawed and pounded and lifted and nailed.

That night I lay in bed with my thoughts drifting this
way and that . . . the pleasure of the day, of the Rourkes'
lively company, of the fact that the roof was on my school.
Jared had stood up to his father about the ranch—perhaps
there was hope that he could talk him into the school. At
least Jared was growing stronger; there was hope. When
sleep came drifting in, I was thinking of Pono's face, and
that it was as handsome, in its own way, as any of his
brothers'.

Liko knew the minute he saw Jenny Coulter that something
bad was about to happen. He and Jared were alone in the
house, while the Colonel and True and the baby had gone to
pay a call on Queen Liliu. Jared was to have gone as well, but
one of his headaches had come upon him at the last moment,
so he had stayed behind.

Liko opened the door and was almost knocked down
when Jenny pushed her way in—as if he might try to stop
her. Her face was a mottled red, so filled with fury that she
made Liko feel afraid.

"Mrs. Coulter, I'm sorry but . . ." he wanted to tell her
that Jared wasn't feeling well.

"You should be," she interrupted, furious. "You should
all be sorry. I want to see True. I have something to tell her.
It is time she heard from me . . ."

Jared came stumbling out of his room, his face pale.
"Liko," he said. "Could you help me? I'm not feeling well
. . ."

Jenny barged on, so angry that she couldn't see how ill he

was. "If True isn't here, I might as well tell you, Jared Wakefield. Something is wrong here. Something is terribly, *unnaturally* wrong."

Jared looked at her, stunned, and for a moment Liko thought he would faint.

Liko put his hand on Jenny's arm to try to stop her, and she threw it off with such force that Liko fell against a table, knocking it over. "You beast," Jenny screamed at him. "You horrible little deformed beast . . . helping her, all of you, pretending that you don't know, making a mockery of a real family. That baby, I've seen that little blond baby of yours. I know—don't think I don't know what you are hiding. And you will all rot in hell for your sins, for your horrible sins . . ."

Jared lay back against the wall and slipped silently to the floor. His stomach heaved and his head jerked back, hitting the wall with a sick, hollow thud. A strangled sound rose in his throat at the same time as his body began to lurch in awful spasms, his arms and chest convulsing in grotesque rhythms. Just as Liko reached his side Jared began to gasp for air, then his head jerked forward, his mouth flew open and a foul bloody yellow stream spew out of him, coursing over the rug and spattering the hem of Jenny Coulter's pink-sprigged dress.

For the rest of her life, True would remember that she came back to the Wakefield house that day with a sense of foreboding. She had hurried out of the carriage, leaving the nurse to bring Emma. The Colonel was only a few steps behind her, because he was late for another appointment—the Queen having kept them longer than he had planned. She had wanted to talk of Kaiulani, had lingered over the details of her funeral—reminded by Baby Emma, born that day, scarcely seven months ago.

A foul smell filled the foyer.

"What the devil . . ." the Colonel began, and then they saw the carpet soiled with vomit and blood.

"Jared," True called out, her voice rising with fear. "Liko . . ."

They found them in Jared's old room, Jared propped up on the bed, blood running out of his mouth, his eyes open and unseeing in death. Liko held Jared's lifeless body in his strong arms, his huge head swinging back and forth in pain and bewilderment. When he saw True he let out a howl of bitter anguish, an animal sound that pierced the sick air of the darkened room and carried out into the world.

25

At Mau'loa, Pono hitched up the carriage to drive me to the ferry to go to Honolulu. Now I was the one who was drowning in silence, unable to speak of my fears. Poor, dear, doomed Jared, dead before his twenty-first birthday. And Liko, who would now be thrown into more grief and despair than I fear he can bear. And True, after so much death in her life, so much sadness. What will this mean to True and the baby, the sweet baby? I began to shudder and I couldn't seem to stop. Pono took my hand and held hard to it, and I could feel his strength revive me.

"The school," I finally was able to say. "I don't know what is going to become . . ."

He held hard to my hand. "The school will be finished when you come back."

"I don't even know if I will come back," I cried out.

He stopped the buggy, took me by the shoulders, and told me, "You will come back." Then he held me to him until my sobbing stopped. My tears left a wet mark on his shirt. When I touched it, he took my hand in his, then he repeated, "You will come back." The memory of his arms around me was to carry me through the hard weeks to come.

Liko and I are staying at Mana'olana with Aunt and Uncle. True sent us here, I think to give Liko a place to grieve. He cannot sleep, and he cannot stop crying. Though the Colonel is touched by Liko's devotion to Jared, he has begun to complain that his grief seems excessive.

True and I have had scarcely a moment to ourselves. She looks harried and worn and forlorn; the Colonel seems unable to contend with the many details of the funeral, so True has had to help him. She did cling to me for a long moment, and whispered, "He was such a sweet boy, Martha, and I cared for him so very much."

"I know," I said, trying to share with her the strength Pono had given me. "We all loved him, and he knew that. Whatever happiness Jared possessed in his life, you made possible. You must never forget that."

She had taken a deep breath before she released me. Then she smiled at me through welling tears and told me how glad she was that I was with her, how much it helped. I kissed her on the lips and sent her back to the Wakefield house, where the Colonel was stumbling around, talking to himself. True found him standing outside of the door to Jared's room, afraid to go in.

He told True that the undertakers would have to preserve the body—he could not bury Jared until his mother saw him. She would never forgive him, never. True brought him a glass of bourbon and sat down next to him in the parlor.

"They cleaned the rug," he said, "and put something on it so it doesn't smell."

"I know," True told him, rubbing his hand.

"A brain hemorrhage," he said, his voice flat. "How could he have died of a brain hemorrhage?"

"The headaches," True repeated, as she had a dozen times in the past five days. "There was terrible pressure in the brain. It could have happened anytime."

"His mother will notice, she always notices those things. The rug, how it smells. We can't bury him, not until she gets here."

"I told the undertakers what you want. They can do it, they say—as long as Jared's mother and sisters arrive soon. Evan came by to say that he spoke to the captain of an Australian ship en route from San Francisco to Sidney who says that the *Polar Star* is two days behind him. And we know she and the girls booked passage on it."

"Two days," he said, shuddering, and she knew then how he dreaded it, his wife coming home to find her son dead. "She'll have two more days of peace in this world," the Colonel said.

True took his hand again. "Jared told me about his brother, about young Toby."

The Colonel's eyes filled. "Both my boys, gone. Both my little boys."

He was gulping down the whiskey when the doorbell rang. "It's the Welderfields—shall I tell them to come another time?" True asked.

He answered, "No, no, let them come, let them all come. The more the better to keep my mind off it all."

Amalie was happy to have me share the cottage that True and I had once occupied, and Uncle fixed up the little room next to the stables so Liko could be alone. More than anyone, Uncle seemed to understand Liko's loss. Taking me aside not long after we arrived, Uncle had said, "I want you to know there is always a place for you here, Martha. And for Liko, too. You are not to worry."

That night at dinner, after she had exhausted her fond remembrances of Jared and the tragedy of his death, Aunt Winona entertained us with an avalanche of details about the school, how many more children they had than when Liko and I were there, and how many more were wanting to come, if only there were room. And if only they could find a benefactor.

"Are things as bad as Aunt makes them out to be?" I asked Amalie that night, before we went to sleep.

"I'm afraid so," she answered. "One of the royal princesses offered to sponsor the school if we would admit only Hawaiian children, but of course Uncle said no. Most of the children who need us are mixed blood. I expect Aunt to start hinting for me to move on, by and by."

"Perhaps you and I should hire out as teachers, or start our own school," I suggested.

"It's the children without parents I want to teach," she answered. "The lonely ones."

I reached for her hand. "Amalie, I hope you don't feel lonely."

"Sometimes I do," she admitted. "But not now. I'm glad you're back, though I'm sorry for the reason."

Mid-morning the next day Evan appeared with Harry, a slender boy of seven with a shy squint to his eyes. Evan seemed preoccupied, but he hugged me close and said he was glad I had come, that True needed me. Then he asked if I would mind taking Harry to find Liko. "I've got some business to talk over with Jameson, and I thought maybe you could talk Liko into giving Harry some swimming instruction."

"I'll bet we can," I told him, smiling at Evan for his trust.

Liko was lying in his cot, his face to the wall. "Young Harry Coulter here and I would like to go sea bathing," I announced, trying to sound cheerful.

"Not now," Liko mumbled, not turning around.

"Come along," I coaxed, my voice attempting to be firm. "A swim will be good for us all. I've been dreaming about a plunge into the surf at Waikiki for months."

"I don't want to," Liko answered, twisting miserably on the cot. "Please leave me alone."

"Leave him be," Harry said, his small voice apologetic. "Don't ask if he doesn't feel like it. My mama's not well either, she stays in her room all day and won't come out."

"I wouldn't wonder!" Liko answered, bolting upright in his bed and glaring at both of us.

The shock on our faces must have surprised him, for suddenly he reversed himself. "Yes, let's swim. Martha and I will teach you how the Hawaiians swim. Then you'll be a better swimmer than your father."

"Nobody's better than my pa," Harry replied, with such certainty that I had to smile.

Liko and I showed Harry how to dive into a wave, how to let it lift and carry you, how to work with the force of the water. For more than an hour we swam and bobbed and let our bodies skim the tops of the waves.

Liko recognized Harry's fears and quickly dispelled them. "I am here. I won't let anything happen to you." The words I had heard him say to Vicky, the words I suppose he said to Jared. Tears came flooding into my eyes; I washed them away with the sea water.

Liko and I sat together on the warm sand while Harry played at the edge of the water.

"What did you mean," I asked carefully, "when Harry said his mother was ill, and you said, 'I wouldn't wonder'?"

Liko looked away.

"Talk to me, please. Something isn't right."

Liko's face crumpled and he made a sudden, strangled animal sound. His eyes found mine and for a moment I thought I could not bear the terrible glare of his pain.

"That's what she said," he told me, and then he choked out in horrible detail the scene with Jenny.

"Dear God," I murmured, watching Harry playing in the water, innocent and happy. "Poor soul," I repeated, not able to think of anything else to say. And to myself, I thought: *poor souls,* Jared and Liko, to think that Jenny might know about their love . . .

Liko interrupted my thoughts. "True said I'm not to tell anyone. But she didn't mean you. She wouldn't expect me not to tell you."

"Yes," I agreed. "But who does know about this?"

"Only me and True. And her, of course"—he couldn't bring himself to say Jenny's name—"I don't know about Evan."

I wanted to ask more questions, but Harry was walking toward us, the scowl gone, his face bright with sun and accomplishment and the excitement of the sea.

True asked me to go with her, and as much as I wanted to resist, I could not. We were allowed onto the *Polar Star* as soon as it docked, the Colonel in the lead and True and me behind, to deliver the awful news to Jared's mother and sisters in their stateroom.

Laiana Wakefield looked at her husband's face and she knew. A terrible wail went out from her. It filled the room and pierced the busy noises of the ship. The girls' faces were frozen with alarm; they did not know what to think. I pulled Rachel aside and whispered, "Your brother Jared, he has . . . he is . . . gone."

The crying and the wailing went on for what seemed an eternity, before we could get them off the ship and into the carriages. In spite of the woefulness of the homecoming, I could see the Colonel gain strength from the reunion with his wife. He pulled himself up; you could almost hear the intake of breath as he stood tall. He began to stroke his beard—flecked now with silver—as if to calm himself. Laiana Wakefield, thick now, more alii Hawaiian in appearance as she approached her fiftieth year, as stately as ever. Her broad, handsome face seemed to absorb the shock; mourning wrapped around her like a feather cloak and she spread it wide, to let her husband in. Hawaiians knew sorrow; she gave herself over to it as her people had always done, letting the tears flow unchecked down her cheeks as her body swayed under the terrible weight. The Colonel put his arms around her, and together they wept.

Simply being in the presence of his wife seemed to lighten the Colonel's burden. True, on the other hand, was on the verge of collapse.

Baby Emma and her nurse had been sent to Ainahau; now True and I joined them, at the Governor's urging and on the pretext that it would leave more room for the Wakefields. Jared's body, packed in ice, had been moved to the front parlor. True could not bear to think of spending another night in the house that had been so filled with pain for her and for Jared. She knew as well that soon enough Laiana Wakefield would begin to question her about Jared's illness, would want to know what she had done, or had not done, to help him. True had absorbed one blow after another, but now she was dangerously close to her limit. She told me she needed me, and Ainahau, to revive her. I wanted to ask about Evan, and if she thought Jenny was responsible for Jared's death, but I could not. Not then.

Three days after the funeral, Evan appeared at Ainahau early in the morning when it was unlikely anyone but the family would be around. The Governor welcomed him, and the two men talked for a time in the library with the door closed. Then the Governor called True and left the two together.

Light filtered into the room through the high eastern windows, illuminating a spot on the floor where an old yellow cat slept, curled up. They sat in chairs next to each other; Evan took her hand and held it in both of his.

"I am so tired of death," she finally said.

He kissed her hand and touched it to his forehead.

"I keep wondering if I had brought him to the doctors sooner, if I hadn't waited so long—but the doctors say no, that it would have happened anyway, but maybe they are just saying that . . ."

Evan looked at her. "You mean they say it would have happened, no matter what?"

She took her hand from his and held hard to the arms of the chair. "You know what Jenny did?" she asked, her voice cracking.

He nodded.

She waited for him to say something, but when he didn't she told him: "She made them think—Jared and Liko—that she knew about them. They didn't understand that she was accusing you and me. I thank God that Jared didn't go to his grave doubting that Emma was his daughter. She was such a pleasure to him, Evan."

Her eyes filled with tears and she turned away. The silence grew.

True did not make him ask. "You want to know if I think it's Jenny's fault. I don't know. Liko described to me what happened, and it seems as if it might already have begun. Jared was just coming out of his room, calling to Liko for help, when she pushed in and began raving. As he lay dying, he asked Liko if he thought Jenny would tell about them."

"God," Evan whispered.

"Yes," True said, bitterly. "Where was God? I keep asking myself that. In his absence, I decided to make some decisions of my own. No one knows about Jenny's visit except Liko and me. I wasn't certain if you knew. Since Jenny hasn't been seen since the day of Jared's death, I assume she is having some pangs—if not conscience, then probably fear."

"She has closed herself away in her room, pleading illness. She won't see anyone."

"She'll see me," True said, softly but firmly.

Evan looked at her but said nothing. They sat in silence for a time, and then he asked, "Have you thought about what you and the baby are going to do?"

She stood, moved to the patch of light so that the sun fell on her face. "The Colonel says that Emma and I must live with them on Mau'loa. He says the Home Place where we have been is too damp and cool for Emma. He says he will find work for Liko, to reward him for his devotion to Jared." She glanced at Evan and shrugged. "And he has always wanted Martha to come teach at his school. So we can all be together, tolerated by the Wakefields."

Her voice was so flat, so dead that Evan stood and took her by the shoulders. "I've been looking into some possibilities," he said carefully. "Jameson and Governor Cleghorn— we have a few ideas. But we need time, and for you to do a few things."

He saw the questions in her eyes and fended them off. "Not now, it would take too long, and I have too much to do. Do you think you can trust me on this?"

"I trust you with my life, Evan, and with Emma's. You know that."

He ran his hands down her arms, pressing them hard. "The most important thing is, don't sign any papers the Colonel or his lawyers might bring to you. You haven't, have you?"

"No," she answered, "but he did say we would have to take care of some things."

Evan started pacing. "It may come up in the next few days," he finally said. "Find some way to delay him."

"I can't stay here at Ainahau indefinitely. I can't impose on Governor Cleghorn much longer. And I have no place else to go."

"I can . . ." he began.

"No," she said, firmly.

The Hawaiian servant who answered the door showed True into the parlor. "Such sadness with the Lord taking your young man," the woman said to True, her whole big body swaying with the sorrow she felt. "If you can just sit there and wait, I'll go tell Miss Jenny you're here. Maybe that will get her up and about, she's been so poorly. Doesn't hardly come out of her room, so you'll have to wait a bit."

According to the big clock in the corner, True waited for twenty minutes. Finally the woman came back in, her face a confusion of irritation and embarrassment. "I'm more sorry than I can say, but Miss Jenny says she can't see you. She says she isn't going to see anyone."

"Not ever?" True asked, smiling. "I guess I'll just have to go see what this is all about." She rose and went striding down the long hall. "Which door is it?" she asked and the woman, astonished, pointed to the one on the end.

Jenny was sitting in a chair by the bed, an old wrapper pulled around her, her hair disheveled. True closed the door firmly behind her; Jenny's face quivered, her eyes bulged in the half light. She pulled her knees up to her chest and averted her face, as if cowering to ward off a blow.

"I am not going to hit you, Jenny," True said, "though I

have thought about doing just that more than once, and it might make me feel better to slap you in the face, hard."

Jenny made some sounds, but True couldn't decipher them, so she went on: "I came to tell you something, and I want you to listen. Are you listening?"

She waited until Jenny raised her eyes. She looked, True thought, like some small field rodent caught in a trap.

"I know about your visit to Jared. I know you made some accusations, I know what they were, and I know that my husband died only minutes after you left. The doctors said it was a brain hemorrhage. Sometimes severe shock brings on such a hemorrhage. You know that as well as I do, and I suspect that is why you are sitting here in this room, hiding.

"You can come out now, Jenny. And I am going to tell you how. The only people who know about your ugly little visit are Liko and me. And whoever you have told, of course. Since you've locked yourself away, I doubt that you've told anyone at all. Liko will say nothing of it, and neither will I. *So long as you accept that my daughter, Emma, is a Wakefield and will stop spreading rumors.* Jared loved her dearly. She was the joy of his life and I will not have your jealousy disturb her life or his memory. So this is the bargain. We will never talk about the part you played in my husband's death, and you will never again try to cast doubt on my daughter's paternity."

Jenny looked up, a flicker of anger in her eyes. She laid a finger across her upper lip and seemed to be thinking. True glanced around the room; the air was stale and smelled of camphor, the bed was unmade and scattered with newspapers. One was opened to an obituary about Jared.

"I see you have been following the news," True said, her voice tight. "Did you expect to see a little note in the paper saying, 'Mrs. Evan Coulter was paying a social visit at the time of Jared Wakefield's untimely death?' Don't you ever wonder if you helped push him into his grave? And don't you ever wonder just what Miss Laiana and the Colonel, and the rest of our old friends would think if they knew what you had done?"

Jenny's head came flying up, her lips seemed stretched tight over her teeth. "I didn't mean to hurt him. I meant to hurt you," she cried out.

"Well, you did that, Jenny. You certainly did," True said, biting off the words.

Jenny seemed to puff up. "I will say no more about your child," she said, as if her mouth were dry and she could barely rasp out the words.

True looked at her with a disgust she did not try to disguise, but she said no more. Walking out of the front door onto the long lanai, she took a deep breath of air perfumed with jasmine, and grasped the railing to keep her hands from shaking. She did not want to think about what would have happened had Jenny refused.

26

January 20, 1900

The new century has arrived, but there can be no celebration. Our private calamity has been overwhelmed by a public one. The maze of warrens crowded against the Honolulu waterfront and called Chinatown, where 7000 Orientals and Hawaiians crowd in upon one another and live in unspeakable filth rife with vermin and lice and flies, has suffered an outbreak of plague.

The first death occurred last month. Since then, dozens more poor souls have fallen. Fifty acres have been sealed off, people are not allowed to come in or go out, and camps have been set up for the refugees. Fear has spread over the city. The *pakes,* with their long pigtails and poles from which dangle baskets full of fresh lotus root and eggplant and all manner of fresh vegetables, are no longer welcomed into the neighborhoods.

Archie will not allow anyone at Ainahau to go into the city, nor does he want outsiders to come here. Not even Evan, who could not come at any rate, since he has been called in to take charge.

This bubonic plague is carried by rats. I know myself— from having gone to Chinatown with Uncle once to rescue a deserted girl—that the place was an open sore, waiting for a deadly infection.

Twelve new cases this month; the death toll is rising. Something had to be done, and the public health officials have decided the infected wound must be cauterized. The first of several deliberate fires was set on New Year's Eve, burning out ramshackle buildings where people cooked over cesspools, and the sewers backed up into the streets.

Five deaths have occurred near the corner of Beretania

and Nuuanu, and every fireman and four fire trucks are there today, to contain the fire that was set this morning. It is said to be the only way to halt the spread of this deadly disease. Several of us walked down the beach for a clearer view, drawn by billows of black smoke that make an ugly streak on the blue sky.

The Governor was with us, and I could see that he was troubled. "The wind is rising," he said. "I hope Evan and the boys can handle it."

But Evan and the boys could not handle it. The fire is out of control, and is burning a wide swath through all of China-town. From our vantage, it looks as if the whole city is ablaze.

January 23, 1900

Disaster. The fire destroyed thirty-eight acres of Chinatown. Seven thousand are without homes and have lost their worldly treasures, such as they were. Some of the buildings consumed, I suppose I should not be surprised to discover, provided rents to such as the Bishop Estate.

Rising winds whipped the fire, causing it to leap the street, set Kaumakapili Church ablaze and roar through the rest of Chinatown. There are whispers that the fire was meant to jump its bounds, that it was a conspiracy by haoles who want the area for themselves. I do not believe that. But certain newspapers do not help; one even goes so far as to say that the fire should be seen as a blessing, giving the white man's business district room to expand. There is a feeling, and a fear—one that at times I admit to myself—that the Orientals will take over the Islands by their sheer numbers. While the native Hawaiians' numbers decline each year, the Chinese and the Japanese multiply.

The Portuguese, brought here to work the fields, seem to hold a position in the public mind somewhere between haole and Oriental. No white man considers them an equal, but neither do they consider them in a class with the Asians. For some time now, Colonel Wakefield has had a manservant who is Portuguese. His name is Manuel; he is strong and proud and more than a little arrogant.

Two days after the fire, this Manuel came galloping the Colonel's big black stallion into the drive at Ainahau, throw-ing up an awful dust and breaking the Governor's ban.

True happened to be sitting on the lanai, examining a rawhide lariat I had brought her—a beautiful piece of workmanship made by one of the paniolos on the ranch. Before she left Mau'loa, True had been learning to rope, and I thought this lariat might be a distraction.

She walked out to meet him. "I'm to give this to you to sign, and return it to the Colonel," he told her, not troubling to dismount. She reached up to take an envelope addressed in Laiana Wakefield's hand, and a packet of papers.

True read: "Urgent that all of us leave for Mau'loa five days hence, at eight on the morning of the 28th. Send Rose back today with the Colonel's man, as you have the girl Martha to help you with the child. Then return yourself by midday on the 27th. You are to sign the papers given here and return them at once." It was signed: "Mother Wakefield," without so much as an "aloha."

True sat down on the steps and opened the packet to find a sheaf of legal papers. She began to read. The man interrupted, "The Colonel says I'm not to tarry. You're to sign them papers and give 'em back to me now."

True looked up at him, still seated on the horse. "I suggest you get off and give the animal a chance to cool down," she told him. "You've ridden him too hard."

He stared back as if he needn't answer. "I go back now with the girl and the papers," he repeated.

True called out to one of the children playing on the lawn to go get Rose, Emma's nurse. Then she returned to reading the document, which seemed rather simple, she thought, in spite of the legal terminology. The Colonel was to be named legal guardian of his granddaughter, Emma Victoria, and be responsible for her well-being.

True had assumed he would see to it that Emma was cared for, as Jared would have wished. True was also well aware that she was dependent on the Wakefields, not only for her own welfare but for Liko and me as well. She had begun to worry that Laiana might dissuade the Colonel from his promise to allow us to come to Mau'loa with her. Best she not aggravate them now, she thought—surely Evan didn't have this in mind when he told her not to sign any papers. She rose to go into the house to get a pen.

The man Manuel, still mounted, raised his voice in challenge, "Where are you going, Miss?"

She whirled on him, and was about to tell him to mind his manners, when Rose came out on the lanai, carrying Emma.

"I'm sorry, Rose," she told her, and explained to her why she must return to the Wakefield house.

Tears welled in Rose's dark eyes and she held Emma close, as if she couldn't bear to part with her.

True put her arm around them both. "It's only for a few days."

"Hurry along," the man called out.

It was too much. True wheeled and shouted, "Just who do you think you're talking to, *driver?*" saying this last word with emphasis.

He held his ground, looking at her with sullen arrogance. "The Colonel says not to come back without . . ."

"Get out. Now!" True shouted at him. She picked up the lariat, felt it hard in her hand, swung it wide over her head and looped it around the man. Then she jerked, hard. He tumbled unceremoniously and sat stunned on the ground, his eyes flashing surprise and anger.

Rose cringed against the house, holding tight to Emma, who began to cry.

The Portuguese reached into his boot; True stepped sideways, putting the horse between them and holding hard to the lariat.

At that moment the Governor came striding out of the house, calling out, "What is this? What is happening here?"

True answered in as calm a way as she could manage, "Governor Cleghorn, Mother Wakefield has sent a message—we're to leave for Mau'loa in five days."

"It's the plague, I suppose," he said, taken aback by the news. "I'd hoped you would be able to stay on until things were more settled."

The Colonel's man was standing, diffident now, hat in hand.

"Go on," the Governor told him, "but walk that horse down the lane. I don't want any more dust kicked up. You've run him too hard as it is, can't you see that?"

True gave the man a scathing glance. "Tell Mrs. Wakefield I will bring Rose back myself this afternoon."

He was looking at the papers she had picked up, afraid now of going back without the girl or the papers, but she pretended she did not notice, and carried them inside with her.

May 1900, Mau'loa

We have been back for four months, very long and difficult months, and I am sorry to say that I am beginning to doubt that life will ever be pleasant again. Although when I went to see Old Auntie Momi a few days before we left, she had rubbed the inside of my palm until I thought the skin would come off, and she had laughed her girlish old woman's laugh. "Oh, it's a good thing that is happening. A good thing, I can see that now."

I wish I could believe something good could come of this; now I only wish to get through each day.

We are living in adjoining rooms in the guest quarters, True and I. Emma is in the nursery in the Big House, in the care of the young German nurse Miss Laiana brought back with them. Rose has been sent to the laundry and scarcely ever sees the baby, though as often as we dare True and I slip Emma out to visit her. We can stay in these rooms until they are needed for one of the Wakefields' big parties, then True is to move into the Big House and I must go to the servants' quarters. It is clear how the Wakefields view me.

I have been sent to "assist" the eighteen-year-old girl who is the teacher at the ranch school here at Kolonahe. She does not want any assistance; the poor girl can scarcely read and write herself, and she needs the job. Thus, she does not want me in her classroom.

Liko sleeps in the stable. He prefers it to living in the bunkhouse, and his job here is to clean the stables. He is, with his experience on Maui, an accomplished ranch hand, but the ranch manager says it is the only job available, and that is that. Liko is the only one who doesn't seem to mind; his despair is so deep that he seems able to do only the most menial work. True thinks it is just that he feels more comfortable with animals.

I have scarcely seen Pono since our return. The school at the old Home Place is finished, I am told. The house has been turned over to the manager and his family because it is closer to the corrals and the herds, and the school is being used as a storehouse. True and I wanted to ride over to see the place, but we were told that horses are in short supply and the paniolos need them. Of course, when the visitors arrive, the paniolos must do without.

It is driving True mad. Sometimes I think Miss Laiana and the Colonel are trying to break her, as a cowboy might break a wild horse.

A few days ago the Colonel asked True into his study and closed the door.

"Come in, come in," he said in his jovial way, as if he had forgotten who she was, and that he was not to be nice to her.

"Shall I have a cigar too?" she joked.

He laughed rather too loudly. "What a spunky girl you are, True. To be honest with you, one of the great jolts of my life was when Jared proposed to marry you." He clipped off the end of the cigar. "Or when you proposed to marry him, if that was the way it was," he added slyly.

True didn't answer, neither did she sit down but chose to wander about the big room, picking up one and then another of the seashells that were collected there.

"It's about Emma I wish to speak," he went on.

True put down the shell she was holding and turned to face him. "It's about the ranch that I wish to speak," she countered, in a polite enough way.

"The ranch?" he asked, as if he didn't understand.

"The ranch," she said. "You do remember the conversation with Jared and Evan Coulter, only a few days before," she paused, "before Jared's death." She had been avoiding the word, now she said it. Death. Jared's death.

"That's not what I asked you in here to talk about. There are some papers I need you to . . ."

"But don't you think we should talk about it?" she pressed, and then she was pleading. "So much needs to be done if the ranch is to prosper. Steps must be taken now. You know! You respect Evan's judgment and he told you."

"What Evan Coulter told me is of no concern to you, not now. While Jared was alive, yes. I admit I was willing to listen, because my son asked me to and I also know that he was doing it because you put him up to it. As for Coulter—I offered him the job of ranch manager and he turned it down."

"Because you wouldn't give him a free hand to make improvements!" she blurted, unable to stop herself.

His face hardened; she noticed the dogged thrust of his chin, Jared's old sign. "Evan Coulter is an important man in the territory, with a wealthy wife and a respected position in

Honolulu society. He could never be convinced to give all that up to come out here and manage a ranch, not even this ranch. God knows, I wouldn't in his place!"

True bit her lip. About that he was right. The Colonel would rather be in Honolulu, respected as Evan was—given the choice, he would choose Evan's lot.

"Won't you at least listen to some of the things we might do?" she asked, plaintively.

"We?" Laiana Wakefield said, entering the room. "I gather you are talking about the ranch again, about what you want done—about how you would save it. If you had spent more time worrying about my son and what was needed to save him, he might still be with us. No. We don't need you to tell us what to do. And you will not. Do you understand? You will not!"

"Darling . . ." the Colonel tried to interrupt, uncomfortable as always by any expression of anger.

"No, Tobias," she answered him, her own fury building, and turned to True: "You are suffered here because of our granddaughter. You and the girl and the stable boy. Remember that."

True turned and ran, blindly making her way down the porch steps, stumbling against the railing as she left and bruising her hip, falling into a hole in the lawn and twisting her ankle, but running on nonetheless, running and running until she reached a canefield and fell, the red dirt marking the side of her that was against the earth. True lay there, sobbing. She did not get up—she could not; there was no reason.

Pono did not know how long she had been there before he found her and carried her a full mile, back to me. He went to the well for cold water and wrapped her ankle in a wet rag and tied it snugly. Through all of this, True said nothing, and I did not question her.

She seemed too weary, even, to move. I sent Pono on his way, then I removed her muddy clothing and bathed her carefully. Like a sad, sick child she did as I asked, turning her face this way, leaning against me for support as I washed away the red mud of the cane fields. She could scarcely find the strength to lift her arms so I could put her nightgown over her head. It frightened me, seeing my friend so complaisant and despairing. I took her hand in mine and put her fingers to my lips. "Pono says we must not lose hope," I told her, working to keep my voice steady. "Just now, that is the last thing he said to me: Don't lose hope."

True looked at me as if she could not comprehend what I was trying to tell her, her eyes half closed. I smoothed away the few pale strands of hair that were clinging to her brow. Her skin felt cool to the touch; I told myself that she was not ill, but that she simply needed rest. As if in agreement, she uttered one small shuddering sigh and closed her eyes as she escaped into the sleep of the exhausted.

27

Rachel Wakefield is peculiar. That is the only word I can think of to describe this big-boned, awkward girl. True says she was odd when she left for England and came back a full-fledged eccentric.

The day after I had been told my services were no longer required at the schoolhouse, Rachel passed True a note marked "secret-secret-secret," summoning us to her room at half past three that afternoon. Rachel has grown excessively fond of secrecy. The last time she called us to her room we found her standing on her head, a skill she says she learned from a Hindu she met in Paris.

Although I should have known better, I thought she might be summoning me because of my lost position. "Calm down," True keeps telling me. "They are not going to send you away. I promise."

"You promise," I said, exasperated, and then the look on her face made me want to bite my tongue. I do not blame True for our sorry situation, but she blames herself.

Rachel opened the door a crack, saw it was us and quickly pulled us in. She whispered, "The map is there—you can see the island, just offshore. The big problem is fresh water; we will have to find a source before we bring in any natives."

"Whatever are you talking about?" True asked in the skeptical voice she uses with Rachel.

"Shhh," Rachel admonished. "They can't know until I'm ready . . ."

She was interrupted by a sharp, pained baby cry, followed by loud wailing. *Emma.* True bolted down the hall to the nursery, Rachel and I fast behind her.

Emma was standing in her crib, screaming. The German nurse was holding her by her arms, shaking her hard.

"Stop that!" True shouted, knocking the nurse aside. She

293

pulled Emma to her and held her close, comforting her with her hands, but her eyes were on the plump, pink-cheeked nurse in her pretty uniform, and her look was deadly enough to make the woman quail.

Rachel was the first to speak: "Whatever have you done to the child to make her cry so?"

The nurse muttered something in German, a sullen look on her face.

Emma was still screaming in pain. "Something is hurting her," I said, lifting her gown. On her delicate little back were bright red fingernail marks. "Dear Lord," I cried out. "She's pinched the baby and drawn blood!"

I thought True would explode; she handed poor little screaming Emma to me, walked over to the woman and slapped her, hard enough to send her reeling against the wall—hard enough, I think, to knock some of her teeth loose.

"If I had a gun," True said, speaking so close to her face that the woman could feel her breath, "I would kill you. If I ever see you anywhere near my child again, I will get a gun and I *will* kill you."

Rachel moved between them. "Go down to Mother's parlor and wait there," she told the nurse, but she wasn't looking at her. She was looking at True with astonishment and admiration.

The nurse was dispatched that same day; Laiana Wakefield would not have a woman on the place who would harm a child. She was so obviously upset that, for once, we were all in accord. It was Rachel who suggested that I be pressed into service as Emma's nurse for the moment, an arrangement which her mother agreed to—especially after True made it plain that she would not trust Emma to anyone else.

We have become something of a foursome: Rachel, True, Emma and I. This arrangement is tolerated by the family, I believe, because Rachel frequently squabbles with her sister, Etta, who is small and plain and speaks with a British accent she managed to acquire. Etta's time is divided between needlework and the miniature dogs she has decided to breed. "Etta is ordinary," Rachel says, stretching out each syllable. On the other hand, Rachel finds True to be "fascinating," as she tells her at least once a day. One nice turn of events: Rachel can request a buggy or sometimes even saddle horses, and we are able to flee the family compound. With this, True's spirits have improved a hundredfold.

Today we took the buggy to go to the little beach where Jared had tried to recuperate. We have enough provisions to stay an extra day; all of us are glad to be away.

Rachel is glad because she can finally talk out loud about what she has labeled her "Grand Plan," but which True calls "Rachel's Folly." She wants to buy a small island off Mau'-loa and turn it into a refuge for native Hawaiians. According to Rachel's plan, they will live and work as they did before the white man came "to sully their paradise," as she puts it. Only the Hawaiian language will be spoken; I've been giving Rachel Hawaiian lessons every day, unbeknownst to her mother, who so far has not seen much value in the scheme—dismissing it as "supremely silly." Since Jared's death, Miss Laiana seems to view many things as "supremely silly." The Colonel is in Honolulu; Rachel believes he will support her plan.

On this day True went running out to dive into the ocean, while Rachel and I stationed ourselves on a large old tapa cloth in the sand in the moving shade of a palm tree, cooing at Emma as she attempted to take her first steps.

"Come ahead, baby girl," Rachel encouraged her, laughing at the lopsided little grin Emma gave her in return. "Such a delicate little thing she is—I hope she isn't like Jared."

"You must miss your brother," I said, realizing that we had never spoken of him before.

"I don't miss him," she answered, flatly. "He never had anything to say to me, and Mama made it plain she didn't want to share him with anybody. Not even Papa. When Jared was around, he was the only child she had. She loved him best and didn't care who knew. That's why she despises True. True took him away. Sometimes I think Mama must be glad he died, so True couldn't have him."

Her bitterness shocked me; not knowing what to say, I played with the baby, holding my hands out to her while she took a few wobbly steps, then fell on her little bottom. Now and then Emma ventured a tiny foot off the tapa, onto the sand heated by the sun, and drew back with an intake of breath and a puzzled baby frown.

"Hot," I said, with Rachel echoing me.

"'ot," Emma said back.

Our cheers brought True running.

"Her first word is 'hot,'" Rachel called out to her.

Laughing, True caught the baby up against her wet body and said, "What a perfectly good first word, darling girl!" and gave her a big, salty kiss.

We celebrated with ripe papayas and a bottle of wine that Rachel had purloined from her father's cellar.

"Here's to 'hot'!" she toasted.

True and I said, "Here! here!" It was good to laugh again, after so long a sadness. For the first time in many long weeks, I went to bed that night listening to the lapping sounds of the ocean and feeling hopeful.

The euphoria was short-lived. Rachel is knocking about the big house in a foul mood because her father will not advance her the money to buy her island, and True is about to claw the walls because she has been banished from the working ranch.

It happened like this: Pono often appears after work at the edge of our compound. True supposes he is coming to see her, and perhaps he is. I always manage to be there as well, in case he has anything to say to me. But in fact, True seldom gives us a chance—she is too determined to learn what is going on with the ranch. Poor Pono is forced to talk much more than he wants to; the man seems never to be exhausted by physical labor, but the act of speech drains him. I can almost see it happening. That he comes at all, I believe, is an indication of how much he cares about us.

Through Pono, True has learned how short the ranch is of experienced riders—and evidently of cash as well, because the ranch manager has ordered Pono to take a crew of Hawaiian paniolos into the mountains to round up some wild cattle that roam there, unbranded—a job that will take five, maybe six days and bring in some fast profit. He expects him to do this with half the men he needs.

"Ask if I can sign on," True said.

Pono's eyes should have told her that he thought it a bad idea. "Ask!" she begged. "You know I am as good a rider as any of the men, even as good as you . . . and I can rope. You've seen me, you know."

He nodded, but doubt flickered across his face as warning.

"I know you don't want to take me along," True said to

him carefully, "but I'm asking you to do it anyway. If I can't get out on a horse with something to do soon I'm going to go crazy, Pono. Purely mad."

He looked at me. All I could do was shrug.

"I'll ask," he finally said.

True fell in place alongside the oxen—the Hawaiians call them *pini*—herding them up the mountains. Pono said she could come along but only to tend to the pini and help with the pack horses; he had made her promise to stay away from the wild cattle altogether.

She breathed in the mixed earth scent of early morning and cattle and eucalyptus from a grove they were passing through; she could almost feel herself coming to life. She lay her head back and looked up through the trees to a sky approaching dawn and she wanted to call out to the universe that she was there . . . alive again. She tightened her thighs and her horse picked up speed, bumping against the side of one of the lumbering pini. She was not on an especially good mount; the Colonel wasn't any more interested in the ranch's working horses than he was in improving the stock.

"Ho, whoa," she murmured, shifting her weight slightly to guide her horse through the oxen. It was twenty miles up the mountain to the base camp. She wished it were a hundred; she wished she could stay in the saddle forever; *in the saddle or in bed with Evan,* she thought and laughed out loud at the idea.

One of the paniolos had been watching her, and when she laughed he called out, "Plenty much fun." She looked down, embarrassed, and he added good-naturedly, "No shame," meaning she need not be shy.

"No shame," she thought. *True Wakefield has no shame.*

Capturing the wild beasts with their long, sharp horns was fierce, dangerous work; True watched as the Hawaiian paniolos tracked them, flushed them out of the low brush of this upcountry, galloped after them with ropes swinging wide. The steers were six, seven hundred pounds and their long horns were lethal. True watched in amazement as the Hawaiian they called Oko—the one who had laughed with her—swung his lariat casually over the horns of a madly careening wild bull, twisted it to a halt and with a few deft movements had it tied to a tree. Quickly then, he pulled a small saw from a slit in his boot and sawed off the creature's wide, sharp horns. So caught up was she in this action that she neglected to bring up the pini, and Oko had to shout to her, "Hele on, missy, get that pini heah."

She moved the tame ox into place next to the wild steer, frantically lunging against the rope that held it—its eyes crazed with fear so powerful you could smell it. True's job was to move the oxen in place so Oko could tie the two together; soon enough the tame creature would calm the wild one, and they could be led down the mountain together.

At night, around the campfire, the paniolos would talk about the day's work; sometimes they would tell stories or chant. For the first night or two, True's presence troubled them and they gave her wide range, but all of them had been watching her work and what they saw pleased them.

She sat a horse as well as any of them, and she did the job she had been given—watching after the pini and the pack-horses—so well that they knew she was doing a full share without expecting any help. Too, it was not a job any of them wanted, preferring to concentrate on the hunt.

Pono was pleased. He had not thought she should come, because he knew how easy it was for trouble to happen on these wild hunts, and he was not certain that she would follow orders. But she had done exactly what he had asked, and she had done it as well as any man. What he hadn't expected was how easily the Hawaiians would come to accept her. "That lady, she dances with that horse," one of the older men had said to him, with a certain dry awe in his voice.

After five days, Pono announced: "One more day."

"Only four pini left," True answered, and added, "I don't suppose you might let me just try my hand at roping a steer?"

His sharp, dark glance made her say, "No, I suppose not. Okay, boss, you are in charge. But when we get them all down and into the paddock, I plan to rope me a few just to get some practice. How am I ever going to catch up to you boys if I can't practice?"

The "boys" had laughed at that, and all of them would remember True's words.

By noon, they were down to the last two pini, and Pono—

thinking about the long drive back down the mountain—
was considering quitting and starting for home. They were
in a long, funneled draw—dry and filled with high, sharp
grasses and great black birds that cried out over them, as if
they had disturbed their precious kingdom. True had been
busy all that morning removing sharp burrowing thistles
from under saddles and from the horses' hooves. She was
able to tell when a horse was having trouble before its rider
knew.

True had dismounted and was examining the foreleg of
one of the pack-horses; she heard the sound—a thunderous
roar, as if the dry mountain air had suddenly expanded—at
the same time that she saw the wild black steer galloping
down the funnel, its yellow eyes wild and its horns lowered
and swinging in a deadly arc. She stood, transfixed, in its
path.

The next instant two ropes were in the air; only one
caught, pulling the beast off course. True wheeled and in two
wild leaps was on her horse; she could feel its terror. The
wild steer, circled now by three more paniolos, pulled up
short, turned and came at her again. Now she had her mount
under control, and she moved out of the crazed animal's
range.

The paniolos closed in, whooping; Pono's rope was the
first to find its mark, then two more. They held it, taut,
between them: the animal let out a sound so fierce that True
was not certain if the shiver she felt was from her horse or
from herself. True moved the pini closer, though she wondered if anything could tame this massive wild creature,
bigger than any they had seen. The pini True led was no
larger than the steer.

As she was thinking this, the wild beast reared gro-
tesquely, twisting in mid-air, shaking off two of the ropes.
The one left was attached to Oko; his horse stumbled, Oko
was jerked from his saddle and was being dragged through
the scrub, bumping and tumbling like some loose sack.

True didn't think; she spurred her horse after them, her
knife unsheathed in her hand. Dust flew everywhere—she
could scarcely see. She raised herself in the saddle and leaned
far over, as far as she could and sliced out with the knife to
cut the rope. She hit out, once and again and again . . . until
she felt it fall away. Only then did she realize the momentum

was too great, she could not stop her horse in time, it was
going to overtake the beast.

She saw the yellow eye, the deadly bestial power, the
need to destroy. It would kill her if it could. She tried to
turn her horse—but it was too late. She heard the horn
slice through her horse's belly, felt the sharp impact, the
warm blood that spurted over, heard the sharp crack of a
rifle, then another and another. Within seconds, she was
lying in a pool of blood between her downed horse and the
dying beast.

Pono reached her first, his face white. "No, no," she was
able to whisper, though her mouth was so dry she could
scarcely speak. "I'm all right. Oko? Is Oko . . ."

"He's alive," Pono told her, and she noticed that his voice
was shaking. Then he added, "Because of you."

They came down out of the mountains that day, the pini
leading the wild animals, who would be penned until they
were tame enough to slaughter. At the end of the procession
came Oko on a makeshift stretcher. His legs were broken
and some of his ribs; he was in pain so terrible that True,
who rode with him, feared he would not live through the
journey.

Tevis, the ranch manager, was there when they rode in. As
soon as Oko was tended to, Pono went to the corral to do
the counts.

"We're one mount short," he told the man who was his
boss. "It got gored in the commotion. Had to put him
down."

"Who was up?" the man wanted to know.

"The one who saved Oko's life."

The man looked at Pono sharply. "That woman," he said
biting down hard on the cigar in his mouth. "She lost her
mount. Don't mean a thing to me how she did it. She's off
the working ranch. Tell her that."

One of the Hawaiians had been standing close by, listening. "It was the horse or *kanaka,*" he said. "She chooses for
the kanaka."

Tevis rolled his cigar from one side of his mouth to the
other, looking at the man all the time but saying not a word.
His silence was damning. What it meant was: *She made the
wrong choice.*

* * *

The Colonel, his wife and Etta are in Honolulu, thank goodness. Though I suspect they will come back with a passel of house guests—that is what usually happens—for now, the ranch is quiet. True walks around, sighing. Or she takes off to walk up to Oko's house, to see how he is doing. His family has gathered True into their ohana.

In the weeks since the drive, each of the paniolos have appeared to say to True what they feel in their hearts. Pono tells me they think she has magic. In a way, I suppose, she does. At least when she is on a horse she becomes a kind of magician. Pono also tells me that the Hawaiian hands are beginning to listen to his brother Patrick, who all along has been urging them to organize and make some demands of the Colonel and his manager.

Pono talks to me quite a lot, when no one else is around. The words seem not so difficult to give up as they once did. Not a few of his words are questions. He asks me about teaching, about my family, about the things that please me and those that don't. Soon Pono will know more about me than anyone, even Old Auntie.

True was in the family horsebarn, and I was in the nursery, giving Emma her bath—she was slapping the water with her hands, spraying us both and having a grand time of it. Rachel, in the downstairs library researching yet another aspect of native life, answered the door.

"Martha," she called up in a voice that warned me of something unusual. "You've a guest. You and True."

Wrapping Emma in a towel and balancing her on my hip, I went down.

"Oh my goodness!" I yelped, scarcely believing my eyes. "Uncle Jameson. Is it you?"

He looked frail and grey and somehow too small for this big house. Rachel towered over him.

"Thank you," he said to her offer of a chair. "The crossing was a bit choppy."

I could not stop shaking my head and smiling. "I'm just so pleased to see you, Uncle. I know how little you like to travel . . . I suppose I didn't think I would ever see you, outside of Waikiki."

He ran his hand through his thinning hair. "You are right, Martha. It has taken a matter of great urgency to bring me here. I do need to speak to you and True. But I fear that first I must lie down for a bit."

He slept for six hours. Most of that time True paced outside of the guest room. "A matter of urgency—could something have happened to Evan?" she asked, twisting her hands. "Or is it Aunt? What would bring him here?"

"Why do you think it must be a disaster?" I asked, just to quiet her.

She sat down heavily in one of the hall chairs and let her hands fall limp on either side of her. "What other kind of news do we get?" she said, so plaintively that I laughed.

Rachel had gone on an errand, but Liko was waiting with us. It had taken some cajoling to get him to come into the big house. Ordinarily, he is not allowed in the family's living quarters, and it made him uncomfortable to be there while they were away.

When Uncle finally came out, looking rested and less frail, he was almost bowled over by our welcome. We sat around him—Liko on the floor at his feet, True on a settee holding Emma and me across from Uncle at the little table where he sat to eat.

Finished, he patted his lips with his napkin, pushed back from the table and took a long, leisurely look around the room.

"Do you know why I do not feel like an interloper in this house?" he asked.

True and I exchanged quizzical glances. "No," we murmured.

"Because Emma is my good little friend. I feel as if she is my grandchild, almost. Isn't that right, Emma?"

The baby gurgled and smiled, as if she understood what he had said, and all of us laughed. We had never seen Uncle in so playful a mood, or so mystifying.

"What is this news you're bringing?" True blurted.

"True assumes disaster," I put in.

Uncle shook his head, smiling still the puzzling little triumphant smile he had been wearing since his arrival. "First I must ask you one important question. Have you signed any legal papers—any at all—since Jared's death?"

True pressed her lips together, then she said, "None. The Colonel has been after me, and I suppose I've been contrary but . . ."

"Good!" Uncle cut in, clearly relieved. "This is good. Here is my news then. Little Emma here is half owner of Mau'loa."

We stared at him.

"Emma?" True gasped.

"Yes, our own dear little Emma. We—Evan and I—have been tracking this possibility for weeks, poring over stacks of legal papers, some of them quite old and obviously forgotten. I must say that Colonel Toby was generous to make them available to us, saved us a good deal of time, you see. Evan made the discovery. He rode out to Mana'olana at three in the morning to tell me! That was just three days ago."

"But what? How?" I asked, while Liko's big face mirrored our disbelief.

"Simply put, since Jared died before reaching his majority—and he was the hanai child of Eben Wakefield—under Hawaiian law his ownership of one-half of the ranch passed directly to his heir. In this case, Emma is Jared's only heir."

Uncle sat back, pleased with their stunned silence. "I know, I know—that was how I felt at first. As if it simply couldn't be, but it is, I assure you. No one can challenge it."

"But Emma is just a baby. It will be ever so long before she can . . ."

"Whoever is named to be Emma's guardian will control her half of the ranch. It must be an adult male. But as Emma's mother you, True, are charged with naming who that person will be."

True gasped. "Are you saying that it doesn't have to be the Colonel? Are you saying I have a choice?"

Uncle smiled again and watched with pleasure as a slow, bright, full smile lit her face.

28

Evan struggled to slide the collar onto his shirt. The laundry-man had starched it so stiff the buttonholes were all but glued shut. He thought to himself, as he did every morning, that he did not like to wear starched shirts and suits, he did not want to go to an office and sit at a desk, and he did not want to spend the whole of his life in rooms. He looked in the mirror and grimaced: thirty-eight years old, he thought, and none the wiser.

Still, there was hope now for True and the baby. They had already taken possession of the old Home Place, and Martha and Liko were with them. Jameson had returned to report that the Rourkes and the Hawaiian paniolos had declared their allegiance to True. The Colonel is going to have a time of it if he insists on breaking up the ranch, he thought. True was on her way to Honolulu. She would be arriving in a few hours to work out the details. Either she and the Colonel would find a way to keep the ranch together or it would be divided. Everything was possible now, he said to himself. But he would have to be careful to stay in the background.

He emerged from his bedroom, stopped to look in on Harry—fast asleep, his bedclothes in a tumble all around him—then braced himself for his morning encounter with Jenny. It had become a ritual; they sat across from each other at breakfast, exchanged whatever information was necessary about Harry or the household and, according to Jenny's mood, discussed whatever else she felt necessary.

This morning she was seated at the far end of the table in the morning room, reading a book. She did not look up as he entered and she had not dressed—both bad signs, Evan knew.

He sat down, thanked the maid who poured his coffee and said, "Morning, Jenny."

She did not answer.

He tried again. "If I can interrupt you—I'm not going to be able to go with Harry today to his baseball practice. He'll have to go on his own. He can ride his pony."

She looked up, appalled. "What do you mean, go on his own? Besides, it is a stupid game. I don't know why you want him to play."

Evan stirred his coffee, studied it. "Harry wants to play. It's fun. He's getting good at it, and it's healthy."

"How can it be healthy? He's only seven years old and the last three times he got hurt . . . his fingers, his knee, he even got hit in the eye."

"Those were just scuffs—all boys get scuffs. I think it's part of being a boy." He smiled, but she wasn't looking at him.

"It's all the way across town—what if he gets lost?"

It was the petulance that annoyed him. "If he could find me on Kauai, he can find a park a mile away," he said and knew at once it was a mistake.

Her hair had been hurriedly pinned on top of her head, and now part of it came tumbling down, giving her a lopsided, unkempt look. Jenny had lost all of the soft, pink prettiness of her girlhood; her skin was sallow and loose.

"You know I went to visit Miss Winona Wright yesterday," she hit back.

He steeled himself and took another sip of coffee.

"She thought I must certainly know about little Emma's good fortune," Jenny went on, feigning innocence. "Since you played such an almightly important role in securing her inheritance. And since you appeared at the Wrights' in the middle of the night not so long ago to tell them all about it."

Evan looked at her but did not answer.

"Don't you think you might have told your own wife?" she demanded.

Evan kept his tone even. "My own wife has repeatedly told me that she strongly objects to the mention of either Emma or her mother in this house."

Jenny seemed to shrug off her anger—she would flail out at him one moment, then be quiet and almost obliging the next. He never knew where her twists and turns would take them.

"Why did she name Jameson Wright to be Emma's guardian? The man can't bear to be away from Waikiki."

"He went to Mau'loa," Evan pointed out.

"Winona said it took all of his courage to make that journey, and she says he vows never to make another." Jenny twirled a strand of hair, a habit that usually presaged an attack. "How did the Colonel and Miss Laiana take the news?"

"I hear they were surprised," he answered carefully.

"Surprised!" Jenny whooped. "I just suppose they were surprised! The Wakefields are such trusting souls, don't you know? They just seem to think everything is what it looks to be, including their grandchild."

The look on his face made her add, quickly, "Oh, I would never say a thing, no. I'm just thinking out loud Evan, that's all. No, I would never ever suggest such a thing." She said this in a high, falsely sincere voice.

Evan stood and folded his napkin, a signal he was leaving.

"Perhaps I'll go to baseball practice with Harry," she said blithely, waving her hand in the air.

Evan hesitated, tried to think of the right words to dissuade her—Harry would be embarrassed, to have his mother along. If he said this to her, she would go into another round of accusations and they would be back into the escalating arguments that he had vowed he would avoid. Not today, he told himself, swallowing his objections.

Jenny Barrows Coulter sat at the table for a long time after her husband had gone. The maid came and cleared the dishes, and still Jenny sat. Sometimes she remained there the whole of the morning, returning to her room just before lunch. On such days she did not dress at all. When this happened, Harry did not knock on her door, did not go near her room. If he did, she always found ways of keeping him longer than he wanted to stay.

When the Inter-Island ferry pulled into the dock at Honolulu that bright morning, True went striding down the gangway; a large swell sent the boat rolling and, in her haste, she almost lost her footing.

"Watch out, miss," one of the hands called to her.

She answered, laughing, "I've been watching out all my life! I'm tired of watching out."

She scanned the crowd that always met the ferry, expecting to see Uncle or possibly Governor Cleghorn. A small kanaka tugged at her skirt.

"Miss True heah?" he asked.

"Yes," she said, puzzled.

"Bettah you come wit me," he told her in the pidgin English the Hawaiians were using in the city.

She followed the boy as he darted through the crowd and followed him alongside the pier and down a narrow street where a carriage was waiting. Evan jumped down to help her in.

She threw herself into his arms and held onto him, laughing and crying with such happiness that the small kanaka, watching, clapped his hands.

Evan gave the boy a coin, brushed him on the head and all but pushed True into the carriage. "We shouldn't be seen together, at least not now," he told her, "but I need to talk to you."

"I need to touch you," she told him, slipping her hand under his coat, pressing against his chest.

He removed her hand, touched her fingers quickly to his lips and told her, "First we have to get out of here without being seen. Make yourself invisible."

She tucked into a corner of the closed carriage and contented herself with watching him. Everything inside of her was expanding; she could not seem to take deep enough breaths. The heat of the day did not affect her; she touched her hand to her neck and her skin felt cool. It was as if some yoke had been lifted from her, as if finally she could stand straight again and breathe freely.

Almost as soon as they were out of the city, Evan turned the buggy down a sandy lane arched over by tall shrubs which led to a small beach. He pulled up alongside an open pavilion. "Some kanaka friends of mine use this for luaus," he explained as he helped her down.

She wound her arms around his neck and brought her mouth to his, soft and seeking.

He kissed her tenderly, stroking her hair, stroking her back. "We need to talk," he whispered as he held her. "There is so much planning we must do."

"You have saved us, Evan. You have."

He shook his head and grinned. "You have old Uncle Eben to thank for that, but I have to say I wish the old man had taken better care of his records. The one we needed was mixed in with a whole passel of stuff that should have been thrown out years ago."

"Were you looking for it? Did you know it existed?" she asked.

With his arm around her waist, he walked her to a place under a tulip tree where two old chairs and a ramshackle table had been left. Evan answered, "I didn't know, but I suspected it might."

"Do you think the Colonel knew?" she asked.

"I'm certain he did not," Evan told her. "The Colonel is many things—convivial, rakish, a little bit thick. But I don't believe he would purposely try to cheat you."

"Does he know you are the one who discovered this?"

"No," Evan answered. "Jameson did all the talking. I want to stay in the background as much as possible. I've a young lawyer who can handle the legal work, but if you need me to . . ."

"No, I agree. I don't want the Colonel to think you are taking sides because I'm hoping we can convince him not to divide the ranch."

He gave her a quizzical look.

"You're surprised?" she said, reaching for his hand because she needed to touch him. "Well, right now we are going to need the proceeds from the whole ranch to make even the most basic of improvements. Splitting it will put us even farther behind, and I don't know that we will ever be able to catch up."

"You've done some thinking."

"And some figuring, as much as I could with the information I could get."

"It's worse than you think," he told her. "The place has been mortgaged to the hilt. Toby's venture into sugar cane was a disaster, and he took out other loans to pay for God only knows what. If we can't find a way to begin to pay off those debts, the ranch could be lost. And you are right; it is going to be three times as hard if the ranch is split. What Emma owns could evaporate if we don't make the right decisions, now."

True stared at him. "Is that right? Is it that bad?"

"It is."

She stood, suddenly angry. "Damn him for not listening! Damn them all with their parties and their silly palaver."

He pulled her into his arms and rocked her back and forth, his cheek against hers. "I feel that way too, my girl. It's going to take some doing."

"Half of that ranch is Emma's, and I mean to see that she keeps it," True told him.

He ran his hands down her arms and walked away from her, standing looking out to a quiet sea with scarcely a ripple of surf. He had trouble getting out the words: "I need to ask you something, True. Understand, please—I must. You say that Jared was Emma's father. But what if that isn't what happened?"

"There is no room in our lives to think of that," she told him, her face set. "Emma belongs to all of us, to Liko and Martha as much as you and me, but her name is Wakefield and Jared Wakefield went to his grave happy that she was his child."

"But tell me, tell me now . . . I need to hear you say it . . ."

She approached him but she did not touch him. Still, her face softened as she said, "I believe that it doesn't really matter, Evan. I believe that by saving the ranch we will be doing a justice for everyone, not just ourselves. The way Colonel Toby is going, he will lose the ranch altogether and then what will they do? How will he earn a living? And what about all the paniolos—the Hawaiians and the haoles alike, where will they go? All I want is a chance to work as hard as I can and make something out of that ranch. I want to be able to sit in a saddle all day long, and all night too, if that is what it takes. I want to see some of the water that floods the leeward side of the island brought over to our pastures, so our cows don't have to walk fifteen miles to get a drink. I want to see paddocks built, and fences strung, and new breeding stock brought in so we can ship beeves that weigh 1000 pounds, not 500. And the horses—we need to get a better grade of working horse. Do you want to hear more of what I want?"

"No," he said, grinning, but she wouldn't stop. "We need a school for all the poor little Irish and Oriental and Portuguese and Hawaiian children who live out in the cane fields, or in shacks so far back in the woods nobody knows they are there. We have the school building and we have the teacher—all we need is to round up the children. And the

ranch hands, we need to help them and their families with
better places to live—have you seen the hovels they call
home? It's awful, Evan. We think the Colonel is such a kind
man, but how kind is he when he lets his help live in those
dreadful places?"

Evan pulled her to him. "You are telling me that you
aren't going to answer my question. All right. For now."

"I love you, Evan. And I depend on you. I have from the
very first day I saw you, and I still do. It will always be like
that. I will always love you better than any man on earth."

"Don't say that."

She answered, "Let's not talk about anything but the
ranch, and what we must do to save it."

For more than an hour they discussed what they would do
and decided on a plan. Jameson Wright and True and the
lawyer would meet with the Colonel and his forces. The
Colonel would expect her to come in fighting mad—knowing that she had seen the books and realizing what a sorry
state the ranch was in. She would surprise and please him by
being conciliatory, would press for keeping the ranch intact.

She would make few demands. She would, however, ask
for a new ranch manager from a list of three names which
Evan provided her. She would not mention Evan, but it
would be good if the Colonel brought his name up, perhaps as someone who might offer suggestions and advice.
If that happened, Uncle would suggest they invite Evan to
come to Mau'loa to tell them what needed to be done to
make the ranch profitable again. Evan would be free to
advise the ranch manager in the open, then, rather than
behind the scenes. True was to use the word "profitable"
as often as possible. It was a word the Colonel would understand.

When they had finished, True simply stood and started to
unbutton the front of her dress. "There's no time, my sweet
girl," Evan told her, but he did not move to stop her. "No
time," he whispered again as she lifted her mouth to his.

"There will never be any time for us if we don't take it,"
she answered, pressing hard into him in the heat of the
afternoon.

Harry squirmed. He did not want his mother to ride along
to the park with him, but he did not know how to tell her.

"I didn't know you could ride," he said, because he couldn't think of anything else.

"Young man," she flared, "I've been riding longer than . . ." She didn't finish because the mare was being skittish, and it was all she could do to hold it.

Harry rode ahead on his pony, not wanting to watch her puffing along, trying to ignore her frequent outbursts at the little mare. He wished Pa had come. They would've thrown the ball back and forth, and then Pa would have pitched to him . . . not so fast as the bigger boys, but slow so he could take his time and remember all the things he was supposed to remember when he was at bat. It wasn't that he didn't want his mother to go but . . .

"Harry," she called. "Come back here with me."

He pulled his pony to the side, then fell in next to her. Her face was bright red, and she was sweating. She would probably be sick tomorrow, he thought, and it would be his fault. Or Pa's, somehow it was always Pa's fault. Even when it should have been his.

"Why do you want to play baseball, son?" she asked.

He ducked his head. "Because it's fun."

"Fun!" she protested. "I don't see how it can be fun. Surely there is something you would rather do?"

He thought about it. She was right in a way, he would rather be doing something else now, with her along, but he couldn't think of what it might be.

"What is it?" she said, smiling widely so he would know she only wanted to please him.

"I guess I'd like to go riding up the Pali. Pa's going to take me there on Sunday but . . ."

"Let's go!" she said. "Now. Right now."

He frowned. "It's too late, Mama. Pa says you have to go early so . . ."

"It's not the least bit too late," she said. "I've made that trip back up Manoa Valley I don't know how many times. Two hours, we can be there. Oh, what fun we are going to have!"

She slapped her horse to a slow trot and he had to hurry to keep up with her, thinking all the while that he shouldn't have said anything about the trip up the Pali. He and Pa were going to do that . . . they had made plans . . . they would leave early in the morning and go to a place Pa knew, with the butterfly nets. Now it was ruined, she was ruining it, and he didn't know how to stop her.

They rode for an hour, Jenny leading the way, without saying anything.

"I don't remember it getting this steep so fast," Jenny called back to him, her voice cheerful.

"I don't know . . ." Harry said.

"We've got plenty of light," she said to reassure him. "Just look how high the sun is—have you ever seen anything so beautiful?"

The sea stretched out beneath them, smooth and gleaming in the afternoon sun. A giant freighter steaming into port looked like a tiny toy tracing a mark of white steam on the sky. "I had almost forgotten how calm it is up here, as if all of the troubles of the world are left down there, below."

Harry patted his pony to calm him. The trail had become a narrow shelf carved out of the side of the cliff. "Shhh, boy, it's okay," he said.

His mother looked back. "What's okay?" she asked.

"Smoky doesn't like the trail, I don't think."

"Smoky is fine. Just let him have his head, he'll do just fine."

Harry couldn't help himself. "I wish Pa was here," he said, his voice breaking.

"Your pa isn't here because he didn't have time for us." He started to cry.

"Stop that," she told him. "As soon as we find a wide place, we'll turn and head back down. Big boys don't cry, so stop that now."

Harry made himself stop. For the past half hour he hadn't been able to look down without his stomach sinking. At times, his pony's hooves had broken loose some small rocks and sent them flying out, dropping far down to the sea below. Harry didn't want to think about the ride down. He only wanted it to be over.

When finally they reached a wide place in the trail the sun made their skins glow a warm orange color. The mare turned easily enough and stood quietly, but Harry's pony balked. It felt safe and did not want to go out again.

Jenny peeled a switch off a bush and leaned to hand it to him. "Whip him when he stops," she said. "Now we do have to get down quickly . . . come!" Harry was glad that she knew what to do. He didn't want to admit that he knew how Smoky felt, he didn't want her to know how afraid he was.

Jenny hurried now; the sun was sitting directly on the horizon, then it was no more than a slim cusp, then only long rays lighting the undersides of the clouds. "Hurry, son," she said, tightening her grip on her mare's sides. She wished Evan had put Harry on a proper little horse, more sure-footed than the pony, forgetting that she had refused to hear of it when Evan brought it up last spring.

"Mama," Harry called out, his voice edging on panic. "Wait. I can't . . . Smoky won't . . ."

"This is the hard part, son. You've got to make him do it . . . switch him a little, show him you know what you're doing." She turned to watch. The sky was now purple tinged with pink; soon it would be grey, and then black.

"Come!" she commanded. "Look at me, Harry, and come ahead. Switch him. We can't tarry."

He made himself look at her, only at her. He would be safe if he looked at her. Not down, not up to the ridge above them, only at her.

The trail gave way in a cloud of dirt and rocks. Pony and boy went tumbling through the air as if freed from the earth's pull, arms and legs rotating in grotesque pinwheels, bouncing off the scrub bushes on the side of the cliff, lit by the sun's purple flares, falling inexorably.

She heard the scream, but she did not know if it came from her or from her son.

29

Colonel Toby joined Evan at the railing as the ferry approached the Mau'loa dock.

"I've been wanting to talk to you, son," he said, laying his hand on Evan's shoulder. "I wanted to say how sorry I am about your boy." He cleared his throat. "I understand his leg is badly mangled and there are some other hurts."

Evan only nodded and looked off to the island as it rose from the sea. He had never imagined that he could see the Big Island without a feeling of excitement, but he felt nothing, only the dull ache that had been lying on his chest since they found Harry. The Colonel pressed Evan's shoulder. "I know how it is to have an ailing son," he went on, "but I hear our Jenny performed a miracle, climbing down the Pali and hanging onto the boy all night long. I have to tell you, I didn't think she had that kind of spunk."

Evan didn't answer. He couldn't if he was going to keep down the rage that was rising in him.

"I hear she says she won't stop until she finds a way for the boy to walk again," the Colonel went on. "I certainly do admire that kind of determination."

Evan broke in to silence him. "They sailed yesterday to see some doctors in San Francisco." He wasn't willing to say more; his throat seemed to close when it came to talking about Harry. He kept seeing the boy's pale, battered face and the look of defeat in his eyes.

"I won't be playing baseball," his son had said. "And I can't ride Smoky anymore. Smoky's dead, Pa. All crumpled up on the rocks, broken."

Jenny was the victor. She had what she wanted. A cause. A son with a crushed leg and a broken arm, and with a scar on his shoulder twelve inches wide. Now she had him back under her control.

"Whatever in the world made you take him up there?" he had asked her.

And she had snapped back, "None of this would have happened if you'd been home to take him to baseball."

Colonel Toby's voice brought him back. "What can you tell me about this Bradley Chin who's going to manage the ranch for us?"

Evan was glad for the change of subject. "He's young and smart and as good with cattle as anyone I've ever known. He worked with me on Kauai. Sometimes he can think of ways to do things that seem kind of crazy at first, but they work. I always liked that about him."

"Is that his real name—Bradley?" the Colonel asked, steadying himself as the boat bounced off the waves.

"No, his real name is Chin Yan Kun."

"So who named him Bradley?"

"I did," Evan told him. "He came to tell me he had decided to become Evan Chin. I said I thought he was more of a Bradley."

The Colonel's big laugh echoed across the stern of the wallowing old boat. When he had finished, he told Evan, "I'd better go round up my guests—they were looking a little green the last time I saw them. I always tell folks that's the price they have to pay to come to Mau'loa. I sure hope you can tell us how to make this ranch do well enough to get our own ferry. This old tub should be scuttled."

Evan and the Colonel rode ahead, as True and Bradley brought up the rear. She had liked Bradley Chin from the moment she met him: his continual grin, his thick black hair falling over his eyes, the perpetual energy that seemed to keep him moving all the time, and his unusual way with English. When Bradley talked, words collided with each other. His mind moved like an abacus, she thought: she could almost hear the clicking.

"Mr. Evan won't going to like this, now too dry, what a shame, terrible terrible sad . . . poor cows walk to water so far, my goodness so many miles."

She spoke quietly, "Evan will tell us what he thinks when the Colonel leaves."

Bradley's eyes rolled around in his head several times, to show her he knew what she meant.

* * *

After ten days of riding over the ranch, Evan came back to
the Home Place. "It's bad," was all he could say. "Worse
than I thought it would be, and I knew it was going to be
bad. The pastures are parched, the fattening paddocks need
to be tripled in size, the cattle have become so in-bred they've
produced every flaw of the species . . . and half at least aren't
branded. I ran into a couple of rustler operations—local
folks helping themselves to an unbranded steer—the whole
ranch, it's a sorry sight."

They were sitting on the lanai at the Home Place, True
and Bradley and Evan. After a while Pono showed up. He
stood at the end of the porch, holding his hat—Pono didn't
wear a big wide-brimmed cowboy hat, but rather something
like a Panama so the bottom of his face was bronze while
his temple was pale. As soon as they noticed him, he was
drawn into their conversation. Liko and I sat on the swing
and listened while Evan and Bradley pelted Pono with questions, and I felt myself feeling proud at the way he answered,
telling them just what they wanted to know and no more. It's
not that he won't talk, I suddenly realized. It's just that he
won't waste words.

After a while Evan stood up and thanked the two men,
and they all shook hands, like they were making a pact.

True and Evan went into the parlor then; it was the first
time they had been alone, and True was filled with worry.
They stood facing each other, awkwardly.

"Tell me about Harry," she said.

He drew a deep breath. "What can I tell you about
Harry?" he answered, feeling the bitterness well up in him,
but this time he was unable to keep it down. "He was becoming a nice, normal boy, and she couldn't let it be." He shoved
his hands in his pockets and turned away.

He had never spoken against Jenny before; now he seemed
unable to stop himself. "She's got him just where she wants
him—in a sick room, and she's in charge. Only her."

"Why?" True asked.

"Because she has the money to take him off to the Mainland in search of doctors who might help him. And because
as much as I might want to stop her, I can't because I'm
afraid she might be right . . . she might be able to find some
new doctor, some new treatment. I don't know, True. I don't

know if it's better for him to be able to walk, or better for him to be out of her grasp."

"She's his mother," True said, simply. "How could he be out of her grasp?"

He shook his head, and she could see how the anger and frustration were choking him. Talking about it was not helping. "I wish you could stay with us tonight," she said, changing the subject, "but I know you need to see Colonel Toby. I still find it hard to believe that he brought twelve guests along with him when he knew you were coming to look over the ranch. Twelve! Bradley thought the request for horses was some kind of mistake. 'This never do, never ever will do,'" she mimicked him, and Evan managed a grin.

She explained, "I thought it best not to face that particular problem today, so I convinced Bradley to give him the horses. He also had to provide wagons for a swimming party, and some of the men who are visiting want to ride with the paniolos—pretend to be cowboys for half a day—that not only means extra horses, but the boys have to watch so the city men don't hurt themselves. It seems to me a bad omen, if after all we've said, the Colonel still asks us to do these things."

Evan stroked her arm. It was the first time he had touched her since his arrival; she felt weak with relief.

"Maybe all of us are going to have to change our ways," he told her, and seeing the flash of fear that passed over her face, quickly added, "Except for you. You have to stay just the way you are." He held her face in his hands and kissed her, very gently, on the lips. "I miss you," he said.

"I know how much you miss Harry, too," she told him. "Both of us count on you. Too much. All you get in return is our love."

At that moment Liko came into the parlor with Emma—he was holding her little hand as she took a few teetering steps, smiling.

"Look who is finally up from her nap!" True laughed. "Let her go, Liko. Evan has to see how she can walk."

The child stopped short, looking at Evan with wide-eyed curiosity. She threw her hands into the air and gurgled a clear, happy baby laugh.

Evan's face broke into a wide grin. He knelt and held out his hands to her.

She went churning toward him, wobbling unsteadily, jabbering away with musical noises until she reached him. He lifted her into the air, then he held her and, looking directly into her bright blue eyes told her, "Miss Emma Victoria, we are going to build you a fine big ranch. Does that meet with your approval?"

True laughed and clapped then, because she had heard the resolve in Evan Coulter's voice, and because Emma had made him smile.

Evan has resigned his position in the government, and now he will take two or three months to finish his work. After that he plans to sail for San Francisco to see Harry. If the boy returns to Honolulu, he will stay with him.

Whatever happens, he will be directing the renaissance of Mau'loa. The last thing he told True was, "Nothing is going to be easy about this. The major problems will be the Colonel and capital. I think I can raise the capital . . . the Colonel is going to be the wild card."

Making herself smile, she added, "I promise not to do anything to make the Colonel mad, though I won't promise not to want to."

You find out a great deal when you start a school. For example, I have discovered that the island has a school board. Yes! Miss Ivy Renford, whose pa left her a big spread just south of Mau'loa, is the chairwoman. Still is, though the board itself came into being twenty years ago, when Miss Ivy wanted to do something about the sad state of education on the island and got the government to send out "inspectors" to make certain the teachers were at least literate. Then, there were seven schools scattered over the island. Now there are five. No one can remember when the last "inspector" was sent out.

My inquiries seem to have stirred up a bit of a hornet's nest. When I rode over to see Miss Ivy to talk about opening our school, I seemed to have jolted her into sending out a new set of inspectors—the island's only priest, a winsome Belgian, and Miss Rachel Wakefield, who volunteered for the job.

Rachel learned about it from me, but I tried to discourage her from taking on the task, warning her that her father's school would likely not meet the requirements. Rachel wouldn't listen, naturally. I believe she had other motives as well. She has not given up on her plan to create an island for native Hawaiians only, and by travelling around to the schools, she thinks she will get to meet the island's native population, particularly the women and children.

It happened. They closed the Colonel's school, and the next day Miss Laiana came riding up to the Home Place with fire in her eyes.

She found me in the schoolroom, and greeted me with, "Have you no shame, girl?"

She did not require an answer, but went right on. "Why you find it necessary to destroy our little school, I cannot say. I do know spitefulness when I see it. We took you in, gave you a place to live, food to eat. But you were too good to help our little teacher out, and you manage to convince my daughter to ride all over the state, closing what few schools people have managed to start."

I knew what to say to her, all the right arguments—they would bounce around in my head, and for days afterward I would find myself speaking them out loud, to the consternation of those around me. But in her presence, I opened my mouth and nothing came out. She whirled and left, having said what she had come to say. Only Liko was there to witness my humiliation.

"Someday she will be sorry," he said to me.

"No," I told him, no longer able to hold back the tears. "She doesn't know how to be sorry."

Opening the school has not been without problems. The Rourkes, all of them, showed up for two Sundays in a row to turn the storehouse back into a schoolhouse. We had a rollicking good time, as before, but when it was all finished two of the wives started to talk about who should be allowed to come to the school and who should not. "You won't want to let the Orientals come," Moira said, as if it were settled.

They were not pleased when I told them the only limitations would be age. A child must be at least seven to start school.

"How will you teach them if they can't speak English?" Moira wanted to know.

I told her what I knew: "They will learn—children do, just being around other children who speak English."

Patrick couldn't keep out of it. "So you want our children to help the Orientals learn English so they can grow up and take our jobs?" Pono let it go on like this for a while, I think until he saw I was being worn down. Then he stepped in and announced, "She's a right to teach who she pleases. Best be glad she pleases to teach the Rourke clan."

They stopped then, but they didn't look glad. After the others had left, Pono stood around a while with something inside of him that had to come out. Finally it did: "It's right to teach them all. I wished I'd of been taught."

I looked at him for a long while, and he looked at the floor. I had suspected, but until that moment I hadn't been sure. "I would like to teach you," I told him. "After your work and mine is finished for the day. Just us."

Thus began our evening sessions. In the schoolhouse, three or four times each week when his work allows. I watch his rough hands trace the lines, learning to read, and I marvel at his intelligence and his persistence. What a strange, good man this is.

Evan had a telephone put in the house so the men at the port can call up when the steamer gets in and order the cattle. That way the paniolos can drive them down that day, with only as many as the ship can take. The telephone rang this morning. That loud bell always sets my heart to thumping. I've not yet had the courage to speak into it, though True tells me you can hear just as if the person is right there in the room.

True put the earphone back in its cradle and said to me, "We have to send the big spring wagon and a team down to pick up a package for you, just come in."

If I hadn't to teach, I would have gone with it—just so I wouldn't have to wait all morning to find out who could be sending me a package big enough to take the spring wagon and a team to haul it back.

Governor Cleghorn and Uncle have sent me a school bell! Not a small, little, no-matter bell. A big bell, one that can ring out for miles around. A proper bell, a great bronze wonder of a bell. Pono is already drawing plans for a bell tower.

How to say how it makes me feel? My bell is going to be

ringing out over this wide green mountain slope, down into
the valleys and out onto the plain, calling all the children on
this part of the island to come to my school. All the children.
To my school.

True fidgets. Almost every steamer from Honolulu brings a
packet from Evan, long lists of things she must do, instructions for Bradley Chin, reminders and observations. First
off, she scans them, looking for the occasional bits about
what is happening with Harry and Jenny.

A month ago, Evan returned from San Francisco believing his family would be following him in three weeks' time.
The San Francisco doctors had done all they could do; they
advised Jenny to return to Honolulu, to continue the hot
massages and other treatments they suggested, and to hope
for the best. *"Hope for the best,"* Evan had written, "is the
doctor's version. A minister would say, 'Now it's in God's
hands.' It means the same. Hopeless." But Jenny wasn't
willing to leave it in God's hands. She has taken Harry to
Boston, where he will see more doctors. At the end of five
pages, Evan wrote: "I have no idea when they might be back.
Jenny has hired a tutor for Harry, and has taken a house on
Commonwealth Avenue. It sounds as if she is settling in.
Boston is a lovely city and I am welcome to visit whenever
I wish, she writes."

True stood, arched her back and grimaced. Whenever the
Colonel is on the island he treats Bradley as he treated his
last ranch manager, as someone to take orders and dispense
cash. When Bradley tries to explain why he can't release any
funds beyond the family allowance, the Colonel pretends not
to understand and simply repeats his demands over and
over. There is nothing to do then except give him his share
of the profits that were to be used for improvements. All
Evan's entreaties, all the time it took for him to get the
Colonel to agree to turn some of his profits back into the
ranch, were for nothing.

True sees Evan's mistake: All along he has assumed the
Colonel would not go against his own best interests. Evan is
convinced that once he understands how much more he can
be earning from the ranch he will listen to reason, will allow
them to rebuild without constantly throwing obstacles in the

way. But she knows reason isn't going to work. The Colonel is going to continue to change his mind unless Evan is right here, on the ranch, battling him every inch of the way. Poor Bradley—he is no match for the Colonel. She ran down the steps and out to the horse barn.

"Hello there, Rusty," she murmured to the stallion she had decided to keep as her own.

The horse nuzzled her and whinnied softly. She stroked its face gently. "The worse thing," she whispered, as if the horse could understand, "is that I almost hope they will stay in Boston, because if they don't he'll never come to Mau'loa."

And so it went, all that summer and fall and into the winter. Letters from Evan, plans, hopes, disappointments. Bradley Chin and Pono work longer hours than ever, and the hands stay right with them. Some fences were put up, some paddocks completed, the fattening pastures have been increased so that the steers are going to market in better condition.

Evan's first idea was to pipe in water all the way down from Mokuna on the wet side of the island, to the fattening lots. That way the dressed weight of the steers can be increased considerably, and the profit on each will go up enough to pay for the pipe in a few months' time. It makes sense to everyone but the Colonel. He says it won't work, that when the last manager wanted to do it, he had hydraulic engineers study it and they say it can't be done. That's all.

It doesn't do any good to remind him that if this drought goes on much longer, we could lose most of the herd. The Colonel is willing to take the gamble. True is tearing her hair, furious that he is risking Emma's half of the ranch as well as his own.

"I wish the Colonel would fall in a deep hole and disappear into China!" she cried out one night at supper. For an instant Liko and Pono and I stared at her, then we all broke out in laughter.

Sometimes I ask Pono to eat with us, so we can have our lesson right after supper. Sometimes I think: If only we had one week together, with nothing else to do, I would have him reading in no time. Writing is going to be more difficult. I watch his big, work-rough fingers trying to trace the loops and circles in the penmanship book, and I sometimes feel a strange catch in my throat. It is an amazement, watching this

man who can rope and tie a long-horned steer with wondrous ease, who can draw plans for a belltower and put up
a barn, struggling to learn his letters.

At first it didn't seem like much. Rachel came walking in
yesterday, the neck of her dress wet with sweat and with a
thirst that came of walking all the way from Kolonahe.

She sat right down by the well and started to drink out of
the dipper. By the third dipper, True stopped her.

"I came and I don't intend to go back," she announced,
her big face working not to cry. "I just left. I told Mama I
was leaving, and she said I mustn't take a buggy nor even a
horse. So I said 'I'll walk, then,' and that is just what I've
done. All the way. And I won't go back," she repeated
miserably, sounding more like a twelve-year-old than a
young woman of twenty-two.

I was surprised to hear True say, "You don't have to.
Come on up and have a cup of coffee and tell me what's the
problem."

When I came back into the kitchen after school was out,
the two of them were still talking. The tiny, tight vertical
frown lines between True's eyes told me that something was
wrong.

True looked up at me. "The Colonel is negotiating, in
secret, to buy Miss Ivy Renford's ranch. That will add almost a third as much land to the Wakefield Ranch—except
he doesn't intend for it to be shared."

Rachel yelped, "And it includes my island. But Pa says the
island is useless, and he's planning to sell it off right away.
He said he wasn't about to promote my 'crazy' idea. Mama
said I'm already a laughingstock, traipsing around the island
closing schools here and there. She's still mad at me about
the ranch school."

I shuddered. If True takes Rachel in, it will be another
wedge between the two households. The way the Colonel
and Miss Laiana will see it, True will be encouraging Rachel
in her madness.

"Why don't you go out to the bathhouse, have a good wash,
take a nap and then see how the world looks?" True said to
her. "If you feel like going back then, I'll ride with you."

Rachel's face screwed up, tears slipped out of her eyes.
"She'll never say she's sorry," she said.

"Probably not," True told her. "Your mother isn't the kind of woman who does. But I think she probably is sorry, especially making you walk all that distance. You showed her you could do it, that took some spunk. I doubt she'll ever feel so sure about you again."

Rachel sniffled, but you could see she liked what True was saying. An hour or so later (saying she wanted to give her mama plenty of time to stew), she and True rode off together in the direction of Kolonahe. True would continue on to the port, hoping to find a ship to take an urgent letter to Evan, telling about the Colonel's plan to buy the Renford ranch for himself.

The next day being Saturday, I was dispatched to speak to Miss Ivy, since I had visited her before when she was heading up the school board and we had gotten on. She was out back near the chicken house, tending to her sweetpeas. "I pulled out the honeysuckle," she told me. "It just got to be such a nuisance, climbing all over everything. Grows like a weed, honeysuckle."

"But it smells so fresh and sweet—like early morning," I said, standing up for honeysuckle.

Miss Ivy's seventy-two years were showing; she was small and frail, bent over now, and her shoulders were hunched. Her skin, once bronze like her Hawaiian mother's, was now the color of parchment left in the sun. Her dress hung on her in loose folds, and her feet shuffled along.

We walked back to the house and settled on the lanai. She folded her hands in her lap and looked at me sharply. "When you're old, you're allowed to ask rude questions, did you know that?"

"Is that so?" I teased. "Then ask away!"

"You're here because you've heard the Colonel's come courting me," she said, coquettish now.

I laughed out loud. "That's so," I admitted.

"He coats everything with honey, the *Colonel*." She went on in a thin, rambling voice, "I suppose you know where he got that title *Colonel*—Kalakaua gave it to him. Made Colonels out of a whole passel of boys he went to school with. Sam Parker's another one. *Colonel* Sam and *Colonel* Toby. Only thing those boys ever coloneled was some shooting parties. My Henry used to say it's a wonder they didn't shoot themselves in the foot."

She looked at me to see if I was shocked. "Well, Mr. Toby Wakefield does have lovely manners," I said. "He's one of these nice people who tell you what they think you want to hear—even if it isn't true—because they can't bear to hurt your feelings."

"Pssshaw," she said, leaning over to spit on the ground. "He wants to buy my ranch, and when I asked him how he planned to come up with the money to pay me, he said it was all taken care of and he didn't want me to addle my head worrying about a thing. That man!" Suddenly she was angry. "Does he think because I'm old I'm too addled to tend to business? Who does he think been's running this place since Henry died?"

I took a deep breath. "I don't know what the Colonel thinks, or what his plans are. But I would like to ask a favor, Miss Ivy. I'd like to ask that you hold off selling until we've had a chance to talk to little Emma's guardian in Honolulu. We think he may want to make an offer as well."

Ivy Renford looked at me hard before she answered. "Since I've been talking plain to you, Miss Martha, I'll tell you that I don't take much with that young Mrs. True Wakefield. I've seen her out riding, and she rides like a man. A woman out here in the ranchlands, well, she has to remember she's a woman and act like one. Otherwise we'll all be heathens. Her own mother, I hear tell . . ." She drifted off and said nothing for a long while, then she started humming under her breath. I began to think she had forgotten my question, and I was trying to think how to phrase it again when she said, "I'll wait for a spell."

Evan met with the Colonel in Honolulu. By the time he tracked him down at the State House, he knew that the Colonel had been turned down by three banks.

"Evan, what a nice surprise," the Colonel had said. "I was just this morning telling Laiana that I had to be in touch with you."

"About the Renford ranch?" Evan had asked, mad enough to be direct.

"Well now, let's see . . . what . . . I'm not certain that . . . what is it . . ." Toby Wakefield bumbled, his smile thin.

Evan came in strong: "I assume you were going to talk to me about this. It makes sense to add the Renford Ranch to

the Wakefield . . . we need the added pasturelands, and it
would be economical to run them as one."

"No," the Colonel said, then, "well, yes, I mean I can see,
but I thought, well, it's been separate for so long. Old Henry
Renford, it seemed like . . ."

Evan stopped him again. "I've already secured the loan to
buy it, for you and Emma."

The Colonel's mouth had dropped open for an instant,
then a practised smile spread across his handsome face. "I'd
forgotten just how well you are regarded in the banking
community, Evan. Of course I meant to include Emma. You
just go right along and take care of it, if you will. I hope
you're being paid handsomely, for all your help to my granddaughter."

"Well enough, Colonel. I'm planning to move to Mau'loa
in a week or two. If I'm going to do a proper job managing
the ranch for Emma and you, I'd best be on hand."

Once again, the Colonel was startled. "But, how will your
family—Jenny and young Harry, how is he doing?"

"They will be in Boston for the next three years, maybe
more. Harry is under the care of three specialists at Children's Hospital. They have a program which is said to be
getting some good results. Harry is willing to do all the hard
work they ask—plenty of exercises every day. And Jenny is
willing to stay."

"I see," said the Colonel, though in fact he did not see. He
had noticed the older Lafferty girl fluttering around Evan at
a luau hosted by the Corps of Engineers' new commander.
Maybe he wanted to remove himself from temptation, the
Colonel surmised at the family dinner table. Rachel reported
this to us, as well as everything else the Colonel said about
us in her presence.

When Evan closed the purchase of the Renford Ranch,
True talked him into suggesting, in such a way that the
Colonel could not object, that the barren island which the
natives called Opihi be deeded to Rachel Wakefield for the
purpose of establishing a reserve for native Hawaiians.

The little beach house is being moved up the port road for
Evan. That puts him pretty much halfway between the
Home Place and Kolonahe. "Halfway between heaven and
hell," he said to True. Rachel says her folks can't figure why

he'd want to live all alone out in the middle of nowhere when they offered him one of the new guest cottages they're building, with running water and a bathroom. They think now that Jenny's leaving, and taking the boy, has made Evan seek solitude.

True is happy to have them think so.

30

From the bell tower of my schoolhouse I can see all the way to that place where the deep blue of the sea meets the lighter blue of the sky. From this vantage, all the soft rhythms of life blend together: The lowing of the herds, the blowing of the trade winds, the air soft and warm against your skin—the great, glowing greenness of it all. There can be, I believe in my heart, no more beautiful place on this earth.

The lulling sameness of our days can mesmerize; yet as soon as that happens, something startles, jolts you out of your complacency. Riding in the mountains you will come upon an ancient burial cave, peer in to glimpse the brutal white of bones against the primitive red of the earth. Or out in the open, riding through belly-high grass, the air will suddenly be poisoned by the decaying carcass of a cow, ripped apart by wild dogs. At times nature itself turns wild and menacing, and threatens to rip apart all that lives so lightly on the surfaces of this earth.

At mid-morning on Thursday last, a hard, hot kona wind struck up from the south and our air, usually cool and sweet, became sticky hot. The children poured out for recess, exploding with the usual energy of healthy young animals kept at bay all morning—but on this day they were peculiarly irritable, poking and arguing and whining. I supposed it was the hot, rustling wind that was causing all of us to be tetchy.

At that moment True came galloping up on her horse. "A kona storm brewing," she called out to me. "Keep the children close by, and get Rose and Emma with you in the schoolhouse. The Hawaiians say it will be bad. I'll send Liko up as soon as we take care of the horses."

I shuddered; I knew kona storms blowing out of the south

could be fierce. "What about the crew that went up the mountain to round up wild cattle?" I called out to her.

She wheeled her horse, anxious to be off. "Pono's with them, so we don't need to worry," she shouted back, knowing full well it was Pono I was thinking about.

The sky, always so wide that you could see rainbows in the mountains and track the showers that spread across hills miles away, now closed in, grey and so thick you could scarcely see across the yard. A wind had struck up, not the gentle trades we are used to but erratic blasts that seemed to spin around and confuse you. I called the children and they came quietly, worry in their faces. Rose rushed in, carrying Emma, who was unhappy because there hadn't been time to put on her shoes.

It was so hot that I did not want to shut the windows, much less draw the shutters across them, until it was absolutely necessary. (I had thought the shutters to be an architectural anomaly, valuable in New England perhaps, but not in our gentle climate. Soon I would learn better.)

Liko came crashing through the door only minutes before the storm hit, not with a few warning drops but with great sheets of water raining down on us as if the heavens had burst.

Somehow, between Liko and the biggest boys and me, we got the shutters fastened and the windows down. Then we crowded together in the center of the big room, unable to speak over the awful clatter of rain on the roof and the banshee screams of the winds. The creaking of the jacaranda trees was punctuated now and then by the sharp crack of a branch breaking; ever so often there would be a hard thump and shudder as something was flung against the schoolhouse. I prayed the giant old Monterey pine in the play yard would hold; if it came crashing in on us . . . As I was thinking this the wind ripped off one of the shutters and sent it sailing. The window shattered, spraying glass into the room and setting off Emma and several of the younger children. No one was near the window, but I gathered them even closer into the circle and away from what I thought might be the trajectory of the pine, if it fell; then I tried to start a song. Liko's voice boomed out, the only one that could be heard at all over the dreadful noise of the storm, singing one of Emma's favorite songs. He was holding her tight, and I could see her little mouth forming the words of the song even as her eyes were wide with fear. Good, I thought. Emma feels safe with Liko. My mind skittered over worries of True and Pono, but I shut them out. Right now all I could worry about were my charges, gathered in a circle as far away from the windows as I could get them.

As the full fury of the storm raged, a tall Hawaiian boy who seemed determined to resist learning English, yet came every day nonetheless, startled me when he started singing "In the Sweet Bye and Bye," a rollicking Christian hymn. Several of the others knew the song as well, even the harmony, and as the refrain was sung the third and fourth time, the Orientals chimed in. They sang: "In the sweet bye and bye (bye and bye) we will meet (we will meet) on that beautiful shore. In the sweet bye and bye, we will meet on that beautiful shore."

I felt like laughing and crying at the same time, wondering if we would have any beautiful shores left when this deluge was over—wondering if the ocean would rise and lift our little school and send it sailing away, across the sea.

When the rain did stop, we could not get out. Both the front and back doors were blocked and immovable. When Liko tried to hand Emma to Rose so he could climb out the window, the child screamed and clung to him so that I sent Jimmy Rourke instead. Soon we heard him laboring, shoving and pushing and grunting, until he was able to open the door enough for us to squeeze through. The trunk of an old tree had been blown clear across the yard, to jam the door.

All of us stood, silent, as we saw the havoc the kona storm had wreaked. My bell tower was askew, the bell leaning at an awkward angle. Tree limbs were everywhere, leaves and dirt and rocks seemed to have been sprayed at random. The earth had been parched, it had been as hard and desiccated as a dried-out old sea sponge. Now you could not step anywhere without sinking in to your shoe tops.

One of Liko's black-and-white banty hens lay drowned in a puddle. A young willow tree had been stripped of its leaves. The air, thick and warm and filled with a sickly promise, began to stir again. Our respite was finished; the sharp crack of a huge limb crashing down from a kukui tree sent us scurrying back into the schoolroom.

It rained without stop for three more hours, then it rained

in spasms for another hour, and after what seemed a terribly long time, splats of blue sky began to show. Before it had stopped altogether, Evan sent one of the hands to see that we were safe, and to tell us that bridges and roads were washed out, water was rushing down the gullies and fields everywhere.

I was to keep the children for the night. Some of them began to whimper. I knew from the worry on their faces that they were thinking of their ohana and how they had survived the storm.

True turned up a few hours later, as we were making pallets for the children; the deerskin chaps she wore over her riding skirt were soaked through and she was exhausted. She spoke to the children: "We've sent men to all your homes to tell them you will be staying here tonight. You don't need to worry about your people—they are all right—we've moved a few into the church, and some of your houses are flooded but it's nothing that can't be fixed."

I could see the worry drain out of their young faces. "They'll be able to sleep now," I told True.

Suddenly I could see the fatigue overtake her. I took her by the hand and led her into the cloak room, where she sank onto the floor, her back propped against the wall. With a haunting look in her eyes she told me, "Sometimes I think the gods need to show us how small we are."

I tried to joke: "Maybe we prayed too hard for an end to the drought. Or maybe the gods wanted to please us too much."

She pressed her face into one of the coats hanging from the peg above her and murmured, "Or maybe the gods don't care."

June 21, 1902

We may have prayed too hard in February, but we didn't pray long enough. The kona storm was the last good rainfall we've had. The ground is bone dry again, and the herds are hurting. The cattle are heading to the gullies and streams and holes where they've always found water, only to find them parched.

Evan is going crazy. He came stomping into the kitchen the other morning just as we were getting up and you could see he was just fit to be tied. "If we don't get that pipe laid and bring some water in up from Mokuna, we are going to lose a thousand head, for certain."

We watched him prowling back and forth across the big kitchen. Evan does this when things get difficult—he paces and he thinks and then he says what he wants to do. It is always what True wants to do as well, but for some reason he says it in such a way that it seems he has to convince her.

"The Colonel says it won't work and that's all there is to it."

True countered, "But you know it will work . . . you have all the hydraulic information. You've studied it until you've worn out the books."

Evan came back with, "It means flat-out contradicting him, moving against his definite instructions. I've not done that before."

"The Wakefields are in Honolulu for at least two more weeks," True persisted. "You are responsible for the herd while he is away. If we can get the pipeline in before he gets back and prove that it works, not to mention save the main part of the herd, he'll thank you."

Evan looked at her for a few moments, then turned and left without saying another word.

With wicked triumph in her eyes, True whooped, "Finally!" and whipped upstairs to pull on the costume she wore most days now: riding breeches and the deerskin chaps she'd had the tanner make up for her, sharp-toed boots with silver spurs like the paniolos wear and a red-and-white-checkered shirt. The only bit of vanity that I can see is in her hats, of which she has several—ranging from a broad-brimmed leather to a small open-weave Panama. Some have fancy feather bands, but most brims are circled with a fluttery band of sweet-smelling flowers and fragrant leaves and berries. All of the paniolos, especially the Hawaiians, decorate their hats with these pretties plucked from the bushes and trees they pass as they roam the far reaches of the ranch.

July 4, 1902

What a celebration! At two-thirty this afternoon we all crowded around when the first water came coursing through the new pipeline, sputtering and gurgling in spasms at first and then steadily and then in a rush: Now it gushes at a rate of 500 gallons an hour. And the Colonel said it couldn't be done. Such screaming and whooping and celebrating, such wild merriment. It started when his rowdy brothers picked Pono up and tossed him in the muddy water hole. Then one by one, they all got thrown in or pulled in, even Liko and Bradley Chin, sputtering "oh no, oh no, oh no." The Rourkes responded with "oh yes, oh yes, oh yes."

Evan was the only man left standing at the edge of the hole, shaking his head at the shenanigans and keeping an eye on the pipe, which spewed water. Even the Rourkes daren't come for Evan.

True just walked up behind him and with both hands shoved him in. At first nobody knew what to do, but when Evan pulled himself up out of the mud, flapping his hat, and turned and looked at True with a grin on his face they all whooped like you've never heard. While all of them were busy flopping around in the mud, I filled myself a bucket of the clear wet water coming out of that wonderful pipe, walked over to True and I threw it on her. The cold of it made her scream, while the men roared.

She got me back by scooping up a handful of mud and smearing it on my face. In the end, we all looked like mud-spattered drowned rats. Evan invited the boys over to his place for a wash and a drink. True and I, giddy as girls, rode for home and some dry clothes.

From the looks of the boys the next day, they had more than one drink at Evan's. I'm glad he loosened up some; I think he doesn't know how hard he drives them. True and Pono and Bradley are the only ones willing to keep up with Evan; those four will drop in their tracks one day. But they are making gains. Even with the drought, the cattle are going to market at a higher dressed weight, and that is quick profits.

August 1902

Without the pump, the ranch would have been strewn with dead cattle about now. As it is, the plains are shriveled and parched—places that were always green are brown now, and even the early morning air carries scarcely a trace of dew. The paniolos have scattered out all over the ranch, searching in the dry gullies and water holes and scrub for cattle too weak to walk. All the hands are exhausted, and as if that isn't bad enough, the tall grass that waves in beautiful green ripples all the way across the plain is now sear and brown, and grass fires have been breaking out. So far the men have contained them, but it is another concern for the paniolos.

In the midst of all this, the Colonel has invited twenty people to Kolonahe for what he chooses to call a "gala." Yesterday he rode over to assure Evan they wouldn't need any extra horses, and Evan said that was a good thing because the ranch didn't have an extra horse to spare, or an extra anything. The Colonel left in a huff, but he was back soon enough—in the middle of the night. Sparks from the barbeque pit lit the dry pasture to the south of the house, setting it on fire—with the wind blowing toward the house. It took all the men and some of the women all night to fight it—not to mention all the ranch hands. Most of the guests are leaving on today's boat. True says that as far as she's concerned, it's a proper end to such a 'gala.'

In the meantime, poor Rachel wilts. She has her island, a longboat to take her there and two hearty Hawaiian families who are willing to try life as their ancestors lived it. Unfortunately, Rachel's island has only one spring and it has dried up in this drought. Rachel languishes, unhappy in a household she believes to be "foolish." It does not help, I think, that her sister has a young man and will soon be married, or that her mother has taken several pretty young cousins into the house "to give the place some life."

"Mother would just as leave toss one of her own out, if she thought someone else's child was more spirited," Rachel told me in a pout one day.

"You don't believe that," I had said and laughed at her, but she said with perfect seriousness that she does indeed believe it.

Evan is off to the Mainland to see his family in Boston and, in California, to buy some breeding stock. As True predicted in the matter of the pipeline, the Colonel proclaimed Evan the hero of the day for "acting expeditiously in an emergency" to save the ranch from disaster. But Evan is not enough of a hero to convince the Colonel to put all of the new profits back into the ranch. Indeed, the

Colonel is expansive these days because he has *more* money to spend.

All of Emma's share goes back into the ranch; it is the only way to make any gains. At three, Emma doesn't mind in the least how much money she has. All we have to do right now to keep our little girl happy is to give her a nice plump peach. With the drought, we haven't much of a crop this year. Rose and I are putting up some peach conserve, not to waste the little hard fruits that managed to survive. Emma loves to wrap herself in an apron and pretend to cook—she sings and entertains us. Her hair is very fine and brown, and is curling now a bit, and she has a charming little coquettish smile, which she reserves for only a very few: Liko, of course, as well she should, because he denies her nothing. Her mother, most of the time. Me, some of the time. Evan, always. And he simply lights up in her presence.

I should also report, though I must say it puzzles me, that Emma seems especially fond of her grandmother and grandfather, who require that she be brought to visit them every Sunday when they are on the island. True tells me that whenever there is a crowd of guests, as is often the case, the Colonel likes to carry Emma around and introduce her as his "ranch partner."

"Does Emma fidget and fuss?" I ask and am surprised at the answer. She does not. She simply sits in her grandfather's arms and looks down on the guests, regally.

We have a new preacher on the island, a Congregationalist named Ned Porthauser—fresh from divinity school in Pennsylvania. He is a blond young man with a touching, burning belief and a surprising gift for preaching. Suddenly, it is a pleasure to go to church on Sundays. Even the Colonel and his entourage show up, and when they do you can just see young Mr. Porthauser puff up and do himself proud. He also has a fine, strong singing voice—and the service is larded with hymns. Even some of the Rourkes, who are Roman Catholic, have shown up out of curiosity—or, like the rest of us, to pray for rain.

Last Sunday Pono was waiting outside the church after the service. I scarcely knew him—all clean shaved and dressed up in a Sunday best I had never seen, since he usually is out working with Evan on the Lord's Day.

I walked right up to him and said, "How fine you look."

"I've the buggy," he said. "Can I drive you?"

"Yes," I answered in a conspiratorial voice. True would be going to the Colonel's big house with Emma, which meant I would have had to ride home with one of the neighbors.

Pono did not take the direct road home, but turned off onto a narrow lane that cut through a meadow toward the mountains. "I come by this place, I thought I'd show it to you," was all the explanation I got.

That was fine with me. The summer had been long and hot and dry, and I was glad to get up into the hills for a change, where there was still a bit of cool and green.

We drove for upwards of an hour. I talked some, he listened as always. It was easy being with Pono; most folks didn't think so, but I did. We've become friends, I thought. Pono and me. Pono and True. Evan and Pono. No, the men weren't friends exactly—not in the same way True and I were friends with Pono. But they had respect for each other. Was that the essential ingredient in friendship, respect? I thought about asking Pono, but I knew there would just be a long silence while he thought about it, and then he would say something like, "Maybe so." Maybe so. I didn't have much better of an answer myself.

As we climbed up the soft slope, the air became cooler and a slight breeze caught so I could feel it lifting my hair. That was nice. All of a sudden we rounded a bend and came upon a wide, flat rock that jutted out over the plain. Next to the rock was a stand of ohia trees. Pono looped the reins over a tree branch and helped me down.

Climbing up on the rock, I shielded my eyes and said, "Just look at that." The island rolled away beneath us, lifted and dipped and rolled until it fell into the sea. Far, far to the north you could even see the path of an old lava flow, vivid black against the blue and green.

"I wanted you to see it from up here," Pono said.

"It is wondrous," I answered, so he would know I was indeed pleased. I turned to smile at him, and that is when I saw the question in his eyes.

"What is it?" I wanted to know.

"Martha Moon . . ." he began.

I can't say why I interrupted him. I almost never did, but

suddenly I felt flustered so I said, "Such a silly thing to be called, Martha Moon. Not even a real name."

Pono's face flushed; I couldn't imagine why, suddenly, he was acting so oddly; I thought we had become friendly enough to be easy together, but today he seemed to be roiled and so awkward with me.

In a strangled voice he managed to say, "Would you like Rourke better?"

I couldn't be certain I'd heard him right, and I couldn't seem to keep silly words from flying out of me, as if they had a mind of their own. "It's a far sight better than Moon," I rattled on. Then I stopped, confused, and pulled up short. My neck flushed hot. "What do you mean?" I asked in a small voice.

He turned away, only the strange, awkward tilt of his shoulders to warn me. When he spoke it was loud enough: "I mean, will you marry with me?"

His question sent me reeling. "What?" I started, then stopped to search for the answer: "I . . . you . . . what . . ." The words tripped over each other, I couldn't get them to go together, my head stopped working, I was sputtering.

He turned to look at me. "It's all right," he said, his voice flat and his face turned away from me. "No matter."

He thought I was turning him down. Panic rose in my throat. I did not think the words would come; I was making harsh, croaking sounds. Then the words flew out like a shout that echoed against the rocks above us: "Pono! Listen to me!"

He stared at me in utter confusion.

A small, weak voice was all I could manage: "Yes, I will marry with you, yes. Yes."

He frowned, as if he didn't believe what he was hearing.

I laughed, feeling the surprise subside and the pleasure take over, rising inside of me. "Pono! I never thought anyone would want to marry me. I thought I was going to have to be a school ma'am all my life. I thought . . ."

I broke into tears then, laughing and crying at the same time. "I am just so happy . . ." I stopped then and looked at him, sober again. "You do mean it? You want me to be your wife? Is that what you said?"

Now it was Pono's turn to laugh. His face brightened, he smiled at me as he reached for my hand.

"I'll say it again," he said, laying his other hand gently against my cheek, "I want you to be my wife. I want to call you Martha Rourke. And I want that a powerful lot, more than I've ever wanted anything in this world."

I put my arms out to him, and he held me—awkwardly at first, carefully. "Well then, Mr. Pono Rourke," I told him, pressing my face against his, feeling where the razor had scraped his skin, "we're each going to get exactly what we want, and won't that be fine?"

We laughed then, holding each other hard, swaying on top of that big rock out there in the middle of the world, all alone but never lonely again. I clung to him, and a feeling flooded into me like none I've ever had, hot and strong, body to body and mind to mind, and the words that went pounding through my head were "home, home, home at last."

31

October 1903

"Can you keep a secret?" True asked, her mouth just above the water in Evan's Japanese tub.

"Can I keep a secret?" he teased, reaching to turn her so he could rub her back in the hot water.

"Oh . . . oh . . . oh . . . that is good," she said in little gasps, leaning back so that she was resting in his arms.

"The secret," he reminded her.

She paused for a long moment to heighten the suspense, then she blurted: "Pono has asked Martha to marry him."

He turned her around, his eyes widening as if to say, "What is this?"

"Yes!" she laughed, pleased to have caught him by surprise.

"Is she glad?" Evan wanted to know.

"Yes again. She is absolutely glowing with happiness . . . I know you could never call Martha pretty, but she is pretty, Evan. She is just blooming." True beamed.

He rubbed her shoulder, pressing into the muscles with his thumbs.

"How old is Martha?" he asked.

"Thirty. She says she was so settled into spinsterhood that she was speechless when he asked her. Pono is two years older."

"When you think about it," Evan said, "they are perfectly suited, a good match."

"Like us," True came back, playfully reaching behind him to pull on his ear. "Except we've our own kind of secret."

"We aren't a secret, woman. Every hand on the ranch knows that when Rusty is tied up out front, nobody comes

339

near this place. Haven't you ever wondered why we are never disturbed?" He laughed.

She moved to the opposite side of the big tub, Evan's one concession to comfort. His house boy fills it each day and lights the fire so the water is hot by evening.

"Maybe the question is, what do the men think?" True asked.

Evan shrugged. "They think that you are a widow-lady with 'needs' and that my wife went off to Boston, leaving me with 'needs,' and that makes it all right."

True looked incredulous. "How do you know they think that?"

"One of the Rourkes told me, the day you so nonchalantly pushed me into the mud and we all got drunk."

True shook her head. "Patrick, probably. Martha says he simply can't keep his mouth shut. Martha and Pono want to keep their betrothal secret because Pono doesn't want to tell his family until everything is arranged, including where they will live. He says Martha worries about having no blood family, while he worries about having too many. Pono is Catholic, of course, and Martha doesn't take to that religion, not after being left with the Sisters at Holy Names. She is worried about the school even more—she wants Amalie to come to teach with her, but first Martha wants to go to Oahu to talk to her and to Uncle and Aunt, as well. I think mostly she wants to go see the old auntie who raised her. She loves the old woman, and she wants her to know how happy she is about marrying Pono. She thinks old Auntie has been holding onto life, waiting for something—and Martha wants to release her, let her go."

Evan climbed out of the tub and turned to help True. She slid down against him and he held her close. "The old ones do that sometimes," he said, kissing her neck. "It is a kind of loving that is so . . ." He groped for a word.

"Tender?" she offered.

"More than that. I was thinking of *infinite* . . ." He thought about it for a while, then he said, "I'm happy for Martha, and for Pono."

They splashed clear water on each other, dried and dressed in silence. Finally Evan said: "If this drought doesn't end soon, we're going to have to lay another pipe—and that is almost certainly going to cause a battle royal with the

Colonel. He's determined to take that position the government has offered him in Washington, even if he has to pay for the whole thing himself. And Laiana is set on going so he's not about to let me have one penny of his share of the profits—the Colonel operates on the 'bird in the hand' theory."

Rachel Wakefield shared Evan's exasperation with her father. Her long months of planning and pleading were beginning to attract native Hawaiians who wanted to return to the old ways in a place free of haoles. The refuge on Opihi Island was about to become a reality when the drought caused yet another delay. Rachel's distress was obvious. The Colonel said to his daughter, "This only proves that some good comes from all travail."

When True, who likes to rile her, asked if she didn't want to ride out the drought in Washington with her family, Rachel exploded: "My parents are mad, and they've about as much sense as warthogs. They have sold off two pieces of Mama's property on Molokai—one was to have been mine, but when I wanted to sell it to buy supplies for my island, she wouldn't hear of it. Oh no, that was my nest egg, Mama said. They've devoured my nest egg so they can prance around and entertain President Theodore Roosevelt—that foolish man."

"Miss Emma Victoria," the Colonel said, bowing low to his granddaughter, "how good of you to come calling. Now, I have a surprise for you—how would you like to take a ride on a nice little pony?"

True said nothing; she had been trying to get Emma onto a pony for weeks, without success.

"Yes, Papa Toby," the child said and took his hand and trotted off with him, leaving True standing in her tracks, amazed and annoyed. "She just needed something more her size," the Colonel told True as they watched Emma sitting happily on the pony's back while a stable hand led the animal around the track.

True grinned. "Well, at least I know now she isn't afraid—I was beginning to worry about her. It would never do for a Wakefield to be afraid of horses."

Pleased with that, the Colonel touched her on the shoulder and said, "Why don't you let Emma come with us to Honolulu for the short time we'll have there before we leave for Washington? It is going to be such a long time before we will see our little granddaughter again and . . ."

True's frown told him she did not like the idea at all, so he quickly added, "You just think about it. No need to make up your mind now."

When Miss Laiana brought the subject up at lunch that same day, True realized they had discussed taking Emma with them to Honolulu. "Do let her come," Laiana Wakefield said. "If you want, send the girl Martha to watch over her."

Emma, listening intently, piped up, "Please, Mama, let me go with Papa Toby and Grandmama."

True gave her a sharp look, which Emma knew full well. She started to cry.

True scolded: "Stop that right now or leave the table." Emma responded by raising the pitch.

When True put down her napkin and stood—a clear indication that she planned to remove the child—Miss Laiana said in a voice meant to cut through the din: "Emma, if you want to go with us to Honolulu, you must stop crying right now. Otherwise you must leave the table and will not be allowed to go." The crying stopped.

Telling about this later, True was furious. "How could she do that—it was the same as promising Emma that she can go. Now what am I to do?"

"Let her go," I told her. "They have said I can come along, so I will. I need to go to Oahu anyway to see Auntie Momi and Amalie and everyone. Pono has been after me to get it settled. He wants everyone to know, so he can begin work on our house."

True wasn't convinced. "I'll need to talk to Evan," she said, as she did about any decision that involved Emma. When Evan said he didn't see any harm in it, especially with me there, it was settled. Four-year-old Emma was ecstatic; she chattered and wore us out with questions about the big city. She was too young to notice how unhappy Liko became when he found out she would be leaving.

I tried to console him by explaining that it was only for a few weeks, and that Uncle Jameson and Aunt Winona wanted to see Emma as well. But Liko would not be consoled. He thought it a terrible mistake, to allow her to leave the island. The third time he complained to True, her anger spilled out and she snapped, "You tell her she can't go— you've always been so good about saying no to Emma. Then you go face the Colonel and Miss Laiana and tell them she can't go. And after that, go tell Evan. You know what he will say to you? 'What's the harm, if she wants to go?' Then maybe the next time Martha or me says no to our little miss and she comes to you and smiles her darling little smile, you might think again before you give in to her. Because that is the lesson, Liko. Giving in to a willful little girl."

"She's like her mama," Liko shot back.

True looked at him, as if he had said something worth pondering. "I don't think so," she told him, thoughtfully.

I didn't think so, either. Emma is winning; pretty and soft, she is a natural little mimic and laughs easily, especially in a group. If more than three people are gathered, she can be persuaded to entertain, usually with a song. Her favorites are the ones Liko has taught her, and which she sings with charming pantomime. Evan delights in her, and the ranch hands adore her; "Little Miss" is everybody's favorite. Few are witness to her quicksilver change of moods; she saves her tantrums for the servants, her mother and me, and Liko when he doesn't do as she wishes. I have to wonder what will happen when she starts school and has to mind the rules like the other children. There are no favorites in my classroom, and there will be none in Amalie's. The thought made me smile. If ever anyone knows how to deal with a willfull little girl, it is Amalie.

The school is much on my mind. Pono worries that I will be unhappy if I cannot teach. Married women do not teach, of course. But they can serve on the island's board of education, and Miss Ivy Renford has asked me to take over her position as chairwoman. It would be a way to improve the other schools on the island. I have visited several of them, and I have to say they need everything: trained teachers, books, tablets—a suitable program. It is the program that interests me most. I want to devise one that teaches students more than reading and writing and figures. I have it in mind to teach them to think. Amalie and I have been writing back and forth about this.

* * *

The trip to Honolulu was awkward. The Colonel is pleasant
enough to me, but Miss Laiana must still be fuming over my
role in the closing of her school, because she speaks to me
only to give me some direction, as if I am Emma's nanny.
Etta and her new husband seem to fuss at each other a good
deal; she seemed annoyed with the pale young man for "ac-
quiesing to mal de mer."

As I was dressing Emma to take her out to Waikiki on the
morning of our third day in Honolulu, we were called to
Miss Laiana's receiving parlor. She was waiting for us with
a woman she introduced as Eveline Statler, "Emma's new
governess."

Miss Statler comes highly recommended. Speaks three
languages. An excellent water colorist and botanist. When
the Colonel and Miss Laiana learned of her availability only
yesterday, they decided to offer her a position. They have
employed her services for a year.

"Perhaps you should speak to Emma's mother first," I
suggested as calmly as I could. "I know she would expect to
be consulted in the matter of her daughter's care and education."

Laiana Wakefield did not answer. She did not seem to
think she was required to reply to me.

It was too much, and I could not have it. "I think perhaps
you should speak to Emma's guardian, Mr. Wright," I said
to Laiana Wakefield in front of the woman. "I'm on my way
there now with Emma. I will explain your suggestion to him,
and he can discuss it with you."

Laiana Wakefield stood, towering over me, with her chin
at its full regal tilt. "There is nothing to discuss. Miss Statler
has been employed. Emma is not to go with you."

"Forgive me," the governess said, looking at me rather
than the woman who had hired her. "I'm afraid I
don't . . ."

"Nonsense," Miss Laiana cut in. "This young woman has
nothing to say about the matter."

"We shall see," I said, turning on my heel and leaving.
Happily, Uncle had sent one of the boys for us in the buggy
and he had driven around back. I whisked Emma out a side
door and we were on our way before anyone could stop us.

* * *

Uncle calmed me. "If the Colonel plans to pay Miss Statler's wages, we should be willing to take a look at her credentials and interview her, to decide if she might after all be a valuable addition to your household. It isn't like you to discount her before you've given her a chance, Martha. If he intends for her wages to be paid from Emma's share—which is what I would guess, given his past behavior—we can explain to the lady that at this moment, funds are not available for a governess."

The children gathered around Emma and she laughed and smiled and sang for them, but when they asked her to go with them to play on the beach she hung back around my skirts.

"I don't want to get my dress wet," she fussed.

"You're not a bit like your mother," Aunt Winona couldn't resist telling her. "She would have been out there romping around, the first one to fling herself in the surf." She started one of her monologues then. I smiled at Uncle to let him know I had missed even this, and he smiled back to thank me. Auntie had only just begun her ramblings when Emma grabbed my hand and said she wanted to go back to Papa Toby's.

I tried to quiet her, but she wouldn't be quieted. She raised her voice, causing Aunt Winona to stop altogether. "I want to go now," she said in the petulant tones of a four-year-old who is accustomed to getting what she wants.

"Stop that right now, Emma. If you don't want to play with the children, you can go over and sit on the chair and read a book. But we are not going to leave now."

Emma glared at me. She looked at Uncle, at Aunt and at Amalie, and when she saw that none was inclined to plead her case, she walked over to a flame tree in the yard, sat on a tiny stool and sulked.

"A little girl with a mind of her own," Amalie offered lightly.

"I suppose so," I sighed, disappointed that Emma should act up just when I planned to tell my news.

"Don't worry," Uncle reassured me. "Surely you haven't forgotten how obstinate four-year-olds can be?"

"When can we go?" Emma interrupted.

"I have a secret to tell Aunt and Uncle and Amalie," I said to her, catching her attention.

"A secret?" she formed the words prettily with her mouth. "Tell me the secret, too."

"All right," I said, looking at her but speaking to the others. "I'm going to tell them about Pono Rourke."

"Pono?" Emma echoed.

"Yes, our luna. I'm going to tell them that Pono has asked me to marry him, and that I have accepted with great pleasure."

"Martha!" Auntie shrieked, and then, "Uncle, did you hear? Our Martha is going to be married."

Amalie came to sit next to me; putting her arms around me she said, "Just look at you; I wondered what had put that happy glow in your face."

Uncle only sat looking at me. I turned, feeling suddenly very shy. *What would he think?* Until that moment, I did not know how much I cared. Uncle cleared his throat. "Since I've heard only good things about this Rourke chap from True and from Evan, I suppose I am going to have to give you my blessing. I do plan to tell him that I admire his judgment. He must be a smart one, to have chosen so wisely."

Emma, confused by all the laughter and talk, came to lean against me. "Do you want to get married with Pono?" she asked.

"I do," I said and laughed, running my hands over her light brown hair; when everyone else laughed as well, putting her back in the center of things, she presented us with one of her bright smiles.

Amalie has agreed to come to Mau'loa within the month, to take over the school at the Home Place. She has trained not one replacement, but two, since Uncle is teaching fewer classes now. I've warned him we may need more good teachers bye and bye.

Returning to Honolulu, we stopped to see Governor Cleghorn at Ainahau, to tell him my news. "Auntie Momi was here, looking for you," he said to me. "Does she know that you are to be married?"

"Yes, I told her first," I answered, puzzled over why Auntie would come searching for me.

The Governor's eyes filled with tears as he said good bye to "our little Miss Emma Vicky." When finally we pulled up in front of the Wakefield house, I braced myself for a scene, certain that Miss Laiana would be angry with me.

Auntie Momi was sitting on the stone floor of the lanai, her head nodding as she chanted a mele.

Emma, frightened by the high wailing sounds, held tightly to my hand. Hearing us, Miss Laiana appeared in the doorway, her alii face composed out of respect to the old one.

A servant took Emma as I knelt before Auntie until her old eyes had fixed on me long enough to recognize me. She put out her hand, and I raised it to my cheek.

"Here is my child Martha Moon," she intoned as if speaking to the gods. "Now we go into this house where they wait."

Miss Laiana and the Colonel were sitting in the little parlor, waiting as Auntie Momi had said. I took long minutes to move her to a chair. As I helped her, we could hear the grinding of her old bones.

Miss Laiana, her face clouded, said: "I had an Auntie Momi once, but she left and we heard she had died." She stopped herself then and asked, "That mele, it is of my family, how do you know it?"

Auntie did not answer. Her voice was high and brittle with age. She had no breath to waste. "This last story I talk," she began, moving her knotted hands in a slow motion. "In year when Pele grew angry and burned her way to sea, I was in house of alii, high chief from Maui and his wife. I care for small boy, one who would be taken from us within year."

Laiana's eyes narrowed; the Colonel had a fixed smile on his lips, as if he didn't know what this was about, but he was watching his wife.

Old Auntie seemed to doze off. I put my arm around her and whispered, "You are tired. Let me take you home."

She pulled herself awake, opened her eyes wide and continued, rasping out the words: "There was beautiful young girl in house, older sister to boy child, and she found young man and they *ipo,* they loved together. But mother, wife of high chief, she say no. Boy fine, but not fine enough for alii wahine. The mother say they no see each other never again."

Auntie was silent. I looked at the Wakefields, curious at the sudden fascination in their faces.

Auntie's voice started again, startling us with its sudden strength:

"Mother made boy go off, and when he came back to see his *ipo,* he sent away. He sad, pretty girl sad.

"Alii girl's belly grows big and big. She stays in house, never goes out, boy never knows. Girl cries, so long. Please, she say to Mother, let me see him, let him know I am hapai. But Mother say no.

"Baby is born, *wahine iki.* Alii girl looks at baby and say, 'So small, so small.' Little mother goes to sleep, and when she wake her mother say that baby is no more, gone now and buried."

Laiana Wakefield's hands began to shake. The Colonel—a puzzled look on his face—took her hands in his, and looked sharply at Auntie Momi.

"Old Auntie, what is this story? Why are you telling us this?"

Auntie's voice filled the room: "Baby never die. I take baby Sister Catherine Joseph at Holy Names."

Sister Catherine Joseph. I felt a sudden flashing hot roar in my ears and my heart seemed to expand in my chest, pushing against my ribs; there was a surging inside of me, as if the tides were streaming in to explode against the hard rock of Auntie's revelation.

Her old eyes filled with alarm as she watched my face, but she had started now. "I stay with baby as she say," she went on, looking only at me. "I never say who is mother, who is father. If I say, my soul go straight to Christian hell. If I tell, my alii will pray to gods never to forgive."

Laiana Wakefield became very still.

Auntie could not be stopped. "Now I tell. Baby is Martha Moon."

A long, tight silence filled the room, the only sound the dry flutter of the fronds of the traveller's tree brushed by the breeze.

I wanted to speak. I tried but my voice broke. It was too much to hold in my head.

Tobias Wakefield blurted, "Are you saying that Martha is our daughter? Is that what you are telling us?"

Laiana Wakefield put her hand, lightly, on his arm. "Yes," she said in a hollow voice. "My hiapo, the first. Born two years before Mother would allow us to marry."

He looked from me to his wife and back again, his face registering disbelief, astonishment and then, gradually, an amused delight, as if someone had played an extraordinary trick on him.

I saw this, and I saw the look on Laiana Wakefield's face as well: calm, cold. There was no delight in her eyes.

The Colonel sat down next to me and took my hand in his. "Martha, my own dear, good girl," he said, pressing my hand hard. "If only we had known, but now, now there is so much we must . . ."

"But we didn't know," his wife broke in, her voice weary but firm. "And after all this time, it would have been better for all of us if Auntie Momi had kept her pledge to my mama."

Auntie studied her. "Better more for you, not for my Martha," she said. "Martha happy now, with good man to give her home. All she needs is who is her Makuahine, who is her Makuakane."

"Are you to marry?" the Colonel asked, a look of confusion spreading over his handsome face. "But we've only just found you, daughter . . ." The word *daughter* drifted out into the room and seemed to hang there, awkward and unwieldy.

"Tobias," his wife broke in, "we've had enough for now. Come."

He looked at me, hesitated. Then he said, "Tomorrow, Martha. We will talk tomorrow . . . there is so much to say," and he scurried off after his wife.

Pono and True and Liko met us at the Mau'loa dock. Emma flew into Liko's arms, happy to be free of Miss Statler and me. Emma's new governess and I agreed on much more than I would have imagined, and especially on the need to maintain a firm hand with the child.

On the ride up the mountain, a terrible fatigue seemed to settle into me. By the time we reached the Home Place, I was so tired that Pono had to lift me down and help me into the house.

Pono sat next to me on the settee, while True and Liko took their places across from us, all of them waiting for the news I insisted they must hear before I could rest.

"Tell us what Uncle and Aunt say about you and Pono," Liko blurted, eager for a full report. "Were they surprised? Tell us!"

True had been studying my face; I could see the worry

mirrored there. "What is it, Martha Moonie?" she asked, and the softness in her voice started my tears.

I sobbed, unable to find the right words. Pono took my arm and held it hard; I knew how badly he would feel, how at a loss he was to help me. Liko threw himself at me and held onto my hands, whimpering, "Don't cry, don't cry please."

"I know, I know," I managed to gasp, taking a sip of the water True had brought me. "There's something you have to know . . ." I tried to begin.

"Take your time," True told me, and Pono added, "No hurry—we've got time—you take it slow now."

A soft silence settled over us. I began: "Auntie seemed already to know about us, Pono and me. She said she had been waiting for me to come to tell her. She believes the gods are glad for us, that we will be good together."

They were looking at me, waiting.

"And then she told me where I came from, who my mama and papa are."

I told them.

True's hand flew over her mouth; Liko stared; Pono gripped my arm in disbelief, his eyes widened.

"The Wakefields!" True blurted. "You are a Wakefield?"

I closed my eyes and sank against Pono.

"Wait," True said. "How can . . . what happened?"

Before I could answer, Liko broke in: "You are Jared's sister? And Rachel, she is your sister too? And . . ."

"Shhh," True stopped him. "Let Martha talk."

I told them the story as best I could, my words seeming to echo out of my body, hollow and loose.

It was Pono who asked me to say, if I could, what it all meant to me.

I laid my head on his shoulder and as the weariness seemed to seep up inside of me, I tried to answer: "Nothing. It means nothing. They are not my ohana. The Colonel, he would like to think . . . but Miss Laiana is right, it is too late . . . here in this room, this is my ohana."

True broke in, "My girl, you need to sleep now. Come, we'll talk and talk tomorrow. You're home now, let's get you to bed."

As Pono left, I heard True tell him, "She'll be fine in the morning. Come early, before you go to the paddock. She will need to see you first thing."

* * *

But I was not fine in the morning. My arms and legs were too heavy to move; the old, awful bleakness had returned. I could not so much as cry out. The greyness reached for me, pulled me into it, would not let me go.

As if to mirror my anguish, the rains started. Not the gentle, bright rains that come shining with rainbows, but a heavy, steady downpour. The wind groaned and moaned and shrieked around the house and there was a hard and steady drill on the roof over my head. One rainstorm followed another; dry gulches filled with water which raced down the mountain, washing cattle all the way to the sea. Roads washed out, valleys flooded; after all the long, dry months the rains came with a vengeance.

Time lost its meaning; day and night drifted together. I could hear the voices: True . . . Pono . . . Liko . . . Evan. Talking, talking over me and at me. True prodding, pulling at me, insisting I do what I could not do.

Pono would cry out, "Leave her be," and True would shout, "No! We cannot leave her be. It's nothing you've done, Pono. You can't think that."

I wanted to sink back into it, to let the grey and the rain swallow me, I wanted not to have to breathe, but I could not . . . because of Pono and True and Liko, Emma and Evan, Amalie and Rachel. My sister Rachel, who sits long hours beside my bed. My ohana.

I lay for the whole of a morning, trying to gather the strength to shove one of my legs off the bed. True sees and shouts, and then she laughs and cries a little, too. "Here she comes," she shouts to anyone who can hear. "Here comes our Martha!"

Christmas Day 1903

Martha gave me this beautiful journal when she left today; it is as much like the one I gave her on my wedding day, five long years ago, as Pono could make it. The cover of koa wood is smooth and lovely to touch.

Martha made her first entry on the day after my marriage to Jared Wakefield at Ainahau. I begin my journal on the very day of Martha's marriage to Pono Rourke.

Not Martha Moon, not Martha Wakefield, but Martha

Rourke. How right that sounds. And what a wonderful, happy day this has been.

Early on this cool, clear Christmas morning we filled the parlor with bright red poinsettias and draped it with shining green maile leaves. Before a bank of orchids and heavenly scented tuberoses, Martha and Pono vowed to love and to cherish each other. Martha wore the simplest of gowns, a holoku of ivory satin, gently fitted at the waist in the Empire fashion with a train sewn with a thousand exquisitely minute iridescent seashells from Opihi. Aunt Winona stitched the dress and the old aunties on Rachel's island spent long hours sewing on the tiny shells. They made as well a glorious eight-strand wedding lei of the shells; if ever there has been a labor of love, this wedding gown was it. And flowers! All the people on the island who love darling Martha and dear Pono brought great armloads of flowers to the house. Never have I seen a more beautiful wedding couple—Martha's black eyes shining, Pono's face bright with love; never have I felt the great swell of emotion that took all of us in, pulled us together, made me know what it is to feel the gravity of family.

Evan felt it, I could see it on his face as he stood witness with me. Tears streamed down Liko's cheeks as he strummed his ukelele and sang the wedding song in a high falsetto. Even little Emma seemed to know how precious this day was; in her blue velvet dress with its white lace collar, she looked like a Christmas doll.

After the ceremony, everyone came to the ranch for a luau—all of the Rourkes, the paniolos, everyone who works on the ranch and all of our neighbors.

Only the Wakefields did not come; the Colonel sent a silver tea service ordered from England, and his regrets. They must stay in Honolulu for an important meeting. They were sorry, he said, adding that he was happy that her sister Rachel would be in attendance. Martha was relieved that they did not come.

I pray that life is kind to these two dear souls, Martha and Pono. I pray that never again will the darkness come to hover over kind, good Martha and pull her away from us, and that the old dread is gone forever. I pray that she can be happy now, she and Pono, in their little house down the road where they spend their wedding night together, this Christmas.

32

June 1906

Here I sit in bed, and here I must stay until this babe I carry is born. Pono frets so over me that I have promised to be very good and follow all of Doctor Frank's orders. We do not want to lose another little one before it can come into the world.

In these past two years I have neglected my journals fearfully; a few henscratches here and there to mark important events—"grand birthday party for Emma" or "Aunt Winona comes to visit." Most of the entries are happy ones; one was so sad I could bring myself to write only: "Our little baby, born dead, was buried today." I shall not attempt to make excuses, other than to say that these have been busy years, and if I must choose between spending an hour with my husband or an hour with my journal, Pono always wins.

Until now, many of my days have been spent working with the district schools—struggling, I should say, to convince the rest of the ranchers and the sugar plantation owners to agree we must educate all of the island children, including those of the Japanese brought in to work in the cane fields.

But I get ahead of myself. At this moment I am propped up in the big koa wood four-poster the Rourke brothers made for us as a wedding gift, looking out onto the pretty little garden with a birdbath in the center, which Pono made for me after we lost our first little one.

True has sent Rose to help me. It is pleasant to hear her bustling about my kitchen, baking bread and making tea for us. Sometime during the day True will pop in, and after school is out Amalie will walk down the road to sit with me and chat about the school day, and probably complain to me about Eveline Statler, Emma's governess, who stands so erect that when she enters a room, you automatically straighten your own back.

In the beginning, True wanted to dismiss her because of the high-handed way the Wakefields had hired her. By then, I had observed enough to ask True to give her a chance. The first time Emma threw a tantrum to get her own way, Eveline surprised us all by picking her up, carrying her to her room and insisting she stay there. When Liko tried to intervene, both True and I stopped him. Eveline does not raise her voice and we know she never touches Emma in anger. She is simply very firm and very patient, and our naughty little charming child has become a sweet, thoughtful and charming girl.

"A miracle," True pronounced early on.

Evan and Liko weren't convinced for many months. Evan finally capitulated when Emma came bounding toward him one day, eager to show him the watercolors of flowers Miss Eveline had taught her to do. Liko gave in when the two brought him daily baskets of food and get-well poems when he was thrown by his horse and laid up with a hurt foot.

Amalie's displeasure with Eveline is more complex. It doesn't help that neither woman has an open, amiable personality. I believe that the problems that rise between them come from the differences in their approach to education. While Amalie is intent on teaching the poorest and the slowest in a classroom, Eveline quite simply prefers to have one student whom she can teach not only the basics of education but the social graces. Amalie believes Eveline to be haughty, on one occasion telling me that, "Our oh-so-important Miss Statler is smug about her command of the French language, when in fact she has a very peculiar accent."

In that case, I had to remind Amalie that in fact Eveline had asked her to give Emma French lessons because she recognized her own deficiency.

"Oh yes," Amalie had retorted, "but she didn't want Emma to be included in the classroom with the other children—she wants only private lessons."

True and I have been troubled by this as well and have insisted that Emma must take some classes at the school. Eveline finally told me that she resists because "Miss Emma is an heiress. It is best to remind her of her position and train her for her responsibilities from an early age."

Evan and True had a long talk with her then, to explain the sort of education they believe Emma should have. Eveline has proved herself to be resilient; since then, Emma attends certain classes at the school and she is allowed to mix freely with the other children and the ranch workers.

I suppose I am the closest Eveline has to a friend on the island; she and Emma will be along today, probably to bring me some wildflowers. Yesterday Pono came in with some early peaches, which he set out on the windowsill next to my bed where Emma would see them right away. I know exactly what she will do: come kiss me, chattering away about the current story she is reading. Then she will see the peaches, will let out a little gasp of pleasure, look first at me to see if she may take one and when I nod yes, she will hold it in her slim hands, turning it over and over again as if examining a present before taking off the wrapper. Then she will ask for a napkin to spread over her dress, knowing that the juice of the peach may spatter her frock. She will be wearing a delicately flowered dimity and a white pinafore. Emma loves the "storybook dresses" pictured in her English books. Eveline's accomplishments never cease to amaze; she is an excellent seamstress and can cut her own patterns. Hence, Emma always looks like a Victorian confection.

She is of average height; her hair is light brown and no longer curly. Sometimes her smile is bright and open, other times wistful and dramatic. Her eyes are her great beauty: they are large and expressive, of a blue that is difficult to define—sometimes quite clear and innocent, other times a darker, more dazzling shade, hinting of storms at sea. She is a child who seldom has the luxury of being left to herself.

Her mother is a wonder to behold. She is in the saddle at sunup each day, working right alongside Evan. I don't know when they find time to be alone. I suspect Pono knows, but we do not talk about this. I also suspect my darling husband believes I haven't a notion in the world about Evan and True, and I do not want to shock him or shake his faith in my naïveté. Still, I would dearly love to ask how he feels about what is obviously a long and passionate love affair.

True, at thirty-two, is beautiful in a careless, wild way. Now and then some eligible bachelor comes to one of the Wakefield house parties, gets a glimpse of True while out riding and simply must meet her. Then he will show up at the

Home Place, where he will discover that True has no time for him at all and precious little civility.

I do know this: True and Evan seem equally obsessed with this place, and one is as determined as the other to make it grow into the finest cattle ranch in the Islands. Sometimes now, when they are working on some new water plan or breeding program, or any of the hundred other things they have in their minds at a given time, True and Evan will show up here in the evening to see Pono.

"Where did the three of you meet before Pono married me?" I asked them one night.

And True answered as pert as you please, "Before Pono married you, Martha Mooney, he didn't want to stay home all the time."

Martha Mooney. I may have been born to the Wakefields, but I am not one of them. The Colonel has made a sincere attempt to treat me as his daughter, and I am touched by his kindness. His wife accepts the truth of Auntie Momi's revelation but says it is best left alone because there is no way to make it up. I agree that there is no way to make it up, but I am grateful to old Auntie for revealing the secret of my birth before she died.

The one Wakefield that I do feel a kinship with is Rachel, and that is because she embraced me with tears of joy as the sister she has always wanted. Since that day she has moved into my life in such affectionate, if sometimes peculiar, ways that I accept her as my sister.

I have to say I am somewhat relieved that Rachel is on her island for the next several weeks, busy with the digging of a new well. There has been a new enthusiasm among haoles in the islands for a movement to "rehabilitate" the Hawaiians by setting them apart, preferably on land nobody else wants, which means land not easily arable. Like Opihi Island. Rachel has been able to acquire the funds to ship in food, since it will be some time—if ever—before the families are able to grow enough to sustain them. Fourteen families live there now, in grass huts like those old Auntie lived in on Oahu. The last time Pono and I went over, we were given our own hut and spent the night battling fleas. Pono believes the only way they are ever going to make the island work is to run some cattle or sheep and pigs to ship to Oahu.

The Wakefields have been back from Washington for a full year, long enough to start a new, more elaborate version of the house party, made possible because the ranch is providing them with triple their income of four years ago. Illustrious visitors have come to our island, we are told—senators and captains of industry, important people the Colonel and his wife met in Washington. President Roosevelt is even said to have accepted an invitation to come for a boar hunt, though he has not yet appeared.

The men hunt and fish—the Colonel has a boat house not too far from the dock with two new, beautifully crafted catamarans; there is almost always a picnic at the beach and a bathing party. Recently, the Colonel built a small paddock near the stables, where his guests can rope bullocks. Evan frowns on this last entertainment, since it means some of the cowboys must be called away from their work to demonstrate. The men don't seem to mind, since they are paid with a measure of whiskey, but Evan says the rest of the day and sometimes the next they're not worth the powder to blow them to hell.

Rachel and I are not invited to these parties, but Emma always is. True does not want to aggravate the Colonel by refusing altogether, so she allows Emma to go for an afternoon or sometimes overnight. Eveline is the escort, and she is careful not to carry tales about these social affairs, but I gather that Emma enjoys them quite a lot.

I have managed to be the source of not a little annoyance on the part of the Colonel's wife—I cannot think of her as my mother. I am told by the lawyer who handled the matter of my "inheritance" that when Auntie Momi died she left to me the deed to some acreage on the island of Molokai. This had been given her by Laiana Wakefield's mother, in return for her long service (and, I suspect, the keeping of her secret).

Pono and I sold the land and with the money bought a parcel just east of the ranch. Someday we plan to run some cattle of our own there. Evan thought it a fine idea and watched over the legal process for us to make sure everything was properly done. But then it turned out that the Colonel, through an intermediary, had been looking to buy that piece for himself, and when they found out it went to us—well—his wife was fit to be tied. She seems to feel that it was impertinent of us to buy land they wanted, with money from an inheritance that she thinks was rightfully hers.

Evan and True are troubled that the Colonel has agents buying up island land for him. From the day he took over, Evan has been intent on enlarging the ranch. Whenever a parcel comes on the market, he bids on it—but always for the ranch, never just for Emma. The Colonel has sometimes refused to agree to these purchases and once at least Evan lost a valuable piece of grazing land. What the Wakefields don't realize is that while they have been off gallivanting around Washington, Evan has been on the island, not only making money for them but working with the people who manage things here. They trust Evan and let him know what the Colonel is up to.

Moira Rourke has just come and gone. She is as big as she can be with her fifth child—three times my size, and we are both seven months along! I do envy her, being able to get out and about—bouncing over these roads in a wagon. She and Tom have three boys, 13, 12 and 9. And now she is producing what she calls her "second batch"—little Malulani, named for Pono's mother, is just two years old.

Moira's visits are trying. Her father and mother came from Ireland, and she is inordinately proud of her bright copper-colored hair and what she calls the "purity" of her bloodline, though from what I can gather they were poorer than church mice in the old country. She seems to think she is giving her Tom a compliment when she says, as she sometimes does, that you would never know he had a drop of Hawaiian blood in him. How any woman can be so stupid is beyond me, but it is Tom's duty to tell her so, and he will not, though it drives all the brothers mad.

What she gets onto me about is encouraging the children of the Japanese field hands to go to school. When Moira started in on it today, Rose swooped in and said it was time for my medicine and my nap . . . and for Moira to leave. Just the way she said it sounded like Pono, so I knew he'd left orders. It was all I could do to keep from giggling.

Still, I was glad when she left. I feel so awfully tired these days, which is perfectly foolish since I do nothing at all.

September 1906

This boy baby pulls hard on my nipple and I can feel something inside of me tighten. It is so strange, having a child at one's breast. So strange.

This is not my child. I grieve still for my own little girl, born dead. She was buried in the Wakefield family cemetery, not far from Jared. And why not? We had planned to call her Momi, and so we did. My baby Momi was an alii, just as surely as the Colonel's wife is. She came to the burial, the Colonel's wife. She came and tears flowed down her face. I say it is too late for her tears; I no longer need them or want them.

The child at my breast is Moira's boy. Big and healthy, with a fuzz of fine bright hair. Moira died birthing him, and my baby died in birthing.

Pono has taken Moira's little Malulani, only two years old, into our home as well. She has the dark hair and eyes of her namesake, Pono's Hawaiian mother, and a solemn little face filled with questions she does not know how to ask. Tom Rourke wants us to take these two little ones and raise them as our own—to be our hanai children. Tom says he has to get away, to leave the island; he says he cannot bear to stay. Patrick and Maude have agreed to take the older boys; now Tom waits for our decision. My decision. Pono holds little Lani on his lap to comfort her and I can see that he wants to be her papa, and the new baby's. But he does not know if I can accept these two as my own.

I cannot seem to make a decision. I am numb. It is beyond me even to decide what simple chores I need to do. Only this baby boy at my breast seems to fix my attention; he nuzzles in hard, smacking and making little wet baby sounds; the milk spills out faster than he can swallow it up. He coughs and sucks and the warm smells of baby and milk fill my nostrils.

Malulani stands close by, watching intently. Her little face is so sad I feel a sudden need to make her smile. "Your little brother sounds like a piggie," I say.

A small smile flickers about her lips.

"But I think we should keep him, don't you?" I hear myself say to the child.

Her eyes look up to mine. "Yes," she manages to whisper.

"Yes," I answer, knowing now what I must do, knowing as well that it is what I want.

"Can you go find Uncle Pono and tell him to come? Tell him Auntie has something nice to tell him. Can you do that, my sweet little Lani?"

33

March 1908

Dear Harry:

The 20th Century Limited took me from New York to Chicago in just eighteen hours, just as they claimed they would. Right now I am rattling along through Illinois on my way to California on the North-western Railroad. My compartment is fitted out with electric lights—brand-new to this line. Now I can work into the evenings, if I have a mind to. Maybe when I get back to the ranch, I'll see about getting my little cabin electrified so when you finally do come out we can sit up all night long if we want. The world is changing in amazing ways, son—each time I come to visit you, the journey becomes shorter and easier.

I brought along plenty of writing paraphernalia, thinking I would get my ranch correspondence finished on this long train trip west. But I find I can't get my mind settled to business. All I seem to be able to think about is you, and how we parted. It seems like we have so little time together, it should be spent without angry words. It pleases me when we can agree, but fathers have to try to think ahead for their sons and not be afraid to tell them when they believe them to be wrong. When a boy is heading in a direction that signals trouble, the father has to try to head him off, move him a different way. I suppose you think that sounds like a cattleman talking, and I suppose it does.

Towards that end, I want to repeat: I believe as hard as I've ever believed anything in my life that you should come live with me now, stay on the ranch for a time. Learn to ride western-style and rope and explore the island. It will give you a new way to look at things, I can promise you that. It

361

doesn't seem to me that any man could ride across Mau'loa, his horse belly-high in grass, with the mountains rising over him and the sea stretching out in all directions below, without a rising spirit taking over in him.

The headmaster agreed with me that it would likely be a valuable experience for you. He said he feels that you would benefit from being with me in a different kind of place. If your mother finds yet another school for you, I think you may well find yourself in the same kinds of trouble all over again. I believe Hawaii—and especially the Hawaiians who work on the ranch—can help you. Your mother did not absolutely forbid you to come back with me. As you know, she was the one who cabled for me to come after this last expulsion. I believe she would allow you to come, if you could tell her forcefully that it is what you want. I know she has found another school for you in New England, as she says. I know she is keen that you finish preparatory school and go on to Yale.

As hard as it is now for you to accept, that goal might better be achieved if you took some time out, came to Mau'-loa with me and sorted out some things. I left instructions with an agent, Mr. I. Samuel Beckwith, 133 Exeter Street, to provide you with train and steamship tickets, as well as spending money, if ever you should decide to travel out here. I pray you will use it. You don't even have to write me to say you are coming. You must, however, let your mother know if you do leave.

Evan put down the pen and flexed his cramped fingers. For a time he looked out of the window, but he did not see the dark landscape of late winter raked by a cold rain. He saw instead the reflection of his own troubled face. He closed his eyes and the scene came rushing back to him: Jenny in the parlor of her brownstone on Commonwealth Avenue, pacing back and forth while Harry sat quite calmly in a chair by the fireplace, now and then reaching into a bowl full of peanuts from the table next to him to toss one into the fire.

"It was not his fault," Jenny said, her color rising, adding, "I had no idea they were about to expel him."

Evan answered Jenny, but he was watching his son. "The list of transgressions was impressive." Then he added, "I've heard what the headmaster had to say. Now, if you want to tell me your version, son, I'll listen."

Harry tossed another peanut onto the fire. He didn't look up.

"Answer your father," Jenny snapped.

Harry glanced up and shrugged. Had the look on his face shown the smallest blush of embarrassment, even a hint of humiliation, Evan would have known what to do, but all he saw was arrogance.

He knew he couldn't break through it, not here in Boston. Evan had been called in when Jenny was still in a panic from the headmaster's dire warnings. Since then she had found time to convince herself, with Harry's help, that once more the fault was not his. While Evan was steaming toward the California coast and then crossing the country, she was able to find another school willing to accept him. The only loss, Jenny had assured him, would be a term.

Evan thought about Harry: At fifteen, he was more fully formed than most boys, probably because of all of the exercises he had done over the past years to compensate for his damaged leg. He walked with a limp but it did not deter him from riding or swimming, both of which he did well. He also had an exceptional vocabulary, when he chose to speak—a result, Evan supposed, of so much reading during his recuperative years as well as sharing the company of his mother's friends, most of whom seem to have some literary bent. The boy was handsome, and he could be charming; he was also, Evan forced himself to admit, deceitful.

"All right, Harry," Evan had said, "maybe it's just as well that you don't give your version of events. Let's pass over fault and talk about what's to be done."

Harry pulled himself up in the chair. "Mother has found me another school."

"I don't think you should go back to school right now," Evan told him. "I think you should come back to the ranch with me."

Both Jenny and Harry had stared at him.

"No!" she blurted.

At the same time Harry asked, "Why?"

There had been an ugly scene then, with Jenny ranting about True and repeating some of the old, angry charges. The boy did not seem shocked; he had seemed more curious than anything, watching Evan. He's heard it all before, Evan reminded himself, feeling the old, sad sickness rising in him. She could not resist making their son her confidant.

Harry would always be the one who bore the brunt. Evan blamed Jenny for the boy's fall from the cliff, but he knew that he was as much to blame for their son's crippling. He thought about True and about Emma. Where was the right in all of this, he wondered.

He turned back to the letter to his son and began to write:

In our last, unsatisfactory day together you asked me a series of questions. One was why I chose to throw away what your mother says was "a brilliant career" in Honolulu to become "a hired manager" of a cattle ranch.

To understand, you must know something about the economic and political situation in the Islands. The territory of Hawaii is all but controlled by five companies, which some call "The Big Five." Each of these, in turn, is owned by white men—haoles—whose parents or grandparents came to the Islands as missionaries in the 1800s. That group was known as the "mission family" and their direct descendants, many of them united through marriage, are now known as "the family." The men are often called the "Mission Boys," and their influence reaches into every aspect of life.

If you take a hard look at every board of directors of every company that does business in Hawaii, you will find the same dozen or so surnames—all of them harking back to the original companies of missionaries who came to save the heathen Hawaiians. No outsider need apply.

Your mother told you that I could have been part of the circle if I had wanted and perhaps she is right.

I believe Governor Dole to be a good man; I admire, as well, some of the Mission Boys. But I question their right to rule so absolutely in what is supposed to be an American territory—where all men are created equal, where there is liberty and justice for all . . . you know the rest. Only a few years ago an attorney general said that the government of Hawaii was about as centralized as France was under Louis XIV. Their hold on the Islands is, I have come to believe, a parody of democracy. The Hawaiian monarchy was overthrown to create what amounts to a family oligarchy. Many of my friends, and your mother's friends as well, are Hawaiians, or of mixed race. Managing a cattle ranch proved to be one way to live a useful life and avoid becoming an active participant in Big Five rule.

You asked me what made me happy. That is the question I've given most thought to—wondering first of all why you should ask. One answer is: being out on the open range, riding a good, solid horse. Making a green, grass-rich pasture where there used to be dry scrub land. Roping a young bull for branding, watching a mare foal—and knowing the foal is going to be a better breed than its mother.

I prefer the active life. Probably I should not tell you how early I am up, or how late I work—it might scare you off. But I can tell you that watching the sun rise makes me happy, and there is nothing in the world like watching it slip into the Pacific when you are high up on the mountain, in the places where there is snow—and see the alpenglow at last light.

Happy is a strange word; I doubt many of us feel it all of the time. Mostly I think it comes in little bursts, or sometimes big ones. The day you were born, I felt an explosion of happiness.

A smaller burst happened to me when I was working on Kauai, where half a dozen big young Hawaiian boys worked for me. I'd been pressing them pretty hard, and they'd never grumbled once. The Hawaiians are like that. So I told them it was time for them to go have some fun, and they looked at each other back and forth and then one, a very big boy of about eighteen named Kaohe, asked me if I wanted to go get turtles with them.

There was something about the way he asked me—a little bit of a challenge, but more than that too, as if there was something about this turtle hunt they wanted me to know.

We set out in canoes, moving up alongside the Pali, heading north into country so steep and wild and thick no roads can go in. I'd been here once in the daylight, but now the only light we had to go by was the moon. It was full and silver bright.

The boys paddled easy and steady, and they kept laughing and joking with me the way the Hawaiians do. Finally we dipped in past a big reef to a lagoon that was as wide as any I've every seen, maybe five feet deep all round and filled with sea turtles. Not the little ones, big ones, swimming all around.

With whoops the boys beached the boats, splashed into the water and began flinging themselves onto the turtles' backs—not to catch them, but to ride them. The turtles would take off, swimming crazily with a kanaka stuck on its back, whooping like anything. The boys would slip off one and onto another, until all of them were mounted and flying around the big lagoon.

"Hele on," they called to me, meaning I should get moving, and I did. It felt strange at first, clinging to that hard shell, and I worried that the turtle would turn around and snap my hand off. But it didn't . . . and pretty soon I was out there in the middle of them. When I think of it now, I have to smile. That was *fun*. Real belly-full fun. And when we went home that night, towing two of the turtles for a feast, I knew better than I'd ever known before something about the Hawaiians and the kind of joy they seem to carry within them that I fear we haoles have lost.

Evan stood, rubbed his hands, turned off the electric light and sat in the dark. Hawaii seemed to close around him, the lagoon in the moonlight, the boys splashing and laughing as they rode around on the turtles' backs.

When was he happy now? Riding alongside True, measuring the canter of his horse to hers, stopping to admire a new crop of bluegrass pasture that was thicker than they had thought possible. Riding out to see the new Percherons brought in to upgrade the utility horses, or one of the Holsteins or Hereford bulls that were fast improving the herds.

In seven years they had separated out the best of the wild cows, tamed them and bred them to the Herefords bulls. Then they kept breeding them until they got bulls from the fourth cross. Those they kept for breeding. This had produced a herd that bore no resemblance at all to the poor straggly, shrub beasts that had roamed the range when they took over.

Now the Wakefield ranch was green and productive; it was on its way to making its owners rich. Evan frowned. He had always thought the Colonel would become easy to deal with, once he had ample income. The trouble was, the more the Colonel had to spend, the more he wanted. The struggle between them continued. If Harry had asked him what made him unhappy, he could have told him about the Colonel. He folded the letter and put it in his pocket.

* * *

True and I sat in the garden, she cross-legged on the ground with baby Tommy plopped in her lap, running her hand over his bright red hair. He smiled up at her, blinking and making nonsense sounds.

"What a big handsome bouncer of a boy you are—a Rourke to be sure," True said. "Don't you think your brother is handsome, Lani?"

Malulani seldom left my side and was so shy she could scarcely bear to have anyone look at her. Now she reached to put her arms around my neck and turned her face away from True. I held her close to me. She no longer asked where her ma and pa had gone, but I could tell that she worried I might leave her, too. The only other person she trusted was Pono. At that moment he came round the barn; Lani saw him and set out running to join him.

"Let me wash up, then I'll take them both down to the spring to draw us some water," he called out, and I waved them off.

I suppose Pono must have known that True wanted to talk to me; he always seemed to sense these things. In a few minutes he reappeared, swung a laughing Tommy up on his shoulders and was off, Lani skipping alongside. Before they were out of sight, True had handed me a sheaf of papers. "Evan wrote this to Harry. He asked me to read it and tell him if he had been wrong not to send it. I don't know, Martha . . . I feel like it's gone so far—Jenny has made things so impossible. But then, well, I have to be honest with myself. I don't want Harry Coulter to come because it will change things. With Evan and me, and maybe even on the ranch. That's terrible, I know, but the thing is—I still don't know if it's duty that Evan feels, or if he really believes he can change Harry, can make him different than he is."

I read the letter. Then I took a deep breath. "He should send it. I believe a fifteen-year-old boy can change his ways, and in this case I think his very best chance is with his father."

True stood, brushed her skirt, looked at me with annoyance. I had not told her what she wanted to hear, but I had said what she knew was right.

Evan sent the letter off on the Friday boat, which delivered thirty guests on their way to Kolonahe. The Colonel was at the landing to meet them, and drew Evan in for introductions and talk about this and that. It was getting late then, so Evan tucked the incoming mail into his saddlebag and rode home before opening it to find a letter from I. S. Beckwith, Esquire, of Boston, and another from Jenny.

"Please be advised," Samuel Beckwith wrote, "that your son, Harry Coulter, has on this day collected a railway ticket to California, with sufficient cash to cover the ticket on an ocean steamer for the journey to Hawaii. The enclosed accounting details also the sum you advised as spending money for the young man, who will, I trust, be safely with you by the time you receive this. We are honored to have been of service and remain your faithful. . . ."

He ripped open Jenny's letter. She did not waste words:

"Harry did not get on in the new school, and has managed to run away again after just one week. I did not cable you on this occasion, because you were not in the least helpful during the last crisis. And also because I know where he is. He has gone with the Charleton family of Newport, Rhode Island, on a tour of Italy. Young Franklin Charleton was a classmate of Harry's. They are travelling with Franklin's parents and his sister. I can't imagine where Harry got the funds for such a trip, since I refused to give him a cent beyond his school funds until he graduates. The Charletons have probably invited him to be their guest, since I believe Harry told me the sister is quite taken with him. I have cabled him to come home at once, but he is not likely to listen to me. I do not know what has happened to Harry. Only a few years ago he was the best, most well-behaved boy. I cannot believe he can be so cruel to his mother. If it had not been for my perserverance, he would never have walked again, and this is how he shows his gratitude. You should have done something when you could have.

"Your wife, Jenny."

34

This day began like any other.

Before dawn, one of the paniolos drove about a hundred horses into the Starlight Corral—named so because Evan and the boys finished it by starlight a few years back. By daybreak the paniolos had gathered round, ready to change their night horses—*ahi*—for a *kau* in the corral. Bradley Chin was waiting by the cutting gate to give the luna of each gang of sixteen men directions for the day.

One gang would go out to repair fences, and another—the young apprentice cowboys—would be breaking horses, while the older hands would head out to ride the range, moving herds from one pasture to another. This day they would be separating three-to-five-month-old males from the mother cows to be castrated. Pono and a Hawaiian named Loe do most of this knifework. Pono says that Loe is the best there is, but Evan told me that Pono works just as fast, and as far as he knows has never lost a calf.

It used to be that the day's work assignments were quick and easy, but that was when the ranch could be run by the Hawaiians and the few hapa haole families—like the Rourkes—who have been around long enough to have several generations working the ranch. Mau'loa runs something more than 10,000 head of cattle; only the Parker Ranch is larger.

Every time Evan adds to the ranch, new men have to be taken on. Some of these are related to the Colonel and hired at his request. None has any claim to the ranch, but that doesn't seem to keep them from feeling that somewhere along the way they have been dispossessed. The spokesman for this group is a tall, tangled man named Jack Owen, the son of one of the Colonel's first cousins. He has a space between his teeth through which he can spit tobacco a far distance and a mean streak that surfaces without warning. Still, he and the others are fine riders, as good with a rope as some of the old hands. To their way of thinking, this and their name should give them their choice of assignments.

Evan doesn't see it that way. Some days these men—we call them "the Cousins"—won't go out until Evan comes and lays down the law. There's a good bit of grumbling, more than anyone likes.

Liko turns up every morning. Sometimes Bradley sends him out with the fence gang, but most of the time he holds him back. When the rest of the men take their day horses out of the corral and are off, Bradley and Liko saddle up and go off to do some chore.

On this morning, one of the range riders had reported water wasn't running into the West Fork troughs, which meant there was trouble somewhere along the pipeline. Bradley took Liko with him to check on it. The gang of young cowboys heading for the breaking pens watched the two ride off together. One said something and another giggled. The old luna in charge of the gang turned and gave them what the Hawaiians call "the stink eye" and they were silent.

Liko didn't see how it happened. They were riding along easy enough, tracing the pipe up into the low hills. The trail was rocky but not too steep. Liko was leading like always, and Bradley thought he could keep a sharper eye on the pipe if his horse could follow Liko's. The horse must have stumbled . . . somehow it fell; there was hardly a sound. That was what was strange. Liko didn't know what made him look back, but he knew it wasn't a noise. He saw Bradley slip off, and the large horse roll over on top of him, and a rise of red dust.

Bradley looked up at Liko, his eyes black with fear. The horse had slid down the hill a ways; it was trying to get up but it couldn't. Liko touched Bradley's chest feeling for broken ribs and moved his legs. Bradley shuddered. His face was white and wet with sweat. Down the hillside the horse whinnied pitifully.

"Shoot it," Bradley managed to gasp.

Liko scrambled to his horse to get his rifle, jumped down the slope, and shot the horse twice between the eyes. He was back kneeling over Bradley again while the animal twisted in its death throes.

"I don't know how bad your back is hurt," he told Bradley. "I can't risk putting you on my horse. It's going to be painful, but I have to carry you. Can you stand it?"

Bradley closed his eyes tight and then opened them wide again. Yes.

He fainted as Liko picked him up. Better that way, Liko thought. He held him close to his chest, so he could feel the rapid beating of Bradley's heart. He would have to carry him to the road. Then he could leave him long enough to ride back for a wagon.

His arms were aching with pain by the time he reached the plain; he sank to his knees in the grass, but he did not change Bradley's position or put him down. His breathing was shallow but regular. Liko touched his lips to Bradley's forehead: it was cool, damp. There was no time to rest. He stumbled to his feet and made himself forget about the pain in his arms, in his back, in his short legs. He had covered one mile, and he had another to go.

Bradley opened his eyes once, looked at Liko's face and, before he could figure where he was, sank back into unconsciousness. Liko tried to take heart. Bradley was still alive, he told himself, please God let him be alive. He could not feel his own arms.

He stamped a bed out of the high grasses at the side of the road and settled Bradley into it, curving his slight body into the soft nest. "I am going now for help," he said, speaking calmly and distinctly into Bradley's ear. "I will be back just as fast as I can." He had to leave—he knew that. If Bradley had any chance at all, Liko had to get him back to the ranch fast, but it was all he could do to make himself go.

He rode as hard as ever he had ridden; he knew he was pushing his mount, but he had no choice. The animal thundered down the dirt path, Liko screaming "Go, go, go" and digging his spurs into him.

When he returned with the vet in the spring wagon, Bradley was as he'd left him. He put his hand under his nose, felt the slight breath and quivered with relief. They wrapped him tightly in blankets, moved him to the wagon and drove him

back to the clinic. By the time they got there, Bradley was
conscious.

The doctor confirmed what Liko and the vet thought: Part
of his spine was crushed. It will be a long time before Bradley
climbs on a horse again.

The old hands have always treated Liko with good humor
and affection; it was the new ones and the young ones who
made fun of him. No more. There's not one of them who
wouldn't ride with Liko now.

Last week we organized a little outing to Rachel's Island—
Evan and True, Amalie, Pono and me and our two Littles.
Emma preferred to be at Kolonahe, and Liko as always is
visiting Bradley at the house he shares with his elderly parents.

My Tommy is such a rambunctious three-year-old, running everywhere and never walking. He will throw himself at
anyone, arms out and laughing . . . as if the whole world
must love him. Everyone in this part of the world obliges, I
must say. He wanders off and is brought back by some
smiling field hand or cowboy or kanaka. Lani is quite the
opposite, fearful of anyone she does not know well. They are
such beautiful children. Sometimes I look at them and my
heart swells to bursting, knowing they are ours to raise and
to love. Moira gave birth to them, but they belong to our
hearts, Pono's and mine.

The seas were high when we left, but the kanakas carried
the women and children out to the whaleboat on their shoulders as if the waves were nothing but an annoyance. I
thought we would all be washed away, but then I watched
the Hawaiians slip the big boat through the waves, and it
settled me. Pono says these big, native men are wizards in the
water, and so they are.

Rachel was waiting for us, arms open and with mounds of
ginger leis to greet us. At first she insisted we speak Hawaiian, and we tried to oblige her but soon enough it was
clear that our conversations were becoming altogether too
laborious. Evan said all he could talk about in Hawaiian was
cattle raising, so we agreed on English, and a little pidgin.

Evan and Pono took off to tramp around the island, and
the rest of us went down to the beach, where a group of old
women occupy themselves making the most delicate and

colorful shell leis I have ever in my life seen. Rachel is hopeful that these shell necklaces can be sold on the other islands, and thus become a much-needed source of income. Neither True nor I responded, but Amalie—being Amalie— spoke her mind. "It is wishful thinking," she said, "to expect beads will support the people of the island." Rachel was crestfallen; I was a bit annoyed with Amalie for putting a shadow on our outing, even if she was right.

Evan and Pono returned to a gloomy group, Rachel having settled into an uncomfortable silence.

Evan sat down next to her. "We have an idea that might help your community," he said.

By the time we left, they had agreed to begin an experiment in sheep farming. Pono would be back with a rig to show the men how to drill two new wells, and Evan would provide the initial stock.

Rachel was the only one who looked skeptical. "It is not what our ancestors did," she said.

One of the old women spoke right up: "Our old ones did not have to pull life from a big dry rock in ocean," and the others all agreed.

When we were about to leave, Rachel drew True and me aside. "I do not mean to seem ungrateful," she began. "I know what most people think of me. I want to thank you."

"You don't have to," True told her, and I put my arms round my big little sister and tiptoed to kiss her on each cheek.

March 10, 1909

Evan found True in the horse barn, brushing down the Appaloosa.

"She's a beauty, all right," he said. "Are you sure Emma hasn't seen her?"

"I'm sure. She seldom comes down to the stables. But maybe she will now—how could she stay away from this young lady?" True stood back to admire the mare. "They call these kinds of spots 'snowflake.' That might make a nice name for her."

Evan laughed. "If I know Emma, she will name her the Grandduchess Gwendolyn or something like that. Nothing so childish as Snowflake."

True glanced around to make certain the stable boy had left, then she reached her hands around Evan's neck and kissed him, touching his tongue with hers. He ran his hands to her hips and lifted her into him. "I have missed you, woman," he said, scratching his beard on her neck.

She laughed like a girl. "I'm not certain I approve of this new beard. I mean, when I turn up all red and raw, what will everyone think?"

He held her away to look at her, his hands resting on her shoulders. "When are you ever going to get old and ugly, so I stop getting worked up every time I see you?"

That's how Emma came upon them, standing close together—Evan's hands on her mother's shoulders, their foreheads touching, laughing about something. Emma hesitated . . . she had come down to the stables to ask her mother something about her birthday party. She had wanted to see Uncle Evan, too—he was always so glad when she came looking for him. She didn't know why she didn't speak up now, it just seemed like she shouldn't. She turned and hurried away before they saw her.

March 12, 1909

Emma Wakefield's birthday was cause for celebration every year, but her tenth was to be marked by events at both Kolonahe and the Home Place. Colonel Toby had invited what seemed like half of Honolulu over for the occasion. By working the men double time and on Sunday, he had finished a polo field in time for an exhibition game. The roster reads like a Big Five family gathering—there were Baldwins and Castles, Cookes and Judds, Doles and Damons and Marstons, Alexanders and Dillinghams, not to mention those like the Athertons and Smiths who had entered the magic kingdom through marital vows.

After the polo game, there was a garden party at Kolonahe and a ball on Saturday evening. Emma reigned over it all in dresses from the City of Paris in San Francisco: a pretty blue silk for the ball, a yellow batiste for the garden party. On Sunday, everyone would move to the Home Place, where the ranch's paniolos would ride and rope for all they were worth and there would be a barbeque and singing and dancing well into the night. The events at Kolonahe were by invitation, but everyone on the island was welcome at the Home Place festivities.

True had never seen a polo match before; standing at the rail next to one of the Dillingham men, she watched the horses wheel and turn. "How do you train them to follow the ball?" she asked.

"How do you train your cutting horses to take a cow out of the herd?" he asked back.

True nodded and asked, "I've always wondered why they're called 'ponies' when they aren't."

Dillingham paused to watch the action. Then he said, "The game is as old as history—the rule requiring ponies went out not so long ago. Any kind of horse can be used but they do have to be hardy. I'm told that in Argentina they've been able to breed a polo horse that is born knowing how to follow the ball. I've been thinking about bringing in some Argentine breeding stock."

True stood transfixed, watching the horses gallop full-out, then wheel and turn as if they understood everything that was happening around them. Archie Cleghorn joined her; she looped her arm in his but did not take her eyes off the action.

"I hear tell you've got a couple of fine-looking foals, sired by a son of True's Surprise."

She squeezed his arm. "Evan found the stallion in California and brought him over."

"Jameson is expecting a complete report," he told her. "If he hadn't been feeling so poorly, I do believe I might have convinced him to come along with me."

At the ball after the match, Carter Dole danced with True twice, to the obvious displeasure of his wife. When he came back a third time, True told him she was winded with so much galloping around and said what she would most like to do was sit down and visit with Mrs. Dole for a spell.

Dole, exuberant from his team's win on the polo field that day and feeling the bourbons he had been sipping all evening, offered her his arm. "Well done, pretty lady," he said as they walked toward his wife. "But before we get there, I wonder if I may say how extraordinarily attractive you are, Mrs. Wakefield, and I wonder if I might make another observation . . ."

True laughed to stop him. "No, sir. No more observations or I'll start asking you some more questions about polo horses, and you told me you'd had enough of that." She settled in next to his wife then, staying long enough to let her know she had no designs on her husband.

Emma interrupted them. "Please, Mama, can I stay just a little longer? Miss Eveline says I must leave, but it's my birthday . . ."

True glanced at Eveline, who gave a small smile in return.

Dole's wife, feeling expansive toward True, took Emma's part. "How can you say no to such a pretty thing?"

At this, Emma preened, smoothing the silk on her dress and twirling around once. True straightened the bow in Emma's hair and told her she had Mrs. Dole to thank for an extra half-hour at the ball. Because of this reprieve, Emma got to hear the Colonel's surprise announcement.

He stood on the small stage built for the band and held his hands high in the air. "Dear Ladies and fine Gents, and of course our lovely granddaughter, whose birthday brings us together," he intoned, "Miss Laiana and I want to take this occasion to share with you some excellent good news." He paused until the room was silent. When he spoke, his voice vibrated with pride: "We have been invited to serve as the honorary representatives of the Territory of Hawaii at the Court of St. James in London, England. Good friends, we are off to meet the King!"

Carter Dole found Evan on the terrace, smoking one of the Colonel's Cuban cigars. "Better light up," Evan told him. "Keeps the mosquitoes away."

Carter breathed in the smoky air and did as Evan suggested—rolling the cigar around in his mouth to wet it. "I almost made a fool of myself with True Wakefield this evening," he said.

Evan looked at him through a smoky wreath.

"She saved me from myself," Dole added, sighing. "I tell you, the True I remember was a skinny, white-haired girl who could ride like thunder. Now she is one fine-looking woman."

Evan offered, "She can still ride like thunder."

"I'll just bet she can," Dole said, shaking his head and smiling. "You know, I've always felt easy around you,

Coulter. I don't know why. Maybe because sometimes I think I'd like to be out here, riding like thunder too."

For a time, both men puffed on their cigars. Then Dole went on, "Some of the boys think you're wasting your talents—or, more precisely, giving them away. It hasn't escaped anybody's attention that you've resurrected Mau'loa and in the process made the Colonel a rich man—anybody except maybe Toby Wakefield and his alii wife. Still and all, this 'honorary' position—that means he gets to pay for it all, and I didn't think he was rich enough to go floating off to England to play with His Royal Highness, good King Edward. Am I wrong?"

Evan flicked the ashes from his cigar into one of the ornamental urns that decorated the elaborate terrace. "What are you worth these days, Carter?" Evan asked.

Dole took a few more puffs, then grinned sheepishly. "Your point is made. Still, in light of tonight's revelations, I thought you might like to know that Toby has been looking into having Jameson Wright removed as Emma's guardian, and having himself named instead."

Evan looked at him sharply.

Dole nodded. "He's trying to keep it quiet."

Evan touched the other man's arm in thanks and turned to go.

Dole held him back. "You have more friends than you know, Evan, in places where they can help. All you need do is ask."

All week long birthday gifts had been pouring in, and Emma had attacked them, shrieking her delight at those that pleased her or repeating—in a high, false voice—a ritual thank-you for those that didn't.

True decided to wait until the morning of Emma's birthday to present her with the Appaloosa. She asked the stableboy to saddle the horse with the beautiful new saddle that was Evan's gift and have it at the Home Place by sunup.

True was waiting when the boy arrived; Liko had made a lei of maile and plumeria which they draped around the mare's neck. Then she stood back to admire the sleek, perfectly groomed black-and-white Appaloosa.

"He wahine u'i," the stableboy said, and True grinned at him. She had never heard a horse called "a beautiful

woman" before, but the praise was fitting. What she would have given for such a horse when she was Emma's age! She could not wait to see her daughter's face.

True clambered up the stairs to Emma's room, making as much noise as she could to alert her daughter, who did not like to be jolted out of sleep. She pushed open the door. "Happy Birthday, Sleepyhead," True called out.

Emma moved under the covers so that only the top of her head could be seen.

"Emma!" True laughed. "Come. Someone is here to see you."

"Too early," Emma murmured from deep inside the covers.

"Never too early for this kind of visit," True tried to coax, reaching under the covers to put her cold hand against Emma's cheek.

"Don't!" the girl cried out in protest. "Go away!"

True stood over her. "Come, Em . . . it's a surprise. A big one."

Emma pushed her face out of the covers, opened her eyes and demanded, "What kind of surprise?"

"I'm not going to tell you. You have to come see."

Mumbling, she pushed her arms into the robe True held out for her and made her way down the stairs and onto the lanai.

The Appaloosa was standing in the yard, picture pretty, waiting to be admired.

"Where is it?" Emma asked, confused.

For an instant, True didn't know what she meant.

"The surprise," Emma pouted.

"Why, right there," True answered. "The horse. It's your birthday present from me. The saddle is from Uncle Evan . . ." her voice trailed off as she watched Emma's face. She could see the girl struggling to hide her disappointment.

"Emma," True began, but she couldn't think what to say.

"Oh," Emma answered, slipping into the automatic words she had learned for just such an occasion. "What a nice gift, Mama. It is a fine little horse. Thank you. I'm just so pleased . . ."

"Good," True said, unable to hear any more, embarrassed at the disappointment that seemed stuck in her chest. "Now you'd best get back to bed and warm up. I didn't realize it was so cold out here. Go on . . ." She patted her daughter on the shoulder to show her it was all right; Emma did not hesitate, but turned and climbed the stairs quickly, closing the door of her room behind her.

That afternoon the riding and roping competitions at the Home Place corral started as usual: the Hawaiians trotting in, smiling and waving at all the folks gathered around the fence, raising their hats decorated with fresh bands of wild-flowers for everyone to admire. We waved back and called out to our favorite riders—two of the Rourke boys were up, and their brothers funned them to the delight of the crowd.

Patrick boomed out, "Sean Rourke, you skinny devil you, your legs so long and your feet so big you watch out or you'll trip up your horse!" The crowd erupted in laughter, all except my Lani, who was upset that one of her uncles would tease another.

"Uncle Sean's feet are not big," she complained to Pono, who picked her up, kissed her smartly and told her she sure was right about that. It was a sweet moment, marred by a sudden whirl of dust as the Cousins came galloping down the road led by Jack Owen, whooping what sounded like a war cry, ready to do battle in the ring.

In years past, these riding and roping competitions had been a joy to watch—some of the paniolos make roping seem like dancing. And Patrick is able to poke fun at his younger brother because Sean is the wildest, most daring rider on the ranch.

Now it was the old group against the new, in what was to come down to Evan's men against Colonel Toby's. By the end of the day, both sides had been bloodied, one horse had broken a leg, three men were pretty badly banged, and fist fights had flared on two occasions.

The Colonel made the best of it, saying he was delighted that his city guests could get a glimpse of "the real Wild West." He pinned a first-place ribbon for roping on his cousin, Jack Owen, and told him he had done the clan proud. Owen pulled his horse around so smartly that it stumbled against the little makeshift reviewing stand built for Emma.

Liko was standing close enough to pull her out of harm's way as the stand tumbled. "Pupule!" Liko screamed.

Jack Owen looked down on him. "You can call me crazy," he said and spat a stream of tobacco that spattered on Liko's boots, "and I could call you something else, but not in front of the ladies."

The two camps tensed, facing off against each other, fists clenched.

"That's enough, boys," the Colonel boomed out. "Back off now, remember this is my granddaughter's birthday party."

Evan appeared beside him. He said nothing, but made a small hand motion that caused the Hawaiians to withdraw. The Rourkes weren't so ready to back away until Pono moved in among them.

The Cousins clustered, a few still on horseback. True went striding into the group. "I want you to leave," she said, looking straight at Jack Owen. "You've all of you worn out your welcome. I want you off this place now."

None, except Owen, would look at her.

"You give the orders on Mau'loa?" he asked.

Evan was watching, but it was the Colonel who moved in. "Maybe you'd better be off, boys," he told them. "Come back when things settle down some."

"Don't come back," True contradicted him.

The Colonel put on his fixed smile. "Well then, I suppose I'll just have to say you'll be welcome up at Kolonahe."

They walked their horses slowly down the road, careful not to seem to be hurrying, the anger vibrating out of them like heat lightning.

Angry, True turned to the Colonel. "Do you think your boys are smart enough to ask themselves why they don't get invited to the parties up at Kolonahe?"

"When you let everybody come, you're asking for trouble," the Colonel told her, as if what had just happened was True's fault.

Evan returned from Oahu with documents naming him Emma Wakefield's guardian in Jameson Wright's place. Uncle is not well enough to do battle with Colonel Toby. True rode with Evan to the county seat at Kailua, to have the documents recorded. By the time they returned to the ranch, the Colonel had left for Oahu. Copies were waiting for him at his solicitor's office. The fuse had been lit.

One week to the day later, Jack Owen backed by twelve of the Cousins walked into the ranch office in town where Bradley Chin, still in a back brace, spent his days doing the book work. The surly cowboys slapped the guns in their holsters and told him they were taking over the ranch on orders from Colonel Toby Wakefield.

"Not at all, you aren't," Bradley told them, in his rapid-fire English, never blinking. "These books you wouldn't understand, anyway, so to take over here means nothing. Go somewhere else, not here. Nothing here at all except numbers in ledgers, words on paper you can't read. Nothing for you."

Liko emerged from the back room with his rifle leveled at Jack Owen's head.

The Cousins began to cough and sputter. It had not occurred to them that they would meet any resistance here, so they did not know what to do. What they did know was that Liko could be fierce. He never made so much as a sound and Bradley stood alongside him, as tall as he could in the cumbersome brace. The room became hot, the sweat smell of their bodies filled the small space. One by one the Cousins filed out of the little room until only Jack Owen was left. Liko's massive arms cradled the rifle with ease.

Owen looked at them with loathing. Finally he said, "You two aren't worth cow dung. Tell Coulter he's out. And get out yourselves. We don't want to have to look at the likes of you."

Evan found Pono and the men in the high country, bringing down the three-year-olds for branding. He told them, "The Colonel claims the ranch is his. Jack Owen and his boys say they have been told to take over, and they're armed. I know some of you are kin to the Colonel and his wife, and I can see how you might not want to be in on this. You can leave now and when it's settled, if I'm still in charge, you can have your places back. You have my word on it."

Pono stood and declared, "I'm with you." The Hawaiians, talking all at once, made it clear they could be counted on, so did the Rourkes and so did all but two of the rest.

The taller of the two—a dusty cowboy of about thirty—said, "We're not putting in with no one."

Evan said, "I appreciate that." Then he told the others, "Better strap on your guns. We're not going looking for trouble. The guns are just in case you run into it and can't get out."

35

We are at war.

It is nothing like the ancient battles that were fought on this island, where warriors met on an open field and clashed until one brute force had beaten the other senseless. This is a war of nerves; the enemy remains unseen until a funnel of smoke marks a fire at one of the homesteads.

Evan's policy has been to encourage ranch hands to homestead; the ranch provides no-interest loans to build. When the Colonel objected to this use of ranch funds and land, Evan argued that it would provide a stable work force. Without the homesteading program, Pono and I would never have had such a fine place.

In the past weeks, five homesteads have been burned to the ground. No one has actually seen a Cousin setting these fires, but no one doubts they are doing it. No one doubts, either, that they are cutting fences and helping themselves to unbranded cattle. If the Colonel ever had control over these angry men, he has lost it.

The Wakefields remain on Oahu, leaving us to contend with the havoc they have wrought. Pono is distressed with me, because I won't take the children and stay with True at the Home Place. I have no intention of leaving our home empty, an invitation for it to be torched. Moving out would be showing our fear.

But I am afraid! Fear is all around us. I wake early and walk out into my garden, the dew making the grass stick wet to my bare feet. Always before I have looked away to the mountains and felt a great calm. Now the mountains loom ominous, the woods at the edge of our clearing hold unknown dangers. When Tommy goes romping off to play near them, I hear myself screeching at him, and my heart sinks at the look on his face.

Our paradise has been corrupted by angry men who feel themselves cheated in life. Never having been given what they want, they have decided to take it—and destroy what the rest of us have done on our own.

Pono is gone all of the day and much of the night. When the children are in bed, I sit in my parlor with a rifle close by. Waiting. Fear and waiting is what this war is about.

Yesterday Sean Rourke—wild, headlong Sean—happened onto three of the Cousins cutting young steers out of a herd in one of the south pastures. It is not in the nature of the Rourkes to obey orders and ride for help. Sean galloped in with a war whoop, gun drawn. An hour later he rode into town slumped over his horse, his arm hanging on by a few long strips of bloody muscle.

Sean will live, but he has lost his right arm.

Evan had already called in the sheriff and his men from Kailua; now he has brought in extra men to round up the outlaw Cousins. He has also sent urgent word for the Colonel to come to the ranch. There is going to be a showdown.

"I want you to be calm," Evan told True.

"Why?" she wanted to know, the anger filling her eyes at the prospect of confronting Colonel Toby.

Evan tried again. "I want you to be calm, because you are going to have to be ready for anything—accusations particularly."

"What can he possibly accuse me of?" she wanted to know, her anger spilling over onto him. "We've worked night and day so he can enjoy himself."

Evan corrected her. "That's not why we've worked night and day. We did that for Emma, and for ourselves. The Colonel will argue that you've made yourself rich in the process, and that you could not have done it without his land and stock."

"He's wrong!" True flared.

"Not entirely," Evan told her.

True stopped and glared at him. "Why are you arguing for him?"

"Because I want you to know how he thinks, and what he

might say to you. I don't want you to say something you might regret. In fact, I'd appreciate it if you could just listen."

"Evan," she said, as if she had run out of patience, "because of Toby Wakefield, young Sean Rourke is without his arm and seven honest hands have lost homes they worked hard for. Don't you think it is time for us to stop being so nice to the Wakefields?"

"Could we at least agree to hear him out first? The Colonel usually has something he wants to say."

"Stop calling him 'the Colonel.' He's no more of a colonel than I am."

Evan gave up. "There's no talking to you."

"I'll hear him out first," she shot back, as if all she could be was contrary.

The Colonel was waiting for them in the library, standing behind a big desk with nothing save a fern and two old magazines on it. True noticed the magazines were covered with a light layer of dust.

"Before you say anything at all," the Colonel boomed out, ready for them, "let me tell you that I had nothing to do, nothing at all to do with this contemptible business of burning houses, and surely you know that I could not countenance the kind of violence . . . or the theft of our herds . . ."

True snapped: "What about the loss of an arm by the best roper on the ranch—who happens to be the brother-in-law of your daughter?"

"Certainly I regret . . ." the Colonel started.

Evan interrupted, "I don't think you had anything to do with those things," he said, "but you did send Jack Owen and his relations to take over the ranch."

The Colonel's face grew red. "Yes, well, my idea was— now that you are legally Emma's guardian—it seemed to me it would be better to have some neutral person as ranch manager. That was my idea. I wasn't certain you would be able to do the best job for me, if you were Emma's . . ."

True erupted. "Are you blind? Evan takes half the salary he deserves—you know that. I've seen the letters you've written him saying as much. And the books are open to you. You get half of all profits, even though from the beginning you put none of them back into improving the ranch. We've

done that on our own—if we hadn't you'd have none of the
bounty you now enjoy. You just go to court and try to prove
to any judge that Evan Coulter has somehow cheated you,
and you will be laughed out of the Islands. And if you are
thinking of shifting the blame onto me, let me remind you
that I was entitled to a widow's share of my husband's estate,
and I chose to put it all in my daughter's name. Don't you
talk to me about bringing in another manager. You are the
most ungrateful . . ."

The Colonel's face froze. He turned to Evan. "Jared was
my son, one of my heirs. My brother's share in the ranch
should have come to me, not Jared."

Evan interrupted again. "Are you saying that it isn't just
a new manager you wanted—it's the whole ranch?"

The Colonel grimaced as if he had a sudden stomach pain;
he had said more than he should have, a weakness he seemed
unable to overcome. He smoothed his moustache with his
fingertips.

True's mouth dropped open. "Are you telling us now that
you wanted to cheat Jared's only daughter out of her share
of the ranch?"

The Colonel frowned. "I would prefer to discuss this with
my granddaughter's legal guardian, a title which now belongs, I am told, to Evan here."

Evan spoke out before True could say more. "I asked
your son's widow to be here today."

"Then my son's mother should be here as well," Laiana
Wakefield said, coming out from the adjoining room where
she had been listening.

True felt the blood rise to her head. If they wanted a
battle, she was ready. She had held it in for so long. She felt
her spine go stiff; it was good, standing here side by side with
Evan.

The Colonel cleared his throat. "It would seem to me that
there remains some reason for some confusion over the inheritance. Emma's place in the family . . ."

"Could you be more specific?" Evan prompted in his lawyer's tone.

The Colonel cleared his throat again, took out a large
handkerchief and mopped his brow. "As I'm certain you
must know, Evan, there have been rumors."

Evan's voice was stone cold. "What rumors?"

"About you and . . ." He coughed. "True. It has been said that the two of you . . ."

True felt her fists knotting. She glared at him, but when she started speaking it was to Laiana Wakefield. She could feel the words leaving her, echoing out into the room: "Your son was my husband and the father of my child. Emma was conceived on the Island of Maui. Do you want to talk about rumors, ma'am? Then I will tell you about rumors and your son. You know that Jared was asked not to come back to Rose Plantation—but you don't know why. I'll tell you why. There was talk that he wasn't quite a man, your beautiful son. There was talk that he preferred the company of his own sex."

Laiana Wakefield's black eyes widened, and she lifted her hand to her mouth, as if she couldn't help it. The Colonel's eyes bulged; his face grew red. True saw, but she did not hesitate: "Jared was confused and pained. He came to me, and I helped him prove that he was a man. That was how Emma came to be. She was his, and he loved her. You know I am speaking the truth, Laiana Wakefield, and you know how your son felt about Emma. But if you aren't willing to tell a judge, I have letters from Jared in which he speaks of his daughter and how grateful he is to me for bearing her. And this will go to court if you try to take away Emma's birthright. I don't have too much of a reputation to lose, as you have managed to point out. If you decide to take this to court, you will have a difficult time proving that Emma is not your grandchild. What you will do is create new rumors where there were none, and malign the memory of your son."

Toby Wakefield sat down abruptly, and his wife moved quickly to him, her hand on his shoulder as if to buttress him. For the first time, they seemed old to True. Old and tired.

It was Evan who broke the silence: "How can we resolve this?" he said, as if he were weary of the subject and wanted to be done with it.

The Colonel breathed wearily. "I need forty thousand dollars."

Evan ran his hands through his hair. "Is that what this is all about?" he said, for the first time allowing a bitter anger into his voice. "You need money to go to England, so you

decide to take over the ranch any way you can to finance
your outing? Is that it? I suspect you have already been
counseled that we can keep you in court for years—and
during that time you might well be without your usual allowance from ranch profits. Certainly you won't be able to leave
the country."

Laiana Wakefield repeated, slowly, "We need forty thousand dollars."

"The ranch doesn't have that kind of money to give you,"
Evan answered flatly.

The Colonel sighed and said, "Then we are going to sell
our half."

Evan and True stared at him, stunned.

"I have a buyer ready, he can give me cash."

Still they stared.

"I have no other choice," the Colonel said.

"You mean you would sell the ranch so you can take some
honorary post in London?"

The Colonel and his lady drew themselves up regally. It
was clear they meant it.

"You are mad, both of you," True murmured, looking at
Evan.

Evan was thinking. "Your half of the ranch is worth far
more than forty thousand. If I can get a loan for that
amount will you agree to make the payments out of your
profits?"

The Colonel looked at his wife, then back at Evan. "I
should tell you that I've already attempted to get a loan."

"I can get it," Evan said.

True turned on him, furious. "No! After all that has happened . . . after the burnings and the shooting and what these
people have said and done to us—why should we help them?
Why?"

Evan looked at her, and when he spoke his voice was
deadly: "Because, Mrs. Wakefield, it is my job to act in the
best interests of my ward. That is what I have done in the
past, and that is what I intend to do now."

Evan would not speak to True that day, or any day for
several weeks thereafter. First he led a small army of men
into the mountains to round up the Cousins. Not a shot was
fired; it was as if they knew their time had run out. Charges

were dropped against all but Jack Owen, on the condition that the Cousins stay off the island for three years. Owens was tried and convicted of the assault on Sean Rourke and sentenced to two years in a labor camp on Oahu.

As soon as peace was restored, Evan left for Honolulu. True knew he was angry with her, and she knew why. She lived with it as long as she could, then she came tearing into my garden, pulling me away from tending my corn patch, and insisted on telling me the whole story.

"Was it so awful, what I said?" she asked.

I sat back on my heels, disappointed and dismayed. "Yes, it was," I told her.

"But don't you understand—I had to do it," she insisted. "I had to prove to them that I was strong enough to hurt them more than they could hurt me."

I just looked at her.

She wailed at me, "How can you possibly defend them, after what they did to you?"

"This doesn't have a thing to do with defending them, but now that you bring it up, they didn't do anything to me, except give me life. Everything else we did—you and me. And I like the life we made for us better than any they could have given me. And I think you like the life you have here better than any other you might have had. Maybe better, even, than if you could have married Evan."

True stood glaring at me.

"You told a lie," I said, unable to spare her. "You wanted to keep this life and you wanted to scare the Wakefields. Maybe you wanted to hurt them, too. It was cruel, telling them about Jared, and you didn't have to do it, True. Not to them, and not with Evan as witness."

"It wasn't a lie," True said without conviction.

"It was a lie. You know it was, and if you are beginning to believe it, I feel very sorry for you—and worse for Evan," I told her.

"Damn you," she said and wheeled and left.

September 1909

Calm has returned to the ranch, but not peace.

Evan has left for the Mainland to buy some new stock and to see his family. True has scarcely had a chance to see him alone since the day they met with the Wakefields three months ago. She is miserable, and when True is miserable, she makes everyone around her miserable.

Liko was the first to come talk to me about it, followed by Emma and Amalie and Eveline Statler.

Finally even Pono asked me what I thought about "Miss True's contrariness."

I can tell none of them the whole truth, not even Pono, because I do not want to risk making him turn against True. She knows her mistake; she blusters and storms and will not come talk to me. I believe it is a way to punish herself.

She is suffering—that is plain. But the one my heart aches for is Evan. True has ripped open an old wound and poured salt into it; I'm not certain that it will ever heal.

I left my little ones with Emma and Amalie, and went looking for True in the tack room. She was hunched over a piece of equipment, her hair trailed over her eyes, and as she pushed it away she glanced up at me, then back to whatever she was doing.

"Hello," I said, making an effort to be cheerful.

She didn't answer.

"Don't you plan ever to speak to me again?" I offered.

"Why should I, when all you do is tell me what I've done wrong?" she muttered.

"I know," I said, breathing out. "I was not helpful. You caught me by surprise, I suppose. But I've been thinking about it ever since."

She threw me a stinging glance.

Determined, I pressed on. "Do you know when Evan is coming back?"

Tears flooded her eyes, catching us both by surprise. I held out my arms, and she fell into them, sobbing.

September 24, 1909

Dear True,

These long sea voyages always set me to thinking. I have, in fact, looked forward to this five-day passage to San Francisco just so I could sort out some thoughts.

All in all, these past years as ranch manager at Mau'loa—

almost nine, though it seems much less—have been good ones for me. I have had the opportunity to do the kind of work I most enjoy with a challenge that at times seemed impossible, in the company of people I admire and feel a great affection for. As I believe you know, I care for Emma as if she were my own. As her legal guardian I will continue to devote myself to her best interests.

Education is one concern. Now that Emma is ten, you should be thinking of sending her to one of the better schools either in Honolulu or on the Mainland. I will bring back information with me when I return, so that a decision can be made. I would assume that you will want to accompany Emma when she does go off-island to school.

Another concern is my son. I hope to convince Harry to come and stay with me for a time, and his mother is welcome to accompany him if she wishes. Since Kolonahe continues to require a staff even though the Wakefields are off to London, I have decided to move into one of the guest houses. Permission has been granted by the Wakefields.

Some weeks back you expressed interest in some Argentinian breeding stock, with the idea of producing polo ponies. It is a small market, but one that seems to be growing, so I believe it to be a sound investment—especially since we already have the playing field where the ponies can be trained.

In reading this over, I see that it sounds much too businesslike for a letter between old and dear friends. Times change, and new challenges arise. As several eligible (as well as ineligible) men who attended Emma's birthday party remarked to me, it is something of a crime against nature for such a beautiful young woman as yourself to hide herself away on a wild Pacific island.

I will cable the approximate day of my return. My fond aloha to you all. Evan.

December 1909

It never rains but it pours.

Nothing has been easy this winter—not the weather or the winds, which blew over the big kukui tree in the garden and scattered the nuts every which way, not the roundups or the drives down to the cattle ship. Last Thursday a week, Pono galloped his horse into the surf, leading a steer—as he's done a thousand times or more. He got the creature lashed to the lifeboat, then went back for another. When they got six cattle tied to each side, they rowed out to the steamer where a belly band was put around each animal in turn, to lift it onto the steamer. Harder work you won't find on a ranch. On drive days, Pono always comes back wet and cold. This time he came back wet and cold and plenty sore, from where a steer had kicked him in the chest. He fussed at me when I tried to help him get off the layers of clothes the boys always wear when they're doing water work, but finally he let me help. When I saw his chest I almost fainted. It was black and blue and so angry-looking I burst into tears.

Then I got stubborn and sent for Doctor Frank. Evan came as well—on his own, because he saw Pono was hurting. The two of them laid down the law, so now Pono is where I thought I always wanted him—at home with us for at least a week. Three days have passed; he grumbles and mumbles and even the Littles have begun to stay away from him. My sweet Pono, kept inside against his will, has turned sour, and I do believe we will all be happier when he returns to work.

When Evan stopped by yesterday, I walked out to his horse with him.

My hand on his arm, I said, "Evan, please . . . True is so miserable. With herself, for what she has done. Can't you please talk to her?"

He was ready to mount, but he stopped, his hand on the pommel, and looked out toward the mountains. At forty-seven, his thick hair is streaked with grey, his face is deeply lined from the sun and he is thicker than he had been, but he is a good-looking man still.

"Martha . . ." he tried, then shook his head. "No, I can't. Not to her, not even to myself. There's just . . . nothing to say." A desolation seemed to sweep out from him and encompass me. Tears sprang to my eyes. He touched my shoulder and tried to smile, but he couldn't manage so he mounted and rode off. I stood for a time, wrapped in the sadness he had not be able to contain, and I ached for Evan Coulter.

True has thrown herself into the breeding and training of polo ponies with the passion of the possessed. She has convinced herself that Evan will understand, in time, that what she did was for Emma. I suppose it is the only way she can excuse herself—by playing the fiercely protective mother. Emma does not always cooperate. Since the departure of her grandparents, she complains that there is little to do on the Islands and wants to be allowed to go to Honolulu to school, as Evan has suggested. True refuses, but she won't be able to hold out much longer. Eveline has said that Emma is ready for the classroom; True and Amalie want Emma to go to our school. I wish I could agree with them, but I cannot. If Emma were as devoted to ranch life as is her mother, I would say to keep her here another year or two. But she is not, and I doubt she ever will be.

36

Summer 1911

True stood in the center of the field, hands on her hips, watching intently as Michael Rourke put Four to Go through his paces—wheeling and turning, stopping short, galloping full-out. Evan stood back; he did not want her to know he was there, not yet. After all these months, he still had to check himself with True, to take time to assume the formality that created a distance between them.

"Let's see if he's still stick shy," True called out to the rider, then stood back and watched with pleasure as the young horse accepted the long, sweeping passes of the polo mallet.

"He was a mean one to break," Michael called out to her, "but it looks like he's going to be worth it."

Evan called out, "Several times over. He looks fine, True. Now that you've got your horses, when are you going to start training?"

True and Michael exchanged glances. "Can you give me Michael here and his brother Patrick, and Kamaki and Manu?"

Evan pushed his hat back on his head and squinted at her. "You planning to field a team?"

True's eyes brightened. "Why not? If our polo horses are as good as we think they are, and we know our riders are as good as they come—why not send them over to Honolulu and give the Mission Boys a drubbing in their hometown?"

Evan stood looking at her, smiling and shaking his head. "Is that what you've had in mind all along? You want to beat the social boys at their own game? I'm surprised you don't plan to play yourself."

"They won't allow women," she came back so quickly that the two men chuckled.

"Our loss," Michael said, gallantly, and True wrinkled her nose at them both.

Evan became serious. "How long do you need?"

True thought about it. "Seven months, maybe eight. The horses are broken and they've been working the cows every day, which is good for them, but we need to get them used to the game—that's four horses to each player. I'd say we should be ready by spring—if I can have the men full-time."

Evan exhaled. "Better tend to that horse," he said, dismissing Michael.

True crossed her arms in front of her, grasping her elbows awkwardly. They were so seldom alone, she felt timid. "Walk with me over to the corral," he said. "I want to have a closer look at these ponies you're so sure can take on the Oahu Polo Club."

They walked in uncomfortable silence; she stumbled against him and, when he reached out to steady her, said "Sorry," as she might to a stranger.

They stood surveying the string of horses she had chosen—quarter horses for the most part. With them were two colts sired by the Argentine stallion Evan had brought in. "In a few years we can be turning out the best polo horses in the Pacific," True predicted.

"Why not the whole of North America?" Evan asked.

"Why not?" True shrugged.

"Why not?" Evan repeated in answer, grinning. "The challenge—it's what you do best." He paused then and added, "Even if you don't beat the Mission Boys on their own turf, the horses will be out there for everyone to see. It should be a good introduction for our line of ponies."

"Good business," True echoed, as if she had forgotten the purpose. "Yes."

He brushed his hands together. "You can have the boys. We'll keep it quiet, if we can. Plan a surprise attack. I know someone—he trained for von Tempsky over on Maui. He knows as much as anybody in the Islands about polo and I think he'll come help us out. But we'll play only that once. That should get us the attention we need . . . after that, the boys have to go back to ranch work. Make sure they understand—we can't afford to field a permanent polo team. If the Colonel were here, I suppose he would say jolly good, or something like that, but right now he isn't even able to make the payments on his loan."

True studied Evan's face. She did not like to think about the Colonel and the loan because it reminded her of the day when, she sometimes believes, she won the ranch and lost Evan.

"Once will be fine," she said.

There was nothing more to add. True ached from wanting to talk to him, wanting to touch him, wanting his arms around her. She felt parched from the withdrawal of his love, dry and brittle and without substance. At night, alone in bed, she made up long conversations between them; she explained everything perfectly and made him understand completely. But when she faced him, the words evaporated and she could scarcely even think of pleasantries. He might as well be a thousand miles away; the messages that passed between them might have been delivered by anyone.

"Emma's school . . ." he began, bringing up a subject she had managed to avoid for almost two years. Even if they had nothing to say to each other, she did not want to be away from the ranch or from Evan. She could not leave the island, not now.

She made motions of leaving. "I know. She is trying to decide which one she wants . . ."

"Emma says you're the one who can't decide."

The color rose in her face. "One day she is determined to go to England, which Miss Laiana Wakefield writes has the only acceptable schools for someone in Emma's position. The next she says she is willing to consider the Priory in Honolulu."

To her surprise, Evan spoke up. "I know this may surprise you since I've been pushing to send her away to school, but I would like to see her stay in the Islands for a few years. It's hard not to remember Kaiulani going off . . . I know you've been thinking about her."

True sighed in relief. "I don't want Emma to be 'trained' to be some sort of princess."

Evan responded, "Even if she is wealthier than Kaiulani ever was, and owns a ranch bigger than some European principalities. And even if that ranch does have its own polo team."

They laughed; it caught them both by surprise, that they

could still laugh together. A small black bug had been walking across Evan's shoulder and threatened to disappear under his collar. She reached up and flicked it off. The familiarity startled Evan and momentarily confused him. "Thank you," he finally said, making himself turn away, moving out of her magnetic field. He could live with only so many lies.

"It's all right," was all she could think to say. But it wasn't all right, nothing was all right.

At the beginning of summer, when Pono went off for the big roundup, I decided to take the children to Opihi to stay with Rachel for a spell. The wells, the sheep and much hard work have made the rocky island infinitely more hospitable. It seems that all you really need do is to plant a few flowers and bushes, give them a bit of water and wait for the greenery to spread.

To tempt us to come more often and to stay longer, Rachel has built a little visitors' bungalow, very spartan but private, and well off the ground, with mats that can be lowered or raised around the whole of the lanai. Not far from our cottage is a pool of brackish water—a mix of salty sea and fresh spring water—which is perfect for bathing. Tommy, in his usual headlong embrace of everything, tumbled in expecting the water to be as warm as the ocean and squealed when he encountered a stream of pure cold spring water.

Lani goes off with the girls of the village, which both surprises and delights me. At home she is so shy; Amalie can scarcely get her to speak out in class. But here on Opihi she assumes a kind of childish abandon that thrills me. It was here that I first realized how *Hawaiian* she is—not just the olive skin, the brown velvet eyes and the soft, wavy hair, but the quiet at her very center, a gracefulness that echoes in the way she sets the table for the noon meal or goes to the well for water, or trails behind her madcap little brother, ready to rescue him from his own exuberance. Lani is more than her grandmother Malulani's namesake; the older she gets, the more she reminds Pono of his mother.

On the fourth day of our stay, Ilima—a slender, beautifully erect woman of perhaps fifty years—appeared at our door to tell me that she should like to take Lani as her pupil. I stood there, struck dumb, not knowing what to say. Ilima has been a *kumu hula*—a teacher of the classic island dance. It was said that she came to live on Opihi Island because she believed that Laka, the goddess of the hula, no longer lived within her. Rachel has fretted over Ilima, worried that she would never chant or dance again, worried that the ancient dances she had learned from the hula master in the *halua* would die with her. Now it seems that she has found a student she must teach. How she discovered Lani's talent I do not know; Rachel seems to think it was as simple as watching her move.

For the rest of our stay, I saw my daughter only at midday, when I took her lunch to her, and after sunset, when she returned, exhausted, to our bungalow. When it was time for us to leave, Lani begged to stay behind for a few more weeks to continue her study with Ilima. Rachel was beside herself with joy when I gave my permission and so was my lovely daughter . . . the very same girl who, just three months ago, was too shy to join in the hula lessons given at the school, but only sat on the sidelines and watched.

When Lani returned, Ilima came with her and stayed until the lessons were done, perhaps six weeks in all. Shortly before Lani's seventh birthday, Ilima announced that she was ready to perform. It was agreed: We will have a luau where Lani will dance for her ohana.

Harry Coulter arrived on the island two days before Lani's luau. True came by to tell me; I was on the back lanai, grating coconut for the party. She was as anxious as ever I've seen her, twisting the leather cord from her hat over and over in her hands, so I gave her a pineapple to cut. Putting her hands to work helped her figure it out. Nothing was said, she told me, but from the way Evan acted, she got the feeling Harry is not here because he wants to be.

She noticed his limp mostly when he had to climb stairs. Other than that he gets around well enough. And he is a good rider, even if he doesn't care much for western saddles.

"Does he look like his pa?" I wanted to know.

True bit her lip. "Some. I suppose Evan might have looked like that when he was eighteen—though perhaps Harry is, well, prettier—more fine boned. But then . . ."

She clamped her mouth tight, shook her head and exhaled. "Then he started to talk, and there was Jenny—the way he moves his hands, the way he has of holding his head when he speaks, even the way he talks."

My knuckles scraped into the grater and I cried out. True took the dipper and poured cold water over my bleeding fingers.

"Poor Martha," she said, patting the scrapes dry.

"Poor Evan," I replied.

True let her head fall on my shoulder. "I know," she whispered. "I want so much to . . . I don't know what to do."

I stroked her hair as I sometimes stroke Lani's, wishing there were words to make things right, and knowing there are none.

The Rourke boys arrived long before the sun was up, to place the pig in the *imu*—a pit in the ground where a fire of kiawe wood has been burning for hours. Hot stones were removed from the fire and placed in the gutted pig. Then the fire pit was layered with wet banana stumps and ti leaves, covered over with more greens and wet burlap and finally with dirt. It will cook for eight hours, into the afternoon. About mid-morning Maude came along in the wagon with her big brood; they scooped up Lani and Tommy and the whole lot of them were off and running to the field behind the barn which Pono had cleared for games.

Baseball is all the big boys can think about; using old oat bags filled with sand for bases, they mark out a diamond and bat balls to each other, allowing the Littles to chase those that go too far. As the day wore on, enough cousins arrived to make up two teams.

I could hear the uproar from the kitchen, where I was overseeing all the preparation that is part of a big luau—the cutting of fresh papayas and mangoes and bananas, heating up the fresh poi one of the aunties had brought, sending someone to the coolhouse for the butter and the lomi lomi salmon we had stored there. Answering questions, stopping to listen when Tommy burst in with something he had to tell me, laughing and joking with the other women, happy to be in the midst of this big, noisy family.

Evan and Harry arrived late in the afternoon. "I have to give you a kiss, Harry, even if you don't remember me," I said, and he obligingly bent to receive my embrace.

"I do remember you," he told me. "You taught me how to swim. You and a little man . . ."

Pleased, I smiled at Evan, but he did not smile back. I recognized the mood: preoccupation with a problem.

"That was Liko," I told him. "I'm sure he is out at the baseball field with the rest of them—maybe you would like to join them?"

"Where's Pono?" Evan asked.

I looked at him sternly. "Taking the pig out of the imu. Evan Coulter, don't you dare talk to him about work. This is a day to play, and every once in a while the both of you need one."

"Work is play for Evan," Harry said, jolting me not just with the sarcasm, but by his use of his father's first name. "I think I'll just arrange myself on your verandah if you don't mind," he added, "to give my leg a rest."

True tugged me into the back bedroom and closed the door. "Evan is seething," she told me. "When I said how glad I was that he was coming today, Harry said he didn't have much choice. He's being terrible—what can I do?"

I shook my head; there was too much for me to think about besides a bad-mannered boy. "He's just being stubborn—let him pout. Or ask Emma to talk to him—maybe she can convince him to join in."

Lauhala mats were spread out on the grassy lawn for everyone to sit on as they ate. The food was laid out on other mats—mounds of everything—and they arranged themselves, our expanding ohana, along with the children from school and their families and some of the paniolos who live in the bunkhouse and have no families. Lani worries about these men and asked that they be invited. It was, according to Amalie, an egalitarian mixing—Hawaiians and Chinese and haoles, and us hapas.

True must have taken my suggestion, because I noticed Emma sitting between Harry and the old Hawaiian cowboy who had taught her to ride. To show his pleasure with her company, the old man took his greasy hunting knife, wiped it on the grass and speared a piece of pineapple, which he offered to Emma. She popped it into her mouth and pursed her lips in a way that made the old man laugh out loud. While Emma might prefer her Grandfather's lavish parties, there is a place in her heart for our homely family celebrations.

The sun was low by the time everyone had eaten his full, and some of the men were beginning to show the effects of regular visits to the horse barn, where several bottles of spirits had been cached.

Ilima walked to the grassy place we had marked off for dancing, sat down with her small, shark's skin drum and began the soft, insistent drumming that signaled the beginning of the dancing. She had stayed to play for her pupil and to witness her first performance. Rachel came to sit next to me and slipped her hand in mine.

Lani walked down the aisle, seven years old, her slender little back straight, her pa'u swirling about her. As she moved we could hear the tinkling of the strands of shells tied around her ankles, a gift from Ilima, who had worn them when she had danced for the King. Two leis circled my daughter's neck and covered her bare little chest.

The drum beat became insistent; Lani lifted her arms and sang out in a high, clear voice the beginning chant. An electric shimmer ran up my spine, exploded in my chest and brought tears to my eyes. She was dancing now, her arms flowing, her fingertips reaching for the softness of the evening air. The drum quickened; Ilima sobbed out the chant; Lani answered her strong and clear. Rachel grasped my hand and a little gasp escaped from her; I could feel it all around me, all of them, transfixed by the young dancer, by my Lani, my precious hanai daughter.

The sounds that began to rise from those watching were pure Hawaiian: a swelling ululation, gentle on the evening air—rising up and circling all around Lani, making her smile and open her arms to us all.

"Look at Ilima's face," Rachel whispered urgently. I did look, and the radiance almost blinded me, and then the tears closed everything out of my sight. I wanted Pono and he was there, his arm around me. We watched together as our daughter turned and moved into the finish of her dance. Then we were on our feet, all of us, brought there by the rapture of the dance, by the glory of the dancer. I blotted my tears on my husband's shirt and looked out at all of the faces smiling and laughing with us. Lani and Tommy moved into our embrace, and then the fun began.

Two big Hawaiian boys brought out their drums, and four kanaka women—daughters and wives of paniolos—stood up to dance. Liko brought out his ukelele and sang all the old cowboy songs anybody could think of. Before the night was done, just about everybody was coaxed to dance.

Evan and Pono. True and me. Rachel, Amalie. Even proper Eveline, who managed to do better than anyone could have imagined, considering that she was locked into her usual governess gown, complete with corsets and high neck.

Several times I noticed Harry Coulter in the background, his white shirt gleaming in the night as if to advertise his separation. Exuberant myself and wanting everyone else to share in the fun, I tried to take his hand and pull him in, but he would have none of it.

"I don't dance," he said. "I've got a bad leg." One of the paniolos standing next to him, a big Hawaiian, grunted pleasantly and tried to encourage him by saying, "All boys heah get bones broke—Pili up there dancing now, he get both legs broke—you no different."

Harry didn't bother to answer, but only turned and vanished into the house.

The next afternoon, Lani rode along when Pono took Rachel and Ilima to the boat to Opihi Island. Tommy, exhausted from so much excitement, had fallen sound asleep on one of the pallets we had put up in the parlor, and for the first time in days I could allow myself to sink into the big chair on the lanai, lift my feet and rest.

I didn't know I had closed my eyes until Emma touched me on the arm. I looked up into her worried face. "Auntie Martha," she said, "could it be true that Uncle Evan is my real father?"

True saddled the Appaloosa. The mare needed a good run; Emma didn't ride her enough, didn't brush her enough, didn't . . . True made herself take a deep breath and wait until the anger subsided. She could not be angry with Emma, she told herself. Emma couldn't help what had happened.

The Appaloosa wanted to gallop, and she let her go; True leaned into the wind and let it sting her face.

She could not be angry with Emma, but she was boiling over at Harry Coulter. *How could he have told Emma that Evan was her father? Why would he do such a thing?* The questions came flying at her from all directions.

She threw the reins around a branch of a māmane tree and ran up the stairs of the guest house. The parlor was empty, the shades drawn. "Evan?" she called out, but there was no answer.

"Harry?" she tried.

She heard voices in the direction of the bedrooms. As she strode down the hall, a door opened and one of the Hawaiian girls who took care of the houses came out, disheveled and laughing. Seeing True, she did not lower her eyes and move quickly away but smiled languorously and murmured, "Aloha."

Harry Coulter came out wearing only white trousers. "We weren't expecting guests," he said, buttoning his pants.

True checked herself, held herself in. "I'm looking for your father," she said.

"Evan left about an hour ago. At least that's what the servant girl said when she came to . . ." he smiled ". . . wake me."

It was the innuendo that made her lash out.

"He's your father—if you can't call him that, call him 'sir' or nothing at all. Just some common courtesy, a little decency, is what we expect on this island, Harry."

He cocked his head as his mother might and pursed his lips. "That's just what your daughter told me at your little luau yesterday—in case you're wondering why I suggested she might consider calling him 'papa' herself."

True slapped him so hard across the mouth that it made her hand sting.

He touched a finger to his lip, looked at the blood she had drawn and smiled a slow burning smile. "My mother believes you are a witch, did you know that?" he said. "She's the one you should slap in the mouth—she tells anybody she can about you and," he hesitated, "my *father.*"

True ran headlong out the door, racing for the Appaloosa, and crashed into Evan.

"Oh God," she gasped, her body shaking uncontrollably. "Oh God, Evan . . ."

They stood facing each other in the horse barn. She took deep gasping breaths, trying not to cry, not to give in.

She managed to tell him, and when she had finished, she studied his face as if the answer would be there.

"What did Martha tell Emma?" he asked.

True bit her lip and then recited like a schoolgirl: "She repeated what I have always told her . . . that Jared was her father. Emma has always wanted to know about him, about Jared . . . she likes us to tell her stories. Martha talked to her about how in Hawaii, children have always had other parents—hanai parents—that they've loved like their own, like Lani and Tommy. She said that, in a way, you have been her father. And Martha told her that you love her as much as any father ever could."

He dropped his head in his hands. True looked at his strong, long fingers roughened by ranch work. She breathed in the smells of the stable: straw and dung and dust, the musty animal smells of the ranch. Light streamed in through cracks in the planks and made stripes across the stacked hay bales.

She clasped her hands together so they would not tremble. "She is yours," she said and listened as the words echoed in the silence.

Evan looked at her and blinked as if he wasn't certain what he had heard.

True repeated in a voice as steady as she could manage: "You are Emma's father."

He stared at her. "Why are you telling me now?"

Her mouth felt dry and her body trembled. She had almost to speak in a whisper. "At first, I thought that if I did not allow myself to say it out loud—not even to you, not even to Martha—then it would be my decision, my burden, my lie. But now I think it wasn't that, or just that. Now I think I didn't say it because I couldn't bear to lose the ranch. And I'm telling you," she paused, wetting her parched lips with her tongue, "because the lie is poisoning so much and I can't . . ."

Evan put his hands on her shoulders and gripped her, hard. "Listen to me," he said. "Look at me, and listen, True. I need time to think about this . . . I need to think." His hands fell to his sides; they faced each other awkwardly, all the unsaid words swirling in the air around them. She dropped her chin against her chest and closed her eyes.

"I knew," Evan finally said. "I always knew, but I needed you to say it." He paused, lifted his hands as if to touch her and then dropped them again. She longed for him to reach out to her, but she knew he would not.

He cleared his throat and in a hoarse and halting voice told her, "I know how little choice you had, in the beginning . . . before . . . I know you did what you had to do. And I . . . did what I thought I could do. It doesn't do anyone much good to talk about mistakes. Sometimes the world doesn't allow for mistakes, there just isn't any way to right them. Now this . . . I'm going to have to do something about Harry. I just need time to figure out what that is going to be."

What Evan did was send all the girls who were working at Kolonahe home. He hired some Chinese boys to take their places, and then he brought Blue Kapua to watch over Harry.

Blue is a Hawaiian, six and a half feet tall and so thickly muscled that the floor virtually shakes when he walks into a room. He is without question the strongest man on the ranch, perhaps in all of Hawaii. He is also one of the hardest working, a man to delight Pono and Evan. Blue never shirks a job, no matter how onerous. His face wears the fierce expression of a warrior; on first sight, children run from him, but those who know him beg to be carried on his shoulders and hang onto his arms. In spite of his heft, he is quick and he is said to be *pili 'uhane*—close to the spirits. Pono is grumbling about Evan's taking one of his best men off the crews, but I believe that choosing Blue to take Harry in hand is perfect.

"If you could not control your actions," I said to Pono, "and you wanted someone close by to watch over you, make sure you didn't go out of bounds, and maybe even show you another, better way to live, who would that person be?"

"If you run off and leave me, you mean?" he grinned slyly.

"Yes," I answered, poking him in the ribs.

Pono nodded. "Blue."

"Yes, Blue," I said, giving him a peck on the cheek for the right answer. Lani walked in at that very moment.

"Are you kissing?" she asked quite seriously.

Pono blushed; I put my arms around her and said, "One for you as well," and gave her a loud smack.

"And one from papa," she said, reaching out to him.

"Blue could take lessons from you," Pono told me as he took Lani in his arms.

I had to smile; dear Pono, always so shy and reserved, now was besieged by females who insisted on kisses.

When I told True that I thought Blue would be able to keep Harry out of trouble, she shrugged and said, "I think it may be too late for that. What Harry did was so mean, so hurtful . . . and he isn't sorry, not at all—except for himself. He complains about his leg whenever he can, and he can walk better than most of the paniolos."

I thought about telling her that Harry's hurt was more than his leg, and that I pitied him as well, for all that he had to endure, but I said nothing. True was in no mood to be charitable to Harry Coulter.

In these past few weeks, things have been settling out on the ranch. Blue and Harry have all but disappeared from view, but Pono tells me they are off fishing and hunting. He said Blue had packed up with supplies, which means he is planning to go far into the mountains. Harry objected to the trip, just as he objects to Blue, but he went. And before he left, he apologized to True and to Emma for what he called his "bad joke." Emma accepted with a wan smile, but True said nothing at all. She treats Harry like a wild boar that can turn on you at any moment. I'm counting on Blue to tame the wild boar; we'll know when they come back from the mountains.

Evan came to talk to me about Emma. It was not easy to tell him, but I felt he should know that Emma has made it clear to me that she would be unhappy were she not the heir to the Wakefield ranch, or the grandchild of the Colonel and Miss Laiana. (How peculiar it all is! They are my blood parents, though I will never be able to accept them as such. And they are no blood relation to Emma at all, yet they are as cozy together as can be.)

Emma knows, I think, that her mother and Evan are something more to each other than old friends. She has hinted that she has seen something, or at least suspects. But she does not want to come out and say the words, perhaps because she does not want to believe that Evan might indeed be her father. She has her mother's practical streak.

Certain things you know will happen, must happen, and you try to prepare yourself and find there is no way. Uncle Jameson has died in his sleep, a copy of Carlyle's essays near his hand, as if he had drifted off while reading. True and I went to Aunt Winona and found her silent. For several long days she said nothing at all, and when she did begin to speak it was in a voice that was cracked and old. We had wanted her to return with us, but she would not. Mana'olana was her home, she said. She must stay and carry on. Yesterday's mail brought our first long letter from Aunt. I can't say when I've felt so relieved to receive one of her long letters—eight pages of her small, feathery hand, detail piled upon detail, tells me that she is emerging from her deep grief.

The letter arrived a few days after Lani's birthday luau. Aunt Winona wrote on about this and that, children I did not know with problems I recognized. When finally she got around to Jenny Coulter, she was astonishingly reticent. "Jenny returned soon after you left," she wrote. "She is opening the house, and has invited me to a tea, because she says it will do me good to get out and about, and she wants to get reacquainted with some of the ladies of certain families whose names you will recognize. She has had a very interesting life in Boston; her friends there were quite accomplished, and I believe she misses them a great deal. She says she is certain she cannot find such interesting people in Honolulu, but she feels she must make an effort to meet with all the good families. I suppose she came back because of Harry—she tells me that the boy needs a man's firm hand, which is why he is with Evan. I am sure she must exaggerate about Harry's scrapes."

"Harry's scrapes?" True said when she read this. "It has to be something more than scrapes. I'd like to know what he did that was bad enough to land him up here."

I frowned at her. "I hear that he and Blue are doing just fine together. Pono says that when they came back, Harry was talking pidgin."

"I say let's just wait and see," she came back.

She was reading over Aunt Winona's letter, not paying much attention. Suddenly I felt annoyed with her. "You sound like you don't want to believe that Harry might change," I told her.

She gave me a hard look. "What I don't want is for Evan to be disappointed again. And two months isn't much time."

"He's only eighteen, True. That's young enough to change course, if enough people believe in him."

She stood, moving into a square of sunlight thrown by the
window. "All I know is that Harry Coulter has caused nothing but trouble since he came here."

I snapped right back, "That may be, but it seems to me
that if you can't find it in your heart to help the son, you
don't deserve the father."

I expected her to stomp out of the room, hair flying and
face set. We'd had other spats, and that is usually what
happened. Then, after three or four days—sometimes as
long as a week—of silence, one or the other of us would
come round, would make up. But this time she only looked
at me with a kind of puzzlement flitting over her face, as if
she was trying to think something out. Then she sighed and
said, "Sometimes you make me tired, Martha." But she
wasn't mad.

Evan came to the Home Place at first light. True was up and
dressed and standing on the lanai; she watched him ride in.
He carried a bedroll, she noticed, and his saddlebags looked
as if he was going to be out on the wild edges of the ranch
for a time.

He followed her into the kitchen, where she handed him
his first cup of morning coffee, an act she had performed
perhaps a thousand times. It reminded her of how much she
missed him.

He took a first sip, swallowed, looked at her and smiled.
Like always. She smiled as well and asked, "Who gave you
the flower?"

He fingered a fragrant white plumeria blossom tucked
into the top button of his leather vest. "Blue," he answered.
"He told me I needed a flower today."

She laughed, pleased with the idea. "I hear that Blue
deserves one himself—for being so good for Harry. I'm glad
for that, Evan."

He seemed to hesitate, then he said, "I'm going over to
windward for a couple of days. If you can come with me, I've
something I want you to see."

She was not certain she had heard him right; the look in
her eyes was questioning.

"Your daughter's father would appreciate your company," he added.

They were on their way in half an hour.

The morning was bright and clear; in the distance, snow flashed white on the mountaintop. Their horses trotted alongside each other through cane fields rustling in the trade winds; as they moved inland they took a wet and narrow trail through thick rainforest jungle, where they felt the spray of a massive waterfall. When they reached the highlands they let their horses move at an easy lope. She was happy riding with him again, just the two of them in the empty landscape, the sea at their feet and the sun in their faces or warm on their backs. Time seemed to dissolve; she took deep breaths and was lulled by the rhythm of the ride. It was as if they were suspended in some peaceful kingdom.

By mid-afternoon they turned off on a path that led to a clearing overlooking the vast expanse of ocean far below; at the far edge of the clearing, placed so that it looked out to sea, was a cabin. As near as she could see, no one was about.

"Who lives here?" True asked.

"No one, just now. There's a caretaker, but he's away this week."

"Is it yours?" she asked.

"I always think of it as ours," he told her. "The cabin came with about sixty acres. I thought someday we might want a place of our own. There never seemed to be a right time to bring you here."

Thoughts began to tumble around inside of her; the slow, happy peace of the long ride up was replaced now with a peculiar excitement. She raised her hands to shield her eyes and looked about her. "I can feel the mana," she told him.

He grinned at her and looked away, as if suddenly he seemed not to know what to say. They were standing across from each other on the old lanai, which was fitted out with rough-hewn chairs.

"I brought the Japanese tub up here," he muttered. "I need to build a fire now if it's going to be hot by sundown."

True's skin felt suddenly cold; she couldn't think why it should be in the heat of the day. She walked around the clearing, looking at the traces of care that Evan had put into this secret place. A mango tree, a breadfruit and a papaya. She walked into a spiderweb and brushed it away. The excitement was tightening in her; she felt it in her thighs. Her arms wrapped around her, she returned to the cabin.

"How long have you had this place?" she called out to him.

"About three years," he answered, surprising her by appearing behind her.

She twirled around and fell against him. He reached out to steady her, and his touch sent electric shocks up her spine. She could see that he was speaking, but she wasn't listening to the words, all she could hear was the roar inside of her. She leaned into him, reaching for him with her mouth. She felt a fierce hunger for him; her body flashed hot. Now she wanted him, had to have him, could not wait.

She went with him, clinging, kissing him, touching him as he made his way to his horse; they stumbled together. He felt the rise of her breasts, and somehow he got the bedroll.

He pretended to fight her off as he spread the blanket on the grass in the mottled shade of an iron tree; she pulled at his vest, at the buttons on his shirt, as he reached up under her blouse and down into her riding pants. Finally, when they were free of their clothes, they lay quietly together, looking up at the white billowing clouds that flew across the sky above them. He took the flower Blue had given him and pressed it between her breasts. She could scarcely breathe from the pleasure; she could feel it building inside of her, power to power, his legs turning her, moving her, his tongue searching hers.

She felt an explosion of silver in the back of her head, as if she were flying with the flume of the waves, skimming in a world of pure air and water and love. She would have held that moment forever, had he not pulled out of her, moaning as his seed spurted onto her leg and over, into the thick green grass.

A tenderness as vast as the sky and the sea wrapped around them, held them. They lay in each other's arms, made love, and bathed in the Japanese tub. Then they ate and slept and woke to make love again. For two days they walked and talked, swam and talked, explored each other, mind and body. Words poured forth with an ease neither of them had ever known.

Late on the second morning they sat close together on the lanai, watching a rain squall move toward them from far out at sea, scattering rainbows as it came. Evan was not looking at her as he spoke; he was watching instead the steady approach of the silver sheets of rain.

"You know that Emma came to see me," he began. "She

was out riding with Eveline. I was up in the hills and I saw them heading for the office—it's easy to spot Emma on the Appaloosa—so I came riding as hard as I could to be there, just in case she was coming to see me." True reached for his hand, kissed his fingers.

Evan went on, "She asked me, very sweetly, if I would take them on one of our 'butterfly walks.' I suspect it was Eveline's idea—or maybe yours?—but Emma seemed agreeable. A bit shy with me, but I think we can get back to where we were without much fuss."

True wanted to look at him, but she couldn't. She wanted to ask if it hurt, not telling Emma the truth. He rubbed her neck, and she knew he had read her thoughts. He went on in the same soft, accepting tones.

"What we want and what we can have are two different things. I have to say you learned that lesson earlier and better than I did. Emma wants to be a Wakefield. We built this ranch for her; we have no right to take it away. I've been a shadow father to Emma, a shadow husband to you. For a long time, that has rankled me, and I suppose I expected you to be as rankled as I was, but you aren't."

She started to say something but he wouldn't let her. "No, listen; hear me out. We need to get this out in the air. You've never felt the same need I feel to be married, to be proper. Even if Jenny would have allowed it, which she never would. I think the way things are suits you as much as it does Emma. Then I started to own up to some other things: I am here with you, I am part of your life and Emma's—at the same time I am doing what I want most to do. Building this ranch has been a pure pleasure to me, nothing else I've ever done comes close to the satisfaction of it. If I feel guilty about the subterfuge—and I do—I also know that I have saved Mau'loa itself and made it a great ranch. What I'm saying is, I've come to terms with the way things are and the way they're going to be. It may not be all that I want, but it is as close as I can come to it . . . and it is enough."

True tried to control her voice, but it quavered nonetheless. "I've never thought that marriage and devotion were the same thing."

He brushed a stray strand of hair from her face, and she could tell by the way he looked at her that he understood, but when he spoke it was about Harry. "Up to now, my son was my worst heartache. I felt sorry enough for Jenny—and I blamed myself for what I couldn't give her, but she brought much of her misery on herself. She never tore on me the way Harry does. But now he is here and it looks like I might have another chance with him . . ."

He paused and sank into thought. The rain drew closer to shore, scattering rainbows in its path. True took a deep breath. "I wondered about Harry. I thought maybe he was acting better because you had found out something, I mean something about what it was he did to get into trouble. I thought you'd warned him off."

Evan's face clouded; the rain swept in, warm and heavy, pelting the roof of the lanai, flooding the grassy plateau in front of the cabin. "I don't think Harry could ever be warned off for long," Evan told her. "He's got to have something more, something to want. And I've got to find out what that could be if I'm going to help him."

"I hope you do," True said. Then she added, "I hope we can."

He pulled her into his arms, held her close and kissed her eyelids. After a while he said, very softly, "I know why he came back, True. But all I can tell you is, I need you to help me save him."

The squall moved over them, the sun came out again and released puffs of steam from the damp rocks. They breathed in the promise of the wet earth and felt at peace.

When they rode out the next day, True paused at the top of the path for a last, long look at the cabin and the clearing. This was her home; she felt it in her chest, in her arms, in her throat. An unutterable sadness fell on her, that they must leave this place to return to a world where they had work yet to do.

37

A new calm, as gentle as an upcountry mist, has settled over
the ranch. These days True and Evan walk together from the
horse barn down to the Starlight Corral like they used to do,
talking and laughing some, and the whole ranch sees and
hears and knows there has been a change. Until Evan
grinned at me the other day, I had forgotten what a funny,
wistful expression it was, and now True waves and calls out
"aloha," where before she was as like to pass without a
word. The waves spread out to all of us. Even my sisters by
marriage, who disapprove of what they call True's "carrying
on" with Evan, have noticed how much easier things are. I
heard Maude say to the others, "Goes to show, we've got
something men just can't do without," and the laughter
erupted. I had to stifle a giggle myself. I happen to know that
the girls attribute Pono's talkativeness—compared to what
he was before—to our marriage bed. I wouldn't say they are
wrong. I do suppose they would be surprised, even shocked,
if they knew how often he beds me, and how much I like it.
Glory, how I love sleeping all curled up with that man!

The game of polo has wrought the other big change on the
ranch. True spends from first light to last working with the
ponies—which aren't actually ponies, but small wiry horses,
most of them mares.

Try as I might, I can't keep my little six-year-old away
from the polo field. Harry and Blue are always there, and
Blue has taken to looking after Tommy for me. Most nights
it is suppertime when they come riding up, the three of them,
with Tommy riding in front of Blue and looking as proud as
a peacock.

If they stay for supper, which they sometimes do, all the

413

talk is about polo. It is the rage all over the world, especially in England's colonies, and it is all the rage on this island as well. Everybody seems to have gone polo crazy, even Harry Coulter.

It happened like this: True and Harry had been avoiding each other; she knew it wouldn't do, but she couldn't seem to find a way to talk to him that felt easy. Then one day she was standing at the rail next to Blue, watching the men in the corral working the ponies; suddenly, Blue was gone, leaving an empty space between her and Harry. She tried to keep her attention on the action in the ring; instead she was preoccupied with the space next to her. She glanced over at Harry; he was following the action. He was not going to approach her; she would have to do it.

She stepped next to him and, unable to think of anything else, asked, "Do you know much about polo?"

"A little," he answered in an embarrassed way, allowing a small silence to gather before clearing his throat and continuing. "At school, I had a friend whose family had a string of polo ponies." There was no bravado in his tone, none of the arrogance she expected. He continued, "My friend's uncle is a number one, he plays with Mr. Harry Payne Whitney."

"Oh my," True said, lifting her eyebrows to show how impressed she was, Whitney being captain of the great Mainland team that won Britain's Westchester Cup at Hurlingham in 1909 and held onto it again last year at Meadowbrook. The American team had run rough-shod over the Brits; it was exactly what she had in mind for the Honolulu team.

"Did you ever see them play?" she asked.

Harry looked down at his hands, which grasped the top pole of the corral. "We used to go out to the farm on weekends to watch, and his uncle would let us play around at workouts."

"You mean you've actually played polo?" True asked, her surprise scattering any remaining reticence.

"I was learning—I didn't get to play."

"That's too bad!" True couldn't keep herself from exclaiming. "Why not?"

Harry squirmed. Squinting up at the sky, he told her, "My leg—it was too risky."

True looked away. She knew full well who had stopped Harry from playing—she could hear it in the accusation that simmered under his words. Jenny had found out; Jenny had put a stop to it.

"Well, Harry," True said, measuring her words carefully, "if you should want to have another go at it, it's fine by me. But if you do, you'll have to put some time in working with the ponies—grooming them and such."

She held her breath, half expecting him to walk away, to reject her offer. She kept her eyes on the ring, but her attention was riveted to the frowning young man standing beside her, who seemed not to know what to say.

"If you don't want . . ." she started.

But he interrupted her with a rush of words: "Blue, could he, too?"

Now True looked at him, and what she saw was a boy—scarcely nineteen years old, so skittery that he could not meet her eyes. The old, tough facade was gone, cracked apart. "Blue too," she said and laughed. "Maybe he can work some of his *ho'okalakupua* for us."

Mr. Jock Gibbons, a native of Australia and a man with a rough mouth and manner to match, has come to teach the boys how to play the game. If Evan didn't set store by him, I would wish him off the island with his coarse language and nasty habits. He keeps a cud of chew in his cheek, and the young boys are beginning to mimic him. Yesterday I found Tommy on the back step, spitting water through his teeth in a long stream, "just like Mr. Jock."

True told me, in hilarious detail, about the arrival of Jock Gibbons. He is tall and rangy, and she hasn't a notion how old he is, though he is not young. His teeth are brown from tobacco, and he smells of sweat and leather. If polo is a gentleman's sport, somebody forgot to mention it to Jock. The first words he said to True were, "I don't reckon to work with wimmin."

Evan, standing behind Jock, had a devilish look in his eye. That made her challenge, "Why not?"

Jock looked at her sideways. "They don't take to my talk, they don't like the smell of me, and they impede my progress . . . ma'am."

True couldn't help it—she laughed. "You can damned

well talk any way you want," she told him. "I spend a good bit of time in horse barns, so I suppose I can handle the smell of you—and as for *impeding your progress,* as you put it, if that happens you can ask me to leave."

Evan clapped Jock on the back. "She's as good as her word," he told him. "Just treat her like one of the boys." At that, Jock snorted and uttered one of the expletives that spew from him with volcanic regularity.

Immediately a polo pit was built, with a dummy wooden horse where the rider sits and, with a long mallet, smacks a wooden ball up an incline into a wire-enclosed court. When the ball comes rolling back, he hits it up again—in this way learning all of the strokes.

The two Rourke brothers and the Hawaiians, Kamaki and Manu, who make up the team were the first to practice on the wooden horse—hitting the ball so hard with the mallets that you could hear the sharp crack a mile away. True and Harry and Blue took their turns, and Evan and Pono have given it a try. Now, the sound of wood against wood ricochets all over the valley as every man and boy takes a turn cracking the ball with the mallet. Even Tommy has been "up," I learned from Blue, who promised me he'll keep him off the real ponies.

Blue and Harry are regulars at the field. At any given time, depending on who can get away from work or school, there will be a dozen or so men and boys gathered to watch. On Sunday after church, almost the whole ranch shows up and stays the afternoon. I must say it is odd to hear young Japanese schoolboys talking of "chukkas" and "foul hooks."

Harry told me, "Jock Gibbons says he's come to spread the gospel of the great god Polo. He says that cow country is the best place to start, with horses that work cattle every day and men who ride as easy as they walk. Jock says you don't have to be a great rider—you just have to know how to ride well enough not to think about it. So many boys show up to have a go on the wooden horse that we have to make them take turns. Jock says that's good."

"Jock says" is becoming a part of everybody's vocabulary. Even True's.

Jock and True had their first and last set-to a week after he arrived. They were on the polo field, and Jock moved out to show Michael, who was on Four to Go, how to ride off an opponent. "You put your knee in front of your opposite's knee," he explained, doing just that. "That way you steer his pony away from the action."

Four to Go snorted and side-stepped and when Michael reined him in, True called sharply, "Watch out for his mouth—you'll ruin it!"

Jock Gibbons turned on her, furious. "Enough from you," he snapped. "I'm in charge here, miss, and I'll be the judge of man and horse. If you want to stay, learn to curb your tongue. And if you're planning on me staying, best you say right now in front of the boys that you'll keep out of my way."

True pressed her lips together to keep her anger from spilling out. The Rourkes looked away, embarrassed and a little pleased; the Hawaiians patted their horses and murmured something affectionate to them, as if to take the sting out of the air. True swallowed and said, as loud as she could manage, "I'm sorry. I won't interfere."

Jock announced, as he might the score of a game, "Apology accepted. Now let's get back to work." At the end of that day he followed True to the barn to tell her, "That pony's got a mouth like silk. Don't think I'd ever let a man abuse it, nor a woman yet." His mouth cracked into what True thought might be a smile, so she smiled back and told him she knew that was so, and that she had spoken out of turn. When he left, she felt not the least angry, but instead strangely pleased. It wasn't until she retold the whole story to Evan that she realized why. "Jock knows more than I do—about polo, and maybe about horses, too. And he wants to take charge. That's a relief. I mean, I don't feel as if I have to do it all by myself."

Evan drew her to him and said, "Old girl, you may be learning at last."

With her fingertips, she smoothed the creases at the corners of his eyes. "Thirty-eight isn't so old."

"Not nearly so old as fifty," he answered, "and I'll be that in a few weeks."

She laughed and tried hard to find some flesh to squeeze around his waist. "Solid as a bull," she told him, wrapping her arms around him and holding tight.

* * *

The next day she was out on the field again, working with the ponies, watching from the sidelines as the boys raced down the field, moving from canter to gallop, turning and wheeling and swinging their mallets all the while. Jock's voice rang out over all the rush and clamour: "Don't look at the pony" he would call, or "don't try to hit too hard." The men who were best at baseball—Michael and Kamaki—proved to be best at polo.

Harry and Blue and Sean Rourke, his poor right arm hanging useless, keep busy as grooms. Now and then they ride together for the fun of it, and pass the ball back and forth. Sean is something to see, the reins clamped in his mouth, swinging with his left hand. He is as daring as ever; it seems like he has it all stored up inside of him, and when he plays this fast-crash game, it comes rushing out.

Late one afternoon, as Jock was standing back, watching the three of them, True rode up on the little chestnut mare she has been training. Jock looked up at her and said: "The boys need some practice games, so we've got to get another team. Sean's a number one, Blue's a natural back, we can make Harry a number two. Now all we need is a three."

True maneuvered her horse in front of him, leaned down so that her head was upside down hanging into his face and gargled, "May I propose an amusing candidate?"

True became number three. Jock told everyone who would listen that it was a bad idea, that she wasn't much to watch and, like all women, would refuse to follow the rules.

Anyone with eyes in their head knew better. That Sunday, the two "teams" met for the first time. Just about everyone on the ranch was gathered round the field. It was hard not to remember the exhibition game the Big Four had played here, all the men natty in their white breeches and shirts and helmets. Then the field had been green and immaculately groomed; now it is dusty and ragged, with tufts of scraggly grass.

The riders came out wearing an odd assortment of bright workshirts and old hats. True wore riding trousers with her usual red-and-white-checked shirt, but on her head was a fancy new helmet, which Evan makes her wear.

As captain of her team, True touched sticks with Michael Rourke, and the field exploded in a gallop of dust and noise. True is daring but she is not so wild as Sean Rourke, who at times seems to fly through the air, his right sleeve tied to his body, his left swinging with a deadly accuracy. Harry and Blue move down the field, doggedly following their opposites, but no amount of daring and doggedness helped, nor any amount of cheering them on from the sidelines. True's team couldn't get near to beating "the Boys."

After eight months of playing together the Boys have become, says the all-knowing Jock, "Scrappy and fast and wily like a fox; no style but plenty of piss and vinegar." Some days he tells the Boys that if they were as smart as the ponies they are riding, we'd have a team that couldn't be beat anywhere, not even in the King's own palace grounds. When Jock gets mad at Michael, he declares he would as soon have Four to Go captain the team. True swears the little mare knows where the ball is when nobody else on the field seems to.

Yesterday Emma came to tell me that she will be going to school at the Priory in Honolulu after all. Clearly, she is not happy with this decision. She walks around my kitchen, picking up a collander, setting it down. She examines a jar of ohelo berry jam I have put out for the children to have with their afternoon bread and butter. She dips a teaspoon in the jar, puts the jam in her mouth, holds it there for a long few moments while she thinks. Finally she swallows it and speaks: "Mama says she doesn't want to be any farther away from the ranch, not for the next few years. Uncle Evan agrees with Mama."

She took another teaspoonful of jam and studied it before putting it into her mouth and slowly withdrawing the spoon. "It is too late to go to England anyway," she went on. "Papa Toby and Grandmama should be back in Honolulu by now. I wish I could have gone to be with them in London," she said and sighed. "Their parties always sounded so very grand."

I did not tell her what I knew: that they had gone through all the money loaned them, that it has been more than a year since they have made any payment on the loan. In fact, Evan has every legal right to claim the whole of the ranch for Emma.

He has spoken at length about this to True and to me. As I am the eldest of the Wakefield children—a position I find both disturbing and distressing—Evan has asked me to consider the family position and help him reach an agreement that will be fair and honorable. What an irony—a daughter is called in to save the "family" that threw her away. Fair and honorable. I can't but wonder what those words mean.

Yet finally True, Evan and I are in accord: Evan will offer to forgive the loan in return for one half of their half interest. The ranch has continued to grow. The profits now are half again what they were five years ago, so the remaining one quarter share should afford the Colonel and his wife a comfortable income, if they stay in the Islands. They are no longer young; this generous offer should please them.

The lawyers did what lawyers do, and the word came back. Colonel Wakefield desires to sell the remaining quarter of his ranch to his granddaughter, Emma Wakefield, for the sum of $80,000.

We were stunned. For two days, True stomped about in such a rage that everybody gave her wide berth. "Those people," she ranted to me. "Those selfish, spoiled, silly silly people . . ."

"Yes," I agreed. "I wash my hands of them."

"Enough to ask Evan to cut them off without another penny?"

I looked at her to see if she meant what she had said. She did. "Evan didn't want to make the loan," I reminded her. "He said at the time that the ranch was worth far more. So it does seem fair to pay them something more."

"After all they've done to us? Don't you remember how they treated us after Jared died? And you, my God, Martha. Liana Wakefield hasn't had a kind word for you, and you are her firstborn! I think they should find out how it feels, finally, to be poor."

"I think," I told her, "that it would be wise of you to consider the history of the ranch, and what Evan feels before you voice those opinions."

Those who knew about the settlement felt that Evan, with the approval of Emma and True, had been too generous. He did not give the Colonel all that he asked, but he gave him more than he deserved. Within a fortnight, Emma was the sole owner of Mau'loa.

* * *

Evan has taken space on the Inter-Island ferry for all the ranch folks who want to go to Honolulu for the polo meet next week, and who can be spared. Though Tommy can hardly bear it, Pono and I have chosen to stay behind to watch after things on the ranch. True and Jock and the Boys will go over with the horses. Everything is very secret; Evan and the rest will follow in a few days. The rest includes Emma, who will be staying on with the Colonel and his lady, but it does not include Harry. We were all surprised when he said he'd rather stay back. He has not been to Honolulu to see his mother; he would rather miss the game than have to deal with Jenny, is what I think. Blue and Harry have promised to play some "real" polo with Tommy; they have assured me it will be gentle and safe, and I must say I trust them. I trust Blue, at least, and Harry when he is with Blue. Maybe that's all a boy needs, a friend who is steady and kind. Tommy has his own pony, a gift from True and Emma, who dearly loves what Eveline calls her "Miss Bountiful" role.

Eveline doesn't mock; in fact, I believe she is the one who instigates many of the "Miss Bountiful" gifts, sometimes in league with Amalie. How else to explain a box of colored pencils for artistic little Charlie Yoshida or the songbooks for Julia Kaae?

Eveline will move to Honolulu with True and Emma; they are taking a house where Eveline will be able to take day students if she wishes, while Emma is at school. Emma is fond of her governess and glad that she will be staying on with them. She is well aware that the Colonel and Miss Laiana prefer Eveline to True. True knows as well and doesn't care a jot. What True does care about is being able to come and go to Mau'loa when she pleases, and with Eveline there to watch after Emma, she will be able to do just that.

There is such hustle and bustle with everyone getting ready to go to the polo match. Since a school holiday has been called, Lani will go to Opihi, to study with her kumu hula, Ilima. I do believe Rachel would keep her if she could!

Tommy and I will be all alone for a few days. Pono has gone up into the high pasture to find an old bull that is wily enough to have escaped several good hands.

* * *

We are going to Honolulu after all, Tommy and Blue and Harry as well. Jock sent word that he needs the boys, that Kamaki has a sore muscle and might not be able to finish a match, and that Patrick Rourke has managed to get a bad bruise in a rough and tumble as well. Pono thinks that Jock is getting skittery, that's all. When Blue and Harry came out to tell us that they'd be going after all, Tommy just went wild and begged to go with them. He wore us down; finally Pono said I should go and take him. Only Harry is gloomy; Jock asked him to come, and that's a mighty pull for a boy. I suppose he figures he might as well go now, that he will have to face his mother sooner or later.

Carter Dole was the first to suspect that something was up, when Evan petitioned for the Mau'loa team to play the Honolulu club in an exhibition game.

"Your boys any good?" Carter asked when Evan stopped by his Honolulu office.

"Good enough to give your team a workout," Evan had answered. Then he added, "Especially the ponies."

Carter Dole wasted no time, and once the word was out, it seemed like most of Honolulu turned out for the game between Oahu's Royals (a strange enough name for the Mission Boys and their relatives) and the cowboys from Mau'loa.

The Oahu Polo Club had never seen anything like it: our Mau'loa Boys, dressed in proper white breeches but with bright flowered shirts, cowboy boots and cowboy hats clamped to their heads with bands. Cheers, jeers and much laughter lifted from the crowd, which had gathered early and pressed forward close to the field with its beautifully tended grass. There were dog carts and carriages and a few open automobiles, ladies sitting inside with their parasols drawn. Hawaiians crowded up to the field, along with a scattering of Japanese and Chinese, until the whole 300-yard length was filled on both sides.

Jock Gibbons' entrance created a stir in the Royals' enclosure. A Marston said to a Baldwin, a note of alarm in his voice, "How long has Jock been with the cowboys?"

Each player had a fresh pony for each chukka. Michael would start on Four to Go. Evan wanted to make certain their prize pony got a good showing, and he wasn't certain how long the Boys would last against the Oahu Club.

The Royals cantered onto the field with perfect assurance, elegant in their brown boots and white breeches and shirts. They called to each other in easy banter, certain of themselves, certain of their place in the world.

"Oh my," True murmured, in spite of herself.

"Steady, girl," Jock told her in a low voice, then added, "and look at their ponies."

True looked and turned back to Jock, a wide, satisfied smile on her lips.

Michael rode out on Four to Go to cross sticks with the captain of the Royals, a muscular young man with a full moustache. There was the click of wood against wood, the ball was rolled out and, with a surprising quick wrist stroke, Michael dribbled the ball over to Kamaki, who smacked it hard down the center in a pattern they had practised for months; Patrick pulled out to the right, his opposite bearing down hard on him; with seconds to spare he leaned forward and passed it to Manu, who tapped it neatly for a goal.

The crowd erupted. Someone shouted, "Three minutes, three hits, one goal" and others picked it up, chanting it out.

Only Jock did not join in. "What's the matter?" Evan asked.

"We've made fools of them. They'll be hoppin' mad now and ready to fight."

Jock was right. When the game resumed, the Royals, faces grim, quickly claimed the ball and ran it down the field. They'd been too lax; now they'd put these cowboys in their place.

Michael could feel the tension in Four to Go; he lay forward. "Let's go, girl . . . stay with me now." As if the pony understood, it sprang after the ball, overtaking its opposite and nudging him away, turning and pulling up short until Michael found himself with a shot under the pony's neck.

Kamaki was waiting; once more the Boys had the ball and were moving with it, but this time they were stopped short. A tall Royal was waiting, neatly skimmed the ball out from under their noses and sent it flying to the opposite goal.

Michael wasn't sure what had happened; all he knew was that they had been out-maneuvered. Four to Go quivered under him. That was when Michael understood: they were going to have to play a fast, galloping game, as rough as they could make it. Let the gentlemen play a gentleman's game—it wasn't for them.

He raised his hand in the air and emitted a war whoop; the others whooped in answer, and so did all who had come from Mau'loa. Jock Gibbons raised his hat to them and spat a dark brown stream into the green grass. War!

No one could remember a game like it, ever. "The wolves are attacking," someone shouted; dirt and curses rent the air; horses went down and got up again. Riders bumped and jostled, the umpires were hard put to see the action through the maze of sticks. Once a ball came sailing through the air, Manu reached high overhead, gave it a solid thwack worthy of baseball and several men ducked as it went sailing straight for the goal and through, to tie the game at two each.

Carter Dole came bounding over to Evan. "These are madmen you've brought," he shouted over the noise. "My god, man, do you know what you've done? You've turned the game into a brawl!"

Jock heard and chortled over the roar: "This is the way the game was meant to be played, brother. Best you get your pretty boys out of there before they get trampled by these upcountry louts!"

At that moment the "pretty boys" scored a quick, clean goal, cheering to each other that "now we've got it, now we're going together." At the end of the third chukka, the score was three to two in favor of the home team.

Patrick Rourke signaled to his teammates. "They didn't think we'd get this far, boys."

And Michael answered him, "It's not far enough, Pat. We need to win." Kamaki and Manu raised their hats to cool their heads.

Then Kamaki said: "All the peoples come too close on the side, the Oahu horses shy from there, did you see? Afraid they go crashing through the peoples. Our ponies do any kine play, near or far don't make no matter, stop short like that."

"It's worth a try," Michael said. "Their best game is smooth and down the center. We've thrown them off with our wild play, but they handle the ball better. Let's see if we can throw them off long enough to score two more goals."

New ponies were brought in, but the men who mounted them were covered with sweat, their shirts soaked through and their white pants streaked with dirt and grass stains.

Frantic galloping and wheeling marked the fourth chukka; the Boys forced the action to the outside rim of the field, so close to the crowd that they sprayed clumps of dirt on them. Kamaki was right; they had that one narrow strip of field almost to themselves, but it took them five of the seven minutes to score the tie goal.

There would be one more chukka to decide who would emerge the victor. The players slid off their horses, their faces streaked with dirt and sweat and tension.

Jock brought out Four to Go, Michael mounted without so much as taking up the reins, guided him with his knees through a classic figure eight. The crowd cheered the little mare, cheered the ragtag team of cowboys who had come rattling into this green haven and turned it into a free-for-all.

The Royals had a look of grim determination. They sat straight, staring ahead, speaking now and then to one another, but to no one else.

Michael, on Four to Go, shot the ball to the far side, forcing the game so close to the crowd that the people scattered. Then Manu flew in from nowhere to send the ball rocketing to the other side and the other crowd.

The Royals would hit the ball out into the mid-ground, but they could not keep it there long enough to score. The Boys would dribble it back over to the boundary lines; after each skirmish they had managed to move it forward some several yards. They would have only one clear shot; it would have to work.

Patrick took the shot. It was blocked by a Royal, and the action moved furiously down the field. Manu streaked to guard the goal, while Michael on Four in Hand wheeled and turned and seemed to dive into the fray. When he emerged, the ball was bobbing toward the side boundary and a solid phalanx of people crowded close.

A Royal was hell-bent for it, his pony racing full-out, but pulled up short before the crowd. Four to Go raced in, under the other pony's nose, to guide Michael to the shot. One long lateral pass to Kamaki, so solid the crack of it electrified the air, and the rest of the field was left behind. The ball went sailing through the posts only seconds before the gun bark that marked the end of the game.

Women screamed, men shouted themselves hoarse, and children raced around squealing. Harry pounded Blue on the back, and Blue let out a bellow that was returned by Kamaki and Manu. Pails of water were poured over the players. Tears flowed down Jock Gibbons' leather cheeks. True saw and touched his arm, then she moved to Four to Go, and the horse nuzzled her.

"What a great girl you are, what a great, good girl," she kept murmuring, over and over again.

When all the shouting and commotion finally settled, Evan went looking for Harry. "He left with his mother," someone told him. "This lady came up to him and said he had to come to her house, and he went."

Evan found Blue sitting at the edge of the road in front of Jenny's house, his broad face forlorn. "He's gone, out the back door she say. Too mad, angry words, plenty pilikia." Plenty *trouble*.

Two days later, Evan was led to a brothel in Chinatown. On the bed was a girl, her face battered and covered with blood, her arms thick with angry bruises. Slumped in the corner was Harry Coulter.

38

May 1914

Emma draped the chain and pendant from her finger and watched as the motion of the ship made it swing like a pendulum. "There is nothing to do," she complained to her mother. "There are only babies and old people. The captain is a bore, and the only handsome young officer has offensive breath."

True looked up from the letter she had just started. "Surely a pretty young lady of fifteen can find some way to amuse herself," she offered.

"I know what you're really thinking," Emma said and pouted. "You want to say, 'I told you to go with that group of Wellesley girls who are touring Europe with three young women teachers.' But I wouldn't have had more fun, because they are older than I am and they've been to school on the Mainland, while I had to stay back in Honolulu. They wouldn't have anything to do with me. Elsie says . . ."

True put down her pen and turned to her daughter. "Please, no more *Elsie says* . . . The only reason I'm glad that you'll be in school in California this year is that I won't have to hear 'Elsie says' anymore."

Emma pouted. "She *is* my best friend."

True thought about telling her Elsie was a nasty little gossip, but she decided against it. She and Emma were going to be together every day for the next eight weeks; best not to argue over things that couldn't be changed.

Emma sighed dramatically. "When will I ever get to be a part of it? Of *life,* I mean."

"Let's go take a turn around the deck; if we're going to talk about *life* we might as well get some exercise."

At that Emma wailed, "You don't take me seriously, you

don't! You think I don't know a thing, but I do know things. Elsie told me . . ."

At mention of Elsie, True frowned and the frown so angered Emma that she blurted, "On our last night, when I stayed at her house, Elsie told me a secret. She said her mother had made her promise never to say a word to me, but she felt that if we were truly best friends we should have no secrets."

True braced herself. She knew what was coming, and she knew that Emma was watching her.

"Elsie said that Harry Coulter was found in a *house of ill repute*. And that he had done something terrible to one of the *people* there. He hurt her. Elsie didn't know exactly what it was that he did because no one would say. Did you know this, Mama?"

"I knew. What else did she tell you?" True asked, her voice tight enough to make Emma start to twist the chain of the pendant.

"She said that Mrs. Coulter came to her mother's house one day. She hadn't been invited—she just came to the door. She was dressed strangely—it was a hot day and she was wearing some of the wool clothes she had when she lived in Boston. Anyway, without even being asked she walked into the parlor and sat down and just started telling these things. Elsie's mother says she is mad. She told her the most awful things."

True looked at her daughter, at the quivering chin and pink mouth. "Do you want to tell me what she said?" True asked.

Emma shook her head.

"Then shall I tell you?"

Her daughter looked up, her eyes bright with fear.

"We were talking about *life* a few minutes ago. Life is sometimes cruel. Last spring Jenny Coulter started going to the homes of some of the old Island families, like Elsie's, to tell in unrelenting detail just how badly life has treated her. She told them that I am the cause of all her sorrow." True took a breath to keep her voice under control. "She even tells a story about your father. About how she went to him to accuse me . . . Jenny Coulter seems to believe that her news killed your father, because he died that day. You know from Harry what the accusation was."

Emma flushed and turned away.

"No, listen now. You've just said how grown-up you are, so perhaps it's time you learned something about the grown-up world. Bad things do happen, Emma. Sorrowful things. You lost your father when you were still a baby. Jenny Coulter didn't cause his death, he died from a brain hemorrhage. You know that because people you trust have told you so. After that—in a way—Evan did become your father. And through the years I have come to care deeply for him, yes. You told me the other day that Elsie told you people called you an "heiress" and said you were the richest young woman in Hawaii. That is so, and it is all because of Evan Coulter. He took a ranch that was nothing and made it the most productive and profitable in the Pacific."

"I know that, Mother. You don't have to tell me again."

True took a deep breath.

"You got the benefit of Evan's attention and care when you were young. Harry's life might have been different, if he had stayed with his father."

Emma cut in, "Mrs. Coulter told Elsie's mama that Harry had hurt two young women in Boston. He smashed one's nose, and her father wanted Harry sent to prison. It was a terrible scandal. That's why Mrs. Coulter had to come back."

"Let's go walk," True said.

The sea air revived Emma. "All the young people seem to be travelling second class," she observed. "Isn't that too bad?"

Paris, June 30, 1914

Dear Evan:

I don't know when or how you will get this letter, but I must talk to you now, this minute, to calm myself. Your worst fears have come to pass. Two days ago the Austrian Archduke and his wife were assassinated and war is imminent. The American Embassy has told us we should leave as quickly as possible. But Evan, we can't. Emma is in hospital with a high fever, and I dare not take her out and aboard ship right now.

I wish we had never come. For a time we travelled with a

group of Wellesley girls, including one of the Athertons from Honolulu and the pretty little Judd girl, and Emma was having such a happy time. They are accompanied by three young women teachers whom they address as "mam'selles," and the prettiest of these seems to have charmed a wealthy American of some influence, a Mr. Winston Snowcroft. He is on the board of directors of an oil company, as well as a shipping line, and has managed to get the girls passage home on an oil tanker. The officers have given up their quarters to them, and the captain was willing to take us as well. Then Emma got a terrible sore throat and high fever, and the hotel's doctor felt she must be hospitalized. As soon as they can bring down the fever, we will move to Calais, where we will get the first boat to England, and hence—if Emma is well enough—home.

We did not get to Deauville, as you must have guessed. I suppose they have fine polo there, but I'm as happy with our rough and ready games on the ranch. I did meet a gentleman in England who saw Four to Go play at West-chester last season, when Harry Payne Whitney rode him against the Hurlingham team. "You Americans are a wild bunch," the Brit said in that oh-so-know-it-all accent. "Your boys aren't pretty horsemen, but even that seems to play to their favor—they sit so far forward they can thump the ball from under the pony's head." I told him that if he really wants to see some wild polo, he should come to our island. So you see, Mau'loa Stables has some fame in the world.

The doctor has just come to tell me that Emma's fever is down, and that he thinks it would be well to move her quickly now. They will have her ready to go in half an hour. The Germans have invaded; the people we meet, in the hotel, in the hospital, are all so distracted by their own concerns, that it is difficult to get them to concentrate on ours. One fine bit of luck: The gentleman who helped the Wellesley girls get out has sent a young American assistant from a shipping line to help us make our way home. If we can get to England within four days, one of his company's ships will take us on. Our automobile is waiting.

July 5, 1914
At sea on board the Housatonic

Dear Martha,

I know Evan has kept you informed of our misadventures, so you know why you have not heard from me all these past weeks. Now we are settled into a fine big stateroom on this American liner, and I've finally time to catch you up.

Emma is feeling fit and sassy again, and the young man who helped us flee Paris, Mr. Devereaux Aldren—who says we must call him "Dev"—has attached himself to us and is doing all he can to make us comfortable.

Emma is delighted, as he is the sort of man young girls find attractive—rather showy good manners, clothes cut stylishly in the French design, scarcely ever a wrinkle allowed, and he does everything with a flourish. He is in his very early thirties, I would say. Emma thinks him "divine," while I find him rather callow.

At dinner each night, he offers each of us an arm and we make a rather ostentatious entrance. Emma loves it, so I go along with the pomp and am glad that she is not complaining about a lack of company.

Since she is still recuperating, I insist she turn in early each evening, to her dismay. Dev joshes her until she leaves, laughing—a charming little flirt, she is. It made me think of Vicky's letters to us from England, and what fun she had flirting with the young men. I can't but wonder how many of those young men of Vicky's are now officers in the British and French armies, on their way to hold the line against the Bosch.

The war in Europe does not seem particularly to interest our Mr. Aldren; it was not until last evening, after Emma went to bed, that I discovered what does interest him. He asked if I wanted to take a turn on the deck; since I do this every night before retiring, I agreed. The questions started rather timidly, but quickly escalated. Devereaux Aldren is not a subtle man.

It took him precisely four turns to discover that I have not remarried by choice, and that I have no interest whatsoever in a romantic entanglement with anyone. His questions were larded with the most obvious compliments: He had thought I was his own age, which is thirty-one. When he first saw Emma and me at the hospital, he had assumed I was her sister. Did you know, Martha Moonie Rourke, that your old friend "is as elegant as a swan" or that she has "hair like the moonlight trail on the sea at night"?

I did not embarrass him by laughing, though I had an awful urge. Instead, I decided to bore him to death with talk of horses and cows; he knows little about the former and nothing about the latter. The next day he went off to play checkers and chatter with Emma. He doesn't seem to have taken my rebuff too personally, though we no longer make our grand entrance to dinner each evening. The curtain seems to have fallen on the courting of the rich widow.

October 7, 1914, Oakland, California

Dear Martha,

Yes, yes and no. Yes, Emma has settled nicely into her studies at Mills Seminary; yes, I am keeping myself busy enough—there are several stud farms within an easy ride, and I am able to do some good work on the thoroughbreds; and no, I will never get used to being away from Mau'loa. People come rushing across this country to get to this place, California, as if it were the end of the rainbow. But the only rainbows I ever think of are those that arch across the mountains in the afternoons, and I miss the green hills and the sweet smell and the trades blowing against my face . . . and I miss all of you. Terribly.

Evan says I must not complain, and I will not. But two long years . . . I don't let myself think about anything but the summer. It helps that Evan is coming to visit in a month; I've collected so much information on new breeds of swine and chickens and cattle that he has to come see them and arrange for shipping. I have asked Evan to talk you and Pono and the children into coming as well; Pono can return with the animals, and you and the children can stay on for a good visit. Please consider. You might enjoy San Francisco—it is a lively place, with good theatres and restaurants. Emma loves to take the ferry across the Bay to the city and will be sure to show you all around. I'm so lonely for someone to talk to—I never was any good about the social niceties. Emma asked that I give a tea for her teachers and some of the other students' parents, and I had to ask the housekeeper how to go about it. Happily, she knew just what to do, and

I suppose the tea was a success, at least Emma felt so. I found it monumentally boring.

Remember my telling you about the young man, Dev Aldren, who helped us get out of France? He has been sending clever little notes to Emma. When at first she seemed to be secreting them away, I asked her to allow me to read them. In fact, they are quite innocent—though if you saw how Emma treats them, tied with ribbons and placed in a velvet box, you would think they contained passionate confessions of unending love. What a romantic little goose she has become! I think you and I were never that way, but then we did not have the sort of childhood that allowed the luxury of romance.

Winona Wright sat on the lanai of her brother's cottage, which she had taken for her own, fanning herself. Jenny was in motion in the rocking chair, her toes just touching the floor to send her sailing back and forth.

"If True comes, you must send her away," Jenny said.

"Now you know very well that True is in California with Emma," Winona repeated, as she did seven or eight times each day.

Jenny wouldn't be mollified. "I won't see True, and I won't see Evan, and I won't see Harry. Not again, not ever. They are lovers, True and Evan. They always have been, since she was a little girl. Not even big enough to know what it meant, but she found out. He saw her without her clothes. Did you know that?"

Aunt Winona cautioned, "Don't talk like that in front of Martha. That's foolish talk. People don't like it, Jenny. Now you know what we said—if you have to say it out loud, no one else can hear. That is what you promised. Don't you remember?"

Jenny looked at me, her eyes clouded and vague. "Tell me who you are again, dear," she asked in an old woman's voice, touching my hand with fingertips that were cold and blue.

"I'm Martha Rourke, Jenny. I used to be Martha Moon. I'm glad you've come to stay with Aunt Winona. It's peaceful out here by the ocean. You'll be good company for each other. And it's so nice to have all the schoolchildren nearby."

"I have no children. Not Harry. He is away. I gave him money and he left and that's all I know. He can't go back to Boston because of what he did, the girls . . ."

"Shush, Jenny. Don't talk about Harry or you'll start crying again. Why don't you play some music, that always makes you feel better."

Obediently, Jenny went into the cottage, cranked the Victrola and put on "Humoresque." You could hear her whistling the melody.

For once, Aunt Winona sat in silence.

"It *was* good of you to bring her here," I told her.

"Oh, it's good for me, too," Aunt said. "Since Brother died, I've needed someone to watch after. And she listens to me, or at least she sits here when I get the urge to talk, and it's not like I'm talking to the walls. We keep each other company I suppose. And she's no longer knocking on all the doors in town, telling her sad tale of woe."

Aunt shook her head. "I hope you will tell True that I did my best to follow Jenny's trail, to explain that she was sick with grief over her boy so that her mind was playing tricks on her. How he turned out so bad, I'll never know. She says he's a beast, and maybe he is. That girl in Chinatown—three times she walked all the way out here to ask for money. Sad creature, her face never did heal right. Harry's in the war, did you know? Signed up to fight with England. Jenny got some sort of official notice, I don't know from where."

The record had finished and the needle was scratching, but Jenny hadn't noticed. She continued whistling, as if she were waiting for someone to turn her off.

Summer 1915, Mau'loa

We met Emma and True at the dock with a Hawaiian band and hula dancers—Lani among them—with piles of leis which we looped around their necks until you could scarcely see their chins and with many warm embraces. Emma's school friends—one large and dour, the other small and cheerful—seemed quite overwhelmed with this Hawaiian greeting. Colonel Toby, his white hair shining in the afternoon sun, led them ashore with great ceremony.

Liko had arranged everything, including a flower-strewn carriage pulled by horses wearing crowns of sweet-smelling plumeria. Evan had ordered the Wakefield home, Kolonahe, cleaned inside and out for Emma's return; in her absence the gardens had been tended by a team of Japanese workmen, and even the polo field had a covering of grass that seemed to set the red earth to glow.

The compound at Kolonahe had never looked better; the Colonel and Miss Laiana moved in for the summer like returning royalty, occupying their old rooms as if they had never left.

Still, if they thought the place belonged to them, Emma soon corrected the impression. She had come home with sketches of changes she wished made: a new pergola in the garden, a conservatory and a music room added to the main house. Two years in Honolulu and one in California had taught her the duties, and the benefits, of being a princess. Vicky had possessed the title but not the kingdom; Emma had the kingdom and took the title for granted. She never doubted, as Vicky had, her mandate to rule.

All summer long a steady stream of young visitors came from the other islands, girls and boys Emma knew from school. There were swimming parties and luaus, hikes up the mountain with telescopes, long horseback journeys up to the volcano. Blue was called in to give polo lessons, and Kamaki and Manu and the two Rourkes would be commandeered to play with the young people. When Emma came riding up to the ranch office, Bradley would tell whatever hands happened to be about to move out if they didn't want to be shanghaied for a roping contest, one of Emma's favorite diversions.

For the most part, the hands took it in stride. Evan always excused them, though it usually meant a gang would go out one or two men short.

Some of the old hands were reminded of the days when the Colonel would pull them away from their work to entertain his guests. But now they did not complain; in the years since Evan came, the ranch had prospered, their families had homes of their own and medical care when they needed it, and there was always plenty of food and an extra pig or a beef for their luaus. Life was better now than any of them could remember, and the men showed their gratitude in their devotion to Emma, the ranch's little princess.

True left Emma and her friends in the care of the Wake-

fields and Evan, in the guest house he has occupied all these
years, and came back to live at the Home Place with Liko
and Amalie. It was good having her down the road again;
often I didn't realize how much I missed her until she was
gone and back again. Then I would wake in the morning and
feel restored.

Early one morning, not long before she was to leave again,
we headed out for a long ride up the mountain. True wanted
to be out with the paniolos, she wanted to see the ranch and
feel how it worked. We were passing the south cow pasture
when she motioned me to stop. A large bull was mounting a
cow, his great pink ule thrusting in and out, the cow standing
passively. It took just a few minutes, and he was down. "He'll
service twenty cows," True said, as if suddenly it had some
import, "and almost ninety percent of those cows will calve."

I offered, "Pono took a gang out on the branding drive—
they'll be culling out the cows today, to take out the barren
ones and those that are too old to bear."

She paused, straightened her back. "Have you ever
thought what a cruel business this is? The females are here
to give birth and the males are castrated and fattened for
slaughter."

I looked at her. "It's a good business just now, because of
the war. With Australia not exporting any cattle it is up to
the ranches on the Islands to provide all the meat for the
U.S. troops stationed here. Pono says we're running about
as hard as we can. That means the profits are as good as
they've ever been."

True pursed her lips. "Maybe I could think that was good
news if I hadn't been in Paris when it started. Then I
wouldn't have a picture in my head. I believe we were in one
of the last automobiles to get out of the city."

We moved off, cantering along through the grasses. When
finally we stopped again we were on a ledge looking out over
the charred volcanic mass of a gigantic lava flow that, a
hundred years ago, made its way all the long miles to the
ocean in the distance.

True shook her head. "I love this place. Even with the
cruelty—the threat of the volcano and the slaughterhouse
and the cowboys that get thrown from their horses and
break their necks. If I could stay here forever, I would. I
dread the idea of going back to Oakland. I wish . . ."

I knew what she wished. That Evan wouldn't insist she go with Emma, that he would allow her to call Eveline back from the position she had taken with a family in Honolulu. They had argued about it more than once, True and Evan.

"It's awful to say," True went on, "but young men—some not so young—are beginning to look at Emma as if she were breeding stock. They study her pedigree, but mostly they study the profit sheet of the ranch. Evan believes I'm the only one who can protect her from predators. That's what he calls them . . . predators. Fortune hunters like Dev Aldren."

I thought about this for a time. "Who's to say what makes a good marriage? I don't think we know. Perhaps you have to allow Emma to decide."

"Emma is a child," she said.

I smiled. "Yes," I agreed, "but so were you when you decided on Evan Coulter."

True dismounted, picked a wild morning glory growing in a creeping vine, handed it up to me. "Emma isn't like me," she said. "Emma is more like your royal parents than either of us are. She loves to be surrounded by people and laughter; she wants to be entertained. The theatre, dancing, concerts, restaurants. You saw it when you came to San Francisco. She enjoys having a good deal of money, she spends it easily, and doesn't ask herself how it is made. That's the peculiar part—Emma *is* a Wakefield."

Three days later, Emma came to say good-bye. She sat in my kitchen, eating ohelo berry jam out of a jar, watching as I kneaded bread dough.

"Don't you know, Auntie, this is one of my favorite places on the island. You always did have time to stop and listen to me, that's why I came here so much. Mama was always at the horse barn. I don't remember once when Mama made bread."

I said nothing; I would not speak against True, as I suspected Emma wanted me to.

"Can you keep a secret, Aunt Martha?" she asked.

"I've been told it is one of my few talents," I answered, then added, "Your mother and I have always trusted each other with our secrets."

Emma laughed, a bright girlish trilling laugh, and said, "Well then, I suppose I'd best keep my little secret to myself."

39

May 1916

It had been washed up and was caught at that place where the waves break on the sand: a mound that moved with the lift of the incoming wave, shifting and rocking this way and back again, a dark offering of the sea.

Winona Wright was drawn to the ocean in the early light; her heart thumped heavy in her chest; she saw it and moaned and prayed as she splashed into the water. She knew the heavy woolen coat, the pale spill of hair.

It was the letter, she told herself. *It was the letter.* She pulled at the weight of it, heavy with death; she cried and tugged and pleaded with God to give her the strength to drag it to shore. A wave crashed, knocking her over. She held hard so she would not be washed out; the force of the wave lifted and shook her. She could hear the thick beating of her heart, throbbing in her ears. Another wave came in, lifting her and filling her mouth and nose. She coughed and choked and, little by little, pulled her burden into the shallows where she sat cradling the lifeless body of Jenny Coulter.

June 1916

Emma stretched out on the deck chair, pulled the robe up to her chin and yawned; it was too early, much too early to be awake and out on deck, but she had promised she would come. She smiled to herself in the morning chill. After so many months, so many letters, finally they would be able to talk together, perhaps to touch. A small thrill moved through her stomach.

She hadn't liked it when Phoebe Penobscot blurted, "He's handsome, but so much older, isn't he?" Phoebe was a child;

she didn't understand. Phoebe and the other girls coming home for the summer spent the whole of their time trying to find a way to talk to the boys in second class, those coming home from a year at Stanford or Yale.

Dev had laughed about it to her. "You can see the reason the parents send their sons second class and their daughters first. They need a barrier to keep them apart—wouldn't do to mix the breeds without expert supervision."

Emma had been shocked, but she managed not to show it. Dev was a sophisticate, and he must think she was too, and it wasn't as if she didn't know about breeding—she had grown up on a ranch, after all. Her mother had thoroughbreds. She wondered what Dev would think if she described to him how her mother and the grooms would be right there when a stallion covered a mare. How the mare's tail would be wrapped and water would be sprayed on her pulsating privates, how the groom would wash the stallion's enormous red ule just before they let him mount the mare. How quick it was, several strong thrusts, the mare quivering. Emma smiled, thinking how shocked Dev would be if she described this to him.

He came carrying a mug of hot tea, and when she put her hands around it to gather in the warmth, he put his hands over hers.

Speaking with slow deliberation, he looked directly into her eyes and said, "I am very happy to be here with you, Emma Wakefield."

They met this way, at five-thirty in the morning, for the first two days of the voyage home after Emma's second year at Mills Seminary. Then Mrs. Penobscot, who was acting as Emma's chaperone, came down with some stomach malady that kept her in her cabin all day long, so that she emerged only for a brief walk on the deck mid-morning and early evening.

Emma volunteered to accompany Mrs. Penobscot on these slow strolls, in part to allay any suspicions she might have about Dev, and in part to placate Phoebe, who spent a good part of her day in second class, where she should not have been, pursuing a Maui boy.

For the rest of the voyage, Emma and Dev Aldren spent every day together. He listened intently as she talked about herself. He asked questions of her and nodded with under-

standing at her long, breathless answers. Her mother had
never married again because of Uncle Evan, she believed. It
was hard to explain; you had to know Uncle Evan to understand. He was so kind to her; he always seemed to know
what she was thinking and feeling, and though he wasn't
really her father, she felt as if he was, she told Devereaux
Aldren. Sometimes she felt as if she loved Uncle Evan more
than she loved her own mother. It wasn't that she didn't love
her mother, she told him. It was that her mother was just so
different. She didn't care a whit about, well, the things mothers usually care about. It was embarrassing sometimes, and
then she felt ashamed for even feeling that . . . but there was
no changing it. And of course, people talked, which drove
her mad but didn't seem to trouble her mother at all.

He observed: "She is diligent, you have to say that for her.
Getting letters through to you has been a major logistical
triumph. How did the Snow Queen allow you make this
voyage without her?" he asked.

"Why do you call her the Snow Queen?" Emma asked,
feeling disloyal.

"All that icy resolve, I suppose. And the fair hair and
glacial eyes. Your mother lacks a certain, how shall I put
it—cordiality. At least where I am concerned."

Emma deflected the subject by answering his question:
"She went back to Honolulu early. Someone died, a friend
of a friend." It was not worth the effort, she told herself, to
explain about Mrs. Coulter. "And I was left in what she
thought was the very competent care of Mrs. Penobscot."

At that Emma started laughing; he pulled her to him to
stifle the sounds, she lifted her face to him and kissed him.
Softly at first, on the lips. And then with a hungry, new
passion. By the end of the journey, Emma was slipping out
at night to meet Dev, to cling to him in the shadow of the
lifeboats, to feel his hands on her body and his mouth on
hers, crushing and urgent.

"My dear, sweet love," he said to her, kissing the top of
her hair and rocking her in his arms. "My wonderful girl."

True did not arrive in time for the funeral. Only Evan and
Aunt Winona and I were there to mourn Jenny, and a few
of the old Barrows family servants. A blanket of white roses
lay over the casket, and I found myself thinking of the pretty

young woman Jenny had been, wearing a crisp blue striped dress, fresh on a warm summer's day. The minister read the Twenty-third Psalm, as Evan had requested, and beseeched the Lord in heaven to take our Sister Jenny unto him, and to give her the Peace that is beyond all understanding for us poor sinners left on Earth.

Aunt Winona sobbed, the old servants wailed, and tears slipped down my face for all the pain suffered, all the disappointment. Only Evan stood stoically, no discernable emotion in his face. Later, Aunt Winona would recognize a slight trembling of his hand as he read the letter.

"Madam," it began, "This is to advise you that your son, Harry, is to be released from hospital within a fortnight and, as I explained in a previous letter, will be sent to his home in the city of Honolulu, the island of Oahu, in the American Territory of Hawaii, under the care of ship's officers. Our country will be forever grateful to those brave young men from other nations who came to our aid, certain of the right of our cause."

Four days later, a short, balding man led Harry Coulter down the gangway of a British merchant ship. He walked haltingly, a summer straw hat pulled low over his face as if to shield him from the bright tropical light, and was delivered into the hands of his father.

"Son," was all Evan could say. A trembling overtook his body, bruising his thoughts, his breath.

Harry Coulter turned toward his father. The flesh of the right side of his face had melted and reformed in sworls, like the lava beds on the scorched sides of Mauna Kea. An unseeing eye peered out through the angry scars.

"Do you think this is enough?" Harry asked.

True paced the length of the parlor at Kolonahe, then back again.

"Devereaux Aldren is in the Islands, in Honolulu?" she repeated, as if she hadn't heard correctly.

On guard, Emma answered, "His company has sent him here. He has a position in Honolulu."

"And quite by chance he came on the same ship that brought you?"

Emma flushed. "I suppose so."

"Don't lie to me!" True snapped. "You knew he was going to be on that ship. You planned it—and you did it behind my back. I have always trusted you, Emma. I never believed you would . . ."

Emma stood; she was not so tall as her mother and could not hold her gaze. Her lip fell into a pouting position. "The only thing I've done behind your back is to write letters."

"And receive them," True added dryly. "Dev is no child, Emma. He knows better. He should have come forward like a man, if he wanted to court you."

Emma walked over to a large fern placed before a window. "I hate these awful big ferns in the house. They belong outside, in the woods. I'm going to ask the plant boy to take them away."

"We aren't talking about ferns, Emma. We are talking about Dev and his skulking around behind my back."

Emma whirled around, angry. "And what would you have said if he had come to you? You haven't liked him from the beginning. He knows that and so do I. You think him silly, foppish. Well, he isn't, Mother. He is thoughtful and kind and he loves me. He does. I know it!"

True simply looked at her. *Love.* Dear God, what had happened in a week at sea? She would have to be careful, now. Emma would be eighteen in a few months; she could make her own decisions then.

True tried to smile at her daughter and succeeded only in a grin. Emma, recognizing this as a signal that her mother did not want to argue, smiled in return.

"I will try to be more understanding, Emma. Sometimes it is hard for me to remember that you are growing up. Evan mentioned it the other day. He wants you to come by to see him this week. Can you do that?"

Emma frowned. "Where is Harry?"

Emma did not want to see Harry. In fact, she would rather he was not on the ranch. Gossip in Honolulu was raging; people seemed to think he was the cause of his mother's death. During the few days she had spent with her grandparents, Emma had been questioned by any number of people—about Evan and Harry and what had happened—and it had made her feel odd, as if she were somehow tainted by it.

"You don't have to worry about Harry," True said, disappointed that Emma did not seem to feel any sympathy for

Evan. "He is on Opihi Island with Rachel and the Hawaiians. Evan has sent Blue Kapua to watch over him. We think he will be there for a long while."

Emma pulled herself up self-righteously and said, "It's too bad he came back at all—it would have been better for everyone, certainly for his poor mother, if he could have died with dignity in France."

True pressed her lips hard together. "Is that what Elsie and her friends are saying?"

She could see from Emma's face that she had guessed right.

"You might tell your old friend Elsie that wishing Harry Coulter dead is something less than Christian. Let me tell you something, Emma, and I want you to listen to this as carefully as you've ever listened to anything. Do you know the first thing Harry said to his father when he got off the ship?" She didn't wait for an answer. "It was to ask a question, and the question was, *'Do you think this is enough?'* " True looked hard at her daughter, demanding her attention, before she went on. Once more she repeated Harry's question: " *'Do you think this is enough?'* The boy's face is shattered, half of it is burned so badly that he is blind in one eye. He has to walk with a cane now, from an old wound. And what he wants to know is, *'Do you think this is enough?'* "

Emma squirmed under her mother's stern gaze. "What does it mean?" she asked.

"Ah," True said. "Finally you ask the right question. Harry wants to know if he has suffered enough, given enough to atone for his sins. And do you know something, my darling Emma? He can't stop asking, because no matter how many times you tell him yes, it is enough, he can never believe it himself. That's why Evan has sent him to the Hawaiians—because they are kind and capable of forgiveness. Your friend Elsie may not be able to understand or feel any pity for Harry, but I expect more of you. Harry is only twenty-three, remember. His life is scarcely over. Dev Aldren is ten years older."

Emma was chagrined; "I'm sorry, Mama," she capitulated. "It is awful, what they're saying about Harry and his mother. And Uncle Evan, how sad for him. Of course I'll go see him this week—I would have anyway—it never seems like I'm home until I've had an *apo* from Uncle Evan."

True saw her chance and took it. "We need to talk about the trust and make arrangements for the ranch. The war has been good for business; we've had to take on more hands. We're shipping more cattle than we've ever shipped—I don't know what we'd do without Evan."

Emma looked worried. "What do you mean, 'without' him? Why would we have to do without him?"

True lifted her hands in a gesture that said she couldn't be certain. "I just thought that he might be considering Harry. He is responsible for him now—I'm not certain what that is going to mean. You know, Evan has a place over to windward. He might want . . ."

"How would we manage without him, Mama? I don't understand. I can't imagine the ranch without Uncle Evan. How can we convince him to stay?"

True shrugged. "Perhaps I'm wrong, but you should talk to him as soon as you can. See what he says."

Two days later Emma sat down with Evan in his cluttered office. She scanned the trust papers that had been drawn up and became impatient when Evan insisted on pointing out all the provisions to her. She told him that he had her full confidence; she wanted him to continue operating the ranch as he had for the past seventeen years, making all business decisions for her and her mother. True had already signed the papers; Emma quickly added her name with a flourish, kissed Evan on both cheeks and went running off, eager to drive down to the dock to meet the Inter-Island, which was bringing Dev Aldren to Mau'loa for the first time.

Harry sat in the shade of a kiawe tree and plaited banana leaves into a rough basket. Down the long arc of beach, women and children poked in the sand, chattering among themselves, searching for the minute, evanescent shells that washed up on this particular beach and nowhere else in the islands, as far as anyone knew. Blue knelt beside him and tucked a red hibiscus behind Harry's deformed ear. He lifted his hand, touched the flower, looked into Blue's big face and smiled with the half of his face that could still move.

"Time to take bath, time to eat, then sing," Blue told him.

Harry sank back on his haunches. "Time to take a bath again? I had a bath yesterday. Nobody bathes that much. Not Americans, and not the French, God knows. One thing's sure, none of them bathe and eat and sing all at once."

"Hawaiians do," Blue allowed, his big flat teeth shining out of his dark face. "Got plenty water, plenty time. Make you feel good, feel fine. Let's go, brother."

Blue had always called him "brother." Harry thought about that, about how funny it was for this hulking, childish brown man to call him brother. Sometimes he wondered what would have happened if he had had a real brother—someone who would have known what it was like. Then he thought that maybe it wouldn't have mattered, that he would have been the "bad" brother, the one who turned up and ruined things, who flailed out and hurt . . .

Blue lifted him as easily as he would lift a child, carried him laughing to the brackish pool and tossed him in. Harry caught his breath at the cold of the spring water, then settled in to let it soothe him. Blue was right, water was good. He ducked under and came up again, blowing water out of his mouth.

Rachel came with a fresh papaya and a knife. Blue cut it in two, scooped out the seeds, quickly peeled it and handed a piece to Harry, still in the water.

Rachel and Blue watched as he ate it.

"Is it good?" Rachel asked.

"Yes," Harry answered, like a polite child.

And then, his tone suddenly flat and measured, he asked, "Do you think this is enough?"

Rachel and Blue smiled down upon him,

"Yes, brother," Blue told him, "this is plenty."

It was the perfect setting for a proposal: the pergola, newly painted and planted all around with pikaki, the bold flash of birds of paradise in exquisite bloom, the softness of the summer night.

Emma closed her eyes and smiled, thinking how perfect it all was, breathing in the sweet scent of the ginger.

"You are amused?" Dev offered.

She opened her eyes. "No, not amused. Happy, just happy."

"How is that?" he asked, positioning himself on the bannister.

Emma thought it a perfect picture—the elegant, hand-

some man in the white suit, the young woman in her rose-
print cotton challis, the green-green grass spreading out,
over the pastureland and to the mountains and to the seas.
She smiled at the idea.

"You are happy tonight, I can see that," Dev joked.

She stood and moved closer to him; her hand brushed his
knee. He caught it and held it and looked at her for a long
moment.

"So serious?" she said nervously.

"It's time to be serious, I think," Dev answered. "Yes, I
am serious. I wonder if you know how very serious?"

She waited. *Now,* she said to herself. This is the right
moment, ask me now.

"Will you be my wife, Emma? Will you marry me?"

She threw herself into his arms, laughing, almost sending
them flying out of the pergola and into the pikaki. "Yes!"
she said, and "Yes!" again, in case he hadn't heard.

Then she kissed him, more passionately than he must have
expected, because after a long moment he held her away
from him and said, as if it was something he had meant to
tell her before, "I couldn't wait until you were eighteen, my
love—I just couldn't wait another day."

"I know," Emma said, moving back into his embrace. "I
don't want to wait either. If you hadn't asked me tonight, I
think I would have burst . . ."

True's permission was required, and Emma was not certain she would give it. She told him they might have to wait
until her birthday in the spring. Dev answered that he would
talk to her mother, talk to her grandfather, talk to whoever
needed to be convinced. He was certain, and if she was
certain too, they wouldn't have to wait. When they could be
alone, he held her and touched his lips to her neck and
breathed his want of her, and she whispered that she wanted
him too, that she could not believe how wonderful it was,
this feeling . . . this roaring in her ears and throbbing in her
stomach.

The interview was conducted, at True's insistence, in the
tack room at the horse barn. She asked him to meet her there
because she needed to be close by for the birth of a prize foal.
In fact, it was because she felt better able to manage in this
place, with its strong smells and rough surfaces.

He stepped into the room, careful to stand away from the dusty table, not to soil his linen suit.

"Mrs. Wakefield," he said, squinting as he came from the bright sun. "So this is where you spend so much time. I remember you telling me about your horses."

"I remember that too, Dev. You called me 'True' then—after all, you're the one who said that I wasn't all that much older than you are, so I think it will be all right if you call me 'True' now."

He frowned and shoved his hands into his pockets. She had struck the first blow. He would have to be direct. "I'm sure you must understand that my interest in Emma, at that time, was no more than what an older brother might feel. She was a charming young woman, and she made the passage a delight for me. But now it has been two very long years, and in that time my feelings—and hers as well—have changed."

True leaned against the table and began to work loose a tangled harness. "How did that happen, Dev? I mean, you a mature man and she an innocent schoolgirl? You didn't see her at all during that time, and yet your feelings changed?" The sardonic tone caused him to grimace; he took his hands out of his pockets and placed them on his hips.

"My feelings have changed," he said, his voice determined, "and so have Emma's. I have a position with American Shipping that allows me now to take on the responsibilities of marriage and a family. My prospects . . ."

True cut in and shook her head in disbelief. "Prospects? Were you going to say that your prospects are good? I don't know what else you are, Dev, but I know you are smart enough to have discovered by now that the prospects are more than good for the man who marries Emma Wakefield. That could not have escaped a worldly man like yourself."

She could see his jaw bulge. *Go ahead,* she wanted to tell him, *get angry, come at me and give me a reason to slap you across the face with this leather strap.*

Instead, he recovered himself and spoke in the cool, detached tones of a lawyer: "Emma and I are going to be married. She would like your blessing, as well as your permission to marry before her eighteenth birthday. You can withhold both, of course. That will make Emma unhappy, but I believe it will not change her resolve. We *are* going to marry, Mrs. Wakefield." It was a threat.

True looked at him with undisguised disgust. "I'm certain that's what you have had in mind all along, *Mr.* Aldren. Or at least since the day you discovered that it was the rich widow's child who would inherit the fortune. Mr. Snowcroft—you remember Mr. Snowcroft? The good gentleman who sent you to help us out of Paris? He has advised me that you have been pressing your company for a transfer to Honolulu for more than a year."

He said nothing for a while, only walked around the small room, stopping to pretend to examine a saddle left on a tall stool. His back to her, he said, "Why do you find that offensive?"

True couldn't help herself. "Because I find you offensive," she said. "Let's be clear. I don't want you to marry my daughter. I question the sincerity of your affection. I don't believe you will make her happy, and I cannot give my permission."

He looked at her and nodded. "All right," he told her, then turned as he was leaving to add, "I'm sorry that's how you feel, True. I had hoped we might be friends."

Emma sat sobbing in the big chair behind Evan's desk. He gave her his handkerchief and waited.

"Can't you please talk to her?" she pleaded. "I love him so, Uncle Evan, I do. She doesn't want to believe that—sometimes I think she doesn't believe me capable of that kind of love. She wants to keep me a child forever, but I'm not a child."

She doubled over, sobbing so that she could hardly catch her breath. Evan waited, rubbing his hands together for warmth, though the day was hot and the office stifling.

"I'll speak to your mother, though I think you should try to talk to her as well."

"She's being so rude to Dev . . . you know how she can be. If she doesn't like someone, she just acts as if they don't exist. This morning when he asked her some simple question, she just turned and walked out the door."

Evan touched her hair. It was a very light brown, more the color of his own hair. There was something about her that caught him in the chest. Dev Aldren was wrong for her, he knew that. And he knew as well as any man the consequences of a wrong marriage, but in the face of her despair he quite suddenly understood that it was going to be impossible to stop it.

"Your mother is asking that you wait, at least until your birthday . . ." he tried.

She shook her head emphatically. "I won't wait, it is so silly. What difference will a few months make?"

He touched her chin and looked into her face. "Exactly, Em. What difference? The Colonel and Miss Laiana are already talking about the celebration for your birthday. Why not wait until . . ."

Her tear-streaked face suddenly turned angry. "I won't have them giving me a party this year," she said. "I won't. They aren't any better than Mama about Dev. 'He doesn't have any family in the Islands,' they said. And 'He doesn't really have any family on the Mainland.' Of course he does; it's just that they don't consider Dev's folks anybody. 'A manager at a woolen mill'—as if there was something wrong with that. I didn't know that Papa Toby could be so mean!"

Evan put his arm around her, held her to him to calm her. "Poor little butterfly," he tried to joke. "As hard as it is for you to understand, they are worried about you—about this marriage—because you are very young, and marriage is for a long, long time. We can do a lot for you, Em, but in matters of the heart, we can't guarantee you happiness—and because we can't, we all get a little bit mean."

She looked up at him. "You too, Uncle Evan? Can't you at least be on my side?"

He touched the back of his fingers against her smooth cheek and suddenly felt weary.

"I have always been on your side, Em. I wish you would wait, but if you tell me you won't, then I'll accept it and help you in whatever way I can."

She threw her arms around him, kissed him on both cheeks and asked him to convince her mother to give permission. They wanted to be married right away, two weeks from Saturday.

At the door she turned back, smiled brightly at him and said, "We'll have to delay our wedding trip, of course. This awful war . . . Paris isn't going to be possible." Then she turned and bolted, sure that he would get her what she wanted, as if the weight of the world had been lifted from her shoulders.

They were married in the garden at Kolonahe, in front of a bank of orchids and white ginger. It was a small, private ceremony, with only the family and a few old friends present. Emma looked as much like an angel as any bride could; she stared at her husband with an overflow of love. Handsome in an immaculate white linen suit, he smiled down on her with what we hoped, in our hearts, was real devotion.

True wore a blue dress Emma had bought for her at the City of Paris and twisted her hair back from her face in an elaborate arrangement executed by the hairdresser brought over from Honolulu. It was not a Hawaiian wedding; a small string quartet played Mozart. Ned Porthauser, our own fine young preacher, was passed over in favor of the Anglican vicar of St. Paul's in Honolulu.

The Wakefields did not make the journey from Oahu. The Colonel sent their regrets: Miss Laiana was not well enough to make the journey. Instead they sent a set of gold-plated goblets, a gift to them from the King of England on the occasion of their fortieth wedding anniversary.

Three hours later Mr. and Mrs. Devereaux Aldren were on their way to Honolulu aboard a boat chartered for the occasion. There was some delay in departure; they stood on the deck and we stood on the dock, waving our good-byes much longer than anyone wished.

They moved into a small house on Beretania Street in Honolulu which would accommodate them until they could find something more suitable.

"Must you go off to work?" Emma asked at the end of their second week of marriage.

"What would you like me to do?" Dev had asked.

"Stay here with me, go swimming, take a ride into the mountains. Go looking for butterflies."

He had laughed. "A man has to work, Emma. I have to pay the rent, remember?"

"No, you don't," she said. "Uncle Evan offered to double my allowance, and I said yes. We have plenty of money to live on."

"Wasn't that kind of your 'uncle'—giving you an increase in your allowance? Such great-heartedness. He can be so generous with your money."

Emma's eyes grew worried. "I wish you wouldn't talk like that about him, Dev. It's his job to take care of the ranch and my inheritance. I've asked him to do it."

"No, love," Dev corrected her. "He was appointed your guardian by your mother. You had nothing to say about it, just as you've had nothing to say about how he runs the ranch. But all that is going to change in a few months—on your birthday."

She looked at him a long moment, dread seeping into her. "But it won't change. I signed trust papers. Mama and Uncle Evan asked me if I wanted to continue our arrangement and I said yes."

Dev put his hat down and walked slowly back into the room. "When did you do this?" he asked.

Emma did not understand the look on his face. "A few weeks ago, when I came back. It was just the kind of thing . . ."

"Who put you up to it?"

She stood, turned her back to him. "I don't like the way you are questioning me, Dev. Please stop it. Uncle Evan built the ranch for me, and he runs it for me, and it is more profitable than any ranch its size in the Islands. Nobody put me up to anything."

He was shaking his head. "Poor little girl, they just tell you what to do and you do it. Is that it?"

She stamped her foot. "Stop it. I have plenty of money, and what is mine is yours. You know that. Nobody—not Mother and certainly not Uncle Evan—is against us."

"But they aren't for me, either, are they? They didn't want you to marry me."

"They didn't want me to marry so young, that is all. They thought . . ."

"They thought I was after your money. I don't give a damn about your money, Emma. Can you believe that? But I do care that they are treating us both like imbeciles, when we aren't. I've worked all of my life. I am as smart as the next man, smarter than most, and I believe that I can and should have some say in my wife's affairs . . ."

Emma came flying to him. "Of course you can, yes. I

know how smart you are and they will too, once they see how . . ."

Very carefully, he pushed her away and left, running down the stairs in a staccato fashion. He was always in a hurry, Emma noticed.

Two weeks later, Dev Aldren resigned his position at American Shipping Company "to devote my attention to family business matters." The first of these matters was to oversee the design and building of a three-story home on Makiki Street, one that would be, he assured his wife, "commensurate with our position in society."

Emma was overjoyed; now they could spend so much more time together, and she loved the idea of planning a whole new house.

40

Emma lowered herself into the big rattan chair on the lanai and sank back against the pillows. Dev, engrossed in what seemed to be some business papers, did not look up. She was not comfortable; she would have liked to have her feet lifted to the ottoman but she could not bring herself to ask him. She closed her eyes and tried to forget the heaviness of her body, the dull ache of her swollen feet.

"How's the little mother?" Dev asked, not looking up.

Emma, pleased for the signal that she could interrupt, told him, "I was thinking about when I was eleven or twelve. At night I would have these pains in my legs—Doctor said they were 'growing pains' because I was shooting up so fast. But I would wake up crying, and then Mama would get up, and she would rub my legs and put hot cloths on them. And sometimes Liko would come and sing to me, to help me get back to sleep."

Dev looked up. "What a charming little tale," he said, in a way that made her wish she hadn't told him. "See what you have to look forward to when Baby comes? Just don't count on me to do any singing—I can't carry a tune."

He went back to his papers before she had a chance to ask him to lift her feet. Tears sprang to her eyes. It was the baby, she told herself—it made her weepy. All she had to do was think of home, and the tears started. She tried to think of something else; Dev didn't like it when she cried.

"What are you studying?" she asked, not so much because she wanted to know but because she knew he liked her to be interested in what he called his "projects."

He looked up, his eyes lit with excitement. "A chance to be in on the beginning of a revolution, but in a unique way. We would be importing automobiles—some racing models.

SHIRLEY STRESHINSKY

We could make a small fortune." Most of Dev's projects, she noticed, were going to make "a small fortune."

She shifted in the chair, trying to get comfortable. "Who is 'we'?" she asked pleasantly.

He frowned. "Who do you think? You and me, ducky. That's who."

"Oh," she said, surprised. "I thought you must have a partner, someone who knows about automobiles and such . . ."

He shook his head and went back to the papers. "You don't have to know about 'automobiles and such' to sell them, goose. What we do need to do, however, is go to San Francisco to talk to the men who are putting together this new dealership. We could make it a delayed wedding trip . . ."

She looked at him, waiting for him to tell her he was joking. "You don't mean it," she finally managed.

He walked over to her chair, knelt to lift her feet onto the ottoman and then kissed her on the forehead. "I do mean it. It's almost three months until the baby comes. We can be there and back long before that happens."

"But I'm already so huge," she moaned. "I can scarcely get around as it is, and to think of being tossed and turned on a boat. Dev, please, I can't . . ."

"It would be like being in a cradle," he told her, smoothing the damp hair from her head. "Just you and me in a big, lovely bed on the high seas . . . rocking our way to San Francisco and back. It will be like a second honeymoon."

Her lowered lip trembled. "We haven't had a first."

Dev laughed. "So there you are—this can be our honeymoon. We'll dance the night away under the moon and the stars . . ."

She wailed. "I can scarcely even walk, I have this horrid taste in my mouth all the time, you're scarcely ever at home and when you are you are always studying some new project, or you're angry because of the ranch . . . I simply can't. You promised I could go home when it was time for the baby and now you want . . ."

His face tightened. "This is your home, Emma. Right here, with me. When we are together, we are home. You are not the first woman on this planet to have a baby, and I have work to do. I can't simply stop everything and hold your hand. If you think I married you so I could live a life of leisure, you are wrong. Your grandfather may think that's a good way to spend a life, but I do not. The fortune is yours, my dear—but it is my responsibility to double it, triple it for you. If that is going to happen, you have to do your part. And that means not always running to your mother and your Auntie Martha—the hired hand's wife."

She bit her lip so she wouldn't cry. "Aunt Martha is my father's sister," Emma whispered, "and Uncle Pono is ohana. We never think of him as a hired hand."

"Ohana," Dev said. "How quaint. Is that the same *ohana* that treats us like dimwitted children—just give them an allowance and tell them to stay out of the grown-ups' affairs?" He stood, looked at her and shook his head. Then he left, running in short quick steps down the stairs and then in long strides across the lawn of the spacious, grand house that was the talk of Honolulu. It happened like this whenever she denied or disputed him, and she had done both. She knew it would be days before he would speak to her again. She closed her eyes and wished herself back at the Home Place, in her own bed with Mama rubbing her back with her hard, tender hands.

"Damn Devereaux Aldren," True said. "Damn him straight to hell. If my daughter weren't on the ship, I'd wish it to sink and Dev Aldren to be devoured by sharks. I despise that man . . . we have to stop him, Evan. We have to get her away . . ."

Evan frowned. "That kind of talk isn't going to help Emma. She decided to go to San Francisco with him. She could have said no."

True exploded. "You can't believe that! She's a child, Evan. And he is a man with a streak of greed a mile wide. He's a beast to make her take a sea journey now. She doesn't know how to say no to him. You can't believe that she would want to go—every letter we've had from her has talked about coming home when it's time for the baby to be born. She's already so big, the doctor says she could be early. Dev just doesn't want her to come home, that's all. She told us as much—he doesn't want her to talk to us without him being here. He's filled her so full of the idea that we are trying to keep her a child."

Evan put his hand on her shoulder and squeezed. "Listen to yourself, True. On the one hand you say she's still a child, and on the other you accuse him of accusing us of wanting to keep her a child. Which is it to be?"

True exhaled and shrugged his hand off her shoulder. She could not understand, after all the accusations Dev had made about Evan's handling of the ranch, how he could still stand up for him. They led their horses out of the barn and mounted. True led off and Evan followed. The ride had been his idea; they hadn't been out together, riding the ranch, for weeks, and he needed to talk to her in the open, from the top of a ridge where they could look out over the vast stretches of the ranch—at a place where all they could see was Mau'-loa. They headed north toward the ocean, on the pretext that he wanted to see the Hereford herd. He was proud of the Herefords; as breeding stock, they couldn't be bested anywhere, not even on the Mainland. He wondered why he couldn't seem to stop trying new things—new grasses, new breeds of cattle, new methods of water conservation.

Emma's husband had not been interested in grasses and breeding programs; he had not wanted to ride the range with Evan and the boys, because he had said that was a job for the people he proposed to hire to make the ranch more profitable. *Profit* was an important word in Dev's vocabulary. Profit and investment. Evan's decision to purchase the Cowdry ranch had infuriated Dev; his "experts" had told him it was a risky venture, too close to the volcano, too many acres covered with lava flow. He had not been swayed by Evan's reasons for buying the property. His last words to Evan had been stiff and full of legal portent: "My wife signed the trust papers without fully understanding the consequences. Had she consulted me, she would never have done so. I am capable of seeing to my wife's best interests, and I resent not being a principal in the administration of her most valuable property."

True held back and waited for Evan to come abreast, so they could ride side by side. "I would like to scream," she said. "Just scream and scream. I feel this great awful rage inside of me. How could we have allowed this to happen to our girl? Why didn't we stop it, Evan?"

There was no need to answer; she knew they could not have stopped it. He pulled up short on a rise and looked down on the herd, strung out in a field of Rhodes grass, grown from seed he had imported from Australia.

"The Rhodes does well on these dry sections of the ranch. I've sent off for some Kikuyu seed from Africa," he told her.

She looked at him, exasperated. "You talk about grasses as if nothing is happening. Evan! Listen to me—we have to fight him. We can't let him take over and ruin everything. We've worked too long, too hard."

He spurred his horse and jolted on ahead of her, moving now toward the horse station. In a few days they would be shipping two hundred head to the Army at $160 a horse. The Army was becoming one of their best customers, as the American military presence in the Pacific grew. "A tidy profit," Dev had said when Evan showed him the contract, "but not good enough." This from a man who knew absolutely nothing about horses or the Army and was disinclined to learn.

Suddenly Evan said, "Let's ride over to the Kala Heiau."

She looked at him in surprise. She had avoided that sacred place since the day, more than twenty-five years ago, when she had gone there with him.

"Why there?" she asked.

"Because that day—when you warned me against marrying Jenny—I remember wondering what it would be like if an earthquake would shake the promontory loose, and us with it, to go drifting off together. I want to go there now to see if I feel the mana again . . ."

She didn't wait for him to finish but kicked her horse into a gallop up and over the hill, past the cane fields, up into the high plateau that looked out over the Pacific, to the great pile of stones that was all that was left of the ancient temple where, long ago, men prayed to the gods. They dismounted and climbed down the sloping cliff and into the magnetic field; the sun caught them at a low angle when they climbed down into the place that had been the altar.

"Remember what we said that day?" Evan asked.

Her eyes looked into his, questioning.

"We decided that we were kindly spirits. Kind friends."

A *pueo* hooted in the distance, as if to punctuate his answer.

"And we have been kindly spirits, all these years."

A frigate bird slid sideways above them. They watched it

and smiled. He held her hands in his, as they stood before the altar. "You have always been my kind friend, my love," he told her, smiling at the words.

"And you mine," she answered, wondering why he was telling her this, now.

"What bound us together was something I can't explain. It frightened me the first time I felt it, here with you all those years ago. I've long since learned to give myself over to it, let it pull me in. We have done what we had to do, I believe that. But now that is finished. It is *pau*."

"Pau?" she said, frowning. "What do you mean?"

"We built and worked the ranch for Emma. Our part of the job is done. We have to let it go. Let them have it."

"Them?" True said, horror registering on her face. "You can't mean let Dev take over the ranch? He will ruin it, you know that. All our hard work, our beautiful ranch—it will be the Colonel all over again. No, Evan. You can't ask that."

He walked away from the altar, turned away from her for a few minutes, then came back and took her hands in his. "Listen to me," he said as she started to speak. "Please, just listen. Harry doesn't ask 'Do you think this is enough?' so often now. I have to hope he is getting better, True—because I have inflicted my share of wrongs on my son, and I need to be forgiven for that, too."

Looking into his face, seeing the pain so close to the surface, her eyes filled with tears. He went on, "I want to bring Harry to our place on the other side of the mountain. He has become good with the sheep we run on Opihi, and I think we can start a small sheep station for him to run. I want to ask Blue and some of his ohana to move up there as well, to work with us. I thought . . ."

She bit her lip and looked above her at the sky and far into the distance to the place where the Pacific made a hard blue line against the lighter blue of the sky.

Something was swelling inside her, hard with sharp edges that were pressing against her skin, making her feel as if it might rip out of her.

"Don't desert me, Evan. Don't do this."

He tried to touch her, but she moved away from him and repeated, "Don't do this to me."

His hands fell to his sides, and he began clenching his fists and unclenching them. "It was never our ranch, True. Never. We were doing it for Emma, which means we were doing it for the future. For whatever the future might be. We didn't hurt anyone by taking over the running of this ranch, and we helped a good many people. But if we cling to it now, if now we are saying it is ours to do with as we will . . . if we shut out Emma's husband, no matter how we feel about him, then it means we've been lying to ourselves all this time."

She shut her eyes, clamped her mouth shut and shook her head. "No," she said, "he will ruin it, all we've done. He won't listen to reason, you know that already. His plan is to bring in new people, people who don't know this ranch, don't love it."

Evan put his hands in his pockets, and a look came over his face that she knew so well she had to sit down, to absorb the shock. He had made up his mind; it was pau.

He told her, "That's how life happens. The first Tobias Wakefield built a cattle empire; his sons and grandson dissipated it; we came in to build it up again. The next generation must be given a chance."

"But Dev Aldren is an outsider; he has nothing to do with the ranch—even the Colonel says so."

"You were an outsider, True. That can't be held against him."

"Oh, God . . ." she wailed, sinking to the ground to rock back and forth. "Oh, God, what are we going to do?"

He lifted her and held her close. "Come with me. Stay with me now. Let it go."

"He'll kill it," she sobbed. "He doesn't understand and he'll kill it."

"No. He may harm it, but he won't kill it. Emma won't let him do that. She is our daughter after all, yours and mine. She needs some time to grow, to figure out things. Don't count Emma out, not yet."

"She has made a miserable marriage," True said, blotting her tears on his shirt. "What if she never stands up to him?"

He took her face in his hands, put his forehead against hers and told her, "She will. And there's a young one coming up, and he's the heir."

"Or she," True said, trying to smile.

"Or she," he admitted.

True felt the breath draining from her, felt herself giving way, knew that it was done. Finished. Pau.

She took a deep breath. "I will come with you. But the horses—I can't give up the horses, I won't . . ."

"Shhh," he said, cradling her in his arms. "You won't have to give them up. We'll get our girl back . . . we'll be able to help her this way. We have to help her, True."

She buried her face in his shirt and cried. It was done. She felt it now, standing at the altar of an ancient temple. Mau'-loa had passed to other hands. It was no longer theirs to care for.

August 12, 1917, San Francisco

Dear Mama,

At last I am feeling strong enough to write you the long letter I have promised. I know Dev has been keeping you well informed, but he is so busy taking care of his burgeoning family and doing a thousand other things that I know you have had none of the details.

First "detail": the twins are the most beautiful babies I, for one, have ever seen. Lucy is growing big and pink and is, I think, quite jolly. She would nurse all day if I allowed it! Tiny Lucien is finally beginning to gain weight, and I worry less about him now. The doctors say he is sound, and they have all manner of extra nutrients to help him get on in this world.

Twins! Can you imagine how amazed I was to learn that one of me was to multiply to three? But I was so very big and heavy, Mama. You should have seen me that last month . . . I could scarcely get out of bed without help. No, I am not going to complain and tell you all the awful little details. But I will admit it is going to be a long while before I decide to multiply again.

I wanted so to be at home when the baby—babies, as it turns out—were born, but our departure from San Francisco had to be delayed a week because of some business involvement. Dev has become interested in importing sailboats to the islands—racing sloops, I believe. We stayed so long and I was so monstrously huge that I felt it could be dangerous for me to risk the return voyage. I was never much good at telling you even white lies, so I shall not try now. Throughout the long birthing, I longed for you and Auntie to be with me. It won't do for me to say more, or this paper will be flooded with tears and the ink will run.

But Mama, I did it! I produced two beautiful little babies, and I can hardly wait to bring them home to Mau'loa. Dev is ready to go at once. All he can talk or think about is the ranch, but now I am the one who delays. Lucien has been helped so much by the doctors here at Children's Hospital, and I won't leave until they tell me he is strong enough for the trip.

The twins have been named for Dev's parents, but each of them has "Wakefield" as a middle name.

I hope this pleases the Eastern parents and the great-grandparents. For my part, I have already dubbed Lucy my "Nani" and Lucien my "Pua." Dev says it's all right to call a girl "pretty," but he draws the line at calling his son "flower." I tell him that he can draw all the lines he likes, Lucien is going to be my pua.

Most of all, Mama, I hope you are proud of me. You've always been so brave, and the doctor said I was too. All the while I kept telling myself, over and over again, "Mama would want me to be strong. Mama would say, 'You can do it.' " And I did.

I need to say something about the letter Dev received from Uncle Evan, explaining that you and he are willing to consider revoking the trust, if that is what Dev and I want.

You know that I trust Uncle Evan more than anybody else in this world. And more than anybody else in this world, he has created the inheritance that Dev is so eager to take over. It was a difficult decision, I know, to turn it back over to us, not knowing if we are capable.

I will admit something in confidence, Mama: I don't know if we are capable, but I do believe we have to find out. You can imagine that Dev is thrilled with your decision. I expect to have a say about whatever changes are to be made. I do not intend to see good people let go, willy-nilly. I expect to make my wishes known on certain things. My next letter will be to Auntie Martha, and part of it will be a plea for Uncle Pono to stay on. Dev may not realize how important he is to Mau'loa, but I do.

I am writing to Liko and to Uncle Evan as well. It pleases

me to know that Harry is doing well and will be working his own sheep station. War fever is raging here on the Mainland, with our boys just off to Europe. But I think of Harry and feel as if I know a little bit about the pain that will be afflicting American boys and their families. So we are to be neighbors, Harry and Uncle and you and I! It wasn't more than a day or two after the births that I realized how much I want my children to grow up on the ranch, to have them know the beauty of it—to take them out on a butterfly search with "the master of the butterfly hunt." How lucky I am, to have such an ohana. I want you to start planning now for the twins' baby luau, one year hence. We will make it a wonderful occasion, with roping contests and a barbeque and we will invite everyone on the ranch to come, and Liko will play the ukelele for us and there will be dancing all night long. (By then I will have regained some sort of figure, I do hope.)

I can't begin to explain to you how much it has worn on me, these past months of struggle between my husband and my mother; my heart is filled with thanksgiving at the great gift you and Uncle Evan have given me. Mahalo, Mama.

Me ke aloha,
Emma

Epilogue

Is a story ever done? I think not. I have spent all this morning and much of the afternoon in my parlor, my journals spread out before me—the beautiful one covered with koa wood that True gave me on the day she married Jared Wakefield, twenty-one years ago, and all the plain notebooks that I have filled since coming to Mau'loa. I have been picking them up at random to leaf through the pages, smiling at many of the memories they evoke, sighing over others.

What I notice most is the monotony of days; the great majority are as common as warm toast—bright sun-splashed summer days, rainy winter days, all of them filled with the clutter of ordinary lives: Tommy's first rodeo and the thrill of a blue ribbon for roping, Pono's long walk from Hilo leading the massive new bull named "Eventide," the first of many such creatures brought in to create one of the finest herds of Herefords in the world. Polo remains a favorite pastime on this island, and it is not unusual to see little boys walking around with mallets just their size. My Tommy, at thirteen, is set on growing up to be a famous polo player. His sister is intent upon becoming a kumu hula. At fifteen, she does have a grace that is rare.

Births are duly recorded in the pages of my journals, and deaths as well: Our dear Governor Cleghorn passed on in November of 1910 and Queen Liliuokalani followed in 1917; the era of the Hawaiian monarchs was pau. Just last year, on the very day of the signing of the armistice that ended the Great War, Aunt Winona died.

Marriages are listed, usually with a pressed flower tucked into the page: My sweet-sour Amalie, to a kindly widower from Kona; Jimmy Rourke to a Japanese girl who was one of my favorite students. Liko helped nurse Bradley Chin's parents through their last illnesses, which came within six

months of each other. Then, when Bradley was dismissed
from his position on the ranch last spring, Liko moved in
with him to share his expenses and his care. Bradley has
never completely recovered from the injuries from his fall;
Dev's new manager could not see that the ranch had any
responsibility for Bradley, or for any other ranch hand who
could no longer "hold up his end of the stick," as the man
put it.

Pono stayed on only because Evan asked him to, but his
patience was worn thin. He missed Evan, just as I missed
True.

Evan and True. Simply thinking about them makes me
smile. Liko and I get together and gossip like two little old
checkered hens. Evan is fifty-seven now, while True is forty-
five, and they are as handsome, to my eyes, as ever they have
been. She laughs so easily; he looks at her and his eyes shine
with pleasure. And oh, it makes us happy knowing that at
last they have found the kind of simple contentment that has
always eluded them.

Emma confided that she had asked her mother why she
and Evan didn't marry, and True told her that the only time
she had felt marriage to be necessary was when she had
married Jared Wakefield. Emma hadn't a notion of what she
meant, and I know True wants it that way.

When Emma told me this, she was cradling poor little Pua
in her arms. The boy is often ill; Emma frequently takes him
to the doctors in Oahu, yet another source of conflict between her and Dev. He claimed that whenever she would
leave the ranch, the servants would make his life hellish. The
house servants told another story; in their version, he was
quick to temper, so they ignored him.

The morning after Emma's twentieth birthday last spring,
we noticed a bruise over her left eye. She told her mother she
had fallen in her bath. That day, Pono and I figured something out: Twice in recent weeks, at Pono's request, Emma
had reversed Dev's decisions. Soon after I had noticed
bruises—once on her arms, another time on her cheek.

We went to Evan with our fears. I do not know what Evan
did, or said, to Dev Aldren, but for a time things seemed to
get better.

That was in March; in September of this past year, a party
of gentlemen who had various kinds of business dealings

with Dev were invited to the ranch for a shoot. Mounted on some of the ranch's best horses, they set out for the high meadows. Along the way they passed a native's shack, and a dog ran out to bark at the pack of horses and men. Dev was in the lead on a fine mare that had been sired by Surprise Party. This horse—descended from True's Surprise—was a favorite of True's; she had offered it for sale for a goodly price and would not have approved its use in a hunt. Perhaps because Dev knew this, he hit at the dog with his whip. He only managed to infuriate the animal, which now came at his mount with bared teeth. Dev called to its owner, an old Hawaiian, to come get his dog. The old man rose and began to make his way out to see what the commotion was all about. At that moment the dog lunged at the mare, the mare sidestepped and shied, and Dev shot the dog through the head.

The rest of the story I have third-hand, from a Hawaiian who is a friend of Blue's cousin, and who works as a yard man at Kolonahe. When Dev stepped out of the back door the next morning, he stumbled on a package wrapped loosely in an old tapa cloth. When he kicked it, some small bones spilled out. Dev cursed and called to an old Hawaiian who was clipping at a hedge of poinsettias to come take the thing away.

The old man looked, dropped his clippers and left, shuffling off as fast as he could manage.

Dev cursed and kicked the thing again; suddenly all the yard workers disappeared. When one of the guests appeared just then, asking what it meant, Dev quickly picked up the package and threw it into a burn pit.

"Nothing," he told his guest. "Nothing but some native nonsense."

It was a kahuna bundle—a curse had been put on Dev Aldren; whether or not he knew is difficult to say, but every Hawaiian on the ranch knew.

That same day, the first of the racing sloops Dev had ordered was to put in at the ranch dock to culminate the week-long party. It was nine months behind schedule, and cost many thousands of dollars more than it should, but Dev remained confident. The group of men, their wives, Dev and Emma waited at the dock with champagne ready to christen the boat, but it did not arrive. It had set out from Honolulu on schedule, but problems in the rudder system had forced it back. When finally it put in three days later, only Dev was on hand to greet it.

He telephoned up to the house to tell Emma to come take the first sail with him, but Emma was not there. She was at my house, and I will not have one of the wretched telephones.

Finally, in a pique, Dev left without her; two days later, the sloop was found shattered on the rocky windward coast of Molokai. All of her crew, and Dev Aldren, were lost at sea.

The Hawaiians will always believe the kahuna bundle had worked its black magic. The men who had worked on the sloop in the shipyards in Honolulu were just as certain it was a result of a badly designed, and poorly executed, craft. For myself, I could only feel relief that Emma had been with me that afternoon, safely out of range of her husband's deadly net.

Emma erected a monument to him in the family cemetery. Soon thereafter, she called Evan and Pono to Kolonahe.

Pono told me about the meeting. He said Emma stood behind the big desk in the library. She asked them very politely to take a seat, rearranged a stack of papers on the desk and proceeded to recount in a businesslike fashion the problems facing the ranch. Then she asked for their help.

Evan could not have been more proud.

"I'm with you," he said, and Pono nodded to show he was with her too.

"Where shall we start?" she asked.

Evan answered, "You're the boss."

And Emma said, "Yes, I suppose I am."

Author's Note

It is impossible, I believe, to go to Hawaii more than once without becoming aware of its history and the remarkable people who shaped these loveliest of islands. By my fourth or fifth visit, I was thoroughly enmeshed in the story of the first Kamehameha—"The Great" one who united all the islands—and with one of his queens, Kaahumanu, who in what must be one of the most courageous acts in all history, stepped forward to seize power when the great king died. These alii fascinated me, but the one who began to haunt me (as I believe she does many Hawaiians, even today) was the beautiful and beloved Princess Royal, Kaiulani, who lived only long enough to see her crown lost forever, the monarchy pau.

These alii appear in this book along with others who are important to Island history: Governor Archibald Cleghorn and Princess Miriam Likelike, who were Kaiulani's parents; Queen Liliuokalani; King David Kalakaua; Princess Ruth; Governor Sanford Dole; Governor Dominis. And, in Kamehameha's time, the explorer George Vancouver. A few other well-known Hawaiian and haole families are mentioned (such as the von Tempskys on Maui and the Parkers on Hawaii).

Everyone else in this book is made up, drawn completely from fiction, as are their actions. Not one person was patterned after anyone who ever lived. This is not to say that there weren't exciting, extraordinary people living on the ranches of the Big Island in the first decades of this century. There were indeed, but they are not the models for the people in this novel.

There were droughts, of course, and kona storms, and roundups and luaus and rodeos and polo matches, and I have tried to portray these as realistically as possible. I spent long hours at the University of Hawaii's library in Honolulu, as well as in several other historical collections and museums in the Islands, and at the Bancroft Library in Berkeley, California. All along the way, the people I met in Hawaii were wonderfully helpful, generous with their time, with information, with encouragement. I hesitate to list them here, in large part because if any mistakes have been made in my perceptions of island history, I would not want them to be held to account. I do want to say that they taught me the meaning of "aloha," and it is the best lesson one can learn.

From the very first time I drove by myself around the Big Island—through its cane fields, across the lava flows, up into the mountains—I understood perfectly how someone like True Lindstrom Wakefield might fall in love with this glorious, green mountaintop out in the middle of the wide Pacific.

Two who deserve great thanks: my literary agent, Claire Smith, and the editor of this book, Lisa Wager.

JILL MARIE LANDIS

The nationally bestselling
author of <u>Rose</u> and <u>Sunflower</u>

___

_____JADE   0-515-10591-0/$4.95
*A determined young woman of exotic beauty returned to San Francisco to
unveil the secrets behind her father's death. But her bold venture would
lead her to recover a family fortune—and discover a perilous love . . . .*

_____ROSE   0-515-10346-2/$4.50
"A gentle romance that will warm your soul."—Heartland Critiques
*When Rosa set out from Italy to join her husband in Wyoming, her heart
was filled with love and longing to see him again. Little did she know that
fate held heartbreak ahead. Suddenly a woman alone, the challenge
seemed as vast as the prairies.*

_____SUNFLOWER   0-515-10659-3/$4.95
"A winning novel!"—Publishers Weekly
*Analisa was strong and independent, Caleb had a brutal heritage that
challenged every feeling in her heart. Yet their love was as inevitable as the
sunrise . . .*

_____WILDFLOWER   0-515-10102-8/$4.95
"A delight from start to finish!"—Rendezvous
*From the great peaks of the West to the lush seclusion of a Caribbean jungle,
Dani and Troy discovered the deepest treasures of the heart.*

___

310